D0012183

**Also available from
Catherine Anderson
and Harlequin HQN**

Sweet Dreams

Catherine Anderson

endless night

HARLEQUIN®
entertain, enrich, inspire™

Recycling programs for this product may not exist in your area.

ISBN-13: 978-0-373-77801-0

ENDLESS NIGHT

Copyright © 2012 by Harlequin Books S.A.

The publisher acknowledges the copyright holder of the individual works as follows:

SWITCHBACK
Copyright © 1990 by Adeline Catherine Anderson

CRY OF THE WILD
Copyright © 1992 by Adeline Catherine Anderson

CONTENTS

SWITCHBACK

As always, to my husband, Sid, because his support has made it possible for my dream to become a reality. And, of course, to his mother, Carolyn, who played a big part in making him the man he is.

To Julie Brinegar and Stella Cameron, because they have been such wonderful friends to me.

To Sue Stone, because she is such a great editor.

And last but never least, to my niece Gerry, who can always make me smile— even when we're hopelessly lost in the wilderness.

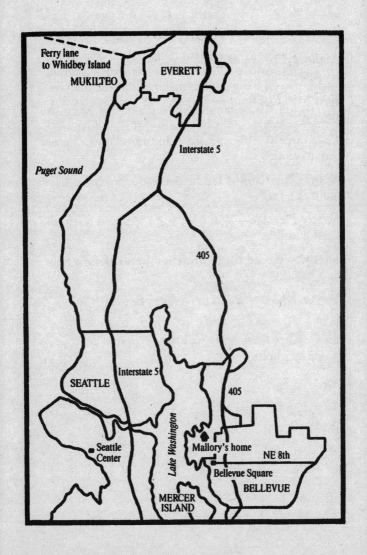

CAST OF CHARACTERS

Mallory Christiani—She was desperate enough to try anything.

Bud Mac Phearson—Was this his chance to even the score?

Pete Lucetti—He's a hard man to find and a harder one to elude.

Keith Christiani—Had he been too clever for his family's good?

Scotty Herman—Was Mac right to avoid his friend on the police force?

Shelby—Would his information network be a help or a hazard?

Steven Miles—Could his ledgers be worth the price?

Emily Christiani—She was the prize in a deadly scavenger hunt.

PROLOGUE

KEITH CHRISTIANI STARED at the telephone, letting it ring three times. As he curled his fingers around the receiver, he gripped the plastic so hard his knuckles turned white. Only a chosen few had the number to his private office line. He knew who was calling. "Christiani here."

Keith could hear breathing, raspy and shallow, underscoring the silence with almost palpable intensity. At last a coarse, cold voice said, "Did you mail the package?"

Keith shifted his gaze to the paperweight on his desk. It was a glass globe with a snow scene inside, a Christmas gift from his little granddaughter, Emily. Knifelike pain cut deep into his left temple. He squeezed his eyes closed. Just a few more hours and this would all be over. He'd fly his family to safety, then notify the authorities of where they could get the key. "Why ask? I know your goons were on my heels all day."

"I have men watching your home, as well. That better've been my package you mailed. If it wasn't, that granddaughter of yours will be stretched out in the morgue by Friday. I guarantee it."

Keith rose halfway out of his chair. "You promised if I cooperated, you'd leave my family alone." If they were watching his house, how could he get Em and Mallory out of there? His vision blurred and he sank back into his chair. "You mess with me and I'll call the cops so fast you won't know what hit you."

"*You* mess with *me* and your daughter-in-law and her brat will be dead so fast *they* won't know what hit them. Nobody crosses me and gets away with it. Not even high-falutin' lawyers. You know that firsthand. You went to the bank today. What the hell for?"

Keith gripped the edge of his desk. Anger, white-hot and searing, coursed through his body. "Probate."

"And that was all?"

"I swear it." A long silence followed Keith's lie.

"For your family's sake, I hope so."

The phone clicked and went dead. Keith clenched his teeth to ward off panic. What had he done? He had been crazy to try outwitting Lucetti on his own. Lucetti was so sharp, so fanatical about detail, so paranoid about leaving evidence, that his mind functioned with the precision of a computer. The man was the worst kind of gutter slime, too smart to be caught and ruthless enough to kill a child without hesitation.

With a shaking hand, Keith dropped the phone receiver into its cradle. He had to get help, but now he didn't dare bring the cops into this. Not as long as Mallory and Emily were still in Seattle where the man could get at them. The panic Keith had been holding at bay threatened to engulf him. Then a rush of hope filled him. Maybe, just maybe, Mac had returned. He was due back sometime today. Pressing the fingertips of one hand against his throbbing head he passed a hand over his eyes. He couldn't remember if he'd taken his pills today or not. These past few days, he'd been so strung out, he had scarcely remembered to eat. Keith lifted his receiver and dialed Mac's number from memory. After four buzzes, Mac Phearson's answering machine broke in. Keith nearly hung up, but desperation forestalled him. He waited for the tone and then said, "Mac, this is Keith."

He paused, unsure how much he dared reveal on tape. An excruciating pain shot up the right side of his neck. Licking his lips with a tongue that felt suddenly thick and rubbery, he frowned. Fragments of sentences danced in his mind. He had to remember what he should and shouldn't say.

"There's—um—a man, a man known as Pete Lucetti." Keith blinked. What on earth was wrong with him? He drew a deep breath. "This Lucetti, he's threatening to kill Mallory and Em. I've got to get them out of town. Tonight. I'd—uh—call the police but he's got a couple of cops on the payroll." The room seemed to spin. Keith struggled for balance, propping one elbow on the arm of his chair. "Don't know who I can trust... I'm counting on you, Mac. You're my only—"

The pain in Keith's head seemed to explode. He heard the phone clatter onto his desk. Then there was a shrill ringing in his ears. The room went dark, then flashed bright as if someone had popped a flashcube in his eyes. The next second, he felt himself pitch forward. A funnel of blackness sucked at him, pulling him deeper and deeper into its center. He couldn't die. Not right now. Not before he could talk to Mac.

With all his concentration, Keith dragged himself back to semiconsciousness and reached for the intercom to call for help. His arm weighed a thousand pounds. He couldn't feel his hand. When he opened his eyes, he couldn't see. The ringing in his ears grew louder.

The intercom. Dear God, where was the intercom?

CHAPTER ONE

THE MOMENT MALLORY Christiani stepped into the Intensive Care Unit, she saw the fear in her father-in-law's eyes. He lay propped against two pillows, the weight of his silvery head creasing the starched cases, his sunken face cast in stark relief against white linen. She took a steadying breath, repositioned the shoulder strap of her leather purse and pasted on a smile.

The click of her heels echoed as she walked toward the bed. She was glad she'd taken extra pains freshening up while she was at the house. Her collarless blazer and matching green skirt were crisp and wrinkle free. Keith would never know she hadn't eaten or slept since he'd been stricken yesterday.

"Dad. It's so good to see you awake." Mallory leaned over to kiss his cheek, holding her amber-colored hair back so it wouldn't trail in his face. As she straightened, she took his right hand in hers. His skin felt cold. The lack of response in his limp fingers shocked her. Until now, she hadn't realized how dearly she had come to love him, how big a part he played in her life now that they shared the same home. Keith was more a father to her than her own had ever been. "You're looking better already, you know? Some of your color's coming back."

A treacherous catch in her voice nearly betrayed her.

Why hadn't she recognized his prestroke symptoms? Any nurse worth her salt would have.

Spying tears slipping down his pallid cheeks, she gave him a careful hug. "Oh, Dad. We're through the worst, right? From here on in, you'll be amazed at how quickly you recover."

Keith's blue eyes followed her as she drew away. Was there something wrong here, something more than anxiety over his paralysis? She glanced at the monitor above his head. It seemed to her his heartbeat was too rapid, but she could detect no irregularities in the configurations. If the fast pulse were anything to be concerned about, the monitor alarm would be going off. Through the glass partition, she could see the ICU nurse sitting at the desk, her dark head bent as she filled out charts. Nothing out of the ordinary, apparently.

Pulling up a chair, Mallory eased her purse to the floor. Spittle ran from the corner of her father-in-law's mouth. Suddenly the nightmare of what had happened to him became a reality. She reached for a tissue and wiped his face, keeping her smile steady, her hands sure.

"Emily will come see you as soon as they move you to a regular room. She can't wait. She lost another tooth, but she won't put it under her pillow until you get home. Holding out for more money, I think. So much for believing in fairies, huh?" She laughed. The sound reminded her of two tin cans clanking. "She's staying with Beth Hamstead until Mother and Dad get home. They're driving back from Texas immediately, but it'll take them an extra day. Dad lost the motor-home keys. Can you believe it? You remember Beth, the lady with all the little redheads?"

Keith's eyes clung to hers, frantic, pleading. His bottom lip quivered as he strained to speak. Spying a flut-

ter of movement, she glanced over to see his left hand
twitching, his fingers extended like claws. A low moan
erupted from him.

"What is it?" She shot up from the chair. "Are you in
pain?" The green graph line was rocketing across the
monitor screen. He was clearly agitated about something.
Her own pulse began to race as she grabbed the nurse
buzzer. "There, there, it'll be okay. Relax, Dad. Take deep
breaths."

The approaching swish of the nurse's polyester uniform eased the tension from Mallory's shoulders. She
turned to watch the plump woman hurry to the bed.
"Problems?"

"I don't know. He was fine and then—" She broke off.
The nurse looked so unperturbed by the racing monitor
that Mallory felt foolish. "I was just talking. And he became agitated."

The nurse smiled. "He's just pleased to see you. Right,
Mr. Christiani?" She slid her twinkling blue gaze to Mallory. "A little too much excitement, that's all."

Another moan erupted from Keith. The nurse flashed
Mallory a concerned glance and lifted her patient's hand.
After studying the configurations on the monitor a moment to be certain nothing was wrong, she said, "You're
fine, Mr. Christiani. Just too many visitors." Turning toward Mallory, she added, "Why don't you have a cup of
coffee? Let him nap for an hour or so. We have a lovely
cafeteria."

"Visitors? I thought only immediate family was admitted."

"Yes, but we make exceptions for clergy. Your parish
priest got your message and came in about an hour ago.
And a few minutes after that, Mr. Christiani's son came

in. You're the third in a short period of time. Even brief visits from family and close friends can be wearing the first day."

A prickle of alarm ran up Mallory's spine. "I'm the only relative and we're Methodists. Are you certain you're recalling the right patient? Mr. Christiani's son is—" She hated to remind Keith of Darren's accident when he was so ill. "I'm a widow."

The nurse looked nonplussed. "How odd."

Mallory was beginning to feel extremely angry. Keith shouldn't be having a parade of people marching through his room so soon after a massive stroke. The priest could have come by mistake, but the so-called son had clearly lied to gain admittance. Who had the man been? Why had he lied to see Keith? "What did this *son* look like?"

The nurse pursed her lips. "He was tall, blond, quite good-looking. The athletic type. Mid to late thirties, I'd say. He was wearing scruffy gray sweats and a blue windbreaker. He asked after you, wanted to know where you were. He seemed like a very nice man."

A very nice man wouldn't have lied to get into Intensive Care. Mallory racked her brain, visualizing all Keith's friends and associates. None she knew fit the description the nurse had just given her. Glancing at Keith, she decided the less said about it in front of him the better. No wonder he was tired.

"If I'm quiet, wouldn't it be all right if I stayed?"

"It would really be better if you gave him a rest," the nurse replied with underlying firmness. "I know he seems distressed about your leaving, but that's quite common the first day. Trust me to know what's best."

"Well… I believe I'll go have that cup of coffee you suggested, then." After stooping to retrieve her purse,

Mallory touched her father-in-law's hand reassuringly. His eyes seemed to beg her not to leave. She felt as though she were abandoning him. "I'll be back soon, Dad. Okay? You take a short nap while I'm gone. When I come back, I'll read to you for a bit. I found a great issue of *National Geographic* in the hall. Would you enjoy that?"

Keith's reply was a dry sob. She forced herself to smile with a cheerfulness she was far from feeling. Once outside the room she drew the nurse aside and said, "Our minister is Reverend Miller. He should be the only church visitor allowed in. And I'm the only relative except for my daughter, Em, who's only seven." Mallory glanced at her watch. "An hour, you say?"

"Give or take a few minutes." The nurse seemed to empathize with Mallory's difficulty in leaving and gave her a kindly pat on the shoulder. In a low voice, she said, "Thank you for cooperating. I'll put the visitor information on his chart."

The sound of Keith's sobs echoed in Mallory's mind as she left Intensive Care and walked down the long hall. She couldn't remember ever having felt so helpless. She wanted to *do* something for Keith, make him better somehow. The shining floor tiles blurred as she blinked back tears. Seeing Keith so distressed made the visit from his so-called son all the more infuriating. Mallory couldn't imagine who the blond man had been, and it was probably just as well. If she knew, she'd be tempted to strangle him. At least she had the consolation of knowing Keith had a good nurse caring for him, that instructions were being logged on his chart so the visitor flow would be monitored more closely from now on.

A good nurse. There had been a time when she had classified herself as one. Memories rushed through her.

Pictures of her husband Darren's face flashed in her mind. *Blood, so much blood.* She lifted her chin and took longer strides. She couldn't let these sterile surroundings get to her. It had been over a year. Long enough for the memories to fade. So why couldn't she put them behind her? When she reached the elevator, she could barely see the buttons. Extending an arm, she jabbed blindly, biting the inside of her lip. Crying was a luxury she seldom indulged in, certainly never in public. *This is what you get for going without sleep.*

"Excuse me, Mrs. Christiani?" a deep voice called.

Because she didn't want to be seen in tears, she almost ducked into the elevator without answering. But what if it was Keith's doctor? He might not make rounds again until tomorrow. She swiped at her cheeks, then turned. The elevator doors closed behind her.

"Yes?"

At first glance, Mallory knew the man loping down the hall wasn't Dr. Stein. He had golden hair, not dark brown, and looked to be about a foot too tall. Gray sweats and a blue windbreaker. Keith's mysterious "son"? Anger flashed through her, and she straightened her shoulders.

As he drew nearer, she saw why the nurse had pegged him as the athletic type. Though she did so begrudgingly, Mallory had to admit she had never seen blue nylon and gray knit filled out quite so impressively. Her gaze fell to a yellow smear on the front of his sweatshirt that looked suspiciously like mustard. Her attention then plunged to his smudged white sneakers. One toe was stained orange.

He shoved a hand into the pocket of his windbreaker and withdrew a business card. As he extended it to her, he whispered, "I'm Bud Mac Phearson, Keith's detective friend. Sorry I took so long. You must be half out of your mind."

Still rigid with anger, Mallory said, "I beg your pardon?"

The faint aroma of hot dogs clung to him. She had a hazy impression of tanned skin, sharply cut features and full lips. She glanced down at the card but didn't reach out to take it. The words PRIVATE INVESTIGATION stood out in boldface type.

Heaving a frustrated sigh, the man raked a hand through his already disheveled hair. "Keith didn't tell you?"

His eyes unnerved her. They were that rare, light shade of gray that seems to see right through you. "Keith isn't able to speak, so he hasn't told me much of anything. The nurse, however, told me plenty. You're the man who lied to gain admittance to Intensive Care, aren't you?"

She didn't miss the guilty surprise that flashed across his face. Without giving him a chance to speak, she rushed on.

"I suppose you're working on a case for the law firm? I've known a few overzealous investigators before, but this stunt takes the prize. The hospital rules are meant to protect the patients. You can't help but know my father-in-law is an extremely sick man." She gave the elevator button another jab. She was so furious her hand was shaking. "What could be so important that you'd bother him here? See his partner, Mr. Finn. He's handling everything until my father-in-law recovers. Now if you'll excuse me?"

He slipped his business card back into his jacket and stepped closer. "Wait. I have to talk to you. It's urgent."

Mallory, whose escape was thwarted by the slow response of the elevator, found herself meeting his unsettling gaze again. "Nothing you have to say could be *that* urgent. Christiani and Finn handles only civil cases."

"Could we find someplace private where we could talk?" He was already looking around as he spoke and reaching for her arm. "Someplace where we won't be seen or overheard?"

She avoided his outstretched hand. Now that she was studying him, she could see a fine sheen of sweat on his face. He kept looking around, as if he expected someone to creep up on him. Not the kind of fellow with whom she wanted seclusion. He turned to glance down the hall again. As he did, the front of his jacket fell back and she saw that he wore a shoulder holster and gun. Since Darren's accident, just being in the same room with a gun made her nervous.

The elevator doors slid open. Before she could react, Mac Phearson stepped forward to block her path with a set of shoulders that suddenly seemed as wide as a linebacker's. She tipped her head back to glare at him. He topped her five foot five by a good ten inches and outweighed her by at least eighty pounds. Her heart sank when the doors closed again behind him.

"Please," he said. "I realize I'm scaring you, but if you'll just give me a minute I'm sure I can explain."

Mallory inched away from him, growing more uneasy by the moment. "So explain."

"I'm an old friend of your father-in-law's. I've been out of town on a case for nearly a week, got back a day later than I planned. When I called in to check my answering machine this afternoon, there was a message from Keith. He said that he needed me to get you and your little girl out of town. *Immediately.* A man named Pete Lucetti has made a threat on your lives." He paused as if for emphasis. "He must have left that message yesterday, before he collapsed, which means I'm a day late as it is. We can't waste any time."

Of all the things Mallory had expected him to say, this wasn't one of them. She didn't like the way this man was behaving. *Terrified* was the only word to describe him. Or maybe *paranoid,* the way he kept checking the halls. "That's preposterous."

"But true. We can call Keith's office so you can be sure I *am* who I say I am, but we can't do it here in the hospital. Right before I went in to see Keith, some guy dressed like a priest visited him, and believe me, he was the farthest thing from a priest you're ever going to see. I saw the guy up close, and I recognized him. The last I heard, he was a strong-arm type who collected on delinquent bets for a local bookie. I watched him through the window and it looked like he was threatening Keith. About what, I have no idea. Do you have any idea how Keith got tied up with Lucetti? Do you know what this is about?"

"I—no—I—" Mallory swallowed. "You're really serious."

"Dead serious."

"Why didn't Keith simply call the police?"

"He said Lucetti has a couple of cops on the payroll. He must have been afraid, not sure who was safe to talk to and who wasn't. Mrs. Christiani, Pete Lucetti heads one of the largest crime rings in Seattle. He's bad news— *real* bad news."

Silence fell over them, such complete silence that Mallory could hear herself breathing. Her gaze dropped to the mustard stain on Mac Phearson's shirt. She hesitated. Christiani and Finn was one of the most prestigious law firms in Bellevue. Surely no one associated with the firm would be dressed so scruffily.

The man heaved another exasperated sigh. "I had a run-in with a kid toting a hot dog. I know I'm a mess, okay? My flight was late getting in. I went directly from the airport to coach baseball—changed into my sweats in the dugout. During break, I went up to the pay phone to call for my messages. After hearing that recording from Keith, I didn't take time for anything. My other clothes are in the car."

"Do you have any identification? Something besides a business card? For twenty dollars, you can have one of those made up proclaiming that you're just about anything, a snake charmer, an underwater basket weaver, anything."

An angry glint crept into his eyes and he reached for his wallet. When his hand skimmed the smooth hip of his sweatpants, he rolled his eyes toward the ceiling. "Mrs. Christiani, if I were some nutcase looking for an easy target, would I pick a woman in a busy hospital? Didn't you hear what I said? An extremely dangerous man has threatened to kill you and your daughter. Do you think Keith would have left me that message if he hadn't believed you were in serious danger?"

"I've no proof that he even called you. Keith and I are very close. If he had been in trouble, he would have told me."

Mac Phearson parted his lips to make a retort, but was cut short by the sharp sound of footsteps as someone came up behind them. Both he and Mallory glanced at the direction of the sound to see a priest rounding the corner up the hall. The priest paused midstride, his gaze coming to rest on Mallory. With a thoughtful frown, he reached a hand under his jacket. Mac Phearson cursed under his breath, seized Mallory by the arm and pulled her between him and the wall. Leaning sideways, he punched the elevator button and then slid his hand under his windbreaker. When Mallory saw that he was pulling his gun, she shrank back.

The priest had drawn a square of paper from his pocket. He studied it a moment, then resumed his pace.

"I thought he'd recognized you and was going for his weapon," Mac Phearson hissed. Hiding her from the other man's view, he whispered, "Don't scream. Please don't scream."

Mallory wouldn't have dreamed of it. This man was clearly suffering from paranoia. He had his gun concealed between their bodies. If he accidentally pulled the trigger, the bullet would go straight through her right breast. She could feel the tension in him, his muscles coiled tightly, his breath coming in short, uneven rasps. She craned her neck toward the priest. The man looked completely harmless to her, just a priest making duty calls to sick parishioners. He had probably pulled the paper from his pocket to check a room number. Mallory watched him, willing him to look her way again. If only he would see what was happening and help her. To her dismay, he walked past, sparing her not a glance.

A heavy ache pooled in her lower abdomen, and she pressed her shaking knees together. Mac Phearson's features swam before her in a dark blur. Her brain kicked into low gear, registering everything in slow motion with super clarity: his breathing, the drumming of her own pulse, the beads of sweat popping out on her forehead. The chime signaled the elevator's arrival on their floor. The instant the doors slid open, Mac Phearson jerked her half off her feet into the cubicle, releasing her only long enough to holster his gun and hit the lobby button.

Mallory threw a panicked glance at the swiftly closing doors. There hadn't been time to run before Mac Phearson had grabbed her arm again. She stood there in frozen horror and tried desperately to think what to do. If she screamed, would she be heard? How well were elevators insulated? And suppose someone did hear her? Was she willing to jeopardize the lives of innocent people? This man couldn't be sane. He might open fire in the busy lobby.

He threw her a look that seemed to mirror her own feeling of terror. "Look, I'm sorry about this, but right now my first priority has to be getting you out of here in one piece. If that means I have to be a little heavy-handed, it's better than you getting killed."

Hysteria closed her throat. She had read about this kind of thing occurring, but she had never dreamed it could happen to her. *Think. Don't give way to panic.* What was the best way to handle someone who had lost his grip on reality? Appearing calm was a must. Angering or frightening him could prove fatal, not just to her but to others.

She ran a cottony tongue over dry lips. Suddenly, insanely, she wanted a drink of water. Visions of her little girl's face swept through her mind. *Emily.* Mallory didn't want to die. Not yet. She had left too many things undone. She wanted to hug her daughter and tell her one last time how much she loved her. There were some dirty dishes in the kitchen sink. She hadn't finished weeding the violets yet, either. And who would take care of Keith?

Mac Phearson was watching the floor numbers flash on the panel above their heads. Without looking down at her, he gave her a perfunctory pat on the back, which she presumed was meant to comfort her. "With any luck, they're all upstairs, Mrs. Christiani. Maybe we'll make it out of here with no trouble."

Mallory had no idea who *they* were. Pete Lucetti? The name sounded like something out of an old gangster movie; it had nothing to do with reality. Who was this man? And where was he taking her? She fixed her gaze on the left front panel of his jacket. Having the gun out of sight did little to comfort her.

"Where's your daughter?"

"Sh-she's staying with friends."

"Do they live far from here?"

Mallory could only pray her face didn't betray her. "A long way."

"How long has it been since you spoke with her? Since you knew for sure she was all right?"

"This morning."

He threw her a sharp glance. "Did she attend school today?"

Surely he didn't know what school Emily attended. "Yes."

"Your sitter takes her and picks her up, I take it?"

"She has kids who go there."

"Does she keep a close eye on Emily?"

Mallory was startled. He knew her daughter's name? Of course, he could have learned it in a dozen different ways, not necessarily through an association with Keith. Indecision held her paralyzed. His gray eyes locked with hers, compelling her to answer him. "I—yes, she watches her closely."

The floor panel light indicated that the elevator was approaching the lobby. Mac Phearson took a deep breath. When the elevator stopped and the doors opened, he looped an arm around her shoulders and propelled her forward into a short hall that opened into the lobby. The lean, hard ridges of his body pressed against her arm. She felt him grow tense, and her heartbeat accelerated.

What if he were telling the truth? As she watched his gaze dart suspiciously around the waiting area, she couldn't help wondering. He seemed as scared as she was, which meant he truly believed they were in terrible danger. Her thoughts flew to Emily again. Mac Phearson was either totally immersed in make-believe or on the level. Her skin prickled. Had someone really threatened to kill her and her daughter? Mac Phearson *had* reached for his wallet earlier, presumably to show her his ID. It wasn't beyond the realm of possibility that he *had* forgotten his wallet in his street pants, just as he had claimed. And there *had* been a priest in the ICU visiting Keith.

What if? She recalled the terror she'd seen in Keith's eyes, the feeling she'd had that he'd been trying desperately to tell her something.

They were halfway across the lobby. Time was ticking by, second by treacherous second. If she was going to scream and try to get away, it was now or never. The click of her shoes against the tile resounded inside her head as her captor led her through the milling people. She fastened her gaze on a toddler fleeing from his mother. If Mac Phearson was unbalanced, he might pull his weapon and fire indiscriminately. On the other hand, what if he was perfectly sane and telling the truth? What if there were killers in the hospital? *Now or never. Now or never,* her mind taunted. A few more feet and they would be out of the building.

Mallory couldn't be sure what it was that finally decided it for her. Perhaps it was the firm but somehow gentle pressure of Mac Phearson's grip on her arm. Or the way he walked, turned slightly toward her, as if he were trying to shield her. She only knew she couldn't risk being wrong. It was broad daylight, after all. There were bound to be people in the parking lot. If he was telling the truth, he had identification in the car. She would simply demand to see it before going anywhere with him.

A sea of parked automobiles stretched before them as they left the loading area. Mac Phearson never broke stride as they crossed the parking lot. His arm felt unnervingly strong vised around her shoulders. He was a tall man, heavily muscled and agile. If he wasn't who he claimed to be, she was in big trouble. *Just as far as the car.* If he didn't come up with identification then, she'd scream so loudly that people on the next block would hear.

He drew her closer to his side. "Lean into me and look down, Mrs. Christiani."

"What for?"

"To hide your face. *Just do it.*"

Mallory almost refused, but the urgency in his voice compelled her. She dropped her chin to her chest and pressed her shoulder against his ribs.

He quickened his pace. "Be sure you don't look up."

"Is there really someone out here?" Now that was a brilliant question. If he was lying, would he admit it?

"In a car to our left, two rows over. Three men. Listen to me and listen close. If I tell you to get down, I want you to drop right where you are. Understand? Don't try to run."

Surely this wasn't an act. Fear inched up her spine.

"They may have a perfectly legitimate reason for sitting there. But it pays to be safe, and they look suspicious. If they have guns, I can't see them. My car's not far." He fished in his jacket pocket for his keys. "Just a few more steps. You're doing great."

He drew to a stop and reached across her to unlock the door of an old, blue Volvo. As he opened the door, he took hold of her elbow and shoved her forward, giving her no time to protest.

"Fasten your seat belt," he ordered as he slammed her door.

On the floorboard was an array of tools, including a hefty screwdriver and a tire iron. An investigator might use such things. On the other hand, so might a killer. Mallory reached for the door handle. She threw open the door, but before she could get out, Mac Phearson had climbed in on his side.

"What are you doing?" he snarled. "You don't seem to understand, lady. This isn't a game we're playing."

He seized her arm, jerked her back into the automobile and leaned across her to slam the door. He glared at her as he fastened his own seat belt, then reached over to buckle hers. The clasp clicked with finality. Mallory dropped her head to avoid eye contact. What if she looked into his eyes and saw madness gleaming back at her? What if there weren't any hoodlums in the parking lot? What if the priest had been just that, a priest who had visited Keith by mistake?

The car engine leaped to life and Mallory leaped with it. Her head shot up and she fastened a terrified gaze on Mac Phearson's taut features. He threw an arm over the seat and craned his neck to see behind them as he backed the Volvo out of the parking space. Despite the mustard-stained sweat suit and tousled hair, he was an extremely attractive man. Were madmen good-looking? She remembered seeing the infamous Ted Bundy's pho-

tograph, remembered thinking how incredible it was that
he'd murdered so many women. The police claimed he
had convinced some of his victims that he was a police
officer and coaxed them into his car. Like Mac Phearson
had just coaxed her?

As the car surged forward, she turned to look back at
the parking lot, not sure whether or not she wanted to see
a carful of men pursuing them. Either way, she was in
a mess. He was driving too fast and the slanting sun reflected off all the windshields. "May I see your ID now,
Mr. Mac Phearson?" she asked as calmly as she could
manage.

"Now?" He threw her an incredulous look. "It's there
in the backseat, but I'd really rather you didn't undo your
belt. As soon as we're someplace safe, I'll get it for you."

Someplace safe? she thought. Safe for who? Him or
her?

CHAPTER TWO

FOR AN ENDLESS moment, Mallory stared at Mac Phearson's profile, acutely aware that their car was picking up speed, heading west. Buildings flashed by. Air whished in around her door. She inched sideways in the seat to face him. He was too busy driving and checking his rearview mirror to notice her.

"I can't see anyone following us. Why should it hurt if I unfasten my seat belt?"

Distracted by the question, he glanced her way. "Give it a few minutes so I can be sure they aren't coming. Right now, ID is the *least* of our worries. Where's your daughter staying?"

Mallory gnawed the inside of her lip, a bad habit of hers when she was upset. His act was convincing, she had to admit, but there didn't appear to be any villain on the scene. "Mr. Mac Phearson, I want to see some ID. *Now.*"

He ignored her, his mouth pressed into a grim line.

Mallory unfastened her seat belt and turned as if to get out of the car. "Either you come up with some ID or I'm taking a quick exit."

His hand shot out to grab the front of her jacket. "Damn, are you crazy? Don't you *dare* open that door."

"Take your hand off me."

"We're doing forty-five, in case you haven't noticed." He checked his mirror again, then narrowed his eyes.

With a curse, he released her and grabbed the wheel with both hands. "That's them. Hold on."

He floored the gas pedal. She stared through the windshield at the heavy traffic, horrified, as he switched lanes and cut off the car behind them. Brakes squealed as he swung across an oncoming lane to reach the north 405 exit ramp.

"You're going to kill somebody!"

"I've got to make the exit."

A blue Lincoln swerved into the guardrail to miss them. Mallory had a death grip on the dash. "We're going to crash!"

"They're on our tail."

They? She couldn't tear her eyes from the brown Bronco that bore down on them. Its steel bumper and winch seemed as formidable as a tank. More brakes squealed. The Bronco skidded sideways and brought the exiting lane of traffic behind it to a quick halt, causing a chain reaction of fender benders. The Volvo careened onto the access road that merged with 405.

Once on the freeway, Mac Phearson darted the car in and out of lanes, driving far faster than was safe, to put several miles between them and Bellevue. "I've only gained us a couple of minutes' head start. They probably doubled back to the exit to follow us. We've got to switch over to southbound."

"Across the divider?"

He flashed his blinker and forced his way over to the middle lane. "It's not a divider once we get down past the bridge, just a sloping ditch. Cops cut across there all the time."

Mallory, unable to believe any of this was happening, saw the overhead bridge coming up fast. She didn't see how Mac Phearson could get over through all this traffic. They zoomed under the bridge and had to travel several more miles before he could manage to squeeze over.

She threw an arm up to shield her face when he finally gained the inside lane. The next second, she felt their tires lose traction on the gravel shoulder. The car bottomed out, bounced and was airborne. They landed with an ear-shattering clunk that jolted her so hard she bit her tongue. Pain exploded through the roof of her mouth. She clung desperately to the dash as the underbody of the Volvo grated its way up the incline to the southbound lanes.

When she felt smooth highway caressing the tires again, she noticed that the glove box had popped open. She reached to close it and froze. A manila envelope in the glove box had come open and spilled an array of glossy plastic squares. Washington drivers' licenses and ID cards, several of them, all with Mac Phearson's snapshot and other names. *Aliases?* She shut the glove box. She was in big trouble. This man didn't work for Christiani and Finn. He was either an undercover man or a crook, and right now, the latter seemed most likely. As yet, she hadn't seen anyone following them. And if no one was following them, everything he had told her was a lie.

Tiny beads of sweat glistened on his forehead. "I don't see them coming yet," he said, "but even so, it'd be a good idea to get off this freeway. We'll be sitting ducks out here."

Visualizing a lonely dirt road and a gun pressed to her temple, all she could think of was getting out of the car while there were still people around. Sudden inspiration hit her. "Pull over. I'm going to be sick. Oh, hurry. Pull over now."

She clamped a hand to her mouth, gagged and bugged

her eyes at him. He swerved into the parking lane and brought the car skidding to a stop. Throwing open the door, Mallory snatched up her purse and made her escape.

"Here they come!" he yelled just as she gained her feet.

Grabbing her arm, he spun her around and jerked her back into the car. She sprawled facedown on the seat as the car lurched forward again. She crooked an arm around his thigh to hold on, too shocked to scream. The door swung inward scraping her calves. When the car swerved back into traffic, all that kept her from spilling out was his hold on her.

"Get in!"

She didn't need to be told twice. With nothing but open air between her and the blur of road, sixty seemed much faster than usual. Scrambling for purchase, she clawed her way in.

"Shut the door." He held her wrist in a steely grip. "I'll hold you."

As she leaned out to reach for the door handle, she could only pray Mac Phearson didn't let go of her. Wind blasted her face and whipped her hair flat against her head. Her fingertips curled on the chrome. *Just one more inch.* She angled her body farther forward.

With the wind pushing against it, the door slammed shut so easily when she pulled that she was propelled backward against him. She felt his muscles tense under his jacket sleeve as he fought for control of the car.

"You okay?"

"No, I'm *not* okay."

"Get that seat belt back on."

She sat up and rammed the buckle together. "Where *are* they? You crazy idiot, you nearly got me killed."

"They're coming up on our left."

There *wasn't* any highway on their left, only a dividing strip. She looked back, not expecting to see anyone. Her heart skipped a beat. Sure enough, there came a cream-colored car, bouncing and swerving inside the ditch, gaining on them at an alarming rate. A man poked his head out the rear window. He held something black in his hands. She couldn't be seeing what she *thought* she was seeing. "They've got a gun!"

In grim silence, Mac Phearson inched up behind an old woman in an equally ancient Ford.

"Step on it! Didn't you hear me? They've got a gun!"

"I can't step on it! We're bumper-to-bumper!"

"Then hit the ditch! You did it before. They're gaining."

"It's too dangerous. I took it at an angle last time. Now I'd have to side-hill. We'd roll."

The cream-colored car was within five car lengths. A rapid splat of bullets riddled the back of the Volvo.

Mac Phearson checked his side mirror. "Hold on."

Swerving to the left, he entered the emergency-parking lane and floored the gas pedal. Twisting within the confines of her safety belt, she peered out the rear window. "They're shooting at us! They're actually *shooting* at us."

His only response was a scowl. Mallory saw the pursuing car hit a chuckhole, do a nosedive and send up a spray of dirt. The Volvo gained several car lengths. Mac Phearson jerked the steering wheel hard to the right and smacked a green Honda broadside. The terrified driver slammed on his brakes, his tires grabbing pavement and spitting blue-black smoke. Mac Phearson took advantage of the open space and managed to move over two lanes. He swiped at his forehead with his sleeve and blinked trickles of sweat from his eyes. He looked as terrified as Mallory felt. "They're trying to follow us over."

Hardly able to believe her own ears, Mallory heard herself say, "I—I could switch places and drive so you could shoot back."

"That's an *Uzi,* lady, not a popgun."

"Wh-what's an Uzi?"

"It puts out about a thousand rounds a minute, *that's* what."

A thousand rounds a minute? Turning, she saw a flash of cream-colored paint in the whizzing traffic. "Who *are* they? Why are they doing this?"

"Lucetti's thugs is my guess. They haven't gotten close enough for me to get a make on any of them and I'd like to keep it that way." He punctuated that statement with a screech of tires. "Scoot down."

Mallory inched down just far enough to hide, but not so far she couldn't see as he took the exit. The Volvo rocked on two wheels around a corner. She saw a red light coming up fast and braced herself. She knew without asking that they were going to run it. As they hit the intersection, she opted for oblivion and closed her eyes. When nothing happened, she lifted her lashes.

He darted a glance her way. "What happened to your cheek?"

She touched her cheekbone and winced, remembering how she'd hit the edge of the seat. "Just a little bump. I'm fine." Sliding up in the seat, she glanced through the back window. The cream-colored car was blocked in traffic. "Can we lose them?"

"We've got the advantage."

"We do?"

His mouth quirked slightly at one corner. "It's called motivation."

"I see your point."

He turned left into a residential area and drove aimlessly for several minutes. Mallory couldn't take her eyes off the rear window even though she soon became convinced there was no longer a car following them. He reduced his speed to twenty-five.

"I think we've lost them," he told her.

She sighed and swept her tangled mass of whiskey-colored hair back from her face. At the end of a cul-de-sac, he parked behind a center island of tall shrubs that would hide them from passersby on the intersecting street. To Mallory's right was a brown house with a lazy cocker spaniel sunning on the lawn. She wished they could go inside, lock all the doors and hide. "Why are we stopping? Is that wise? If my daughter's in danger, I want to go get her."

"We have to stay out of sight for a while. Besides, I need to get my stomach back down where it belongs." He leaned his head back against the rest and closed his eyes. His hands remained clenched on the steering wheel. "As for wise? If I were wise, lady, I wouldn't be here."

Now that she knew he was telling the truth about Keith's message, Mallory was plagued with more questions. "Why, exactly, *are* you here, then?"

"Keith's a good friend. He asked, I'm here."

Bitterness laced the words. After several uncomfortably quiet minutes had dragged by, he released the catch on his seat belt and rose to his knees beside her. She turned to watch him sift through piles of assorted junk in the back of the car. She'd never seen such a collection. Boxes, baseball bats, rumpled clothes, a battered suitcase and various fast-food cartons. After a search that led him clear to the bottom of the pile, he lifted a white plastic case and a spray container.

"What's that?"

"First aid. For your scrapes." He gestured to her legs.

She hadn't even noticed. "I'm fine. Please, can't we go get my daughter now?"

"I told you, we have to give them time to get off the scent. Might as well take advantage of it." He crooked his right leg under himself and sat down, motioning her to turn sideways as he gave the can a shake. "Hand me a foot."

Catching hold of her skirt to cinch it tight, she lifted her legs and swiveled on her bottom to put her feet on the seat. Her eyes widened when she saw she was minus a shoe. It must have fallen off when she was dangling from the car.

"No great loss. High heels spell nothing but trouble anyway. I'll get you something practical. No fashion shows where we're going." He ripped a larger hole in her nylon and doused the back of her leg with cold spray. "Your ankle is pretty bruised."

He made it sound as if he thought fashion was the be-all of her existence. Mallory shot him a glare, then leaned forward to assess the damage to her legs. "And just where are we going?"

"Eastern Washington. A cabin in the mountains. You and Emily will be safe there until I get to the bottom of this."

Capping the spray can, he tossed it in a careless arc into the backseat junk pile. Her spine went ramrod straight when he pursed his lips and blew softly on her skin until the disinfectant dried. The play of muscle in his shoulders stretched the cloth of his jacket taut. His hands were gentle as he smoothed stick-on bandages over the worst of her scrapes. He'd obviously done this before. Perhaps he had children? He wasn't wearing a wedding ring, but that didn't always mean anything.

She watched his bent head, feeling suddenly ashamed of herself. Most men would have dumped her from the car and said good riddance when she'd faked being sick. "Mr. Mac Phearson, I—I didn't mean to call you names back there. I was just so scared, they popped out."

"Names? Crazy idiot, you mean?" He raised his eyes to hers, his mouth twisting into a humorless grin. "I've been called worse, believe me." He snapped the first-aid case shut and threw it over the seat. "You weren't really sick, were you?"

"When I saw those fake IDs, I thought—" Mallory broke off and licked her lips. "Well, I—"

His gaze flew to the glove box. A slight frown pleated his forehead. "I can't always go by my real name in my line of work."

"Yes—well—investigators for Christiani and Finn don't usually go undercover. And if not undercover investigators, most people who use aliases are—"

"Crooks?" He grabbed his street pants from the pile of stuff on the backseat, fished for his wallet and tossed it in her lap. "Christiani and Finn isn't my only client, you know. In my line of work, I've even worn a chicken costume to catch a thieving employee at a fast-food joint. Believe it or not, if people know who I am, I don't always get the answers I need. I'm Bud Mac Phearson, just as I said. You almost got us both killed pulling that stunt back there." When she didn't open the wallet, he snapped, "Go ahead and check me out. Blood type, political affiliations, licenses, permits. It's all in there."

"I don't really need proof, you know. After all that's happened, how could I not believe you?" But even as she said it, to satisfy him and herself, Mallory opened the wallet and glanced at his identification. She couldn't afford mistakes.

"I'm glad to hear it." He flopped back down behind the wheel. "If we're stuck with each other, a little trust can't hurt."

A heavy silence settled over them. "I said I was sorry."

"Yeah, me, too."

From his tone, she couldn't be sure if he was sorry for something he'd done or if he just regretted his entanglement with *her*.

"I should have had my ID with me. I was stupid to forget it in the car. When I lecture on crime prevention, I warn women never to—" He swiped at a hank of hair that waved across his forehead, getting in his eyes. "Let's just forget it, okay?"

Mallory offered his wallet to him. He took it and shoved it into his jacket pocket. She studied him for a moment, then said, "I feel as if I'm having a bad dream and can't wake up. Why are those men doing this? I can't understand it."

"For now, I'm not going to worry about why. A gun in my back has a way of dampening my curiosity. As for dreaming, I wish."

She rolled down her window and inhaled a bracing draught of spruce-scented air. The sound of children's laughter came to them from up the street. The sound reminded her of Emily and unbidden tears welled in her eyes. "Shouldn't we be going? I'd like to get my daughter."

He stuffed a rumpled handkerchief into her hand. "In a few more minutes. They'll comb the streets for a while. Let's make sure we're safe."

Mallory searched for a clean spot on the handkerchief.

"Sorry. Toby's hot dog and orange slush is all over it."

"Who's Toby?"

"My pitcher." He grabbed a dog-eared notepad off the dash, unclipped the Lindy pen attached to the bent spirals and jotted something down. "Was that a Buick they were driving? An '88?"

"There was a *gun* hanging out the window. That's all I noticed."

He didn't even look up. "It was at least an '88. I think the first three letters on the plate were LUD."

"Are we going to the police?"

"Keith said no."

"Then why write the tag number down?" She stared at his taut face. "Every cop in King County can't be working for Lucetti."

"Do you want to take a chance on trusting the wrong one?"

"Do you know what you're saying? That there are policemen who know about this and aren't doing anything to stop it?"

He tossed the tablet back onto the dash and braced his arms on the steering wheel. "That's right."

"This is Seattle, not Miami Vice."

His eyes locked with hers. She had the feeling that he thoroughly disliked her.

"You say *Seattle* like it's smack dab in the middle of *Disneyland. Most* cops are on the level, probably ninety-nine-point-nine percent, but it only takes one. Bellevue, with its manicured streets and fancy houses and fifty-thousand-dollar cars, isn't the real world. I know that's hard for you to digest, but take a stab at it."

"Just what *are* we going to do, then?"

"We're going to go pick up your kid and then get out

of town." He gave her a challenging glance. "Unless you can come up with a better suggestion?"

For the life of her, Mallory couldn't think of a single one.

CHAPTER THREE

THE RIDE TO Beth Hamstead's house, where Emily was staying, took thirty minutes, during which Mallory felt the tension in her neck and shoulders beginning to ease. She couldn't think of any way anyone could know where Emily was. That thought and the peaceful country scenery along the Woodinville-Duvall Road soothed her as nothing else could. Leaning her head back against the rest, she watched the green hillsides whiz by, relishing the cool caress of the early evening breeze as it rushed in through her open window. In a few more minutes, she would have her daughter safely in her arms, and Mac Phearson would spirit them away to a safe place where they could wait together until he could find out what was going on.

Turning her head, she watched him as he maneuvered the car, one shoulder propped against his door, one hand loosely curled around the steering wheel. At a glance, he appeared relaxed. Only his eyes gave him away. They darted continually from the road to his rearview mirror. His watchfulness reminded her that the nightmare from which they'd just escaped was far from over.

"See anyone?"

"Not yet. Mrs. Christiani—"

"Mallory, please. Mrs. seems so formal."

"Mallory," he corrected. "I want you to think back over the last few weeks. Has Keith said or done anything odd?"

She shook her head. "He's been horribly tense, that's all."

"Any strangers been calling the house? People who've never called before? It's extremely important."

Again she shook her head.

"Has Keith been gone at odd hours? Has he, um, had a sudden increase in income?"

Mallory stiffened. "Just what are you implying?"

"Nothing. I'm just trying to—" He narrowed his eyes. "Get something straight, okay? Keith's like a father to me. I'm not maligning his character, just looking for answers."

"He *isn't* dealing in anything criminal, not Keith."

"Has he had an increase in income?"

"No!"

"Don't just say no, *think.* Like it or not, he's tied up in something pretty nasty and there has to be a reason for it. Not everyone runs in your circles, you know. Keith didn't meet Lucetti over a friendly game of handball at the athletic club."

Mallory sat straighter in the seat. He made affluence sound like a sin. It wasn't as if she were one of the rich and famous, after all. Her dad was an ex-congressman— so what? She had been raised in a town where the wealthy greatly outnumbered the middle-income families. Again, so what? People didn't pick their parents, after all.

"You don't like me, do you?" she ground out.

His jaw tensed. "I just met you. Why wouldn't I like you?"

"You tell me."

He turned his attention from the road to give her a lazy perusal. "If I had to describe my feelings toward you, I'd have to say I'm indifferent. I haven't known you long enough to form a personal opinion of you. I'm here as a favor to Keith. Which brings us back to my question. Let's stick to that."

He didn't sound indifferent, he sounded contemptuous. And for the life of her Mallory couldn't see what it was he found so revolting. Her expensive green suit was a mess, no doubt about it, but he wasn't going to take any fashion prizes himself. In frustration, she decided to let the issue drop. Indifference could be mutual.

She forced her mind back to his question, Keith's income. Could her father-in-law have become involved in something shady? No, she couldn't believe it of him, not for an instant. "There's been no increase in income that I'm aware of. No strangers calling. Nothing. He's been tense…that's all."

"How about strange cars in the neighborhood?"

"No, not that I noticed. Our neighborhood is pretty quiet."

He frowned. "There has to be something we're missing."

Mallory had no answer. "Keith's a good man, an honest man."

"I know that." He squinted to see out the dirty windshield. "You said to take a left at two hundred and twenty-sixth, right?"

She nodded and tried to read the street signs. They still had about a half mile to go before their turn. "It's not finished yet, is it? They could still find us."

"Assuming Lucetti doesn't already know where we're heading. It's possible that he's been having you followed."

Sweat sprang to her palms. So much for her calm assumption that Emily was safe. Thank goodness they were only a short distance from Beth's. "You think that he might've?"

"It's possible. But let's not borrow trouble."

He was right. She had problems aplenty already.

He glanced over at her. "You look exhausted. How long since you slept and ate?"

"I'm fine."

Remembering the bitterness that had crept into his voice earlier, she fastened a curious stare on him. One minute he sounded almost as if he hated her, the next he took her off guard by being kind. Did he have some particular reason for disliking Bellevue people? He seemed loyal enough to Keith, referring to him as a surrogate father, which meant he must have grown up in the Seattle area. Intercity, probably. But what part? She shifted her gaze to the pile of junk on his backseat. The baseball bat caught her eye. "I take it you like kids?"

"They're okay."

"You must think they're a little better than okay or you wouldn't coach ball."

He checked the rearview mirror again. "We can't all do our good deeds at fancy charity dinners."

She ignored the dig. "Still live in your old neighborhood?"

"My mom does."

"Is that where you coach?"

He hesitated before answering. "That's right."

"Is it a school team?"

He looked over at her. Something flickered in his eyes, something so cold it almost made Mallory shiver. "You want to know what part of Seattle I'm from, right?"

"Is there something wrong with that?"

"Nope. Just predictable."

It was several seconds before she realized he hadn't answered her question. *Just predictable.* What was that supposed to mean? He took the sharp left turn off the Woodinville-Duvall Road. She pointed through the trees toward Beth's two-story white house. "It's the third right, up there on the hill." Glancing at her watch, she added, "The kids are probably out in the pasture with Lovey. It's not quite supper time yet."

"Lovey?"

"The Shetland pony."

Mac Phearson steered the car up the narrow, winding driveway. Trees blocked Mallory's view of the house. She strained her neck to see the upper pasture, hoping to spot her daughter. When she looked back at Mac Phearson, he was staring straight-ahead, his eyes flat and hard. He braked to a stop.

Mallory immediately knew something had to be wrong. Her heart leaped when she saw the police car angled across the driveway. Beth Hamstead was standing beside a tall policeman out in front of the garage. Mallory threw off her seat belt and wrenched her car door open. Mac Phearson cut the engine, pulled the emergency brake and piled out his door after her. She felt his hand clamp down on her arm. "Be careful what you say."

Mallory jerked away from him. Beth's brood hovered around their mother. But where was Emily? Mallory searched for her daughter's amber-colored braids among the bobbing redheads. Oh, dear God, where was Emily? A call came over the police car radio, and the officer left Beth to go answer it.

Beth stiffened when she spotted Mallory running up the steep driveway. "Oh, Mall, thank heaven you're here. I've been out of my mind, trying to call you. Em's wandered off."

It felt to Mallory as if the ground had disappeared from

under her. She didn't realize she'd nearly fallen until a hard, strong arm caught her around the shoulders. *Mac Phearson.* Forgetting that she barely knew him, no longer really caring, she leaned into him for much-needed support. "Wh-what do you mean, she's wandered off, Beth? How long has it been since you saw her?" Mallory dreaded hearing the answer.

Beth lifted both hands, blue eyes apologetic. "I only turned my back for a few minutes. The phone rang and I ran inside to answer it. That's all, I swear it. You know how closely I watch her. She was right here playing with the others and then—then she was just gone." Running her fingers through her red hair, Beth flashed an unconvincing smile. "I'm sure she's just lost her way in the woods. No need to panic. In this thick brush, it happens sometimes. I can't count the times my kids have gotten turned around. Of course, they're more familiar with the area, so they've always gotten back before I felt it was necessary to call the police."

Fear sluiced down Mallory's spine and pooled like ice at the small of her back. An image of her daughter's face swam through her head, and she felt a scream welling in her throat. She clamped her arms around her middle, clinging desperately to her self-control. Mac Phearson's hand clasped hers where it rested at her waist and she threw him a pleading look. The dismay she read in his eyes only intensified her fear. "Lucetti?" she whispered.

"Let's not jump to conclusions," he cautioned in a low voice. "It doesn't add up."

He threw an uneasy glance at the policeman to make sure he wasn't listening.

Ignoring his warning glance, Mallory continued her questions. "You don't think Lucetti took her, then?"

Mac Phearson's gaze slid to Beth before he answered. The redhead was busy speaking with one of her children, not listening to them. "When professionals make a hit, they do it quick and clean, Mallory. They couldn't have found a more ideal place than here, remote, no witnesses. Why take her someplace else and risk being seen while they—" He broke off and swallowed.

Mallory knew what it must be that he had left unsaid, but she couldn't let herself dwell on it. What he *had* said was what she must concentrate on and that was bad enough. If Lucetti was out for blood, he couldn't have found a better place to spill it. Which meant what?

The police officer turned away from the car, his face lined with concern. He stared at Mallory's torn stockings and bare feet for a moment, then lifted his gaze to Mac Phearson's smeared sweatshirt. "I assume you're Mr. and Mrs. Christiani?"

"I'm Mrs. Christiani. This is my friend, Mr. Mac Ph—"

"Pleased, I'm sure," Mac Phearson said, cutting the introduction short and extending his arm for a handshake.

"I'm Officer Maloney. It looks as if your daughter has wandered off into the woods, ma'am."

"Did you already question the children?" she asked.

"Yes, but they weren't much help. It seems they left Emily holding the Shetland's halter while they ran into the barn to get some oats. Evidently the pony isn't a very cooperative riding mount unless she's bribed. They had trouble getting the feed-room door open and took longer than they meant to. When they came back out, Emily was gone. Mrs. Hamstead had gone inside and wasn't watching them, as I understand it."

Beth approached, her eyes taking on a glint of anger. "I *was* watching them. I just went in to answer my phone."

The officer cleared his throat. "I don't think there's any cause for alarm. She's been gone less than two hours. We have four squad cars on the roads, three officers on foot. We've asked all the neighbors, and no one has seen her. But most people are busy this time of day preparing dinner, so that's not really odd. We'll have her home for her own dinner if my guess is right. Too many roads around here for her to wander far."

Mallory nearly groaned in exasperation. Em wouldn't take off without permission. The child *knew* better. And Mallory never left her here without cautioning her against leaving the yard. In one direction, there was a busy highway, and in the other, a lake.

There was a horrible, quivery feeling in the pit of Mallory's stomach, a feeling that seemed somehow connected to her throat. *Emily?* She searched the faces of the other children, willing her daughter to appear. This was every mother's nightmare, the sort of thing you read about in the paper but never dreamed would happen to you. *Oh, please, God, not my baby.*

"It's not like my daughter to leave the yard without permission," Mallory said, struggling to keep her voice calm. "Have you considered the possibility that she might have been kidnapped?"

Mac Phearson stiffened and cast Mallory a warning glance, which she presumed was meant to silence her. She lifted her chin and met his gaze head-on before returning her attention to the policeman.

"Kidnapping is always a possibility, Mrs. Christiani, but we've no reason to suspect that at this stage. Mrs. Hamstead hasn't noticed any strangers hanging around.

This is a quiet area, not much off-the-highway traffic. Who'd be up here to spot an unattended child and take her that quickly?"

"Unattended?" Beth protested. "What are you implying? I watch the kids more closely than most mothers, especially with a lake so close."

Mallory doubled her hands into fists. Her nails bit into her palms. Her daughter was missing. This was no time for Beth's ego to get in the way.

"I— Don't misinterpret what I'm saying, Mrs. Hamstead," the officer said patiently. "I didn't mean that you were neglecting the child. Kids will be kids. They forget rules sometimes and wander farther than they realize. Unfortunately a turn of the head is all it takes and they're gone. Especially in a wooded area like this. Emily probably didn't intend to go more than a few steps and simply got turned around. Where is this lake?"

"Right up the road."

The alarm that flashed across the officer's face was impossible to miss. "Did Emily know about the lake?"

"Yes!" Mallory cut in. "I've warned her about it."

"Does your daughter like the water?"

Mallory stared at the policeman, scarcely seeing him as she pictured Em standing on the diving board at home, poised to do a backflip. *Mommy, look at me!* The memory made her eyes burn with unshed tears. The trees in her peripheral vision seemed to be closing in, spinning. "Yes, she loves the water." Her voice sounded as if it belonged to someone else, calm and reasonable, completely at odds with the panic churning inside her. She wanted to charge off into the woods—scream, cry—beg someone to tell her this wasn't really happening. "We have a pool. She's an accomplished swimmer. She's already in intermediate lessons."

"Excuse me just a moment." The policeman walked back to his car and leaned through the open window to grab the mike to his radio. After talking a few minutes, he strode back to them. The expression on his face spoke volumes.

Mallory couldn't breathe. It felt as if a thousand-pound weight had hit her square in the chest. *The lake.* Em *was* a good swimmer, but what if she had fallen in? Her woolen school uniform and shoes would soak up water like a sponge and hamper her.

Mallory began to tremble. She could almost feel Em's soft little body hugged tightly in her arms, smell her shampoo, see her twinkling brown eyes and freckled nose. "We have to find her," she said, glancing up at Mac Phearson. Fear made her voice sound slightly off-key. "She's only seven. It'll get dark soon."

"We'll find her." Mac Phearson's arms slipped around her reassuringly. "There's plenty of daylight left."

Mallory nodded and sucked in a breath of air, holding it until her temples throbbed. Exhaling with a shaky sigh, she forced herself to relax. She had to stay calm. Think. Where might Em have gone? She glanced over the bushy hillsides, trying to see it from a child's perspective. What could have enticed Em from the yard? A squirrel, perhaps? A pretty bird? Mallory couldn't imagine her daughter disobeying the rules on a whim.

"Better?" Mac Phearson's arms loosened and she felt him smoothing her hair. "She's okay. Count on it."

Lifting her head, Mallory looked deep into his gray eyes. The low timbre of his voice bolstered her. He sounded so certain. *Oh, please, let him be right.* Again she turned to stare in indecision at the semicircle of trees that hemmed the property. Emily's name ached in her throat. Could Lucetti have tailed them here last night, as Mac Phearson had mentioned? What if he had? What if he had taken Em? If he had, they'd be wasting time searching the woods.

But what if Lucetti doesn't have her? Em *might* be lost. They had to search for her here first—just in case. She might panic, fall and hurt herself. That thought spurred Mallory into action. She took several steps toward the trees, only to be dragged to a stop by Mac Phearson's strong grip on her shoulder.

"You can't take off on foot, not without shoes."

"I have to. She'll be getting scared by now." She tried to slip out of his grasp. "She'll come if she hears my voice. Hearing a bunch of strange men yelling her name might frighten her. She could start running and fall or—"

His grip on her wrist tightened. "We'll take the car. You can drive up and down the roads while I search the brush. If you keep your window down, she'll be able to hear you just as well as if you were walking, and you can cover more ground that way. She's bound to stumble out to a road sooner or later, right?"

Mallory glanced at the car, anxious to start searching. If Em did come out onto a road, she would surely stay on it. Mac was right. Looking for her in an automobile might prove to be the fastest way to find her.

The policeman turned to Beth. "Someone should stay here." Beth nodded. Glancing at Mac Phearson, the officer said, "We're sweeping up from the highway in this direction. As soon as the men get here, we'll go on up the road."

It went without saying that "up the road" meant the

lake. Despite Mac Phearson's reassurances, Mallory's stomach lurched.

"Then that's where we'll head first," Mac Phearson replied.

AN HOUR LATER, Mallory stood beside the car. Mac wove his way toward her through the thick brush, never taking his eyes off her. Standing there barefoot in the dusky light with her tousled hair framing her face, she looked like a scared twelve-year-old. The bruise along her cheek was a dark shadow against her white skin.

His stomach tightened as he drew closer. The fear in her sherry-brown eyes reached out and coiled itself around his heart.

He had hated Mallory Christiani so venomously for so many years that the sudden wave of pity he felt for her confused him. Time after time today, he had found himself forgetting who she was. Now was getting to a point where he didn't much care. She wasn't at all as he had imagined her. Admitting, even to himself, that he might have been wrong about her didn't sit well. But the truth was staring him in the face. She wasn't the empty-headed, spoiled little rich girl he'd expected. She had more guts than most.

And now he had to kick her when she was already down.

The news he had wasn't good. A few minutes ago, he had run into one of the policemen beating the brush. The general consensus was that if they didn't find Emily soon, there was only one place she could possibly be, in the lake. There were so many houses and fences peppering the woods that they didn't think the child could have wandered past them into open country.

After beating the brush as thoroughly as he had this past hour, Mac was inclined to disagree with the lake theory. He'd circled the body of water himself, and there wasn't any sign that a child had been playing along the shore. After leaving the lake, he had worked his way back toward the Hamstead place.

He'd found a dirt road above the property that looked down on the Hamstead house, a cul-de-sac where some new homes were being constructed. There were tire tracks on the road's shoulder where a car had been parked. Judging from the scattered cigarette butts, someone had sat there a good long while, chain-smoking. There were also a man's shoe prints in the dirt going from the car toward the pasture where Emily had been playing right before she disappeared.

Mac knew what must have happened to Emily. But he still didn't know why. Lucetti must have taken her. Who else? Like the cop had said, there was no throughway up here, no random passersby who might have taken the opportunity to snatch a child.

Now, after having assured Mallory that Lucetti probably wasn't involved, Mac hated to have to tell her he had been wrong. And, boy, did he dread the confrontation he knew was coming when he told her he didn't want the cops involved.

Being afraid your child might be dead was bad. But to know she was alive and probably in the hands of a heartless criminal? That would be enough to send anybody over the edge. There was a steep bank at the shoulder of the road. Mac paused below it and gazed up at Mallory. In the next few minutes, he would find out just how much strength Mallory Steele Christiani really had.

Most people would be basket cases after the day she'd

been through, but she stood with her chin lifted, mouth set in a grim line. When he looked closely, he could see that she was shaking, but she hid it well, arms crisscrossed over her small breasts, trembling hands tucked out of sight so they wouldn't give her away. She had grit, he'd give her that.

"Anything?" Her voice quavered as she spoke.

He tried to shake his head in reply to her question and found he couldn't. A shiver ran the length of her, and she hugged herself more tightly, hunching her shoulders against the cold breeze blowing in off the water. Mac knew she was thinking of her child, wishing she had her arms around her. He'd never had a kid of his own, but he could imagine the agony she felt. There was nothing he could think of to say or do. Not one damned thing.

She turned her pale face toward Lake Tuck. Her mouth worked for a moment, no sound coming forth. "D-do you think th-they'll drag it?"

He sighed and raked a hand through his hair. "She isn't in the lake, Mallory."

"Then where is she?" She lifted her hands in supplication. "It's been three hours." Her voice grew shrill. "There are so many houses around here, how could she have gotten lost? Where is she?"

Mac squared his shoulders. "I think Lucetti has her."

Dead silence fell between them, broken only by the breeze whispering through the tall spruce and fir trees that crowded the hillsides. The sky had darkened to slate. The wind-twisted evergreens in the background loomed like black sentinels, casting Mallory and the light blue car in stark relief.

As briefly as he could, Mac told her about the car tracks and footprints he had found.

"Lucetti." Her voice rang hollow now. "But you said that didn't make sense. That he would have—have just done it here." Her voice broke and a low cry erupted from her throat. "You said you thought she was just lost."

"I was wrong. Don't misunderstand and start thinking she's dead. If he took her—and I'm pretty certain he did—I don't think he did it so he could kill her. He must have had other reasons. Like I said earlier, this is the perfect place if he meant to—" He sighed and gestured behind him. "There are houses in every direction going away from Beth's. She couldn't have stayed lost this long. The cops think she's in the lake, but I don't buy it. They have no reason to suspect foul play, so they probably didn't take notice of the tire tracks up above. If they did, they more than likely thought it was one of the home builders' vehicles that had been parked there."

"Then why didn't you call their attention to them?"

"I didn't feel I should, not until I had spoken with you—explained the possible consequences."

"Consequences? My daughter is missing. We should tell the police everything so they can find her. If someone took her, we've no proof it was Lucetti. It could have been anyone, couldn't it?"

"I'd say that's unlikely. Extremely unlikely. Knowing what we know, we have to assume it was Lucetti."

"This is my *daughter* we're discussing. I don't want to assume anything. I *can't*. We should go back to Beth's and tell the police."

"They're convinced she's in the lake. To convince them otherwise, we'd have to tell them *why* we think the tire tracks are significant, *why* we feel the footprints going off the road might indicate a kidnapping."

"So we'll tell them!"

"About Lucetti? Mallory, if they even once get wind of it, they'll be in on this case for the duration. We can't risk that."

"But—" She stared at him, no longer able to conceal how violently her body was trembling. "You're supposed to get help from the police when things like this happen. That policeman—the one at Beth's—he looked really concerned. I'll bet he's got a little girl of his own. He's not one of Lucetti's men. He'd help us, I know he would. They won't let Lucetti know the police are involved. They're trained to handle things like this."

Mac wiped his mouth with the back of his hand and stared into the woods for a moment, trying to consider the situation from all angles. "I'm sure you're right and the cops we've met tonight are all on the level. There are probably only a couple in the whole county who aren't. Finding men we can trust isn't the problem. One of my best friends is on the King County force. I could trust him with my life, Mallory. But not with this. It's the grapevine *inside* the police force that we're up against. Stop and think about it. No cop likes to believe the cop next to him is on the take. They *have* to trust one another to survive. Even my friend Scotty might be working with someone who's crooked and not realize it. If we turn this matter over to them, the wrong cop could get wind of it. And if he clues Lucetti, it could be dangerous for Emily."

"Dangerous?"

"If Lucetti thinks the police know she's missing, he'll dispose of—of any evidence."

Even in the dusk, he could see the pupils of Mallory's eyes dilating. "K-kill her, you mean? You're saying we should tell the police nothing, just leave? And what if someone besides Lucetti took her?"

"I don't think that's the case."

"You don't *think?* I don't want you to think, I want you to know. My little girl could die."

"Mallory, whoever has her will have to call if they want ransom. If it isn't Lucetti, we can contact the police then. Sometimes you have to weigh everything and go on gut instinct. I'm telling you what I feel our next move should be. No cops, period. I told them I was taking you home to get some rest so you wouldn't see them dragging the lake, and I think that's exactly what we should do."

"And what if you're wrong? What if we don't go to the police and Lucetti just kills her? That's what Keith said he had threatened to do."

"That's the key word, *threatened*. Men like Lucetti don't bother with threats, not unless they're trying to coerce someone. So we have to assume Keith either had something Lucetti wanted or that he was in a position to do something Lucetti needed done. Now Keith's in the hospital and your daughter is missing. Like I said earlier, if Lucetti had wanted to kill her, he would have had it done here. There's a lot of cover for a sniper to hide in and several back roads to use to get out of here afterward. It's the perfect place for a hit. But instead, they took her? They wouldn't have bothered unless they needed her alive for some reason. That convinces me that Lucetti believes *you* can do whatever it was he needed Keith to do. You see what I'm saying? He's taken Em to use as leverage against you."

"How can you be so sure you're right?"

"I don't *know* I'm right. I'm only making an educated guess. I grew up on the streets. I know the kind of people we're dealing with, how they think."

Her eyes widened. "You're saying you're one of them?"

"In a sense. I used to be."

"What did Keith do, post your bail once? Get you off on a lesser charge? What?" The words shot out of her mouth before she could call them back, then hung there like a cloud between them.

She saw something flicker in his eyes. Pain? "I—" Running a hand through her hair, she averted her face for a moment. "I'm sorry, Mac Phearson. I didn't mean that. I'm just so scared."

He sighed and switched his weight from one foot to the other. "It's your decision. She's your child. I could be wrong. My theory makes sense, but that car chase today doesn't back it up. If Lucetti wants you to do something or give him something, he needs you alive."

"Maybe he was just trying to scare us."

"That's a risky way to scare someone. If I'd lost control of that car, we both could have been killed." The torment in her expression was so pronounced, Mac could almost feel it. "Mallory, it's your daughter who's missing. It should be you who weighs the risks and makes the decisions. If you want to drive back down to Beth's and tell the police, I'll go with you."

She thought for several seconds before she replied. "No. Keith trusted you. For now, at least, I'll do what you say." Her eyes sought his. "You don't think Lucetti will hurt her, do you? If we don't call the police and we cooperate?"

Mac could scarcely bear to look at her. There was no gentle way to tell her the truth, so he chose to say nothing at all. Before he realized his feet were moving, he was nearly up the bank. Two more steps and he was standing ver her, feeling like a cumbersome clod as he grasped houlders. She wasn't a very large woman. Her collarbone felt fragile under his hands. The flood of tears he was expecting didn't come. Instead of leaning against him, Mallory pulled back. Taking a deep, shaky breath, she raised her chin.

"If he touches a hair on her head, I'll kill him," she said evenly. "Come on, let's go."

Mac took a moment to respond. For some reason, he'd always equated small with weak. Now he realized he couldn't have been more wrong. "Where?"

"To find him."

There was a deadly gleam in her eye. If it hadn't been such an awful situation, Mac might have laughed. "Mallory, people like Lucetti are roaches. They crawl out of the woodwork after dark. We can't just drive into Seattle and look him up in the phone book. He keeps an extremely low profile. He's renowned for it. I've never even seen him. I don't even know anyone who has."

"Then how do we find him?"

The question took him off guard. She was serious. If he pointed her in the right direction, she would take off without hesitation. "We have two choices. We can hit the streets. Start asking questions, which could take days and might get us nowhere, or we can wait for him to find us. That would probably be a lot quicker, judging by what happened this afternoon."

"In other words, we should stay extremely visible?" She turned decisively toward the Volvo. "Then I'm going home. I can't get much more visible than that. You don't have to stay involved in this, Mac Phearson. She's not your daughter."

He grabbed her arm, steering her away from the driver's door. "It's my car, remember? Where it goes, I go."

"You'd be wiser to walk back to Beth's and call a cab.

They'll be watching for the Volvo. I'll leave it parked at the hospital and you can pick it up after things have calmed down." She looked up at him. "I'm serious, Mac Phearson. Why should you risk your neck? This isn't your problem."

"Nobody ever said I was smart." He studied her face for a moment, then shook his head and gave a halfhearted grin. "Keith asked for my help. He's my friend so I'm making it my problem, okay? You can't do this alone."

"And why should you care? You scarcely know me. You've never even seen Em. Keith wouldn't hold it against you if you backed out now. He isn't that kind of fellow."

"You forget I know what kind of fellow he is, probably better than anyone does." Mac felt a strange tightness rise in his throat. "He did me a favor once, a big one. I owe him."

"That's ridiculous. No matter how big a favor Keith did for you, you don't owe him your life."

"Oh, I owe him, all right. There are some things you can't put a price on. Let's just leave it at that. Besides, you and I were nearly killed together this afternoon. You don't go through something like that with someone and then just walk away."

"If it was me, I wouldn't be *walking,* I'd be running."

"I doubt that." Mac was surprised to realize he really meant it. "If it was my kid, you wouldn't rest until we had her home."

"You're crazy, Mac Phearson," she said softly.

"So you've been telling me most of the day." He gave her a little shove and stepped toward the car. "And *please,* stop calling me Mac Phearson?"

"Bud?"

His gaze met hers over the top of the car. "My friends call me Mac."

She paused by the passenger door, peering at him through the gloom. His friends? All day long, she'd been getting the distinct impression that he didn't like her. She tried to read his expression, but he was standing in the shadow of a tree, which made it impossible. Perhaps it was just as well. If he was making an overture, she should accept it and leave it at that, not wonder what had happened to change his mind. "All right, Mac it is."

Once they were inside the car, she leaned her head back and closed her eyes. Again he braced himself for a deluge of tears. Shoving the shift into first, he eased the car forward, casting uneasy glances her way. "You okay?"

"No." She straightened. "I—want to thank you."

"For what?"

"For staying."

"No big deal. A few thrills every once in a while keeps life interesting."

From the corner of his eye, he saw her wiping a tear from her cheek. He pretended not to notice. She pressed the back of her hand to her mouth for a moment, then dropped her fist onto her lap. "I'm going to get her back. If it's the last thing I do…"

"Correction. *We* are going to get her back. I told you earlier that I'd find her for you. That's a promise I intend to keep." He sighed and adjusted his side mirror. "The way I figure it, Lucetti will get in touch if we make ourselves available, probably by phone."

"To make a ransom demand?"

Mac frowned. "My gut instinct tells me it's not money he's wanting."

"Earlier, you said you thought he needed me to do

something, that he'd taken Em to use her as leverage against me. What could he need done that only I could do?"

Shaking his head, Mac threw her a puzzled glance. "I wish I knew."

"Whatever it is, I'll do it. When it comes to my daughter's safety, the word *no* isn't in my vocabulary."

"Then broaden your vocabulary," he retorted softly. "*No* may be the most important word you can utter. We can't let him bully us. When he calls, you'll have to insist on speaking to Em, so we know she's all right. That's her life insurance. Unless you insist on that and keep insisting, he has nothing to gain by keeping—" He broke off and looked uncomfortable.

"No reason to keep her alive?" Mallory finished for him. Fear rushed through her, but she refused to give in to it. "Don't pull your punches, Mac Phearson. I need to know exactly what to expect."

"If we don't talk to her, he can get rid of her without our realizing it," he said hollowly. "There's no way we can second-guess what he wants or what he might say, but on that one point—assuring ourselves that Em is safe—we have to stand firm, no matter what he threatens. Think you can handle that? He's liable to get nasty."

"I can handle anything if Em's life might depend on it."

She sat quietly for a moment.

"You know," she added thoughtfully, "I have a phone that's equipped with a speaker. We should probably turn it on when he calls so both of us can hear. If we listen closely, perhaps the background noise will give us a clue as to where he is keeping Em."

"Good idea. We also need to find out everything else we can manage while you're talking to him. What he wants. Why he needs you. How Keith became involved with him. Any tidbit of information you can get out of him may help us find Emily."

She murmured her agreement. In the darkness, he saw her face crumple before she turned to gaze out her window. He gripped the gear shift until his knuckles hurt. His first inclination was to stop the car and take her into his arms to comfort her, but he instinctively knew it wouldn't be wise. She wasn't the type who wept easily. Before she would break down in front of him, her pride would have to go. And right now, her pride, and fear for her child, were all that held her together.

CHAPTER FOUR

MALLORY WAS QUIET as Mac Phearson pulled his Volvo into her driveway. The windows of the house yawned black against the white siding. A shiver raised goose bumps on her skin. Without Em and Keith here, the place looked as lonely as a tomb, an impersonal mass of wood, plaster-board and brick. As they climbed out of the car, he shot uneasy glances over his shoulder to check the cul-de-sac. Her heart lifted with hope. Surely Lucetti knew where Keith lived. Coming home had to be the smartest move.

"Got a key?"

As she climbed the steps, she unzipped her bag and became so engrossed in her search she stubbed her toe. Mac snaked an arm around her waist and steadied her. Too tired to care, she leaned against him, letting him guide her up the remaining steps. "My keys aren't here."

"What?" He released her and grabbed the purse. After rummaging a moment, he swore and dumped the contents of her handbag onto the porch. He sorted through the pile and then said, "Well isn't that great. Did you leave them in your car?"

"No. The alarm goes off if I leave them in the igni-tion. I know I had them when I went into the hospital. I do have a spare set in the house for all the good it does me." Mallory groaned and plopped down on the top step, hugging her bent knees. "I've heard of Murphy's Law, but this is too much."

"I can get in. That's not what bugs me. Was there an opportunity for someone inside the hospital to have had a moment alone with your handbag?"

Mallory pursed her lips in thought. "I left it for a couple of seconds—right before I went into the ICU to see Keith, I stepped up the hall to a sitting area to get a *National Geographic* that I had seen earlier, lying there on a table. I wasn't gone but a second, though. And there wasn't anyone else in the hall."

"A second is all it would take if someone was watching you, waiting for the right moment."

"What makes you think they were stolen? I could have dropped them by your car when we left."

"No, I would have heard them fall. Let me go check the floorboard." He left her for a moment to search his car. As he walked back up the steps to the front yard, he called, "Nothing."

"They could have spilled out when we were on 405. When the door was open. My purse might have gotten dumped."

He leaned over to eye the assortment of odds and ends. "Pretty selective dumping. Besides, you had it zipped."

"I could have zipped it while I was driving around the lake tonight. I remember looking for a tissue."

"I still say that if the keys fell out, other things would have, too. Someone's rifled your purse. Look at all this stuff. And there's not a scrap inside the car."

He lifted a wad of tissue and several other pieces of paper as if to use them to prove his point. One of them was a small photograph. He stared at it a moment and then dropped it onto the pile, but not before Mallory glimpsed her daughter's face. Her hand flew toward the photo. A small cry escaped her before she could bite it back. *Emily.* Mallory could almost hear her giggle, smell her hair and the curve of her neck where silken curls escaped her braids. Was she alive? Hungry, cold? Not knowing was awful. Funny how clearly she could remember her first smile, her first tooth, her first step. And, oh, how the memories hurt. Like a knife twisting in her guts. Wrapping her arms around her waist, she rocked forward until her chest nearly touched her knees.

Mac sighed and crouched next to Mallory, placing his hand on her hair at the back of her neck. The warmth of his touch was nearly her undoing. Tears burned in her throat, forming a huge lump that suffocated her. Closing her eyes, Mallory clung to what little self-control she had left and conjured a vision of her mother to put some starch back into her spine. Crying in front of a stranger would be the unforgivable sin in Norma Steele's books. *Ladies* didn't make spectacles of themselves, *not ever.* And her mother was right. How could she help Emily if she was falling apart?

Keeping her head bowed, she straightened her shoulders. "I'm handling this badly. Just, um, give me a second. I'll—"

"You'll what? Pretend everything's fine for another hour? I think you're handling this better than most people could."

"No, I'm not."

Her voice floated up to Mac no louder than a whisper. He studied her bent head and wished he knew what to say to her. There was no shame in tears, after all. But she seemed to think so. Who had done this to her? Beneath his hand, he could feel her shaking, feel the brittle tension in the column of her neck.

"I'm not real good at comforting people, but I've got a great shoulder to lend you. Absorbent, anyway." Mac watched her, feeling inept. Why couldn't he just say what he meant, that he wouldn't mind holding her? The words caught at the base of his throat. "I—Mallory, come here."

She shook her head emphatically. "Crying never solved anything. In my family…" Her voice trailed off.

With a heavy sigh, he cupped her chin and lifted her face. His touch felt sandpapery and warm against Mallory's skin, so strong and solid that she wanted to lean into it. In the moonlight, his eyes shimmered silver, delving so deeply into hers she felt as if he knew her every thought.

"Crying may not solve anything, but it sure can make you feel better sometimes."

"How would you know?"

"Experience. When my little brother—" He broke off and shrugged one shoulder. "There have been a few times. Over in Nam. Here. We all have to let go sometimes." He tightened his grip on her chin. "The point is, you don't have to pretend with me, okay? There's no sin in having feelings."

Drawing away from him, Mallory dragged in a deep breath of air, acutely conscious of his other hand where it still rested against her hair. "It's just that I feel so helpless, so alone. When something happens to your kids, you expect to have the other parent to share it with. You can lean on each other, you know? I'm so *scared*. I wish it was me instead of her. If only it was."

He slid his hand to her shoulder, draping his other arm across his bent knee. He studied the brick pattern of the porch for a long while. "I know I'm a poor substitute for your husband or Keith, but you're not alone. And if you need that shoulder I offered, I won't think any less of you for it."

"I'm afraid that's not saying a lot."

He looked up at her. "What's that supposed to mean?"

"That you don't think much of me anyway."

She felt his thumb rasp along the arm seam of her jacket, saw the corners of his mouth quiver with a repressed smile. "It's a bad habit, I guess, judging people by their addresses."

A peculiar awareness electrified the air between them. Not sensual, but powerful just the same, a drawing together, a feeling of having known one another always. It frightened her. They had been thrown together by crazy circumstances, then shaken up for most of the day like the dried seeds in a *maraca*. There hadn't been time for the usual proprieties, and now it seemed too late for them. Her emotions were roller coastering out of control. She wanted him to set her world right again, to put his arms around her, to hold her, to stroke her hair, to make everything better. It was stupid, ridiculous, childish, but she wanted it with such an intensity she ached. The fact that he was a complete stranger made that realization pretty scary.

He seemed as uneasy as she with the feelings erupting between them. She was relieved when he broke the building tension by giving her shoulder a pat and standing.

He gazed down the street, his expression thoughtful. "It's scary to realize how close you came to trouble today. Before I ever got to the hospital, one of Lucetti's men got near enough to you to go through your purse."

Until this moment, Mallory hadn't thought of it that way. She had been in danger and hadn't even known it. She threw an incredulous glance at the pile of junk from her purse. "I wonder why they wanted my keys? To strip the house? Steal my car?"

"Lucetti isn't into small-time theft. My guess is, he wanted to get into the house to search for something. Or he thought you might have the key to something he needs opened."

"Like what?"

"Beats me." He turned and patted all his pockets. Pausing next to her, he said, "I need my lock picks. Be right back."

Lock picks? Mallory watched him lope to his car. After rummaging in his trunk for a moment, he returned, carrying a key ring with a number of small tools attached to it. She watched him select and try three picks before he found the right one. Seconds later, she heard the door latch assembly click.

"Do you have any idea how much money we invested in that lock?" she asked.

He smiled and pocketed the key ring. "If it's any consolation, the average burglar probably couldn't pick it. It's a high-quality lock."

"Which you just opened in a matter of seconds."

"Dead bolts are a better investment. For night security, I recommend the type that locks from the inside and doesn't have an outside keyhole."

She scooped everything back into her purse and stood, not at all sure she was pleased that he was so adept at breaking and entering, or that he knew so much about locks. What kind of man was he? As she walked toward the open door, she realized that it didn't really matter to her what kind of person he was, not as long as he would help her find Emily. "I don't suppose I should ask where you learned to do that."

He stepped back so she could enter. "Probably not." Pausing behind her, he glanced around the large entry. She sensed a sudden wariness in him. "Come back out to the car a sec. I want to take another look for your keys. I need you to hold the light." He motioned toward the porch. Once they were outside with the door closed, he whispered, "Another reason just hit me why he might have wanted your keys. To plant bugs. With your keys, they could get right in without alarming any of your neighbors by picking the lock or breaking the door."

"Listening devices? In my house?"

"I should have thought of it immediately. If he's going to hold Em for ransom, he'll want to be sure you don't call the cops. The best way to do that would be to listen to everything you say. Which puts us in a spot. We can't let him know who I am."

"Why?"

"I'm a professional. He won't like me being in on this."

"Then maybe you'd better leave."

"No way. We'll just have to be careful."

"But if he learns who you are, it could endanger Em."

"And if you do the wrong thing, it could endanger her even more. You need my help, Mallory. There has to be a way."

"Like what?"

He thought for a moment. "We'll be lovers."

"We'll be *what?*"

He clamped his hand over her mouth, then slowly lowered it. "Lovers. Say we've been seeing each other for six months. Things have gotten cozy. It'd seem natural for me to be here. Keith's in the hospital, your kid's been snatched. I'd hang around, stick close, give you moral support. All it'll take is a little playacting."

"How *much* playacting?"

"Enough to be convincing." He caught her shocked expression and rolled his eyes. "Not *that* much, for heaven's sake."

"It's not that. It's just that I'm afraid I can't do it."

He pressed his fist against her chin jokingly. "Hey, it'll be easy. Just don't call me Mac Phearson. He might recognize the name. Mac or Hey-You, but not Mac Phearson. I'll do the rest."

The front door swung open beneath his hand with a loud creak. He preceded her into the entry, the soles of his sneakers grabbing the tile.

For some reason, the thought that there might be monitors in her house was the final blow to her self-control. She began to shake and couldn't stop. All evening, she had fought off tears and hysteria, telling herself there would be time for that later. Now she realized there wasn't going to be. Her only sanctuary had been invaded.

Mac must have seen her trembling. He paused and curled his arm around her to draw her against him. Being closer to him helped somehow. The tremors running through her body subsided. She pressed her face into the hollow of his shoulder. Soap, cologne, leather and the faint aroma of hot dogs—a nice smell, ordinary and comforting. The steady beat of his heart lulled her fears. His arms were hard and warm. He ran a hand over her hair and she felt his callused palm catch on the strands. He was wonderfully sturdy when nothing else was, and she dreaded the moment when he would move away from her.

"You okay?"

She found the strength to nod. He gave her back a pat and left her again, disappearing into the shadows. Sudden light blinded her. She blinked and tried to focus. With detached curiosity, she watched him move about the hall, running his hands along the door frames. When she realized he was searching for hidden microphones, she began to help, sliding her fingertips under the edge of the table, behind the painting of the Puget Sound, through the dried flowers. They found nothing, but that still didn't mean there weren't bugs in a nearby room.

"I really appreciate your staying over," she said, praying she didn't sound too stiff and formal. "Good friends make times like this bearable. Are you sure it's not too much trouble?"

She saw a gleam of approval flicker in his eyes. "I wouldn't have it any other way, sweetheart."

They walked the length of the entry into the kitchen, which adjoined a breakfast nook to the left, a formal dining room to the right. Mac hit the light switch as they passed through the doorway. Mallory turned to stare at the rose-and-cream tiles on the counters, at the oak cupboards and trim. Day before yesterday, she had made breakfast in here. Em had stood chattering at her elbow. Now it seemed like a lifetime ago.

Mac motioned toward a chair in the breakfast nook. Then, shrugging out of his jacket, he draped it across the bar. He took quick stock of his surroundings and began to check the kitchen for hidden listening devices. Taking her cue from him, Mallory ignored his signal to sit down and searched the two adjoining rooms. This *was* her house, after all. She would notice if anything was out of place when he might not.

When she returned to the kitchen, Mac was just stepping through the hall doorway. She guessed that he had been checking the remainder of the first floor. It had been a long while since either of them had spoken. Afraid that the silence might strike an eavesdropper as odd, she said, "It's amazing how much better I feel knowing you're staying over for the night." No sooner had the words passed her lips than Mallory realized she sincerely meant them. Having Mac there *was* a comfort. "With Keith in the hospital and my folks gone on vacation, I would have been alone."

"Maybe you can be there for me sometime," he replied. "That's what friends are for, right?"

He jabbed a finger toward the ceiling to let her know he was going upstairs. She followed him up, searching the rooms off of one hall while he checked the ones off the other.

Nothing. As Mallory slipped silently from Keith's bedroom into his upstairs study, a deluge of memories swept through her mind, pictures of Keith and Emily together, laughing, playing, filling the rooms with sounds of happiness.

Now, with nothing but silence around her, Mallory could appreciate how truly blessed she had been. Had the refrigerator always hummed so loudly? She could hear it, even from up here. Had the floors always creaked like this when someone was walking? The horrible sense of emptiness inside the house made her feeling of loss all the more acute. She might never again see Keith sweep his granddaughter into his arms, never hear Em's carefree giggles or see her eyes light up with excitement at the sound of her grandfather's voice when he came in at night. The list of losses seemed endless.

When they had finished searching the second floor, Mac met her on the landing. Together, they returned to the kitchen. Grabbing a notepad and pen off the bar, he wrote, *Nothing that I could find. As far as I could tell, the house hasn't been searched, either.*

Mallory lifted her hands to let him know that she also hadn't found anything. Then she took the pen from him and wrote, *Maybe they wanted my keys for something else? To open something, perhaps?*

He scanned her response, his frown deepening. Shrugging one shoulder, he motioned for her to sit at the table. He seemed more relaxed as he opened the refrigerator. She sat down and watched him, too heartsick to care what he was doing or why. She even forgot to worry about his gun, despite her fears. Em's voice rang in her ears. *Mommy, will you cut my toast into hearts? With jam on top?*

Mac's voice sliced through Mallory's memories like a knife through tinfoil. "How do eggs sound? Eggs and toast."

"I'm not hungry." She closed her eyes and tried to sort the voices in her head, Em's, Mac's, her own. "A drink, maybe."

"Just because you don't feel hungry doesn't mean you shouldn't eat. My cooking may not be up to your usual standards, but it'll fill your hollow spots." He located a skillet and placed it on the stove. Flashing her an encouraging smile, he began taking food from the refrigerator. "You'll be surprised how much better you feel once you've eaten. Take it from me. When things like this happen, you make it through one minute at a time. When you can't do anything else, you fuel up for the next round and rest."

"I—I really don't feel like eating."

"I want you to try, sweetheart."

Mallory gazed at his broad back, at the crisscrossed leather strap of his shoulder holster. The endearment unnerved her for a moment. Then she decided he must still think it was necessary to keep up the pretense that they were lovers. She watched him move around her kitchen with practiced ease. Clearly he was a man with many talents, as adept at acting and cooking as he was at picking locks and tending scraped legs. He located the silverware drawer and pulled out a fork to whip the eggs he had cracked into a bowl. Seconds later, she heard a loud sizzling sound, followed by the methodical scraping of the spatula against the cast-iron pan.

The cooking smells reached her and turned her stomach. She fastened her gaze on the tabletop. In the reflecting light, she could see smudges on the polished surface. *Fingerprints.* Tiny ones. Everywhere she looked, she saw something to remind her of Emily. She could hear Mac taking plates down, sticking bread in the toaster. Everyday sounds. She wanted to scream at him to stop. She couldn't eat. Couldn't even think about eating. Was Em hungry? Had someone fed *her* yet? It was past her bedtime, and Mallory didn't know if she even had a blanket.

A ringing sound pealed through the room. Mallory stared at the telephone on the bar, her body frozen. Mac jerked the skillet off the burner. "Answer it," he urged.

She pushed up from the chair and took a halting step. The phone clamored again, the sound running along her nerve endings, making her skin quiver. "Do you think it's him?"

"I don't know. Just answer it." Mac strode across the floor and seized her elbow to pull her forward. "Just play it by ear."

By the third ring, Mallory was standing directly in front of the phone. For some reason, it seemed to have taken her much longer than usual to cross the room. She stood there and stared, willing herself to move, so filled with dread of what she might learn that she couldn't. Mac flipped the panel control on to intercom. She lifted her arm, forcing her fingers to curl around the receiver and lift it. Trembling uncontrollably, she pressed it to her ear. "H-hello?"

There was a long silence. Then a voice crackled over the speaker and filled the room. "Mrs. Christiani? I have your daughter. If you want to see her alive again, listen very carefully."

Mallory clutched the phone with both hands, like a lifeline. It was her only link to her daughter. "Where's my little girl? Who *are* you? What have you done to her? She's just a baby!" Her voice broke. "Please, don't hurt her, please—"

"Get a grip on yourself, Mrs. Christiani," the man snarled. "I have no time for hysterics. Whether or not I harm your daughter is entirely up to you."

Mallory held her breath until her temples throbbed. She could hear Mac whispering, "Stay calm—stay calm." The words eventually sank in and she exhaled in a rush. "What do you want? Money? How much? Just name a price. I'll get it for you. Anything. I'll do anything."

"Not money, just a package."

"A package?" Incredulity swept through Mallory. She hadn't expected him to say that. "What kind of package?"

"The day your father-in-law collapsed, he was supposed to have mailed it to me. Unfortunately for you, the package I received was a fake, filled with nothing but blank sheets of paper. I have reason to believe he put the documents I had requested in his safety-deposit box, hoping to retrieve them later."

"What makes you think that?"

"Shortly before he collapsed, he was seen entering the vault at the bank with a package under his arm. He reappeared without it. I have tried, without success, to find his deposit-box key. That leaves me with no options. I want that package, Mrs. Christiani. I need you to get it for me."

Someone had stolen her baby to get a package? Hysteria swelled in her throat. "A package? Why did my father-in-law even have it? What connection does he have to you?"

To Mallory's dismay, the man ignored the questions. "It's a large manila envelope. At the upper left corner, you'll probably see the name Steven Miles, Accountant, with the return address stamped in red ink. Inside you will find several sets of ledgers with the same accountant's name in the headings. You don't need to know anything more. Find that key and get the package, Mrs. Christiani. When you return it to me, you get your child."

"B-but I don't know anything about a key."

"You'll find it, Mrs. Christiani. You have access to your father-in-law's files, his belongings. You know what his habits are and where he might have hidden something important. Oh, yes, you'll find it. If you don't, your little girl will die."

For an instant, all Mallory could see was Darren's face after his accident, the blood in his hair, his empty eyes staring up at her. She heard Mac curse beneath his breath, felt him tighten his hold on her. "Y-yes, I'll find it… I'll find it. Let me talk to Emily. I want to talk to my daughter."

"You'll talk to her when I have the package, not before."

"But how will I know she's all right? That you haven't—"

"I guess you won't," he replied coldly. "Now put your friend on the line."

Mallory glanced up at Mac and handed him the phone. For a horrible moment, it occurred to her that he might be in on this, that he had duped her from the start. She gazed up at his chiseled features, at the grim set of his mouth. His eyes locked with hers, as if he had guessed what she was thinking.

Averting his face, he said, "Hello?"

"Let's cut right to the heart of the matter, shall we, Mr. Mac Phearson? I ran a make on your car. I know you're a private investigator. Take this as fair warning. Don't mess with me. I don't care if you hold your little friend's hand, I don't care if you help her find the package for me, but don't interfere. If you call the local police or the Feds in on this—or even *look* like you're going to—your girlfriend's child is dead. Have I made myself clear?"

"Perfectly clear." Mac's eyes darkened to a cloudy, turbulent gray. "Is the child okay?"

"Yes, and she'll stay that way as long as you cooperate."

"You're going to have to do a little cooperating yourself."

"You're in no position to make demands."

"I think that depends on how you look at it."

A long silence crackled over the speaker. "What are you asking?"

"Two things. Number one, call off your thugs. We can't find the key, package or anything else while we're dodging bullets."

"I don't know what you're talking about."

"Then *find out* what I'm talking about. Three men tried to kill us this afternoon."

"A man in your profession is bound to make enemies, Mr. Mac Phearson." A horn honked in the background. Thus far, that was the only external sound Mallory had detected. "I can't be held accountable for that. Whoever those men were, they have no connection to me."

Mac's eyebrows drew together in a scowl. "I want the kid put on the phone."

"That's impossible."

"No, that's just good business. No kid, no package."

Mallory held herself absolutely rigid. She knew Mac had to take a firm stand. They'd discussed the fact that it would ensure Em's safety, but that didn't make it any less frightening. Mac glanced over at her, his face unnaturally pale, the only sign that he, too, was afraid. "So do we speak to the child or not?"

"Tomorrow morning, eight o'clock."

The phone clicked and went dead. Horror flooded through Mallory, and she grabbed the receiver from Mac's hand. "No—oh, please—don't hang up!"

Silence hummed over the intercom. Mac felt Mallory's body go limp. As she slumped against him, only her hand on the phone seemed to retain some life. He had to pry her fingers loose to return the receiver to its cradle. He had done his best. And it hadn't been good enough. It was going to be a long, miserable night for her, an eternity—wondering if her daughter was alive.

CHAPTER FIVE

MAC DIDN'T LIKE the expression on Mallory's face after he pried the phone from her hand. Her eyes had a blank, dazed look. Her skin was chalk-white. She stared at the phone, her head tipped to one side as if she was listening for something. "Mallory?" he whispered.

For several seconds she didn't seem to hear him. Then she lifted her liquid brown eyes to meet his gaze. He could tell that she wasn't really seeing him. He stepped behind her and grasped her shoulders to steer her back to the table. Like a lifeless doll, she sat when he told her. Hunkering at her feet, he gazed up at her and tried to reconcile this woman with the one who had been so resilient all day, surprising him at every turn. She still hadn't really cried. A few stray tears, but she hadn't broken down. He had a feeling that was coming, though—probably soon.

How could he have been so wrong about her all these years? Mallory Steele, wife of the promising young attorney, Darren Christiani, the daughter of a wealthy congressman, a woman who had it all. Self-centered, shallow, as cold as ice. That was how he had pegged her. As useless as a paper dress in a downpour. A pretty little darling with charm-school manners who went every week for a fifty-dollar manicure, who drove a brand-new sport Mercedes around town with the top down, her salon-conditioned hair flying in the wind.

The Mallory he was getting to know held no resemblance to that imagined girl-woman. Hadn't all day. And now? An ice maiden didn't love this deeply. Her hair hung in a tangled mass of whiskey-colored curls that reached her shoulders. Her clothes were wrinkled and soiled. Her stockings were torn. Her legs were scratched. She looked like an abandoned child, eyes bruised, mouth quivering, hands limp in her lap. Not even Mac could dredge up resentment toward her.

He cupped the side of her face, brushing his thumb along the fragile contour of her jaw. The blue smudge along her cheekbone was turning a darker color. Her gaze shifted but didn't focus. It was as if she had slipped into another dimension, a nightmarish place that wouldn't release its hold on her. "Mallory, come on, sweetheart."

Awareness at last flickered in her eyes. He could almost see her picking up the threads of her self-control. He had never been good with crying women, but this was one time he would have welcomed tears.

With a sigh, she said, "Well, now we know why he stole my keys, to see if the safety-deposit-box key was on my ring."

He sat back on his heels, still concerned about her pallor. "Which means I was probably wrong about the bugs. At least we don't need to be so worried about what we say now." Weariness weighed heavily on his shoulders, ached behind his eyes. "I want you to listen up, okay? Look at me and listen. Emily is Lucetti's ace in the hole. He won't hurt her. Not if he wants that package."

"What if he already has? He wouldn't put her on the phone. If she's all right, why wouldn't he let me speak to her?"

"Scare tactics. She's leverage, Mallory. He's deliberately trying to make you come unglued so he can be sure you'll do as you're told. I know it's hard, but try to think positive. Without Emily, he can't bargain for the package. He'll handle her with kid gloves, believe me."

She passed a tremulous hand across her brow. "Do you really think so?"

Mac nodded with far more certainty than he felt. "He said we could speak to her in the morning. Now would he have promised that if he couldn't deliver?"

"No, I guess he wouldn't. A package? He took my little girl! Why would anyone want a set of ledgers that much?"

"I don't know. Maybe the information in them is incriminating. Mallory, I don't know. I wish I—"

"Then why would Keith have them?" Her voice was shrill, quavery. "Keith doesn't handle criminal cases."

"I assume that Steven Miles, the accountant, gave them to him." Mac frowned. "That name rings a bell. I wonder why."

While he was lost in thought, she pushed up from her chair and went to open the top drawer in the cabinet under the breakfast bar. He watched her rummage through it, her slender fingers sifting the smaller items, her gaze intent.

"What are you doing?"

"Looking for that key." She glanced over at him, her lips set with determination. "Keith might have kept it here in the house. It's certainly a possibility, anyway."

A very slim one, Mac thought, but he hated to say so. Searching for the key would give her something to do tonight, give her hope. Personally Mac thought Keith would have been more likely to keep the key someplace where it would have been more readily accessible to him during the day while he was at work. Lucetti's people had seen Keith going into the bank vault with a package shortly before he collapsed. Could he have returned home after leaving the bank and left the key here? Or was it at his office? In his car, perhaps? Surely he wouldn't have been so careless as to hide it in a junk drawer at home.

Mallory had worked her way down to the third drawer. There was a feverish look on her face, a desperation in her eyes. Mac finally joined her and began searching the cupboards. "You know, to search everywhere in a house this size could take days. We should at least go about it systematically."

She nodded. "Like Lucetti said, I know Keith's habits, how he thinks. Tonight, we'll look in the most obvious places first."

"But, Mallory, it stands to reason he probably would have *hidden* it if he didn't want Lucetti getting his hands on it. Someplace no one would ever think of looking."

"Not Keith. He deals in human nature, remember. He has always maintained that people usually fail to see things that are right in front of their noses. If he really wanted to hide a key, he'd probably put it someplace so obvious that Lucetti would look everywhere else first." A faint smile touched her mouth. "Think of all the places no one in his right mind would hide an important key. *That's* where we'll find it."

Mac rocked back on his heels, his gaze coming to rest on a ginger jar on top of the refrigerator. It was a short drive to the house from Keith's office. He *might* have brought the key home and hidden it here. And a ginger jar was pretty darned obvious. After all, Mallory did know Keith better than anyone. Beginning to feel hopeful, Mac stood and went to check the jar. Next, he looked on the key rack by the back door. None of the keys there were for a deposit box.

While Mac wandered from room to room, Mallory finished searching the kitchen and moved on to the dining room. Even though she was busy looking for the key, her mind was filled with pictures of Emily. There was an ache inside her chest the size of a melon. *Hold on, darling,* she thought. *I'll come through for you. If it's the last thing I do, I'll come through for you.*

With each passing minute, Mallory searched a little more frantically. Room by room, she eliminated every hiding place she thought Keith might have chosen. *Nothing.* She headed upstairs, praying Keith's rooms would turn up something.

After searching fruitlessly for four hours, Mallory and Mac returned to the kitchen. Mac shook his head, his eyes filled with discouragement. Mallory sank onto a chair, fighting off a wave of disappointment so acute that she could scarcely bear it. Without that key, she couldn't get her daughter back. She had to find it. And she had to find it soon.

Mac hunkered beside her, gazing up into her pale face. He wished he could think of something to say, something that would make her feel better, but there was nothing. Taking her hand, he asked, "Hey, you all right? Would you like something? I could get in touch with your doctor. He could prescribe something to help you sleep. We wouldn't have to tell him why—just that you're upset."

Mallory shivered. "How could I sleep? No. If I took pills, I couldn't wake up. Something could happen and she might need me and I wouldn't be able to—"

"Okay, okay," he interjected. "No pills. Just a thought." He gave her cold fingers a squeeze. "How about something to eat now? You're running on sheer willpower."

He returned to the stove to finish making the meal he

had begun earlier. He didn't like this, not a bit. He had dealt with distraught parents before, managed to keep them glued together when things got tough, but he'd never been with the parent of a small child right after a disappearance, never seen that horrible fear in a mother's eyes or heard the desperation in her voice. Television didn't come close to depicting the agony of it. Watching Mallory, touching her skin and feeling her clammy fear, made him feel physically sick.

What kind of a man did something like this? That question frightened Mac more than anything. Lucetti would clearly stop at nothing to get what he wanted. The day's events kaleidoscoped in Mac's head, bits and pieces that jostled for position, none making sense. Those three men who had chased them today had been professionals. To believe, even for an instant, that they were connected to him and had nothing to do with Lucetti stretched credibility to the maximum. Mac had been in his line of work too many years without having any complications. Why would he suddenly be on someone's hit list? Mac had a few enemies, but they weren't after blood.

And that wasn't the only thing. The voice on the phone hadn't rung true, either. Born and raised in a poor section of Seattle, Mac knew a two-bit hood when he heard one. Lucetti might have climbed the ladder to the top, he might be rolling in dough by now, but unless he had attended college somewhere along the way and changed his circle of friends, he would still slip into old speech patterns, especially when tense. Mac knew he did himself, probably more than he realized, though he tried not to.

The man on the phone hadn't.

Granted, Mac had never seen Lucetti. But the man was

a known racketeer, and Seattle lowlifes weren't renowned for being articulate. Which meant—what?

It meant trouble, that's what. And he didn't know for sure what kind. Stabbing the knife into the butter, he turned from the stove and slanted a concerned glance at Mallory. From the looks of her, he had trouble enough already. She was just sitting there again, staring at nothing. Shock, maybe? He hoped not. Striding to the table, he slid a plate in front of her and cleared his throat to get her attention. She didn't even look up. He poured them both some milk, then slid her plate closer.

"Come on, eat up," he said gruffly. "You won't be any good to Emily sick. And sick's what you'll be if you don't eat."

She turned on the chair and picked up her fork. Giving the steaming scrambled eggs a tentative poke, she whispered, "I have to find that key."

"Yeah, but first you have to eat." He straddled a chair and scooted forward, propping an elbow by his plate. Watching her from the corner of his eye, he took a bite of toast, tucked it aside in his cheek and said, "Come on, just a few bites. Then you can go upstairs and maybe grab a shower, get some sleep. We can't do anything more tonight."

She stiffened, her fork hovering midway to her mouth, a clump of eggs perched precariously on the tines. "Sleep? I can't sleep. I have to keep looking. Can't you understand that?"

Mac swallowed the lump of toast and grabbed his milk to wash it down. "Name me a place we haven't already looked."

"There are hundreds."

"But is it likely Keith would hide a key there? No. The

best thing to do now is get a little rest. After we speak to Emily in the morning, we'll be free to leave the house. We can search the office and Keith's car. If we come up empty-handed, *then* we'll tear this place apart again. That's a promise."

"If you think searching here for the key is useless, then shouldn't we be trying to find Lucetti?"

"Pete Lucetti isn't an easy man to find, Mallory. I've told you that. You have to understand the sort of person we're dealing with. He's the man behind the scenes, faceless, impossible to nail, a fanatic about never leaving evidence. If the cops can't find him, how do you think you can?"

"Won't you help? You're good at finding people, aren't you?"

Her voice held a pitiful note of hope.

"Drink your milk."

She lifted the glass to her lips. When he glanced at her, he found that she was watching him over its rim with the most vulnerable brown eyes he had ever seen. Shoving the remainder of his toast into his mouth, he concentrated on chewing and tried not to look at her.

When the toast was finished, he said, "The smart thing for us to do is to wait for that phone call. Eight in the morning isn't so long to wait." *Just an eternity of not knowing.* "After that, we'll have a better idea what we're up against. Right? You don't know. We might find that key and have Emily home by noon."

"Do you really think so?"

Mac hated liars, but he managed to put some assurance into his voice to help her through the night. "Absolutely."

She studied him until he wanted to squirm. "I think you're just saying that to make me feel better." That empty, dazed look had crept into her eyes again. "What are the odds? On the level."

"Mallory—"

"I want to know the truth. The odds of getting her back alive aren't good, are they?" After watching him a moment, she set her glass down with a thunk. "That's what I thought."

An uncomfortable silence rose between them. Mac saw a glint creep into her eyes. Rage. He couldn't blame her. But, even so, he felt uncomfortable, as though he might take the brunt of her anger if he said the wrong thing.

After an endless moment, she cried, "I can't accept that. Pete Lucetti may be slick, but he can't be that slick. I'm going to find him, just you watch. He's going to be sorry he ever did this."

A tremor ran the length of her. Mac tried to imagine how frustrated she must be feeling and realized no one could truly understand without having first lived through it. She looked completely drained.

"Maybe what you need is a long, hot shower," he suggested softly. "I know it'll be hard to lie down, but you have to think of Emily." Mac felt like a heel for using Em's welfare as a bargaining chip, but it was the only way he could think of to convince Mallory she needed sleep. He would have been willing to bet she hadn't so much as napped since Keith's collapse. And he doubted she had eaten much, either. "If you aren't rested tomorrow, you won't be able to think clearly. And you're going to need your wits about you. Why don't you go on upstairs. I'll clean up here."

Though clearly reluctant, she nodded and stood. He watched her as she left the kitchen. How many times had he wished that Mallory Christiani and all women like her would get their comeuppance? Well, he was getting his wish. Daddy's money couldn't buy her way out of this one. Mac crushed the napkin in his hand.

GEORGE PAISLEY COCKED his gray head to one side and stared at the crumpled napkin in his plate, considering what his friend, Paul Fields, had just said. In a low whisper, he replied, "The problem is, I don't like wasting broads. Call it what you like, but it doesn't sit right. It's one thing when you get a direct order to rub out some whore no one cares about. It's another to decide to do it on your own, especially when the victim is a—"

"Lady?" Paul supplied in a snarl. A compulsive stirrer, especially when he was nervous, he clanked his spoon in his cup, driving the other two men at the table and everyone else in the restaurant half crazy with the noise. As always, he ended the stirring with two loud thunks on the edge of his cup. "Will it sit better if it's you who gets it? If the boss sees what's in those ledgers, we're all three goners. Do you think I've come this far to get caught because you're feeling chivalrous? I say knock her off. Better her than us. It's the only way I can see to stop her. Look at the facts, man. The boss has her brat. She'll do anything to get that kid back. Nothing will stop her, not as long as she's alive."

Dennis Godbey sighed and propped an elbow on the table, his blue eyes sliding from one of his friends to the other. "My vote is to take her out tomorrow. I'll do it if George can't."

"It's not that I can't handle it!" George snarled. "I just think there ought to be another way, that's all."

Paul laughed softly. "Right. Why don't we simply call her and tell her our problem? I can hear it all now. 'You see, Mrs. Christiani, we were in cahoots with Miles, cheating our boss. Those ledgers you have will finger us. If that happens, we all die. The way we see it, it's your daughter's life or ours.' Come on, George. Do you think she's going to care? He's got her *daughter*. We have to take her out. When the old man leaves Intensive Care, we'll get rid of him, too. End of problem until after everything goes through probate. When the box is finally opened, we'll find out who gets the contents and arrange to steal the ledgers before anyone reads them. It's simple, clean, and we come out smelling like roses."

"Just like the boss would do it?" George said softly. "No loose ends. Don't you ever get sick of it? That's why we got ourselves into this mess in the first place."

Paul began stirring his coffee again, his hazel eyes intent on the swirling liquid. "Oh, I'm sick of it. We're all sick of it. But I'm not so fed up that I'm willing to go swimming in the sound with bricks tied to my ankles."

"I vote we do it from a distance," Dennis inserted.

"I'm game," Paul replied. "And you won't hear any more arguments from George, either." He gave his spoon a final clank, skewering Paisley with a meaningful glare. "Right, Georgie Boy?"

AFTER MALLORY WENT UPSTAIRS, Mac placed two phone calls, one to the King County Police and one to Beth Hamstead. He hated lying, but he had to be sure well-meaning cops or friends didn't unwittingly do something to panic Lucetti. Emily was home, safe and sound, Mac told them. They had found her wandering one of the back roads. No more searching necessary. He apologized profusely for all the trouble that had been caused. Kids would be kids. Seven-year-old girls didn't always stay in the yard as they were told. There was another call Mac wanted to make, to his best friend, Shelby. He needed to find out who those three men in the cream-colored car were. *Fast*. Shelby could do the legwork for him. What if Lucetti had tapped the phone lines, though? A call like that could be disastrous. He'd have to phone Shelby from a booth in the morning.

Once Mac felt certain he didn't have to worry about the Hamsteads or the police complicating matters, he did the dishes, one ear cocked toward the stairs to listen for Mallory. When twenty minutes passed and he hadn't heard water running through the pipes, he began to worry. Was she all right? He hated to go up. If he caught her half-dressed, they'd both be embarrassed, but if he didn't go up and she was sick or something...

He dried his hands and tossed the towel on the countertop. Indecision held him rooted for a moment, then he moved through the entry hall until he stood at the bottom of the stairs. The house was eerily silent now that he had stopped rummaging around. No, not completely silent. He turned his head slightly and listened. There it was again. She was up there someplace bawling. And trying very hard not to be heard.

Mac put a hand on the banister, took a step up, hesitated. If he were smart, he'd stay down here and let her cry. He took another step. He was lousy at mopping up tears. He took another step. Then another. He might be clumsy, but nobody else was around to take care of her.

The house was like a maze. Two long halls when most places had one. Doors everywhere. He homed in on the soft sounds. At last he found the right room. The door was closed. From the other side, he could hear the sobbing clearly, not quite so soft now that he was so close.

He stood there and shifted his weight from one foot to the other. Then he raked his hand through his hair. *Here goes nothing.*

He opened the door and peeked inside. The shaft of light from the hall spilled across Mallory, who knelt by a canopy bed. Pink ruffles and lace. A little girl's room. She held something clutched in her arms. Mac couldn't see what. She was rocking it like she would a child. His guts twisted. He had seen a lot of heartache, experienced his share, but never had he seen anything like this. The raw, jagged sounds coming from her chest sounded as if they might tear something important loose.

He didn't feel himself move toward her. Suddenly he was just there. Going down on one knee behind her, he placed a hand on her back. She jerked away, surprised, then averted her face and shrank from him. Now that he was closer, he could see that she had a tattered stuffed dog in her arms.

"Mallory...."

"It's Ragsdale," she sobbed.

"It's what?"

"Ragsdale. She c-can't sleep w-without him."

"Oh, Mallory. Come here."

Mac thought she might resist. Instead he got an armful of woman and stuffed dog. He caught her to his chest and buried his face in her hair, shocked because some of the tears flowing were his own. He had never felt anyone shake the way she was shaking. He could almost feel her pain.

"My baby. They're going to kill my baby." She clung to him as if she were about to plunge off a cliff. "I love her so much. She's afraid, I know she is. How can he do this? Oh, Mac, I can't bear it. Not my little girl. They can have everything—all of it. But not my baby... Sh-she never did anything to anyone."

"I know."

He wrapped his arms around her. Now it was him doing the rocking. There was a first time for everything. Mac dipped his head to wipe his cheek dry on her blouse. She smelled like the lilac bushes that bloomed in his mom's backyard each spring. He closed his eyes. "You listen to me, okay? I'm going to do everything I can to bring Emily home. You hear me? Safe and sound. Back to you. Back to Ragsdale. I promise you that."

"But you said Lucetti can't be found."

"No, I said he would be hard to find. There's a difference. I'm good at what I do, Mallory. Give me a chance to prove it. If he can be found, I'll find him." Catching her face between his hands, Mac set her away from him so he could look into her eyes. "I'll do everything I possibly can to bring Em home. Trust me, okay? Just trust me."

He felt some of the tension drain out of her. She hiccuped and sniffed. "D-do you r-really think you can?"

"Of course I do. You and I are going to find that key and get the package. We can find it. After that, getting Emily back will be simple."

He drew her back into his arms and after a long while, she quieted. When she did, he rose to his feet and pulled her up with him. She swayed sideways and he caught her, tucking in his chin to look at the tattered toy between them. A little girl smell drifted up from the lop-eared dog, shampoo and powder and fresh-washed flannel. He could picture Emily fast asleep with the toy nestled in the crook of her arm. Moving toward the bed, he whipped back the covers and lowered Mallory to the mattress. For an instant, she looked startled to find herself lying down, then she peered up at him through the gloom, her eyelashes fluttering. Mac knew exhaustion was about to take its toll. As he straightened, he hit his head on the canopy frame. He bit back a word that should never be uttered in a little girl's bedroom and shot a glare at the ruffled contraption above him. The child obviously had no father, or he'd have gotten rid of the darned thing.

With the back of her hand, Mallory made a halfhearted swipe at her nose and sniffed. There weren't any tissues on the nightstand. He felt for his handkerchief and couldn't find it. Sighing, he drew the covers over her and sat down. She sniffed again and made another swipe. He wasn't sure where a bathroom was, and he was afraid to leave her just yet. Tugging up one corner of the sheet, he mopped at her face. She was beyond caring, and so was he.

"Blow."

She made a snuffling noise into the sheet and he gave the tip of her small nose a careful squeeze.

Mac sighed and smoothed her hair back from her cheek. The strands were every bit as soft and silken as he had always imagined.

Her eyelashes drifted downward, wet and spiked. He watched as her lips parted slightly and her breathing changed. Her hand relaxed its hold on Ragsdale and slid partway down the dog's back. Mac touched her hair again. Rubbing it between his fingers, he smiled to himself. Definitely salon-conditioned, he decided. Hair didn't come that soft naturally.

His gaze dropped to the unused half of her pillow. Weariness and the soft sound of her breathing made him yawn. There was room enough for two. If he slept beside her, he wouldn't have to worry about her getting up in the middle of the night. The house was locked up. He stripped off his shoulder holster and laid it beside the bed. Just for a few minutes, he thought, as he stretched out next to her. An hour, tops....

CHAPTER SIX

JUST BEFORE DAWN, Mallory awoke alone in Emily's bed. In the farthest reaches of her mind, she remembered the feel of Mac's body stretched out beside her during the night, the heavy warmth of his arm slung across her waist, his other hand cupped beneath her head. She lifted her lashes slowly, aware of the relentless ache in her chest before she fully opened her eyes. She had escaped the pain for a few hours, but now she had to face it.

She didn't want to. Part of her longed to stay unconscious until Em was home. Ah, but that was the catch, wasn't it? There was no guarantee that Em would ever return. Mac's reassurances had worked their magic last night, giving her hope, but now that her head was clear, she had to accept facts. The odds weren't good.

Determination filled Mallory. It was up to her to tip the scales in Em's favor. And she would. Somehow... No price was too dear, not even her own life, if it came to that.

The room was cast in shadow. As she rolled over in bed, the covers slipped down her arm and exposed her to the predawn chill. She had forgotten to turn up the thermostat. Passing a hand over her eyes, she blinked to clear her vision. As her surroundings came into focus, she spied Mac's silhouette at the window, his shoulders delineated against the charcoal gloom of the sky. She lay there and studied him, making no sound.

It made no sense, but seeing him there was a comfort. At a time like this, Mac should seem a poor substitute for Darren or Keith, but strangely enough, she no longer felt so alone. Mac had been there for her in all the ways that counted last night. Many men would have been incapable of that kind of tenderness, especially with someone they scarcely knew.

As if he sensed her watching him, he glanced over his shoulder at her. Even in the dim light, she could see the clear gray of his eyes, feel their impact. Eyes like his touched. She knew it had to be her imagination, but that was how she felt—touched. Yesterday at the hospital that had unnerved her. Now she wasn't certain how it made her feel.

"What time is it?" she asked.

"Five. We have another three hours to get through."

Three hours…one hundred and eighty minutes… forever. She swung her legs over the edge of the bed and planted her feet on the floor. Glancing down at herself, she saw that her blouse had come partially undone and that her skirt had twisted until the sideseam was in front. She stood and quickly straightened her clothing, aware that Mac's eyes never left her, that he was watching her fumble with the buttons. She wondered what he was thinking, but when she looked up at him, she could read nothing in his expression. All she knew was that the closeness they had shared last night had evaporated. That left her feeling strangely desolate.

Mac leaned against the window frame, aware of the woman behind him with every pore of his skin. What would she say, he wondered, if he turned to her right now and told her he was Randy Watts's half brother. Because of the different last name, she probably didn't know; not unless Keith had mentioned it. And even if Keith had at some point, Mallory probably didn't remember. Fourteen years was a long time.

But Mac remembered....

Judging by his behavior last night, perhaps he hadn't remembered quite vividly enough. If he closed his eyes, he could see that cheap headstone of Randy's as clearly as though he were there, feel the rain pelting his face, hear the wind whistling. A very lonely place, that graveyard, Randy's eternal reward for having dared to believe in the great American dream...that the sky was the limit, even for poor boys. When Randy was at last forced to accept that he wasn't quite good enough in some people's eyes, the disillusionment had killed him. Mac wouldn't make the same mistake. Women like Mallory were lethal.

"Mac?" Mallory could see the rigid set of his shoulders, the knotted muscle along his jaw. He looked angry and remote. She didn't mean to sound pitiful when she said his name, but her emotions betrayed her, making her voice tremble. "I—are you—is something wrong?"

"No."

The word hung there between them. *No.* Sometimes, no meant yes, and she sensed that this was one of those times. Her first thought was that something had happened while she was asleep, that Mac was trying to work up the courage to tell her. *Emily.* She clasped her hands and pressed them against her stomach. Words slid up her throat and caught right behind her larynx, words she couldn't utter. *Emily.* Mallory felt as if she might be sick. Cold sweat trickled from her armpits down the sides of her breasts.

"It's Em, isn't it? Something's happened."

Mac shot her a puzzled look. "No. Why?"

Mallory stared at him. Running a hand through his

hair, he moved away from the window. "I was just thinking, that's all. This time of morning does that to me, makes me gloomy. I didn't mean to upset you."

"You—there's nothing—they didn't—she's not—" She could hear herself babbling, but couldn't stop, couldn't sort the words once they began to erupt.

Mac laid a hand over her mouth. "She's all right, Mallory," he whispered. "I'm sorry if I frightened you."

She had an unbalanced feeling, very like when waves washed the sand out from under her on the beach. She was losing her grip, and this was how it felt to go insane. She could feel her body twitching. Taking a deep breath, Mallory quit breathing and clamped her mouth shut. Little black spots bounced in front of her eyes. She wondered if she might faint.

Mac slid a hand behind her neck to pull her face against his shoulder. He kneaded the spasm-stricken muscles in her shoulders. "You're all right, Mallory," he murmured. "It happens sometimes. Happened to me once, in fact, after a grenade hit near our foxhole. The old muscles go crazy. Stop trying to control it and just let go."

After a minute, her body began to respond to the gentle massage of his hands. The twitching slowly subsided. She stood there with her face buried against his shirt and wished she didn't have to lift her head. She had *never* in all her life acted like such a complete idiot. What was happening to her? What must Mac think? She had to get a hold on herself. She'd be of no use to Emily or anyone else if this continued.

Forcing her head up, Mallory pushed against his chest and took a wobbly step back. "I don't know what's gotten into me. You must think—I'm really sorry."

His eyes probed hers. "I think you're a mother who loves her child, that's what I think."

Hugging her breasts, Mallory averted her face and avoided looking directly at him again. "I'm going to take a shower and dress. Keith's room is down the hall. You're welcome to use his things. He's a little shorter than you, but his shirts might fit."

"I still have my luggage in the car, remember?"

"Oh, yes. Your trip. Baseball practice." Her gaze shifted to the mustard stain on his shirt, then to his sneakers, and she managed an anemic smile, remembering her first impression of him. What a great judge of character she had turned out to be. "There's a bathroom two doors down, or you can use Keith's."

She turned and walked to the doorway.

"Mallory?"

She glanced back, one hand on the doorknob. "Yes?"

His eyes locked with hers. After a long moment, he said, "She's going to be home before you know it. Try to remember that."

She nodded. "See you downstairs."

AFTER TAKING THEIR SHOWERS, Mac and Mallory utilized the time until eight o'clock to search both of Keith's studies, this time looking everywhere, even going so far as to remove the covers from the furniture cushions. Their thoroughness turned up nothing. At seven-thirty, they headed for the kitchen to await the phone call.

Stepping to the sink to fill the coffeemaker's reservoir, Mallory said, "We should be thinking of alternate places to search, don't you think, so we don't waste time once we talk to Em."

Mac drew a chair to the table and sat down. "I'm not

so sure where we search is as important as *how* we go about it. There aren't that many places he might have stuck a key, are there?"

"Here," she replied. "Or in his office. Possibly his car. Other than that, I can't think of anyplace, unless he rented a locker somewhere or put it in still another deposit box."

"Let's not borrow trouble."

She flipped the brew switch on the coffeemaker, and turned to face him. "He probably won't give us much time, will he? So *how* we go about looking will be crucial. Let's face it. Something as small as a key could be hidden almost anywhere. Under some loosened carpet. Inside a book. In his mattress. We could spend weeks looking."

He nodded.

"Then I say we use the process of elimination. Let's search only in the likely places first, so we can make an initial sweep. If that turns up nothing, we can backtrack and take rooms apart, piece by piece, if we must. His office first, then his car, then back here."

Mac glanced around the kitchen. "You're right. In this room alone, we could spend hours. For all we know, he could have stuck it in a cereal box or something."

"So we're agreed, a superficial search first in the obvious places, then we go deeper?"

"Agreed."

When the coffee was made, Mallory poured them each a cup, then joined Mac at the table to wait. It seemed to her that each minute was an hour long. She watched the clock. Fifteen before the hour. Then ten. Then five. Her breath began to catch as she measured off the remaining seconds. At last, the large clock hand moved forward onto the number twelve. She braced herself, her nerves raw with expectation. Nothing happened. The silence seemed deafening. And the minutes crept by.

When it became apparent that Lucetti had no intention of calling at the agreed time, Mac leaped up from his chair and let loose with a string of expletives that expressed Mallory's sentiments exactly. Then he began to pace. She counted the steps he took. Back and forth, his fist smacking his palm each time his right heel hit the tile. Just when she felt sure that the sound would drive her mad, he stopped and turned to look at her, his blond head cocked to one side, his gray eyes almost blue with anger. Leveling a finger at her nose, he said, "He'll pay for this, I promise you that."

Mallory believed it. He looked furious enough to rip someone apart. He was a big man, lean of waist and hip, with heavily muscled shoulders and arms. Sunlight poured in the sliding glass doors and surrounded him with a golden aura, creating an almost mystical effect. Even in pleated gray slacks and a fresh blue shirt with tie, he managed to look formidable. His anger surrounded her and emanated an almost electrical charge, tingling on her skin. She was glad he was in her corner; she wouldn't have wanted such a man as an enemy.

By this time, Mallory felt as if she had been injected with a gigantic syringe of novocaine. In a hollow voice, she asked, "Do you think she's dead?"

He planted his hands on his hips. "It's a mind game. He'll call. We'll talk to Em. But he wants to make us sweat first."

"But why?"

"So we'll jump when he tells us to, that's why." He grabbed a chair, turned it around and straddled it, folding his arms across its back. After studying her with a fierce intensity that unnerved her, he said, "I know I've stressed this once before, but it's worth saying again. You can't let him bully you. Emily's life might depend on it. Insist that you be allowed to speak to her, not just this time, but every time you talk with him until we find that package. Ask her at least one question each time. We don't want him playing us a recording. He'll want to refuse. For one thing, he'll be afraid we'll put tracers on the phone. No matter what he threatens, you remember four words. *No kid, no package.*"

"But—what if he gets angry and kills her?"

Mac lifted an eyebrow. "Mallory, you and you alone can deliver that package to him. Whatever's in it, he wants it so badly that he's nabbed Emily to get it. He's desperate or he never would have done it. You *have* to remember that. You can't let fear do your thinking for you. If you want your daughter back, you're going to have to get tough."

She knew he was right. To get Em back, she would have to maintain control, bargain, threaten if she had to. She couldn't let Lucetti sense her fear. If she did, he would use it against her, and Em would be the loser. "Right. Tough, I'll be tough." She ran a hand over her hair. "I just wish he'd call."

Mac reached out and caught her hand. His fingers closed around hers, warm and strong. "Just for the record, I think you've done great so far."

Heat crept up her neck. "After last night? And then this morning?"

A slow smile lifted one corner of his mouth. "Yeah, before, during and after. Believe me, I wouldn't say it if I didn't mean it. I don't dish out praise much, especially not to—"

His eyes darkened. He let go of her hand and turned his head to gaze out the sliding glass doors at the pool deck. Mallory watched him and wondered what it was he had left unsaid. Especially not to who? Her? She nearly asked, but something about the rigid set of his shoulders forestalled her.

An hour passed. Then another. When the clock in the hall chimed ten, Mallory knew firsthand what hell was like. She also knew now that you didn't have to die to go there. There was nothing Mac could say to make her feel better, so neither of them said anything. They just sat there at the breakfast table and stared at the phone on the bar. And they waited....

Mallory thought of little else but Emily. It was strange, really, the things she found herself remembering about her daughter, silly things that she scarcely noticed day to day. The way her mouth drew down at the corners when she felt disappointed, the dimples in her plump elbows, the silken hair that shimmered like gold on her upper lip when she stood in the sunshine. She remembered how it felt to snuggle with Em beneath the warm folds of her Winnie the Pooh sleeping bag on Saturday morning, their fingers sticky from eating hot Pop-Tarts, attention glued to the cartoons on television. Silly things...the sort of things only a mother would recall, things Mallory knew now she might never do again. She found herself wishing she could do them all just one more time—just once—so she could memorize every precious moment.

When the clock struck ten-thirty, the phone rang almost simultaneously. Both of them leaped from their chairs and whirled to stare at it. Then sanity returned. Mallory crossed the room, made sure the speaker was on and lifted the receiver. "H-hello?"

"Mrs. Christiani? I trust you slept well?"

The voice on the other end of the line was so smug that anger flashed through Mallory. She tightened her grip on the phone. "I slept quite well, thank you."

The silence that followed her cool reply gave her a sense of satisfaction. Mac had been right. Lucetti had delayed calling to gain an emotional advantage. For once, she was grateful to her mother. She might sweat, but Lucetti would never know it.

"Listen carefully. I have reason to believe that—"

"Excuse me," Mallory cut in. "You're forgetting I requested that my daughter be put on the phone. First things first."

"Have you ever visited the King County Morgue to identify a body, Mrs. Christiani?"

Mallory's legs quivered. She glanced at Mac, licked her lips and said, "Yes, as a matter of fact. I'm a retired nurse and I've worked in the hospital morgue." Mac's eyes locked with hers and he gave her a thumbs-up signal as he walked toward her. A proud grin slanted across his mouth. She pressed a trembling hand to her throat. "I think perhaps we've reached a stalemate. Mr. Mac Phearson made our position quite clear last night. Call back when you can put my daughter on the phone."

With that, Mallory hung up. For a moment, absolute silence resounded in the room. Then Mac let out his breath in a rush. Mallory threw him a frightened look.

"Oh, Mac—" She clamped a hand over her mouth and closed her eyes.

Mac came over to stand beside her. "You did the right thing. He'll call back, honey. And when he does, he won't play mind games."

Mallory nodded and made an odd little sound behind her palm, half sob and half hysterical laughter. She prayed he was right, that she hadn't just signed Em's death warrant. The phone rang again, making her jerk. Her eyes flew open. Mac put an arm around her and held her clasped to his side as she reached out for the phone.

"Just stay cool," he whispered.

Mallory gulped down panic and lifted the receiver. "Hello?"

"Mommy?"

Joy welled within Mallory, so intense that she couldn't speak for a moment. She moved closer to the phone, as if somehow she could get closer to her child. That precious little voice ran over her like sunshine. "Em? Oh, Em! How are you, princess?"

"Fine. Mommy, why didn't you tell me I had to stay someplace new? I felt awfully angry with you at first. Is Gramps better yet? I'm tired of staying places. I wanna come home. I miss you, Mommy. And you forgot to bring me Ragsdale." She made a clucking sound with her tongue. "You promised you would when we found out I forgot him, remember. I've had bad mares for two nights now."

The scolding note in her daughter's voice brought a fresh rush of tears. "Nightmares, you mean? Not bad ones, I hope? I wanted to bring you Ragsdale, darling, but something came up and I—I couldn't. Em, are the people there treating you nice?"

"Yes, but I'm—" Emily's voice broke off "—homesick. I can't talk more, Mommy. We don't got enough quarters."

"Em? Em!"

"Satisfied, Mrs. Christiani?"

Mallory leaned heavily against Mac, drawing strength from him. "For the moment, yes."

"I'll call back with the instructions."

The phone clicked and went dead. Mallory threw Mac another panicked glance. "He's afraid to stay on the line too long in case we're trying to trace him," he explained. "It'll be a few minutes. He'll call from another phone so he can't be located."

Mallory grabbed the back of a bar stool and swung into it. "That was the hardest thing I've ever done in my life. The very hardest."

"I know, but you didn't show it. That's what counts. I thought you were the lady who couldn't act?"

Mallory leaned her head back. "That wasn't an act. It was just—" She broke off and licked her lower lip. "You'd have to know my mother. A regimental upbringing comes in handy."

Mac lifted an eyebrow. "Regimental?"

Mallory met his gaze. "How long before he calls?"

He glanced at his watch. "Another five minutes, probably. So we wait again." He studied her for a moment. "I'm curious. What is a regimental upbringing? Tell me about your mom."

Mallory hesitated, but something in his expression— she had no idea what—made her start talking. When she finished, she couldn't remember exactly what she had said, but Mac's expression, which had started her talking in the first place, had subtly altered. "Do you like your mother?"

"Of course I do. I love her."

"That isn't what I asked."

"I admire her."

"But do you like her?"

Mallory frowned. "That's a terrible thing to ask."

"Only when you can't say yes." He caught her by the

chin, his eyes searching hers. Then the phone rang and interrupted them. Mallory turned on the bar stool, her heart slamming.

"Wait for the third ring so we don't appear too anxious."

Her hand shook as she reached for the receiver. "Hello?"

"Listen carefully," the now-familiar voice hissed. "As I mentioned last night, I have reason to believe your father-in-law put the package in his safe-deposit box. You find that box key and get the package. Once you have it, return with it to your home. I'll phone you there to arrange a meeting place for the exchange."

"How will you know when I've gotten the box opened?"

"I have you under constant surveillance, so I'll know."

"And what if I can't find the key?"

"For your child's sake, find it. You have twenty-four hours. Countdown begins now."

The moment the phone went dead, Mallory dropped the receiver and made a fist in her hair. "Twenty-four hours! He can't expect—what kind of miracle worker does he think I am?"

"That's not what has me worried. Are you on the safe-deposit contract at the bank?"

"The what?"

"The contract. It just occurred to me that if you aren't authorized to open that box, key or no key, they won't let you touch it. Did you ever go in to the bank and sign a release?"

Pressing her hand to her forehead, Mallory tried to remember. "I—I don't know. I've signed so many things. After Darren died, there was so much red tape, so many contracts and releases and affidavits. Keith, being a lawyer, was relentless about having everything done to the letter."

"Let's hope he didn't forget any minor details, like giving you access to his deposit box. If you aren't on that contract, it would take a court order to get the box opened even with a key."

Mallory's hopes lifted. "But, Mac, if I *am* on the contract, couldn't I have the box drilled myself?"

"Sure. But it might take too much time. One locksmith is authorized by the bank chain to drill their boxes, and it'd be our luck he'd be in Spokane or someplace. Let's see about the contract first."

Mac leafed through the phone book, ran his finger down a page, then punched out a phone number. A woman's voice came over the speaker, "Good morning, Ann speaking."

"Yes, Ann, this is Keith Christiani. I'd like to do some checking on my safe-deposit box contract. I need to find out if my daughter-in-law, Mallory Christiani, is down as an authorized user?"

"One moment, please." When the woman came back on the line, she said, "No, Mrs. Christiani's signature isn't on file. If you'd like for her to be, it's a simple matter of signatures."

Mac closed his eyes for a moment in disappointment, then angled a meaningful look at Mallory. "I might do that. Well, um, thank you." Dropping the receiver into its cradle, Mac turned and leaned a hip against the counter. "That's not good news."

Mallory could feel her blood pounding in her temples, hear the pulse beats going *swish-swish* in her ears. "But we *have* to open it. What are we going to do? Does that mean that even if we manage to find the key, we can't get the package?"

A distant, thoughtful look crept into his eyes. "No, it just means we can't get it legally."

"Meaning?"

"Meaning that once we find the key, I'll have to forge Keith's signature and pray I'm good enough they don't suspect."

"Couldn't you get in trouble? What if they caught you? Someone there might know Keith on sight. He isn't exactly a nobody in town, you know! If they're that strict about who can open those boxes, you could be arrested or something."

"It wouldn't be the first time." He chucked her under the chin. "Don't look so horrified. It isn't a hanging offense."

"You mean it, don't you? You'd actually risk jail."

"Don't pin wings on my shoulders. You can't pass for Keith, so I'm elected, simple as that. So where do we start? His car or the office? We have to start searching. Like you said, a key could be almost anywhere."

A key. A cold prickle began at Mallory's nape and crept up to her scalp. Keith's face flashed before her. She remembered how his hand had clawed the air when she had mentioned that her father had lost the motor-home key. Now she realized what he had been trying to tell her. "Mac!"

He glanced over at her. "What?"

In a rush, she told him what had occurred yesterday. "Do you suppose we could set up some kind of signal to question him?"

Mac shook his head. "It's no use. I tried that yesterday before you arrived. He hasn't got enough control over his body. If he could open and close his eyes upon command—anything like that—we could set up a signal, but he can't. Trying just frustrates him. Unless he improves dramatically, we're on our own." He sighed. "Well? Where do you want to look first?"

"My vote is his office. He was there when he collapsed, so it seems the most logical starting point. And if the key isn't there, maybe we'll find a clue to lead us to it."

CHAPTER SEVEN

THE MOMENT MAC and Mallory stepped into the lobby of
the law firm, they froze. The elegant room looked as if a
quake had hit: furniture upside down, plants dumped on
the rug, paintings hanging askew. Trudy, the secretary,
sat at her rifled desk speaking on the telephone with the
insurance adjuster, one hand buried in her graying blond
hair. Her tortoiseshell eyeglasses were perched on the
end of her nose so she could see over the rims to assess
the damage.

"Nothing valuable was stolen, and nothing seems to
be missing from our files." She rolled her eyes. "And
how long will that take? I can't leave things like *this,*
you know."

"What on earth happened?" Mallory asked, the moment Trudy hung up.

"Vandals," she replied with a groan. "This is how I
found it this morning. Awful, isn't it? All three offices.
Keith's got it the worst." She shrugged one shoulder. "I
wasn't going to tell you. I figured you had enough on
your plate."

Mac stepped over a pile of potting soil and the wilted
remains of a fern. "How many offices in the building
were hit?"

"Only ours. I guess we were the most convenient."

Mac's gray eyes met Mallory's in silent communication. Turning simultaneously, they headed for Keith's office. The mess in the lobby didn't prepare Mallory for the destruction that greeted them. Nothing of Keith's had been left unmolested. Even his law books lay scattered on the floor. His files had been dumped, his desk gutted, the phones disassembled. The top had even been pried off the IBM Selectric. His sofa and chair had been slit open, the stuffing strewn everywhere on the rug. With a grim scowl, Mac planted his hands on his hips and surveyed the wreckage.

"Well, I wonder if they found it."

Mallory could only stare. The photos of her and Em had been taken apart. Keith's snow globe was shattered. Clearly the intruders had been searching for something small, like a key. "What if they did? Why is he doing this? I don't understand."

"Doesn't make sense, does it?" He sighed and gave the room another once-over. "From the looks of things, they didn't miss anything. That's a good indication."

"It must be Lucetti. It has to be. Who else could it be?"

"That's a question I can't even start to answer. And, given the time schedule, I don't have time to find out. Tunnel vision, Mallory. We have to stay focused on one thing, finding that damned key." He scattered a pile of papers with the toe of his loafer. "Why is he undermining you like this?"

She walked to a file. "Looking now will be twice as hard. He must realize that. Maybe it wasn't even Lucetti who did it."

"And if not, then who?" He shook his head. "No point in even bothering to look here."

She knew he was right, but desperation made her refuse to admit it. "They might have missed it. A key is so small."

"Mallory." Mac's voice was low pitched and persuasive. "Come on. It's hopeless. They put everything through a sifter."

"Let's check his car, then."

"Where is it? We've got to get ahead of them."

"Out back."

Trudy was on the phone rescheduling appointments when they returned to the lobby. She excused herself and said, "Awful, isn't it?"

"Sure is," Mac agreed. "Did you call the police?"

"First thing."

He gave a brisk nod. "We'll be in touch, okay?"

"Tell Keith I'm thinking of him. I hoped to go see him today if they moved him from the ICU, but this—" she waved her hand at the mess "—has changed my plans." Her green eyes rested on Mallory's pale face and clouded with sympathy. "Keep your chin up, honey. He'll pull through."

Guilt washed over Mallory. She hadn't given poor Keith much thought since yesterday. Not trusting herself to speak, she slipped out the door ahead of Mac. Leading the way down the hall to the front exit, she blinked back tears. Tears wouldn't help Em. Like Mac said, she had to get tough. If only it were her in danger instead of her child. She felt so helpless. All her maternal instincts were screaming at her to do something. As she drew near the door, it seemed to her that the tapping of her heels sang, *The key, the key, you have to find the key.* If someone else had found it, how could she ransom her daughter? How much of their twenty-four hours had been wasted by coming here? Time was slipping away, each second taking them closer to deadline. Her mind stumbled on the first half of that word. *Dead. Oh, Em, I love you. I couldn't bear losing you.*

She felt Mac come up behind her, felt his sleeve brush the back of hers.

"You okay?"

Mallory sighed and glanced over her shoulder at him. How many times had he asked her that since last night? Concern lined his face. Well, that was all about to change. A person could only become so scared. Then numbness set in. After that came resignation. Lucetti had Em, and there was nothing she could do to change that. But that didn't mean she couldn't fight back.

When she stepped outside, the morning breeze touched her cheeks and whispered softly through her hair. Above her in a gnarled elm, a pair of birds twittered and hopped from branch to branch, celebrating the sunshine. Tipping her face skyward, Mallory absorbed the warmth and parted her lips to take a bracing draught of fresh air. The expanse of blue overhead was the color of robin eggs, the clouds fluffy wisps of white. "Do you believe in God, Mac?"

He studied the branches silhouetted above them, the azure sky, as if the answer to her question lay there. "Not the way you probably do. I don't attend church and go to pancake breakfasts, that kind of stuff."

Her gaze rested on his upturned profile, on the crooked bridge of his nose, the tiny scar above his eyebrow, the rock-hard line of his jaw. He was incredibly handsome, but not in a refined way, more rugged and rough, like one might expect an ex-boxer to look. She tried to imagine him at a stuffy church brunch and found herself smiling the first real smile in days. Did he really think the sum total of her life revolved around linen napkins and place settings? "But you do believe?"

His gray eyes fell to hers, eyes so clear, so transparent that a reply wasn't necessary. "He watches out for fools and children, you know. She's going to come through this okay."

Taking another deep breath, she stuffed her hands deep into her blazer pockets. "Yes, I think she is, too. I *know* it. I've already lost my husband. It wouldn't be fair if I lost Em."

"Nope, sure wouldn't."

"Besides," she added lightly, "we have you on our side. I'd say that stacks the odds in our favor."

With that unsettling vote of confidence, she turned and struck off down the walkway toward the corner of the building.

Spying a pay phone, he asked her to wait.

She slowed her pace and fell in beside him to walk to the booth. Mac quickly scanned the area, then left her outside, digging in his pocket for a quarter. Dropping the coin into the slot, he punched out Shelby's number. *No answer.* With a sigh, he hung up and left the booth, shrugging one shoulder.

"It figures. Good ol' Shelb. Never home when I need him."

He trailed her to the back parking lot, his gaze shifting constantly, alert for movements between the cars, in the shrubbery. He didn't want to remind Mallory of the men who had tried to kill them yesterday, especially not right now when she seemed to be rallying, but it was something he couldn't afford to forget. Someone else searching for the key might prove to be the least of their problems.

She led the way to a silver Lincoln, then stopped to stare at it in dismay.

"What is it?" he asked.

"Keys! My set was on the ring that was stolen yesterday."

"I carry a master key in my car. Be right back."

She watched him take off at a lope toward the client parking area on the other side of the building. A master key? Until now, she hadn't known such a thing existed. Moments later, he returned with two long pieces of flat, flexible metal with yellow handles at one end and cutout hooks at the other. "Slim Jims."

"I thought those were illegal unless you worked for a company that had uses for them."

"I'm a company, and I definitely have a use for them." A flush crept up his neck as he worked the pieces of metal through the crack of the car window and fished with the hooks for a hold on the lock switch. "Mallory, there are two things you need to learn. Turn your head and don't look if I ask you to, and don't say the word *illegal* loud enough for a cop to hear. Even when I'm completely legitimate, it makes me nervous."

A grin curved her mouth. "Then they *are* illegal."

Teasing laughter lit up his eyes. "Only if I get caught or someone yells *illegal* at the top of her lungs in a public parking lot." He stepped back and opened the car door. "The end justifies the means. Scouts honor, I don't steal stereos."

He muttered something else under his breath as he leaned inside the car. "Pardon me?" she queried. He muttered it again and she moved closer. "Sorry...what?"

He threw her a glare. "I said I don't, anymore." He was

fanning his arm under the driver's seat, so the words came up from the floorboard muffled.

"You don't what anymore?"

"Steal stereos."

Mallory's grin disappeared. "Oh, come on, you've never robbed people's cars with those."

"It's called thugging, not robbing. And no, not with these. My old set had black handles. Yellow would show up after dark like a beacon. *These* are legally in my possession and I only use them for legitimate purposes. In my line of work, getting into cars is often a necessity. I've cracked a lot of cases from clues I found in locked automobiles." When he straightened, he hit his head on the steering wheel and cursed under his breath, rubbing his temple as he fell back against the seat. He hesitated when he saw her staring at him, and his scowl deepened. "What's the matter? Did I just lose my angel wings?"

Was that hostility she saw flaring in his eyes? She avoided looking directly at him. "Not at all. I'm simply curious. You're saying you were a thugger of automobiles?"

"A *thugger?* Mallory, thugging is something you do, not what you are. And I really don't want to get into my history."

Her eyes flew back to his. "That isn't fair. Why say something like that if you don't want to elaborate?"

"Because I didn't want to give you a false—" He broke off, his jaw muscle knotting as he clenched and unclenched his teeth. "Elaborate? You spew big words like a walking dictionary."

She hadn't imagined the hostility. It glowed like banked embers in his eyes. What had she said or done to set him off?

"You know what bugs me the worst about people like you?" he snapped. "You're *relieved* I got the car open, *glad* I had the Slim Jims, but you'll still stand there and look superior because my having them may be on the shady side of legal." He pressed the panel button to unlock all the Lincoln's doors, his eyes narrowed. "I'm sorry if I offend your refined sensibilities. Don't worry. I'm not breaking the law, okay?"

The contempt in his expression was unmistakable. Since *sensibilities* wasn't exactly monosyllabic, she wondered what his problem was. "What do you mean, people like me? Just what kind of a person am I?"

"Let's just drop it." He slid out of the car and loomed over her, the Slim Jims dangling from his right hand. In slacks and a sport coat, he looked too respectable to have ever engaged in street theft. "We've got a key to find, remember? No time to discuss your character faults." He slanted her a look that spoke volumes. "Or *mine*. Don't worry. I won't rub off on you. Hopefully the same will hold true in reverse."

She felt as if she had been slapped. He was already back inside the car, running his hands along the underside of the dash. She went around to the passenger side. As she rifled the glove box, she said, "You think I'm a snob, don't you?"

He jerked down the visor. "You said it."

She slammed the box closed and nearly stood on her head to check the underside of the seat. "Well, I'm not. You shouldn't judge people before you know them."

"If that isn't the pot calling the— Oh, never mind. I don't want to argue with you, Mallory, okay? We have enough trouble."

"When have I behaved like a snob to you? Name one time?"

"You need me right now, though. Naturally you'll treat me nice. Let's see how thick we are when this is over, shall we?"

"Are you implying that I'm *using* you? That I'm only being civil because I need you?"

He made no reply. His silence was all the answer she needed. He opened the rear door on his side of the car. She did likewise and watched him pull on the backseat. When she realized he was trying to remove it from the car, she grabbed handholds to help him. "One question, Mr. Mac Phearson. If you dislike people like me so much, why are you doing all this?"

Stony silence was his only response.

"Are you going to answer me? Why put yourself out for a Bellevue *snob* that spews words like a walking encyclopedia?"

"Dictionary." He tipped the seat at an angle so it would fit through the door opening. Seconds later, he pulled it free. "I told you, I owe Keith. Isn't that good enough? Or don't you people repay favors?"

He made it sound as if she came from another planet. "Someone *did* try to kill us yesterday. I suppose that's an everyday occurrence to *you* people." It gave her a perverse satisfaction to see him flinch. Served him right. There was such a thing as reversed snobbery, and he had a bad case of it.

She marched around the rear bumper, her heels snapping smartly on the asphalt to emphasize her anger. Unfortunately Mac was too busy looking the seat over to notice. That infuriated her all the more. In the back of her mind, she knew she was overreacting and tried to calm down. Grabbing an end, she helped him turn it upside down. "Hold your side up higher," he ordered.

She obliged, watching as he poked and prodded the springs and frame. "It must have been a big favor Keith did for you."

"Big enough."

"Well, I'm not sure I like being a payback. Especially when you so clearly dislike me."

His eyes lifted to hers. "Have I said I don't like you?"

"Yes."

"I have not."

"Yes you di—" A hissing pop filled the air, and a *twang* resounded as something hit the metal framing inside the seat. Bits of leather and cotton batting pelted her face. She stared at the gaping hole in the upholstery where an instant ago there had been gray leather. There wasn't time to wonder what had made the hole. Before her brain could register what her eyes and ears took in, Mac sacked her in a football tackle, his arms locked around her waist as they fell. Mallory landed on her back, Mac sprawled on top of her, the force of his weight flattening her. Lights flashed before her eyes, then black spots. She couldn't breathe. When her vision cleared, she saw Mac above her, his upper body supported by his elbows, his eyes scanning the parking lot. He focused on something and went pale.

"Son of a—" He sprang to his feet, back hunched, knees bent, and jerked her up beside him. Mallory's rubbery legs failed her and she slid along behind him on one knee, ripping her panty hose, scraping herself from shin to ankle. The sheer force of his forward momentum finally hauled her to her feet. He shielded her with his body as they ran the length of the car. "Stay down! When we reach those shrubs, make a dive for them and roll until you're covered by branches."

Another muffled pop. Air whooshed from one of the Lincoln's tires and the car rocked. A gun? In her terror, even with a silencer, it sounded more like a cannon. *Oh, please, God...* "Someone's shooting!" Another bullet splattered asphalt right in front of them. "Dive!" he cried. She saw the shrubs looming ahead of her. *Safety.* She dived, landing chest first on the lawn two feet short of her mark, and did a third-base skid on her stomach into the bark chips and juniper needles. Pain washed through her. Clawing for purchase, she slithered farther into the foliage, unaware of Mac beside her until she felt his arm across her back.

Mallory inched her head up. At the end of an adjacent building, she glimpsed a man as he eased out from around the corner to point something long and dark brown in their direction. Sunlight glinted off something shiny. Before she could react, Mac pushed her down hard.

"Keep down," he whispered.

"You don't have to be so rough."

"You'll know what rough is if half your head gets blown off. That's a high-powered rifle he's taking potshots with." Two more muffled shots rang out. He took a shaky breath and let it out slowly. "Do a Marine crawl to the corner of the building."

"A what?"

He threw her a look that plainly said any idiot should know what a Marine crawl was. "A belly crawl. Dig your elbows into the dirt to pull yourself. Use your knees and toes to push." With a nod of his head, he indicated that she should go first. Mallory pushed off. The next instant he smacked his palm on her bottom. "Keep your butt down!"

She threw him an incredulous glance over her shoulder. Nobody had dared to slap her on the behind in over a quarter of a century, but this wasn't the right time to argue with his methods. Burying her elbows in the bark dust, she pushed forward with her toes. Just as she did, there was another explosion of noise and the ground ahead of her geysered in her face. She stared at the crater left in the dirt. Suddenly it hit her that the noises exploding around them were *real* bullets being fired, the kind that blew holes in you, and one had just missed her by mere inches. Fear held her rooted.

"Move!" Mac snarled behind her. "Now!"

His snarl prodded her forward. She could feel him crawling next to her, keeping his body between her and the sniper. She kept hearing a strange noise—a panting, whining sound. After several feet, she realized it was her. She clamped her mouth shut, not wanting to give their position away, but the noises came out through her nostrils. Her blouse had either ripped or come unfastened, and every time she dragged herself forward, bark scraped and poked her bare skin. A sheared off branch jabbed her collarbone.

By the time they made it to the corner, she felt certain all her hide had been rubbed off. A sharp piece of wood had gotten inside her bra, but she didn't dare rise to remove it. They crab-walked around the building and inched their way toward Mac's Volvo.

"You stay put," Mac whispered. "I'll bring the car to you."

Mallory didn't have a chance to protest. Mac lunged to his feet and sprang forward in a zigzag run. Another shot rang out and a bullet zinged through the air where he had been only a millisecond earlier. It plowed into the

building, spraying mortar and bits of brick. She dug her
fists into the loose bark and held her breath, terrified for
him. Two more shots rang out.

In all her life, she had never seen anyone move with
such precision, powerful legs thrusting his body from
side to side, eating up distance at an incredible speed even
though he took an indirect path. This wasn't the first time
he had dodged bullets. His military training? She closed
her eyes for an instant to send up a fervent prayer. And
not just because she needed him. He was a very special
man. In the past day, he had proven himself to be a loyal
friend to Keith—and to her—at least a dozen times.

In the distance, she heard police sirens. Someone must
have heard the shots despite the silencer. Probably poor
Trudy. Mac reached the Volvo, threw open the door and
literally dived inside. The next instant, the car engine
roared to life. She stared through the juniper and watched
as the car bounced onto the walkway. When he cut the
tires toward the shrub beds, she realized that when he
had said he would bring the car to her, he had meant exactly that. He was coming straight at her. The front grill
snowplowed through the evergreens and bent a small fir
tree double. Mallory jumped up and out of the way just in
time, not sure even then that he wasn't going to drive right
over her. The car swerved at the last second. He leaned
sideways to throw the passenger door open, his harsh
"Get in!" nearly drowned out by the roar of the engine.

She scrambled to obey. The moment she hit the seat,
she slammed the door closed. A pop rang out, and a star-
ringed hole splattered the windshield. She slipped down
between the seat and the dashboard. The Volvo scraped
bottom over another twenty feet of shrubs, then grated
over the walkway curb as it dropped to the asphalt.

Grabbing the dash, Mallory eased her head up. Mac was guiding the car deftly in and out around parked vehicles. She knew what to expect this time and wasn't surprised when they careened into westbound traffic and headed toward Hunt's Point.

Several minutes passed before either of them realized they weren't being pursued. The sounds of the sirens had become more distant. Mac eased up on the gas pedal and blew air like a surfacing whale. "They must have decided to back off when they heard cops coming. You can get up now."

She slid back onto the seat and fastened her belt with shaking hands. "Who do you think they are? Lucetti's men?" She raked a hand through her hair. "It's bad enough that he gave me only twenty-four hours. Does he have to complicate matters by trying to kill us?"

Mac said nothing. From the frown that pleated his forehead, she knew he was trying to think. He drove aimlessly, taking a narrow road around the lake. After several miles, he relaxed. When he glanced over at her, he did a double take. "You're cut."

She glanced down and saw blood on her chest. She also saw that her top had indeed come unfastened and she was sporting scrapes from her waistband to her collarbone. She plucked the sharp piece of wood out of her bra and tried to do up her blouse, only to find that three buttons were missing. In defeat, she tugged her blazer together in front and buttoned it instead.

He looked over at her and chuckled. "If you could only see yourself. A day in my company and you're ruined for life."

She glanced down. "You're not exactly a prize winner yourself, you know."

Their eyes met and held for an instant, then he returned his attention to his driving. Perhaps coming so close to death was making her magnanimous, or maybe it was simply the bond of friendship that she sensed was developing between them, but their recent quarrel suddenly seemed ridiculous.

"Mac, I—" She licked her lips. "About the Slim Jims. I didn't mean to be judgmental. And I'm afraid I overreacted."

One of his eyebrows arched as he executed a left turn. "Slim Jims? Judgmental? What are you talking about?"

He reached over and placed his hand over hers, his grip warm and all too fleeting. He said nothing more, but he didn't need to. Whatever it was that she had done to rile him, he seemed as sorry as she about what had been said. She took a deep breath and sighed. "So what's our next plan of action?"

"I say we go back to the house. The office is out. We've checked the car. It's time to execute Plan B."

She didn't miss the troubled expression that lined his face as he made a U-turn. "What's wrong?"

"I'm not sure. It just doesn't make sense. You're cooperating in every way possible, right down to not calling the cops. So what's Lucetti stand to gain by having you killed?"

"Nothing," she agreed. "In fact, I'm the most likely person to succeed in finding the key and getting him the package. I know more about Keith's habits and personal affairs than anyone."

"Exactly. If you're out of the picture, he may never get that package. That's what bothers me."

Mallory considered that a moment. "Maybe it has nothing to do with Lucetti. It could be someone connected with your work."

"No way. For one thing, I don't have any deadly enemies. And for another, those fellows have pro written all over them. They're sharp. This whole mess has Lucetti's stamp on it. Besides, if it *was* someone after me, why would they ransack Keith's office? Doesn't make sense."

"Maybe there's someone else involved, someone connected to Lucetti, who doesn't want me to give Lucetti the package."

"You took the words right out of my mouth. All we have to do is figure out who. And why. Which is an impossible order, considering we have so little time. We're caught between a rock and a hard spot. The only option we have that I can see is to continue searching and be more careful about guarding our backs so we stay alive while we're doing it. Meanwhile I'll keep trying my friend Shelby. If I can get in touch with him, he can run some feelers out for me and, with some luck, find out who the people after us are."

"And then?"

"Well, if we're right, and they're somehow connected to the racketeering, we can give Lucetti some names the next time he calls, have a little more fact to back us up. Then maybe he'll get them off our backs. As it stands, he doesn't believe me, thinks they're connected to my work. We won't have much luck convincing him to take care of the problem unless I can convince him we *have* one."

CHAPTER EIGHT

THE DRIVE BACK to Mallory's went without a hitch. With the sun shining and the wonderfully warm air gusting through the open windows, it seemed like any of a hundred May days when she had driven home through downtown Bellevue. Businesspeople emerged from the mirrored skyscrapers and hustled along the sidewalks. Shoppers from Bellevue Square juggled packages as they scurried across the streets. The world continued its regular schedule. While Mac stopped to make another unsuccessful attempt to contact his friend, Mallory waited with a feeling of unreality. It didn't seem possible that someone had tried to kill them.

Before turning into the cul-de-sac where Mallory lived, Mac drove up and down the adjacent streets. They saw nothing suspicious. A few minutes later, when Mac pulled the Volvo into her driveway, the house looked so cheerfully ordinary she almost expected Em to come bounding down the steps. She could picture her against the rose-pink rhododendrons, tendrils of hair slipping out of her braids, eyes twinkling. After Mac parked, they sat there in silence and listened to the crackle-pop of the cooling engine. There was no through traffic here at the end of the cul-de-sac, so they felt safe enough to take a moment's rest.

He turned to look at her, his gray eyes gentle. A mus-

cle in his jaw flickered as he touched the cut on her collarbone. His hand drifted up the side of her neck to lift
her hair. She loosened her grip on the door handle as
he traced the hollow of her temple where her pulse had
suddenly begun to throb. Maybe it was almost dying, or
maybe it was simply a need to be held, but she felt like a
wax figure that had been placed too close to a furnace.
She let her eyes almost close.

Behind the veil of her lashes, she studied him, remembering how he had looked dodging bullets. A po-
tent combination of good looks and rugged, old-fashioned
masculinity, that was Mac. Nothing like her father in his
expensive suits and silk ties. Garrison Steele would have
lain beside her in the shrubs and quivered with fear if
someone had been shooting at them. She couldn't quite
bring herself to think of her arrogant, overbearing father
as weak, but he fell short somehow when compared to
the man beside her.

"I didn't mean to be so rough when we were crawling
through the bushes," he said huskily. "I know I hurt you
a couple of times. I don't have a light touch when I get
scared, I'm afraid."

"Oh, Mac…you didn't hurt me."

"Then why does the end of your nose look like I
smacked you? Seems to me I remember shoving your
face in the dirt."

The rasp of his fingers against her skin sent a shiver
over her. With a feeling akin to horror, she recognized her
body's reaction, and it had nothing to do with nearly dying
or needing comfort. Perhaps fear and sensuality were
like hate and love, divided only by a thin line. She had
read about a syndrome—couldn't remember the clinical
term—where people became infatuated with one another

in dangerous situations. Was that what was happening? Terror playing havoc with her hormones?

She tried to break eye contact with him and was powerless to do so. What if he read her feelings? He was reaching out to her as a friend, nothing more. His fingertips stilled on the curve of her neck. Almost imperceptibly, his face drew closer. Then his expression became quizzical, uncertain, and he withdrew as though the touch of her burned him. Throwing open his door, he exited the car in a rush.

She pushed her own door open and climbed out. He threw her another look over the top of the car, then turned to gaze at the house. He stood with his back to her, head tipped back, arms akimbo. His hair shone like burnished gold. She walked around the front of the car, her face averted, her cheeks scalding hot. What must he think?

"Mallory?"

She ignored him and climbed the steps. The only explanation for her behavior was that she was losing her mind. She had only known him for a day. Keith was gravely ill. Em's life was in danger. And he had been the one to pull away?

"Mallory, for Pete's sake—" He was right behind her.

She reached into her purse for the house key. The moment she pushed it at the lock, the door swung in. Fear flashed through her. When Mac saw that the door was ajar, he seized her by the arm and spun her away, pushing her against the house as he stepped sideways. He slipped his hand under his jacket and pulled out his gun.

He moved back to peer through the now yawning doorway. "Don't move," he whispered to her. "I'm going in. If anything happens, run to the nearest neighbor's."

She wanted to tell him to stay with her on the porch

where he'd be safe, but he had already moved beyond her reach, disappearing across the threshold. She held her breath and listened. The sound of her own pulse seemed deafening. Seconds dragged by, and stretched into minutes. Her fear mounted. Where was he? She imagined someone leaping out and hitting him over the head, pictured him lying unconscious someplace inside while she stood here, letting him bleed to death or something... like Darren.

When she could bear the waiting no longer, she inched out from the wall and peeked into the silent entry. She couldn't just stand there. She *was* a nurse, after all. *Nothing*. Emboldened, she crept inside, her skin aquiver as she moved the length of the hall and angled frightened glances into the rooms as she passed. The house had been ripped apart, paintings pulled off the walls, lamps overturned, furniture slashed, books thrown from the shelves. Where was Mac? The kitchen was a disaster, drawers dumped, food spilled, flour everywhere.

Mallory couldn't believe so much damage had been done during their brief absence. Forgetting to be silent, she spun and ran back into the entry hall. As she came abreast of the den, someone stepped out the doorway directly into her path. She screamed as she plowed into a broad chest. Strong hands grasped her shoulders.

"I thought I told you to stay put?"

Her knees almost buckled. "Oh, Mac, you scared me to death."

"Good," he growled. "Next time, do what I tell you."

"I was afraid you might be hurt."

His grip grew so tense she could feel him trembling. From the look on his face, she had the feeling he wanted to shake her. "You do what I tell you, *exactly* what I tell you, is that clear?"

As recently as yesterday afternoon, an order issued to her with such undiluted arrogance would have galled her. However, as short a time as had passed since, she had come to know Mac quite well. He was angry, all right, not so much over what she had done, but because she might have been hurt doing it. Knowing that, she was able to bite back her retort. She disliked playing the role of helpless female, but she supposed he was justified in thinking of her as one. Deadly skirmishes weren't her area of expertise.

Apparently satisfied that he had drilled his point home, he sighed and planted his hands on his hips. "The house has been ransacked."

She had already ascertained that much but it didn't seem wise to say so.

"They went through everything, even the pillows and your talcum powder. The lids are off the toilet tanks. Every place where something could have been hidden has been checked."

"Do you think they found it?"

"Not from the looks of this house. They even tore up Keith's jackets." He raked a hand through his hair. "This has got me worried. Somebody wants that key awful darned bad. Which leads us back to the original question. Why are those ledgers so important? Could someone not want Lucetti getting them? Do they want them for themselves? Who is Steven Miles? Could it be him behind this? Two of those guys must have come here while the third was at the law firm trying to blow us away."

"I've never heard of an accountant named Miles."

He groaned with frustration and threw up his hands.

"We don't have time for this. I wish I could have reached Shelby. At least he could do some legwork, ask questions."

"I think we ought to search here again. Plan B, remember? Take apart the light fixtures, the bedposts, everything. They might have missed something we won't." She was afraid he might disagree. "It's a big house. They couldn't have looked everywhere."

"Where do you think we should start?"

"You take Keith's bedroom. I'll take his study. We'll spread out from there."

"Maybe not. We might find it by then, you know." He flashed her a grin and touched her chin gently with his fist.

SUNLIGHT GLINTED OFF the cream-colored paint of the car's hood and momentarily blinded George Paisley. He squinted to see the traffic light. "Well, what's our next move?"

On the passenger side, Paul Fields slanted a questioning glance at Dennis in the backseat. "You're the brains, Godbey. What next?"

Dennis gazed out his window. "We're back at square one."

"Eliminating her isn't going to be as easy as you guys thought, though." George glanced sideways at Fields. "Mac Phearson is a problem. What did you dig up on him?"

"Mostly just bad news." Fields shuffled through some papers on his lap. "Several brushes with the law as a kid, all misdemeanors. Lied about his age and joined the Marines at fifteen. Rated an Expert Marksman when he finished boot camp in San Diego. Came home from Vietnam with honors, would you believe? Just what we needed, a real live hero. Single. Got out of the service, became a security guard. Lost his only brother at twenty-five. Took to some serious drinking." He glanced up. "This isn't documented, but I went by the firm where he first started doing P.I. work and a lady there told me that Keith Christiani hauled him out of the gutter, dried him out and helped him get his life back together. Later, he footed the bill for some classes in law, vouched for his good character and got him on at his firm as an investigator. He opened his own agency eight years ago."

"I wonder if he can be bought off?" Dennis mused.

"Have you gotten a load of the Christiani woman? Come on." Fields chuckled. "And he's in to his eyebrows, even without that. Probably feels beholden to the old man. Heroes can't be bought. They're too damned dumb."

"Hey, it'd be worth a try," Geroge argued. "Money talks. With a healthy bribe, he could buy a dozen pretty broads if that's one of his weak spots. And we wouldn't have to kill his little friend. The kid would be the only casualty, and that's not on our conscience."

"Does he have any experience with explosives?" Dennis asked.

"None in his military profile. Why?"

Dennis just grinned.

THREE HOURS LATER, Mallory had her arm elbow deep in a Cheerios box, feeling for small, foreign objects in the cereal. Mac was sweeping up the last of the flour. When he finished, he dusted off his hands and emptied the dustpan into the trash. "I can't think of one place we haven't looked. I even went through his other car out in the garage. It's just not here."

She set the box on the counter with a thump and, from

sheer habit more than anything, grabbed a cloth to wipe the counter. *No key.* She had to face it, think of somewhere else to look. A vision of Em's face crept into her mind, and she blocked out the picture, knowing it would only make her frantic. She had to be calm, make every second count. "I was so sure we'd find it."

Her voice rang with such discouragement that Mac turned to look at her—really look. Her hair hung in tangled, unruly waves around her small face. Her previously flawless ivory skin was now marred with scratches and bruises. Her smart blue suit, fresh that morning, was dirty. Bits of bark were snagged in the fabric. There were circles under her eyes, she was pale, and she looked exhausted. Alarmed, he went back upstairs to the front bathroom where he had seen a bottle of disinfectant and a package of cotton balls. Mallory was poking around inside a refrigerator container of applesauce when he returned. *That* was getting desperate.

"Time for first aid," he said in a deliberately light tone.

She frowned. "I can clean myself up. I *am* qualified to do that much, at least."

"You can't see all of the cuts that well. Come on, sit down. Afterward, we'll go check the clothes and belongings Keith has with him at the hospital."

As she sat by the table, he strode toward her, holding the disinfectant bottle up so she could see it. "Does this stuff sting?"

"No, I keep it on hand for Em."

Her mouth trembled slightly at the mention of her daughter, but she quickly suppressed it, controlling the emotion that was undermining her. He put the bottle and cotton on the table and leaned over her to examine the deep gouge on her collarbone.

"Tip your head back."

She obliged and met his gaze with those beautiful brown eyes of hers. A completely irrational response swept through him. *Careful.* He couldn't understand the feelings erupting within him—this almost compulsive urge to gather her into his arms. When this was over, the last guy on earth she'd want to spend time with would be him. And the feeling ought to be mutual. As he separated the edges of the wound, he tried not to notice how silken her skin felt. What *was* his problem, anyway? *Randy, remember Randy.*

"Ouch!" She pulled away and threw him an accusing glance.

Mac realized he hadn't been paying enough attention to what he had been doing. He apologized and uncapped the bottle of disinfectant and saturated a cotton ball. Leaning over her again, he dabbed gently at the cut. She kept her head tipped back to afford him a clear view, her face only inches from his, the sweet steaminess of her breath feathering on his cheek. His guts tightened.

"Undo the blazer so we can see what else we've got."

She started to do as he asked, then hesitated. Mac met her gaze head-on. He had to get those cuts cleaned. No telling what chemicals might have been on those shrubs and the bark dust. Weed killers, insecticides. He hated to think about it. She could medicate most of the abrasions herself, but he'd seen a couple of deep-looking cuts that she couldn't get at unless she was a contortionist.

She unbuttoned the second button and her jacket fell open. He hunkered next to her and peeled back her ruined blouse. Keeping his gaze on the lacerations, he tried to ignore the fact that her small breasts were right at eye level. What was he, a Class A creep? She was numb with exhaustion and worry. What she needed was tenderness and caring from a friend. Only a heartless heel would let his eyes stray. Especially when she probably felt desperate to stay on his good side. Her daughter's life hung in the balance. And if he allowed her to see how she was affecting him, she'd not only feel uneasy around him but also trapped, afraid to reject him because she needed him. The woman had enough problems.

Mac had to accept the fact that, like it or not, he was a Class A creep. Whenever she wasn't watching him, his eyes were drawn to the embroidered pink rosebud on her bra. Right above it was her cleavage and a wealth of creamy skin. The cups of the bra were a tease of filmy white over nipples the same delicate pink as the rosebud. How had he gotten himself into a situation like this? His hands began to shake. He tried to think about Randy—a sure cure for what ailed him—but Randy had been dead fourteen years and Mallory Christiani was here, just inches away.

To even think about making love to her was contemptible. Subconsciously was he seeking some sort of sick revenge? Randy had been used, then thrown aside. Did he want to use Mallory? Was that why he felt this sharp yearning to hold her? It was a possibility he couldn't ignore. He kept telling himself he just felt sorry for her, that his protective side was rearing its head, but that didn't hold water. The ache low in his belly wasn't in any way chivalrous.

He shoved the bottle of disinfectant into her hand and stood so fast he felt dizzy. He had done some things he wasn't too proud of in his lifetime, but using emotional blackmail on a vulnerable woman wasn't going to be added to the list. "You can get the others by yourself. I think I'll clean up a bit before we go to the hospital."

Mallory straightened in the chair, clearly startled by his abrupt withdrawal. Mac ignored her and strode away, loosening his tie with a vicious jerk, tempted to strangle himself with it.

MALLORY WASN'T SURE what it was that she had done to make Mac angry with her, but there was no question that he was. Ever since… She tried to remember and decided it had begun in the kitchen when he was cleaning her cuts. Ever since then, he had been as cold as a blast of arctic air, scarcely speaking, keeping his distance, his expression unreadable. During the drive to the hospital, he had ignored her presence in the car.

Now that they were inside the hospital and approaching the ICU, the temperature still hadn't reached thawing level. Mallory walked along beside him, aware of every brush of his sleeve against hers, every sharp rap of his heels. She grew more than a little irritated. The long strides he was taking forced her to a near run just to keep pace. In an attempt to dress as much in character as possible, so as not to upset Keith, she was wearing high heels and a brown suit. The narrow skirt and heels didn't lend themselves well to a foot race. She didn't mind someone becoming angry with her, but it would be nice to be told why. Fat chance of that when Mac would hardly talk to her—as if either of them needed added tension. Just being back at the hospital was enough. For all they knew, there could be a man with a gun lurking behind one of the closed doors…or stalking them.

When they reached ICU, Mac requested admittance

over the intercom and was promptly denied it. Mallory would have to go in alone.

"Try to question him," he instructed her before she went in. "I'm sure he can't speak yet, but if he can even manage a blink upon command, you could set up a yes or no signal."

The moment Mallory stepped inside, the attending nurse cautioned her not to upset Keith. The doctor had been keeping him sedated because he seemed agitated. Mallory hated herself for what she was about to do. She had no choice, though. Em's life was at stake. If Keith was able to communicate in any way, she had to question him. Her only comfort was knowing that Keith would have had it no other way. Em was everything to him.

Keith's eyes widened when he saw her and promptly filled with stark fear. This time, she knew why the sight of her upset him so badly. She took his cold hand in hers and told him, in as steady a voice as she could, that he mustn't worry. "Mac told me everything, Dad. He's been wonderful. He's taking care of it."

Keith's eyes drifted closed. He was clearly exhausted. Mallory's stomach twisted with guilt. "Dad, can you blink your eyes for me?" His eyelids fluttered crazily. "No, I mean just once."

Again his eyelids fluttered. Not one blink, but a dozen.

Mallory gave his hand a squeeze and tried not to reveal how disappointed she was. She glanced at the monitor. Did she dare press him? "Dad, can you move any of your fingers?"

Keith's body strained as he tried to comply. Mallory forced a smile. What movements he could manage were uncontrolled. In a few days, he might improve, but she didn't have a few days. Again she checked the monitor.

His heartbeat was accelerated. She was upsetting him... endangering him. And for what reason? Unless she could think of a way to communicate with him, there was little use in continuing. Because of her medical training, she knew how easily he could have a second, possibly more severe stroke.

There was no point in telling him Em had been kidnapped, not if he couldn't communicate. Better that he believe Mac had somehow taken care of everything. Not so hard to believe if you knew Mac. "I, um, can't stay, Dad. I wish I could, but something has come up. I'll try to come back tomorrow when I have more time." She prayed he didn't wonder why she wasn't haunting the hospital, that he didn't realize something had happened. Bending to kiss his cheek, she whispered, "I love you so much. You remember that, okay?"

A tremor ran the length of his body. Mallory left his bed and walked to his locker. Her hands shook as she lifted the latch. Hopefully he wouldn't become alarmed when she began searching his clothes. She ran her hands into all his pockets first, praying with each thrust of her fingertips that she would find the key, fighting back disappointment when she didn't. She felt the lining of his jacket. Again nothing.

Panic rose in her throat. It was a quarter after five. In the morning, Lucetti would call. She turned and looked at Keith, holding herself rigid to stop herself from pouring her heart out to him. Her eyes burned with unshed tears as she shut the locker door and leaned her back against it. He looked as though he was sleeping. She hoped he was. Hurrying by his bed, she gained the door and shoved out into the hall, one palm pressed to her waist.

Mac stood with his shoulder propped against the opposite wall. He straightened and took a step forward when she came out. Their eyes met, and his mouth tightened. "Nothing?"

She shook her head and blinked frantically, dashing a hand across her cheek. "I'm going to have to get his wallet from the hospital safe. I figure you might need his ID later when you go to the bank to try to get into his deposit box."

"Good thinking." He took hold of her elbow and guided her gently along the hall. His strides were shorter now to accommodate hers. She knew he must feel her trembling. He let go of her elbow and encircled her shoulders with an arm, pulling her snugly to his side. "Hey…it was a long shot, right?"

"Yes, but what are we going to do now?"

"Keep looking. We'll ask for more time." He hit the elevator control. "Don't panic. Lucetti wants that package. He has nothing to gain by being unreasonable."

The walk through the hospital and the ordeal of retrieving Keith's wallet passed in a blur. Once inside the car, Mallory handed the wallet to Mac. He quickly removed the pieces of identification from it that he thought he might need and transferred them to his own billfold. Then he leaned his head back and closed his eyes, his hands braced against the steering wheel. She knew he was trying to think of someplace else they might search. At least he could still think. Mallory's mind felt like congealed gelatin. She closed her eyes, too. How could she feel tired? Or think of sleeping? There wasn't time to rest, to eat, to do anything.

"She loves Pop-Tarts," Mallory blurted out. "On Saturday mornings we cuddle under her Pooh bag and watch cartoons. Sometimes, Keith even joins us."

A lump rose in Mac's throat. "Maybe she'll be home by Saturday."

He heard Mallory make a strange noise, but when he glanced over at her, she looked composed, her head back, eyes still closed. "You like Pop-Tarts? There's room for three under the Pooh bag. It's kind of fun, actually. Some of the cartoons aren't bad."

"Now that sounds like a date I wouldn't want to miss. Not often I get to cuddle with two beautiful women under a Pooh bag. What *is* a Pooh bag, by the way?"

"A Winnie the Pooh sleeping bag. You've seen them."

Mac hadn't. He had no nieces or nephews, so he wasn't familiar with things like Pooh bags. "I like Pop-Tarts."

He heard the strange little noise again and tensed, not sure what to say. If only she didn't fight showing her emotions. He wanted to throttle her mother. He sighed and reached to start the car. He no sooner turned the key in the ignition than she sat bolt upright, eyes wide with excitement.

"His shoes! I didn't check his shoes."

At this point, Mac's mental clock was ticking like a time bomb. He was willing to look anywhere. If they didn't find the key soon, Lucetti might make good on his threat and kill Em. When Mallory leaped from the car, he wasn't far behind her. She broke into a run, crossing the parking lot at dangerous speed for a woman wearing heels. He loped along in her wake.

Just as she reached the automatic doors, a deafening explosion rocked the parking lot. The ensuing blast of air knocked Mallory off her feet and she staggered against the building. Mac whirled. Orange flame shot into the air above his Volvo. The doors hung at crazy angles. The glass was all blown out. *A bomb.* Reaction set in immediately. His legs felt as limp as hot rubber and his stomach heaved. If they had remained in the car a few seconds longer, they would both be dead. Someone had wired the doors or starter with a timer.

No one had been injured, but the fire was bound to set off a chain reaction of explosions in nearby cars, and their luck wouldn't hold forever. Spinning on his heel, he grabbed Mallory's hand and together they dashed into the lobby. "Call the police and the fire department!" he roared at the woman behind the information desk. "There's been an explosion. Hurry! Other cars are gonna blow!"

CHAPTER NINE

Mac's hand was gripping hers firmly as he dashed through the lobby, hauling her in his wake. Veering down an intersecting hall, they raced by doorways so swiftly that everything seemed a blur. Up ahead, Mallory saw a sign with arrows pointing to the Emergency Room. Mac turned the opposite way, toward an exit.

"Where are we going?" she asked as they paused outside.

"Anyplace. If the guys who put that bomb in my car aren't still around, the cops soon will be." As if on cue, sirens wailed in the distance. "The minute they find out that's my Volvo, they're going to want to question me."

Before Mallory could catch her breath, he struck off again at a dead run, this time dodging through the emergency parking area to an adjoining business lot. He didn't stop until he spied a public phone booth that was not easily visible from the street. Throwing the door open, he stuffed Mallory inside and wedged his way in behind her. The space was so confined that his elbow poked her as he dug in his pocket for change. Through the thick glass, she could barely hear the sirens.

He dropped a coin into the slot and grabbed the phone book to find a cab company number. He was breathing as hard as she was. He had to gulp and swallow before he could speak to the dispatcher and arrange for a taxi.

After hanging up, he shoved his hand back into his pocket and then fed a second quarter into the slot. "Keep an eye out for me," he ordered as he dialed another number. "I'm going to try that friend of mine again."

As she checked the area around them, tremors shook her legs. This wasn't a bad dream she was having. She wasn't going to wake up and make it all go away by telling Keith about it over breakfast. It felt as if a balloon were being inflated to bursting point inside her chest. *Panic.* Even though she recognized it for what it was, she still had difficulty staving it off. *My baby. Terrible men who blow up cars have my baby.* The words echoed in her mind, a funereal litany. Men like that wouldn't hesitate to kill a child.

Steady. Don't think. Not about Em, not about anything. She scanned the parking area again, craning her neck to see around a stand of shrubs that blocked her view. A woman with a toddler on her hip came out of an insurance office. A man pulled his car up near the phone booth and studied a street map.

Mac listened intently as the call he'd made went through. No one seemed to be answering. Then he gave her a thumbs-up signal and started talking. "Hey, Shelb, you're finally home. Can we talk?" He shot one quick look at the parking lot, then glanced at Mallory to make certain she was still standing guard for them. She heard the sound of male laughter coming over the wire.

"Shelby, this is no social call. I'm sorry I didn't call before this, but I was afraid our lines were tapped and every time I've tried to reach you from a phone booth I couldn't get you." Mac listened a moment. "Shelb, I don't—you took it off the hook?—no, I don't—" He held up a hand. "Shelb, really—this is *serious*—would you quit clowning?" He cocked his head, listening again, and began to look mollified. "First off, how long's it been since you saw Corrine?" He sighed. "Yeah—no, me neither. Okay, forget that idea, I guess. I need you to do a little street work for me. Find out what you can on a guy named Steven Miles. An accountant, connected somehow to Pete Lucetti."

Mallory heard snatches of the other man's voice coming over the line, the most pronounced word being *Lucetti*. Mac nodded his head every few seconds. When at last he got another opportunity to speak, he explained their predicament, leaving nothing out. The intermittent voice on the other end of the line grew louder.

"Yeah, yeah, I know that, Shelby. But sometimes trouble comes knocking, you know? While you're at it, dig up anything you can on a newer model cream-colored sedan. A Buick, Washington plates. If I remember right, the first letters were LUD. I had it written down, but my car just got blown up. We want to know who the guys are that use it. There are three of them, businessmen types, wear suits. Slick operators."

Shelby's voice had risen to such a level now that even Mallory could make out what he was saying. "You *did* say Mallory Christiani? Maiden name Steele? You done lost your mind?"

"No, not yet, and I don't intend to if I can keep from getting my brains blown out. You be sure to watch your back, okay?" Mac's scowl deepened even more as he listened to his friend's reply. "No lectures, Shelb, just check around for me. Did you write that info down? I'll call you late tonight to see what you've got, okay?"

He snapped his fingers with sudden inspiration. "Say, you might try Teddy down at the gun shop. Have him call around to his competitors. At least one of them packs a modified Uzi with a clip. And today one of them took some shots at us with a seven mag—my guess is a Winchester—mounted with a scope. They have to visit an indoor practice range on a regular basis unless they go outside the city. There can't be many guys packing that kind of weaponry and driving around in a cream-colored Buick. Tell Teddy I need anything he can dig up on them."

More yelling ensued from Shelby's end, but Mallory couldn't be certain of what he was saying because Mac was running interference with a number of *uh-huhs* and *yeahs*.

"She's standing right here listening," Mac cautioned. When his friend didn't take the hint, he said, "Shelby, you're yelling loud enough to be heard in Tallahassee! Do you mind?"

After a moment's dead silence, Shelby resumed yelling. "That's because I'm upset. I *yell* when I'm upset. You're my best friend. What am I s'posed to do, keep my mouth shut? Let little Miss High 'n' Mighty take care of her own problems. She's got plenty of bucks. She can *buy* her way out of trouble."

Mac tipped his head back and stared at the ceiling of the booth. "Shelby, I'm counting on you to come through for me. I'd go myself, but I've got Mallory with me and it would be too risky to take her down there after everything that's happened."

"Lucetti? You're talkin' *way* out of my league. And even if you weren't, why would I risk my neck for the likes of her?"

"Yeah, but when a kid's involved, it's a different ball game, right? I knew you'd see it my way."

"That's blackmail, Mac. Don't go puttin' no guilt trips on me about no kid, man."

Mac grinned. "Big brown eyes and freckles. She's got a stuffed dog named Ragsdale."

"That's dirty pool. That's not even *playin'* fair."

"It's times like this, Shelb, that I know the true meaning of friendship."

"Yeah! It's a real pain in the neck."

A loud clunk came over the receiver. As Mac hung up, he met Mallory's startled gaze and said, "Shelby... he's really a nice guy. You just have to get to know him."

Mallory couldn't help feeling alarmed. How did Shelby know her maiden name? And why did he seem to harbor such dislike for her? "Mac, what was that all about?"

"Nothing." He flashed her a smile. "Nothing I want to get into, anyway. Don't worry. He squawks a lot, but he comes through. I trust him with my life."

The question was, could she and Em?

They left the booth and stood behind a bushy evergreen so no one would see them while they waited for the cab. The wailing of sirens grew increasingly loud. They could smell rubber burning. The Volvo's tires? The thought made her sick. A police car careened around the corner and sped past. Seconds later, two fire trucks went barreling by. Mac drew her closer to the tree. She noticed he kept looking over his shoulder to scan the parking lot. A cold feeling crept up her neck. Even now, they weren't safe. She began to sneak glances over her shoulder, too. Black smoke roiled above the hospital parking area.

The minutes crawled by. Her feet began to hurt, and the prickly fir needles made her back and legs itch. Her thoughts drifted to Mac's conversation with his friend Shelby. Did Shelby know her? Was Mac hiding something from her? Should she question him about what she had overheard? Glancing up at him, she decided to keep her mouth shut. Mac was her only hope of saving Em. Antagonizing him would be stupid. If there *was* something he was holding back from her, he'd tell her when he was ready.

At last, the cab came. As Mac opened the back door for her and she slid onto the seat, she tried to read his expression.

Mac climbed in after Mallory and slammed the door. He leaned forward to give her address to the cabbie. As he sat back, he felt her watching him. He was going to scalp Shelby for mouthing off. She had enough to worry about. For an instant, he considered telling her the truth, that he was Randy's half brother, but the words caught in his throat. The old hurts ran too deep for him to glibly tell her about them and pretend they were water under the bridge. They weren't. Never could be.

"What's goin' on there at the hospital?" the cabbie asked.

"I'm not sure," Mac said. "We heard an explosion of some kind. I wasn't about to get close enough to see what it was."

"Smart thinking. One thing's good. If anyone got hurt, they chose a great place." With a loud guffaw at his own joke, the driver merged the cab with traffic. "Lots of doctors handy," he elaborated when neither of them laughed. When that still didn't get a chuckle, the man settled down to drive in silence. Mallory simply didn't have a laugh in her. All she could think of was Em.

They were halfway home before Mac realized that he was holding Mallory's hand. He didn't know if he had initiated the contact or she had. It didn't really matter.

Some things just felt right, and her hand in his was one of them. He didn't want to analyze that right now or think about the implications. Shelby's question rang in his head. *You done lost your mind?* Mac was afraid maybe he had.

MAC WAS SILENT all during the drive home. Mallory knew there must be risks involved in returning to her house. At first she wondered if that was why Mac was so quiet. But by the time they stepped into the entry and closed the door behind them, she was convinced that he was just still angry at her. There was an empty look in his eyes, a grim set to his lips. He backed her into a corner and pressed a staying hand to her shoulder.

"Stay put," he ordered, his tone brooking no argument.

She stood there in the cool semidarkness and watched him creep up to the doorways along the hall one by one, gun in hand. Each time he exploded into a room she flinched and held her breath until he emerged unhurt. When he finished the first floor and went upstairs to check the bedrooms, she really began to sweat. She hated feeling so helpless. As much as she detested guns, right now she wished she knew how to use one, just so she could help.

If there was one thing she couldn't stomach, it was feeling useless. If she came out of this alive, she was going to learn to shoot a handgun and take lessons in the martial arts. The next time something like this happened— heaven forbid that it should—she'd be better equipped to handle it. Better equipped to protect Em.

When Mac came back downstairs, she led the way into the kitchen and located an unopened container of Folger's in the cupboard over the stove. She lifted her chin and swallowed down a wave of self-disgust. Her daughter was being held for ransom and her big contribution to finding her was to make coffee? After opening the can, she stepped to the sink to fill the reservoir of the coffeemaker. Menial though the chore was, she knew caffeine would do them both good. They couldn't keep going on sheer willpower. She imagined Mac was as exhausted as she. He was sitting at the table, long legs stretched in front of him, arms folded across his broad chest. She filled the filter cup with grounds, inserted it into the coffeemaker and turned around. Something was on his mind; she sensed it.

"I know you too well. Something's wrong. What is it?"

It seemed a silly thing to say. *I know you too well.* She scarcely knew him at all by normal standards. Yet somehow, inexplicably, she felt that she knew him better than she had ever known anyone. She knew all the important things, at any rate. That he was kind, that he had more courage than anyone she had ever known, that he cared about little girls he had never met, that he noticed things like freckles on noses and remembered a stuffed dog's name was Ragsdale.

He sighed and said, "I'm just wondering, at this point, if you don't want to cry uncle and go to the police for protection. The guys after us are getting into some pretty serious stuff."

Fear mushroomed inside her. Had he already decided they couldn't save Em? "Are you saying you want to give up?"

"No, I'm just giving you the option. You could be killed, you know."

"Better me than Em!"

He smiled. "Just checking. Some people would be re-evaluating things at this point. Be wondering if it was worth the risk."

Mallory couldn't imagine doing that. She loved her daughter so much that no risk was too great. No matter how nasty this situation grew, Mallory would keep fighting.

"You know that friend I was talking to—Shelby?" Mac asked.

"Yes, what about him?"

"I'm going to take you over to spend the night at his place."

"Why would I want to go there? If I leave the house, who will be here to take Lucetti's call?"

"I don't want to leave you here alone. They know where you live and there are places I have to go before morning. I don't need any extra baggage slowing me down."

Extra baggage? That wasn't very complimentary. Mallory caught her lip between her teeth and bit down hard. As much as she hated to admit it, she knew she *was* a burden to him. Had been from the start. He knew it, she knew it. She had no business letting her ego get in the way. Em's safety was the only consideration.

"Would you stop that before you make a sore?" His gaze was fastened on her mouth. "You're constantly gnawing that lip."

She immediately stopped. "It's better than grinding my teeth like you do. My lip will mend. Molar enamel won't."

He tightened his jaws and ground his teeth. When he realized he was doing exactly what she had just accused him of, he rolled his eyes and tried to stop. Perverse though it was, she was pleased when she saw his jaw begin to ripple again.

"I guess it's not a good time for either of us to swear off a bad habit," he admitted. "It just worries me, that's all, the way you go after that lip. It's going to be hamburger by the time this is over."

Her mouth was the least of her worries, Mallory thought. The gurgle of the coffeemaker was the only sound in the room for several seconds. At last he ended the silence with another heavy sigh and glanced at his watch. "I've been doing some thinking, Mallory. We only have a few hours left. The key would have been found if it was in Keith's shoe, and whoever undressed him would have put it with the other valuables. I'm fresh out of ideas where else to look for the key. There's not much point in my sitting here doing nothing when I could be working the streets. We may not be able to deliver that package to Lucetti, after all. And if we can't, there's only one other way to rescue Em."

"What's that?"

"I have to find her. To do that, I have to find Lucetti."

"But you said he'd give us more time. You said you couldn't find him, that no one could, that—"

"I *know* what I said. But what if he won't give us more time? It wouldn't be a smart move on his part to refuse, but neither was kidnapping Em before he knew we had the things he wanted. Getting information on him won't be easy. But if I hit the streets and grease enough palms, I should be able to get some leads. Between Shelby and me, we should come up with something. I have a few—" he paused and cleared his throat again "—a few *friends,* old connections. One of them, a gal named Corrine, could probably give me something on Lucetti if I can find her."

"But—" she lifted her hands "—why can't I help?"

"It's not your kind of neighborhood. Look…I've done it a hundred times. I don't need you along."

"Maybe I need to go. Did you think of that? It's my

daughter we're talking about. I can't just sit someplace—in some stranger's house—doing nothing." It was on the tip of her tongue to add that she didn't feel welcome at Shelby's, but she swallowed the words back; how she felt about *that* wasn't important. She'd do it in a minute if she thought it would help Em. "How would you feel? I'd go crazy. I want to help, Mac. Even if I can't do much, I'll feel better trying."

"No!" An angry glitter crept into his gaze. "Mallory Christiani combing the streets? It'd be like parking a Rolls-Royce in a junkyard and expecting no one to notice. And don't forget, someone's trying to kill you. You shouldn't be going anyplace where you stand out."

"I've got slacks and stuff to wear."

"Slacks? You think that'll make you—" He broke off. "I'll be questioning prostitutes. You just don't have the look."

"Meaning?" Mallory glanced down at herself. "I don't have the right equipment or what?"

Mac certainly hadn't meant to infer that she was sexless. Far from it. If she stood on Aurora Avenue to advertise her wares, she'd draw passing cars like a tollbooth on an expressway. Twice today, she had nearly been killed. To knowingly put her at risk again would be insane.

He clenched his teeth. He was having trouble dealing with this fierce feeling of protectiveness she brought out in him. Talk about acting like a jerk; he deserved an award. How could he have been so cruel? Was it necessary to hurt her? *Yes.*

Ordinarily taking her into downtown Seattle wouldn't have been a concern. It was rough, but not *that* rough. But with killers after them? That was a different story. He understood her need to be actively involved in trying to save her daughter. He knew how miserable she would be sitting at Shelby's. But miserable or not, at least she wouldn't get hurt there.

"You aren't going," he said in a reasonable tone.

"How do you know we won't be followed to Shelby's? The minute you leave, I could find myself facing three men with guns. Mac, please, I won't get in the way. I could stay in the car."

"Won't be any car. Yours is still at the hospital, remember? And mine no longer exists. I'll be taking a cab, then walking."

"But that would leave you stranded. We can take Keith's BMW. The one in the garage."

He studied her pale face with a sinking feeling in his guts. She was right about a lot of things. He didn't want to be stuck downtown without a car. And someone might follow them to Shelby's. It was so obvious a possibility that it scared him to think he had overlooked it. Was he so exhausted that his brain was no longer functioning? If he left her, he might return to find her dead. At least he could watch out for her if she was with him. Or make arrangements for someone else to. It would make his job much more difficult, worrying about her every second while he was dealing for information, but the more he thought about it the better it seemed than the possible alternatives.

"Oh, all right. But no slacks. Don't you have some jeans?"

"Um…some designer types. Would those do?"

Mac hated to think what Mallory's idea of designer jeans were. "Go get them on. And go heavy on the makeup. You don't want to stand out any more than you have to."

He rose from the chair and stepped over to the bar.

"Who are you phoning? I thought the lines might be bugged?"

"If I take you along, I won't be able to stay with you every second. I'm calling in some recruits. I'll watch what I say."

AN HOUR AND A HALF LATER, Mallory stepped across the threshold into Mac's downtown Seattle apartment, where they had stopped so he could change into what he called street clothes. As he shoved the door open for her it pushed aside the heap of mail that his landlord had been sticking through his mail slot this past week. She sidestepped the scattered envelopes and cast a curious glance around. The mail-littered entranceway stretched into an equally untidy living room. She remembered all the junk in his Volvo and realized neatness was not one of Mac's strong suits. Neither was interior decorating. She had never seen such a hodgepodge. Nothing matched, not even the two end tables.

He scooped a pair of running shoes off the floor, grabbed some sweatpants and several newspapers off the brown recliner, then smiled. "Excuse the mess." He dumped everything on the sofa, looking a little embarrassed. "Have a seat."

Mallory eased herself into the recliner and watched him disappear through a doorway. Drawers thunked. She could hear him stripping off his clothes. His change jangled as he tossed his slacks—probably onto the bed or a chair. Her gaze trailed around the living room. Lived in, but not really dirty. The furniture didn't reside under layers of dust, so he apparently cleaned, or had it done, on a regular basis.

Restless, she rose from the chair and wandered around

the room. Along one wall, he had a bookcase. Law books, a dated preparation course for a general equivalency diploma, several blockbuster novels—the lusty variety—a book that promised perfect spelling with an investment of ten minutes a day, a dog-eared Bible, and books on investigation. A pile of gun manuals rested on the bottom shelf with three large and very expensive volumes on the works of great painters. She trailed her fingertips down the spine of the GED preparation book. *You spew big words like a walking dictionary.* The accusation came back to haunt her. Had Mac been deprived of a high-school education?

She wandered over to the component stereo system and portable television, which were housed in an entertainment center along the opposite wall. As she scanned the albums and tapes to see what kind of music he enjoyed—mostly outdated rock and roll—her attention was snagged by a flash of metal. Midway up on a right-hand shelf, a photo of a lovely, gray-haired woman smiled down at Mallory from a gold filigree frame. Moving closer, Mallory wondered if this was a likeness of Mac's mother. Looking into the woman's clear gray eyes, she guessed it must be and found herself envying Mac for having been raised by someone so plump and huggable looking. A real "mom" type who probably still wore an apron when she made pies, the kind who would probably say "I love you" at least once daily. Mallory's gaze shifted to another photo, a candid shot of a much younger Mac standing with his arm around a slightly built boy with platinum-blond hair and blue eyes.

Randy.

Mallory's heart felt as though it stopped beating. Randy Watts? Her late husband's best friend in college? She stared at the picture, at the two youthful faces, one startlingly similar to the other when you saw them so close together. Mac's face, even in his early years, had been rugged and masculine, but his mouth and chin resembled Randy's. Their noses had even been alike before Mac's had been broken so many times. *Brothers.* The truth hit her hard, right between the eyes.

She remembered now that Randy had told Darren he had an older half brother, an ex-Marine. Whirling away from the irrefutable evidence, Mallory clamped a hand over her mouth. All the snide remarks Mac had made to her since yesterday came back to taunt her. No wonder. She had once been Bettina Rawlins's best friend. Bettina had killed Randy Watts as surely as if she had held a gun to his head and pulled the trigger. Mallory and Darren had seen it coming, but they had been helpless to stop it.

Oh, no, please... She turned to look at the picture once more. It was terrible of her, but as much as she regretted what had happened to Randy, her foremost feeling now was desperation. She needed Mac. So did Em. If he abandoned them, what would she do? What should she say to him when he returned from the bedroom? *I didn't know you were Randy's brother. My, it's big of you, helping me like this.*

She dragged her hand from her mouth and pressed it to her waist. Mac had known who she was from the first. Looking back, she felt sure of that. For some reason, he had chosen not to talk about Randy. Maybe it was cowardly, but she wouldn't risk alienating him by forcing the issue. Not *now*.

She could hear him rummaging in his bedroom. At any moment, he would come out. She couldn't be standing here looking like she had just seen a ghost. He would guess why. She looked around for something constructive to do so he wouldn't think she'd been snooping. She stepped into the kitchen and found where he kept his empty paper bags. Returning to the living room with one, she began gathering his mail, stuffing it into the sack.

When Mac reappeared, she was just finishing. Face flaming, she turned to look at him. "I, um, thought I'd pick it up for you, take it along. Maybe you can go through it later."

He had undergone a transformation in the other room. Gone were the respectable jacket and slacks, replaced by tight, faded blue jeans and a red sport shirt that revealed a sexy V of tanned, muscular chest. At his throat was a heavy, gold chain. The outfit was capped off with a black leather jacket, the collar tipped up around his neck. Showing below the frayed cuffs were thick leather wristbands, peppered with brass brads. Even she had seen enough television to know the wristbands were to protect the forearms in a knife fight. They were wicked looking, so uncharacteristic of the Mac she knew that they made her shiver.

His blond hair was tousled, curling across his forehead in lazy waves, slicked back on the sides. He looked like someone she wouldn't want to meet in a dark alley, hard and ruthless. For an instant, she almost felt like laughing. But the way he stood, one lean hip slung outward, shoulders hunched, doused her amusement. That tough-guy air wasn't something he'd acquired by practicing in front of a mirror. For an instant, an icy tendril of alarm coiled in the pit of her belly. Which was ridiculous. This was the man who had held her in his arms last night.

She folded down the top of the sack with tense fingers, acutely aware of Randy's picture smiling down at her only a few feet away. Mac's attention dropped to her hands. She prayed he wouldn't see how they were trembling. "Ready?" he asked softly.

"I—" She licked her lips. "Sure. I'm ready if you are."

He studied her for a long moment. Then he glanced over his shoulder at the entertainment center. When he looked back at her, there was a question in his eyes. She averted her face and prayed he wouldn't choose to confront her now. She had no idea what to say. *I'm sorry?* That seemed pitifully inadequate. *I had nothing to do with it?* That wasn't entirely true. Both she and Darren had known how Bettina operated, that to her Randy was nothing but a passing fancy. A poor kid, someone she never would have dared take home. The Rawlinses had planned for their daughter to marry a local senator's son. Randy wouldn't have even been in the running. Darren had tried to warn him, but Randy had believed Bettina's coquettish lies, that she loved him and would one day defy her father to marry him. No, Mallory couldn't honestly claim she was blameless. She could have done something more. What, she wasn't sure, but there must have been something. Wringing Bettina's neck, for starters.

Mac didn't glance toward Randy's picture again, but she still had the feeling he knew why she was suddenly so nervous.

"Before we leave, let's go through a few ground rules," he told her in a low voice. "Number one, in case there's trouble, I want you to promise you'll do exactly what I tell you."

She nodded in agreement.

"Number two, don't call attention to me by looking surprised or asking questions. We'll be hitting the waterfront area, Aurora Avenue and the intersecting streets. If that's a dead end, maybe the airport. As I'm sure you know, those areas draw lowlifes this time of night. To get information, I have to be part chameleon."

Again she nodded.

He ran a hand over his eyes. His weary sigh was the only indication he gave of how unutterably tired he was. "When we get near there, we'll have to leave the car a few blocks away and strike out on foot. That expensive BMW would be a red flag to anyone who saw it. And since it's registered in Keith's name, I don't dare leave you sitting in it for fear those three guys might recognize it." He settled his cloudy-gray eyes on her. "There'll be times when I'll have to leave you. Some of my contacts are reluctant enough about talking to me when I'm alone. I'll be leaving you with those friends I called earlier. They'll meet us downtown." He hesitated and gave her a long study. "They aren't exactly the kind of kids you're accustomed to. They may even seem a little intimidating to you. But I trust them. Because you're a friend of mine, you can, too. When you're with them, you listen to Danno, the oldest boy, just like you do to me. If something should go wrong, Danno knows his way around."

Mallory forgot all about Randy's picture. "A boy?"

"He's nineteen. A very old nineteen when it comes to that neighborhood."

"Mac, I'm thirty-four years old. Born and raised in the Seattle area. I *am* capable of taking care of myself. I have been in rough areas before, you know."

"Oh, I'm sure you have. But have you ever gone down there looking for trouble? There's a big difference." His eyes searched hers. "Put your pride in the backseat a second. Somebody's trying to kill you. We've already decided that it's somebody connected to Lucetti. We're going down into the roughest part of town to ask questions. About Lucetti. About Miles. And about the three guys who have been after us. At the best of times, hanging around in those places isn't the wisest way to spend an evening. Tonight, it could be downright deadly if the wrong people see us or get wind of why we're there."

Put like that, Mallory was beginning to see his point.

"Shelby's apartment is still an option for you if you'd rather not go. If you are going, though, then Danno gives the orders and you stick to him like he's covered with superglue."

Mallory could see that Mac meant it. And he had her over a barrel. The realization rankled.

Stepping closer to her, he touched her hair, his expression softening. "I know it's hard on you, being kept out of the thick of things when you want to be helping. But you have to remember there's a very important third party involved in this. If something happens to you, she's sunk. Danno knows how to blend in down there, who he can trust, who's trouble and who isn't. This way if anyone comes looking for us, I won't have to worry about your being seen."

Mallory suspected that he would be protective of her no matter what, that he was using Em as a smoke screen, but regardless, he had a point. She couldn't afford to risk herself until Em was safe. "All right, Mac," she at last conceded. "You win. Danno's the boss."

He lowered his hand and hooked his thumb in his hip pocket. "I just don't want anything to happen to you."

"If something happens to me, it'll be my own fault for having insisted on going, not yours." A flutter of panic blocked her throat. This conversation was dangerous. It could flow so easily into a discussion of blame about Randy's death and they didn't have time for that. She tucked the bag of mail under her arm and turned toward the door. "Besides, it's not my welfare I'm worried about. Finding Em and getting her home safely is the important thing… the only important thing."

CHAPTER TEN

MALLORY HAD NEVER ventured into this part of Seattle after dark. Respectable people avoided the area once dusk fell. Even driving through here with the car doors unlocked could be risky. The sidewalks weren't as crowded as she had expected, but because the people seemed intimidating to her, she felt as though she was walking through a solid wall of humanity, bums, drug pushers, runaways, streetwalkers. There was no light in their faces, no hope. Life was a struggle to survive and if you got in their way, they would walk over you.

When Mac stepped into a grimy tavern to buy a pack of cigarettes, his hissed order "stick tight" was one she hastened to obey. Some of the men standing under the flashing neon sign outside of the establishment were staring at her as though she was an all-you-can-eat special. She didn't know if it was her appearance that appealed— she found that hard to believe—or if she looked as though she might have money.

"Hey, Bro," Mac said to the barkeep. "I'm lookin' for Corrine. She been around?"

"I ain't seen nothin'," the man snarled, his brown eyes gleaming with hostility as they fastened onto Mallory.

Mac tossed his quarter of change into the air, palmed it and slapped it on the bar. "Tell her I'm lookin' for her."

"I'll tell her if I see her, Mac." The bartender, who

seemed to know Mac well, took the quarter and tossed it into a jar of coins, muttering something under his breath that cast serious doubts upon both Mac's generosity and his legitimacy.

"Guilty on both counts," Mac called over his shoulder.

The bartender guffawed and rubbed his sizable paunch. Walking past the occupied bar stools, Mallory noticed that the men and women patronizing the establishment looked at her as if she was a cockroach in the center of a banquet table. Were these the kind of people that Emily was being held by? People who whiled away their lives staring at rows of bottles?

Mallory doubled her hands into fists and dug her nails into her palms, picturing her daughter's guileless brown eyes.

"I didn't think you smoked," she said to Mac as they emerged from the bar. *I can't think about Em. I have to keep my perspective, stay calm.* Tears burned in her eyes, and she blinked rapidly to keep them from falling.

"Chameleon, remember? I don't inhale." He dipped his head toward his cupped palms to light the cigarette. As he straightened, a purple-haired youth dressed in skin-tight black leather veered in Mallory's direction. Mallory's face flamed when he directed an insolent look at her breasts. Mac draped one arm over her shoulders, his face settling in harsh lines. Snuffing the match with his fingers, he met the kid's gaze. It was an unspoken challenge. The younger man turned sharply away.

Glancing down at her, Mac said, "I'll say this for him, he's got good taste."

Mallory tried to smile and failed. The vision of Em's face still floated in the back of her mind. "Do you think she's down here? With men like these?"

Mac placed his hand on her hair and threaded his fingers to her scalp, his touch warm and soothing as he traced circles above her ear. "I don't know, Mallory. We just have to pray that whoever has her is a decent person. There *are* some down here, you know. A lot of them."

"I've never told her about the really ugly things that can happen to little girls. The closest I ever came was warning her not to talk to strangers. I didn't prepare her for anything like this."

"She'll be okay, Mallory. Think positive, hmm?" His eyes met hers and, imagination or no, it seemed to her that some of his strength flowed into her. He placed the cigarette in his mouth to free his other hand, then smoothed the wetness from her eyelashes. His eyes narrowed against the trailing smoke, and the lines that bracketed his mouth deepened as his lips tightened on the filter. Dropping his arm back to her shoulders, he drew her close. Glancing around them, he said, "Not getting fresh, just don't want anyone deciding you look lonesome."

When they first began to walk, her hip bumped against his thigh, but they quickly fell into a rhythm. She slipped an arm around his waist. "Not getting fresh," she said. "Just don't want to *look* lonesome."

He chuckled.

A drunk staggered toward them. Mac swerved to avoid a collision, but not in time. The man bumped her shoulder and would have sent her reeling if not for Mac's steadying arm. She swallowed, her throat parchment dry. She looped her shaky fingers under Mac's wide belt and moved even closer to him. Being an unattached female down here was clearly not wise. Mac struck off down the sidewalk again. His hand curled warmly around her upper arm, his fingers making light circles on her sleeve. That absentminded caress was the only sign he gave that he was even aware of her. When she looked up at him, she noticed that his face had assumed the harsh and unreadable expression she had seen before, the cigarette dangling from the corner of his mouth as if it were a permanent fixture.

A young girl sidled up to them. She jutted out a hip, her denim-clad leg brushing Mac's as she flashed him a smile. "Hey, honey, ditch Goldilocks and I'll show you a good time."

Mac's arm tightened around Mallory as he sidestepped the girl and continued walking.

Shock coursed through Mallory. "She's not that much older than Emily. Thirteen, fourteen, maybe?"

"They grow up fast down here. And as much as you might want to, as hard as you might try, you can't rescue all of them."

From his tone, Mallory knew he had learned that lesson the hard way. The longer she knew this man, the more she liked him. *Liked?* She pressed closer to the lean hardness of his body. No, what she felt for Mac had already gone far beyond mere liking. The feeling had sort of snuck up on her. She wasn't quite ready to pin a name on it. Her practical side, which was and always had been dominant, told her she hadn't known him long enough to feel anything for him. Was it gratitude? Desperation? Those were possibilities she couldn't ignore. Mac was her one and only hope when it came to saving Emily. Mallory sighed. What did it matter? The feeling was there, nonetheless, waiting to be faced, a one-way street to heartache. Even if Mac could forgive the fact that she had been Bettina's friend, he was never likely to forget it. Randy *had* been his brother, after all.

His gaze shifted back and forth, taking in every person, checking every dark doorway. "The boys should be down this way someplace. As soon as we meet them, I need to find Corrine."

"Who is she?"

"An old school chum. She's worked the streets for over twenty years. Started at about the same age as the girl back there. Has her own stable now. I hope she still runs a string down here. From what I've heard, the big money is made out by the airport."

"A stable?" The question no sooner left her lips than she knew what he meant. Em was so much in her thoughts that Mallory's brain seemed to be functioning at half capacity.

Mac took a drag on the cigarette and squinted as smoke drifted from the corner of his mouth uninhaled and got into his eyes. "Corrine's got more connections than the governor. If anyone knows who works for Lucetti, it's her. The problem will be finding her. She doesn't work herself anymore, just manages her girls. And she doesn't go for rough stuff. If someone wants to quit or move on to greener pastures, she doesn't get nasty. Lucetti, unfortunately, doesn't deal that way. She hates his guts, which is why I figure we can count on her for information."

Mallory bit her lip. They were going to comb the streets looking for a woman who supported herself managing prostitutes? For a moment, she felt appalled. Then she shoved the feeling aside. She didn't care who Corrine was or what she did for a living, not if she could help them find Emily.

"Hey, Coach!" someone yelled.

Mac stopped walking and pivoted on his heel. His change of direction was so sudden that Mallory lost her hold on his belt and fell out of step, dislodging his arm from around her. Four teenage boys converged on them. Mallory, who was following closely on Mac's heels, took one glance at the youths and faltered. They looked as rough as dirt roads after a torrential winter rain. Mac greeted them with a ritualistic bumping of elbows and clapping of palms. Then, as if he missed the weight of her hand at his waist, he turned to look for her.

Feeling intimidated, just as he had predicted she might, Mallory was hesitant to join them. Mac held out a hand to her. When she walked over to him, he put his arm around her. She groped for a hold on his belt, acutely aware that she was being looked over by four pairs of impenetrable eyes, two sets of blue, one of green and one as black as obsidian.

The boy with the black eyes appeared to be the oldest, a tall young man of Indian or Spanish descent with shoulder-length ebony hair. He regarded her with an almost contemptuous curiosity, his youthful and extremely handsome face cast in light, and then in shadow by the bar's neon sign that flashed on and off above him. A thin scar angled across his right cheek. From a knife fight, possibly? A length of chain dangled from the hip pocket of his tattered blue jeans, and the handle of what she guessed was a switchblade protruded from his waistband. Unlike Mac's, his wristbands were adorned with sharp little spikes.

With a snort of anger, Mac plucked the boy's knife from his waistband and hefted it in his hand. "What's this, Danno? You know what will happen if you guys are caught packing blades. You don't run the streets anymore."

"You said it might be dangerous. We came prepared."

Mac held out his hand. "No way. Hand them over." He snapped his fingers at the other boys.

"Coach!" Danno cried. "Do you know how much those switchblades cost me? We walked ten blocks one way to get them."

"Next time, you won't buy them, then, will you? When I said it might get dangerous, I didn't mean it as a call to arms. I just thought I should level with you. Besides, the danger will most likely be to me. You can't violate your probation. You know better. Come on."

With sullen glowers, all four boys handed over their knives. Mac tossed them into a nearby trash receptacle. When he returned, he inclined his head toward her.

"Danno, I'd like you to meet Mallory Christiani."

Danno shifted his unreadable black eyes to her. After a tension-laden moment, he extended his hand. Just as hesitantly, she placed uncertain fingers across his palm. His grasp was loose and noncommittal but warm. She tried to smile with stiff lips, then forced herself to meet his gaze. With a shock, she realized he was afraid, afraid of being rejected. The realization made her heart catch. He was too young to be so bitter and suspicious. Mallory's smile relaxed and spread across her mouth. "I'm pleased to meet you, Danno."

The obsidian glassiness left his eyes, revealing a vulnerability that disarmed her. His mouth tipped into a crooked grin. Glancing at Mac he said, "Hey, Coach, she's *choice*."

The next boy, Mark, was a scruffy redhead with freckles, which made him seem a tad less ominous. Mallory shook hands with him and suffered through being referred to as *sweet,* another term she knew was popular with teenagers. Then she was introduced to Eric and

Toby, blue-eyed with shaggy brown hair, on the shy side of fifteen. Toby pumped her arm up and down with so much enthusiasm that her shoulder felt as if it might become dislocated.

"Mark and Danno are college boys this year," Mac informed her. The pride in his voice made the boys stand taller.

Danno smiled and arched his bushy black eyebrows. "So what's up, Coach?"

"I've got to do a little street work tonight. When I have to leave Mallory, I need you guys to watch over her."

Danno threw Mallory a curious look. "She in trouble?"

Mac quickly briefed him. "I want you out from under the lights, staying low. Think you can handle it? I don't want her getting hurt, and you're the only friends I can completely trust to watch out for her. I won't color it. These creeps on our tails mean business. My Volvo got blown to smithereens this afternoon. We've been shot at. Just being in the same vicinity with us could be bad for the health."

"If there's anything we're good at, it's gotta be blending in." Danno grinned and slid his dark gaze toward Mallory again. She was beginning to suspect he had practiced that crooked smile for hours, perfecting the lazy, careless twist of his lips so it had just the right effect. The way he stood somehow reminded her of Mac, his hands shoved into his pockets, his shoulders slouched, one hip angled outward. "I'm real sorry about your little girl. All of us are."

Not trusting herself to speak, Mallory merely nodded. She fell into step beside Mac as he struck off down the sidewalk, the four boys flanking them. She noticed that oncoming pedestrians, rather than walk through their number, preferred to spill into the street and brave the traffic, which was considerable. The first time it happened, she wondered why. Then she remembered who she was walking with. If she had met these four boys on a sidewalk, she would have taken her chances in the street, too. And now that she came to think of it, Mac didn't exactly look like the kid next door.

Within the safe circle of his arm, Mallory absorbed the sights and sounds around her. Though it was night, the city seemed bright and glaring to her. She found herself searching every face and wondering if that person knew where Em was. Pain swelled within her. A few hours, that was all they had left. Every step they took measured off a second, the seconds accumulated into minutes, minutes into hours, taking them closer and closer to the deadline.

"Try not to think about it," Mac whispered.

Taken off guard, Mallory threw her head up and stared at him, wondering how he had known. "It's hard not to."

"Think about the welcome-home party we'll throw for her. I have a friend who's a clown."

"Seriously?"

"Yeah, me!" Toby interrupted.

Mac smiled. "What's her favorite cake?"

"Chocolate." Leaning her shoulder against his side, Mallory took a deep breath. Visions of Em at home drifted through her mind, and the frantic feeling inside her slowly subsided. She was lucky to have Mac on her side, she thought. So lucky.

As they walked, the boys relaxed enough in her presence to talk among themselves, including Mac in their teasing banter. Mallory deduced from their conversation that they were on Mac's baseball team, which he had begun coaching several years ago, volunteering his time to an organization for underprivileged, delinquent boys who were thought to be still redeemable. Now she understood why Mac had been so hesitant to discuss the area of Seattle he had grown up in. She also discovered why Mac's end tables didn't match. He was paying for Danno's and Mark's tuition at the University of Washington. Little wonder he drove an old clunker Volvo.

Danno's major was going to be law. Mallory had trouble picturing him in a suit, sitting behind a desk like Keith's. Mark proudly announced he planned to be an accountant. Just when Mallory was beginning to be impressed, Mac winked at her and said Mark already had a job lined up keeping books for the local fence. Mark roared with laughter, then skipped back, doing the elbow bumping thing with Danno.

Watching them, Mallory could see why Mac would fork out thousands of dollars for their education. They were just kids like any others, no matter how they came across when you first met them. Had Mac been a Mark or Danno once? She suspected he had. Glancing at the surrounding throngs of humanity, she could even see why all five of them worked so hard at looking mean. Down here, the weak weren't going to inherit much of anything. A kick in the teeth, maybe.

That thought brought Mallory full circle, back to worrying about Emily. On the upper floors of some of the taller buildings, there were low-rent apartments, their grimy windows mirrored by the lights below. Was Em up there someplace? Was she gazing down, even now, hungry and afraid? Could she see them? Mallory's steps faltered but Mac hauled her relentlessly forward.

They walked several blocks, until they reached a cluster of even taller buildings with graffiti on the exteriors. As they wove in and out of the throngs of people, Mac became watchful, his eyes scanning the women who advertised their wares curbside to passing men in swank cars. Every half block or so, he left Mallory in a shadowed doorway with the boys while he approached one of the girls, slipping her money as he asked her questions. Each time, he came back looking discouraged.

They finally came upon a young woman who whispered something when Mac slipped her some money. Mac thanked her and returned to them. "Pay dirt," he said, satisfaction gleaming in his eyes. "Hey, Danno, do you know of a new—" Breaking off, Mac threw a glance at Mallory. "A new *house* around here?"

"Over two blocks. Why?"

"Corrine's set up there."

Danno's grin vanished. "The redhead?"

Mac nodded. "Lead the way. We'll follow."

Danno clearly found this to be an unacceptable turn of events, but he finally shrugged and struck off down the sidewalk. A few minutes later, he pulled up and glared at Mac over his shoulder. "This is it."

Once more, Mac left Mallory standing on the sidewalk with four grim-faced boys. He went inside a large, rundown house. A quarter of an hour later, he emerged from the building, reclaimed Mallory and lifted an eyebrow at a glaring Danno. "I have to go back downtown and find a fellow called Chapin."

Danno planted his hands on his hips and jutted out his chin. "What's up, Coach? You flipped or what? First we come here. Now we're going to find Chapin? He's a pim—"

"I *know* what he is," Mac cut in. "We don't need it spelled out."

Danno stood there, head cocked to one side, questions

shining in his eyes. "You're always preaching to us about avoiding trouble and now you—"

"Danno, trust me," Mac said, reaching out to grip his shoulder reassuringly. "I wouldn't talk to him if I didn't have to."

By the time they had walked clear back downtown, exhaustion was beginning to take its toll. Mallory had had little sleep for days, and it was starting to show.

Mac approached a young woman dressed all in red. Money changed hands and with a slight nod, she indicated a man up the block.

"Thanks." Whirling, Mac walked back to them, giving Danno a thumbs-up. "If something goes wrong, Danno, take her straight to Shelby." Mac's eyes locked with Mallory's. "You remember our deal? Stick to Danno. He'll take care of you."

Mallory grabbed his jacket sleeve. "What do you mean, if something goes wrong?"

He tried to pry her fingers loose and flashed her an unconvincing grin.

Panic flooded her. Until this moment, she hadn't realized just how dangerous this might become for him. It wasn't his fight. "No! Mac, wait. If it's that dangerous, let me go."

Mac cradled her face between his hands. "Mallory, I didn't mean to scare you. I've done this a hundred times."

"But never to get information about someone like Lucetti. This is just as much out of your league as it is for Shelby, isn't it?" It seemed to her that his hands pressed harder against her cheeks. "Answer me! You could be killed, couldn't you? For asking questions about him? I—I don't want you hurt. Em's *my* daughter. It should be my risk. Keith wouldn't expect you to do this." His face started to swim, and she realized she was looking at him through tears. She struggled to keep her voice firm. "Let *me* do it. All you'd have to do is point him out and I'd—"

He was looking down at her as if he had never really seen her before. "You really mean that, don't you?"

"Well, of cour—"

Her words were smothered midstream by his fingers on her lips. His eyes seemed to look down into hers and see forever. Then he released her. Stepping back, he pried her hand from his sleeve. "If I get hurt, it'll be my own fault for having insisted on going," he said softly, echoing what she had said earlier when he had been afraid to bring her along. "Besides, I intend to come back. I have an important date to keep, remember? Watching cartoons and eating Pop-Tarts with two beautiful ladies. Now do like you promised me, Mallory, and stay with Danno."

With that, he slipped away through the crowd, leaving her with the boys. She watched his bobbing blond head. About a quarter block north of them, he approached a man wearing black slacks and a vest over a leopard-patterned silk shirt. Mallory glanced at her companions. They were all four staring at her.

Danno motioned for her to follow him back to the darkened doorway. She fell in beside him. "If something happens to him, I—" She gulped and made a helpless gesture with her hands.

"Nothin'll happen. The coach is too slippery." He drew her deeper into the shadows. "You watch. He'll be back before you know it."

Eric and Toby stood guard, one on each side of the doorway. Mark joined Danno and Mallory in the darkness and reached inside his jacket for a pack of cigarettes.

He lit up and took a quick succession of drags, keeping an eye out for Mac.

"The coach will snatch you baldheaded if he catches you," Danno warned him. "You're on your honor to quit."

"I'm tryin'," Mark snarled. "Give me a break." When the cigarette was about half gone, his gaze fastened on something beyond the crowd. He quickly tossed the cigarette. "Whoa, Danno, look sharp. We got trouble."

Danno stepped from the shadows to see. Mallory followed. Standing on tiptoe, she saw Mac grab the man in the leopard-patterned shirt by the front of his vest, lift him off his feet and slam him against the cement wall of the building.

Danno stiffened. "Uh-oh, he's got company comin'."

Mallory's stomach dropped. The people who had gathered around Mac fell back to let a flamboyantly dressed man get through. She saw metal shimmer. Mac threw the man in leopard print onto the sidewalk and whirled, leaping back just in time to avoid a flashing arc as the newcomer swung a knife at him.

"Whoa…" Danno started forward, then turned to look at Mallory. Their eyes met in silent communication. She nodded encouragingly. Grabbing Eric by the sleeve, Danno shoved the younger boy toward her. "Eric, Toby, you guys make like her shadow. The coach needs help."

Eric did a nervous little jig on the sidewalk, jumping to see what was happening. Toby, who was even shorter, grabbed his friend's shoulders and bounced around behind him, his chin lifted. "Oh, man. They got blades! I *knew* we were gonna need ours. The coach is such a priss sometimes."

Mallory craned her neck. Danno and Mark were running at breakneck speed, turning sideways and shoving

their way through the throngs, their long hair flying behind them. Mac was now surrounded by three men, the
man in leopard print and two others. Jumping into the air,
Mac delivered a kick to one man's chest. As he landed,
he did a backswing and caught another guy with a stun-
ning blow to the side of his head. The third man slashed
with his knife and connected with Mac's side. Mallory
clamped a hand over her mouth. Before she realized it,
she was running along the sidewalk, Eric and Toby right
beside her.

She saw Danno break through the crowd that had gathered to watch the fight. He leaped into the fray, whipping
his chain from his jeans as he landed beside Mac. The
chain seemed to come alive in Danno's hand, snaking
through the air to pluck the knife from one man's fingers.
The weapon no sooner clattered onto the cement than
Danno spun and whacked another man in the temple. Mac
took advantage of the confusion and let fly with another
kick to one fellow's chest. After delivering that blow, he
followed up with a fist to the man's unguarded midriff.
Mark hurtled through the crowd at that point, evening up
the odds. The confrontation was over in short order. The
two men who had attacked Mac from behind disappeared
among the spectators, leaving the man in the leopard-skin
patterned shirt alone.

Mac grabbed the man's vest again and shoved him
against the building, planting his fist in his midsection.
The man grunted under the force of the blow and expelled
his air in a gush. "Now start talkin', mister," Mac hissed.
Drawing his gun from under his jacket, he pressed its nose
against the man's ribs.

Danno and Mark flanked Mac and stood guard to
make sure no one interfered. Danno wrapped his length

of chain around his arm, prepared to use it as a weapon again if anyone stepped forward. Mallory elbowed her way through the crowd, then stopped, caught up in the breathless tension. A chill slithered over her skin as she glanced at the faces around her. There was a thick eagerness in the air, so thick she could have scooped it with a spoon. They *wanted* Mac to kill the man, were hoping he would. Especially the prostitutes. From the hatred gleaming in their eyes, Mallory suspected they would like to rip Chapin apart. She couldn't blame them. Looking at him, Mallory felt the same primal thirst for revenge. Chapin might not have been directly involved in Emily's abduction, but he was still an associate of Lucetti's. That gave her cause enough to hate him.

Chapin started to shake. "Miles is dead, Bro. That's all I know."

"How did Lucetti figure into it?"

The man rolled his eyes toward the gun. His larynx bobbed and he cried, "He'll have me killed if I say. Give me a break, man, please."

"Talk!" Mac gave him a threatening shove with the gun.

"Lucetti had three of his goons waste him. Miles was gonna double-cross him. That's all I know. I swear it."

"How was Miles gonna cross him?"

"I—Lucetti killed somebody, some professional fellow. Miles found out about the killing! I don't know all the details. All I know is Lucetti got wind that Miles had gone sour on him."

"And how did Miles fit into the organization?"

"I—I think he kept the books. Yeah, that was it. He kept the books. The head accountant."

"Where can I find Lucetti?"

"I don't know."

"You'd better tell me, friend, or I'll blow a hole in you the size of a baseball diamond."

"I—I don't know. I'd tell you if I knew. I would. I never see Lucetti, just the guy under him. I swear it."

"And who is that?"

"Andrews, Jake Andrews. You can find him at Longacres on the weekends. He likes to bet on the horses. Otherwise, I don't know. That's where I always meet him."

"Okay. What about the three men who wasted Miles? What were their names?"

"I—I don't know. One was a guy named Fields, I think. They work together—on the financial end—collecting I think. I'm not sure, man. I'm not lyin'. I'm just not sure."

Apparently satisfied, Mac released his grip on the man's vest. The boys backed off and continued to check out the crowd. Mac ran his hand down over his eyes, blinked, then gave his head a shake as if to clear it. He spotted Mallory then and moved toward her, Danno and Mark closing in behind him. The moment he reached her, Mac seized her arm.

"We have to get out of here," he growled, pulling her forward into a run.

Mallory knew that Mac was afraid the other two men had gone for help. As they sprinted up the sidewalk, the boys fell in around them. The pounding of their feet on the cement seemed deafening as they took the corner and headed east.

"Mac, are you cut?" she asked breathlessly.

"Just my jacket. *Miles.* I knew I recognized that name!"

"What d'you mean?" she panted.

"Dead, he's dead. I read about it in the paper right before I left town. They found his body in an alley. Beaten to death."

Jerking her half off her feet, Mac took a sudden left turn down a dark alley. When Mallory saw the looming swath of blackness ahead, she nearly balked. If the streets were dangerous, a dark alley like this was suicidal. Then she remembered who she was running with and decided they were probably at home in dark alleys.

They spilled out at the other end of the alley onto a street that intersected with the block they had just fled. Cutting through traffic, ignoring the many screeching brakes, they picked up the alley again on the other side. Mallory lost all sense of direction. Mac was circling, backtracking to throw pursuers off their trail. It seemed to her they ran for hours. She reached the point of exhaustion and passed beyond it into blessed numbness. She couldn't feel her legs, couldn't tell if her sides were still aching. But she was keeping up.

When Mac drew up beside the white BMW, she fell across the front fender and labored for air. It was some comfort that Danno looked like a blob of jelly beside her, his mouth gaping as he fought to breathe. Mark leaned against the building and slid down it to sit on the sidewalk. Holding his belly with one arm, he groaned and started coughing.

"That's what cigarettes do for you," Mac said with a growl as he unlocked the passenger door of the car. "Come on, pile in. I want to get out of here."

Mallory skirted the open door on quivery legs, so weak she felt as though she might collapse before she made it onto the seat. Danno boosted her in by placing a hand on her back. He slid in beside her and sank low, throwing his head back and gulping for air. The other three boys climbed in back. After Mac got in, he gave everyone a quick once-over, then cranked the engine. "Everybody in one piece?"

"Yeah," Danno assured him. "Fine, Coach."

"Good, that means I can wring all your necks. I thought I told you to stick with Mallory?" He swerved the car out onto the street. "What did you think you were doing, Danno? You could've been killed. Or what if the cops had come? Assault with a deadly weapon? I asked you not to carry chains anymore."

"Sorry, Coach. We'll trash them, I promise." He took several deep breaths and swallowed. "Tomorrow. We'll do it tomorrow. Right, Mark? I'm sorry."

"Sorry? Sorry wouldn't comfort your mother much if you ended up hurt! That wasn't a game out there. Those guys were trying to kill me. And what about Mallory? How would you have felt if you'd gone back and found her with her throat slit?"

Eric leaned forward to peer over the seat. "Coach, Danno didn't leave the broad alone. I stayed with her."

Mac reached back and smacked Eric's forehead with the heel of his hand. It was more an affectionate thump than a reprimand. "Apologize, idiot. You don't call women broads."

"Why not? I've heard you—"

"Er-rr-ic! Just apologize, please."

"Sorry."

Mallory closed her eyes. "Apology accepted." Glancing at Mac, she said, "And it was my fault Danno left me. I could have stopped him."

"I'll wring *your* neck, too, then. If I get into a spot, I don't want the *diaper* brigade coming to help." Glaring into the rearview mirror, he said, "I'm trying to get you guys straightened out, not killed. A serious offense for any of you and it's going on your permanent records. End of career. Is that what you want, Mark?"

"I'm nineteen," Danno protested. "That's not exactly the diaper brigade. You were fighting in Vietnam when you were younger than me."

"Just old enough to go to trial as an adult, that's what you are. No more juvenile hall and a slap on the wrist for you, Danno. You do realize that an attorney can't be a convicted felon? You keep your nose clean, understand?"

"I have! I've been so straight, my back aches!" Danno jackknifed forward so he could see around Mallory. "You were in trouble. What was I supposed to do? Let them cut you to pieces? You wouldn't have deserted me, law or no law."

Mac took a right turn and pulled the car up next to a curb. Mallory peered out the window at a two-story Victorian row house that had been converted into apartments. Many of the windows were patched with cardboard. Trash was strewn across the porch and small yard. Dim lights shone through tattered curtains.

"Danno, I'm counting on you to keep these yahoos off the streets tonight. Got it? Those guys might recognize you."

"Consider it done," Danno replied sullenly.

"Coach…" Mark's voice sounded strangely off-key. "Coach, I think maybe I'm bleeding."

Even in the dim light, Mallory saw the color wash from Mac's face. He twisted in the seat. "You're what?"

Mallory had seen Mac scared a number of times, but never had she seen such stark terror in his expression. He loved these boys as much as he would his own. She could feel his body going taut. Struggling for room to turn around and battling a suddenly writhing ball of frightened boys, Mallory at last managed to get on her knees so she could look over the seat. "Open your door, Danno," she said crisply as she reached for Mark's uplifted arm. "I can't see anything in the dark. Mac, give me some room."

The cool authority in Mallory's voice brought Mac's head around. The dome light flickered on. A little amazed, Mac did as she said and scooted aside, watching as she gently slipped Mark's jacket off his shoulder and freed his arm from the sleeve. "Don't look so scared, Mark," she said with a grin. "If it was serious, you would be pumped dry by now." She turned his arm to examine a long slash that ran from his elbow toward his wrist. Placing a thumb on each side, she pulled at the edges of the wound. "It'll hurt like the devil, but it's not going to need stitches. Hardly more than a scratch. You were lucky."

Mac realized he was shaking. The calm in Mallory's voice soothed him like a balm. Passing a hand over his eyes, he let out a breath of pent-up air. Some of Mark's color was returning. The boy grinned. "Yeah, I figured it was nothing."

Danno laughed. "Which explains why he's green. Admit it, Mark, you thought you'd got it bad."

"Well…" Mark's voice rang with anger. "I couldn't feel anything. When it doesn't hurt, it's usually real deep."

Mallory gave his shoulder a pat. "I think you were just too scared to feel it. Have you had a recent tetanus shot? Good." Turning toward Danno, she said, "I want you to disinfect it—"

"Not with merthiolate, either," Mark cut in.

"—and wrap it with clean gauze," Mallory went on. "By morning, it won't need a bandage."

"It's not *that* teeny a cut," Mark cried. "Whatcha think you are, a doctor or something?"

"A nurse. Used to be, at any rate. Not a very good one, I admit, but I do know enough to recognize a life-threatening wound." Mallory gave him a reassuring smile. "Trust me, Mark. It's superficial. Your jacket got the worst of it."

Mac's attention snagged on what she had said. She was a nurse, but not a very good one? There was an underlying bitterness in her voice. From where he sat, watching her in action, he would have said she was top-notch. Even before she had known how serious the injury was, she had reacted with calmness and decisiveness. Which was better than he had done. She was a natural, able to instill trust in others, take control.

"I'll take care of him," Danno teased. "Once I finish with it, he'll *think* it's life threatening."

The boys piled out and slammed the car doors, plunging the interior back into shadow. Mac lowered his window and reached out to collar Mark as he walked past. Drawing him toward the car, he ruffled the boy's hair. "Thanks, my friend." After giving him a light punch on the chin, he plucked the cigarettes out of Mark's shirt pocket. "I'll be in touch."

"Coach, don't you know how much those are a pack now?"

"Yeah, too expensive for a college kid. So quit, huh? And the next time I see you, that chain better not be in your pants. Clear? I'm serious, Mark. No weapons, period, no matter what. I have too big an investment in you."

"Yeah, yeah."

Mac leaned his head out the window. "Hey, Danno! Come here a minute."

Mallory sat down and leaned across the seat to roll down the window so the boy wouldn't have to open the door. Danno braced his hands on the top of the car and bent at the waist to bring his face on a level with theirs. "Yo?"

"I owe you one," Mac told him huskily. "If you hadn't come along when you did, I wouldn't be here. If I came across as ungrateful, I didn't mean to. You saved my bacon. Thanks."

"What goes around, comes around. It's called a pay-back, Coach. I'm sorry I left your lady. It just seemed like the thing to do at the moment, you know?" Even in the dark, Danno's teeth gleamed as his mouth slanted into the lazy grin. Extending his hand to Mallory, he said, "I hope I see more of you."

"I'd like that." Mallory was faintly surprised to realize that she actually meant it. She gave Danno's hand a friendly squeeze, then dug in her purse for her business-card case. "Hold on a sec." She found a pen and scribbled notes on the backs of two cards, signing off with her initials. Handing them to Danno, she said, "There's one for you and one for Mark. Go to that address and tell them I sent you. You can both get on-the-job training there with fairly good pay. After school, summers. When you get your degrees, get in touch with me through Mac. I know a couple of influential people who may be interested in promising young graduates."

"No lie? Hey, that'd be radical. Why would you want to do that?" He tipped one card toward the streetlight so he could read the print. "Attorneys at Law? Hey, it's right downtown. Me and Mark can walk there. You sure they'll hire us?"

"Guarantee it." Mallory snapped her purse closed. "As

for why? It's called a payback, Danno. Thank you for all your help tonight."

With a chuckle, Danno threw his chain on the seat beside her. "She *is* choice, Coach. Don't let her get away."

Mac bumped the horn as he pulled out into traffic. Craning her neck, Mallory watched the boys until the car rounded a corner and she could no longer see them. Turning back to Mac, she sighed. "Quite a baseball team you've got there."

"They're especially good with bats."

She wished she could manage a smile, but it simply wasn't in her. Leaning her head back, she closed her eyes. "Now what?"

"Now we can relax until Lucetti calls in the morning. I have enough information on him to hang his—" he cleared his throat "—to hang him. Because of that he'll have to give us the extra time we need. At least if he doesn't want the wrong people to hear he wasted Miles and that other guy. Which I'm sure he doesn't. Knowing his penchant for keeping his trail swept clean, he wouldn't like the heat it would generate. Even if the cops couldn't find him, they'd sure make a massive effort to." Her shoulder was touching his. He glanced down at her. "Hey, you okay? You're skaking."

Mallory tried to smile. She wasn't at all okay. Mac's line of reasoning seemed sound, but that was all it was, a line of reasoning. He didn't have an insight into the future. He couldn't predict Lucetti's next move with any certainty. She knew he meant to comfort her, but a new kind of terror had her in its grasp. If Chapin was the kind of man who had Emily, was her daughter still alive?

CHAPTER ELEVEN

BEFORE THEY WENT home, Mac stopped at a pay phone to call Shelby. Thus far, his friend had learned nothing about the identities of the three men chasing them. Teddy, the gunsmith, had come up with zilch. If the men did business anywhere on a steady basis, it was outside Seattle. Shelby's luck had been no better. A friend of his had run a tracer on the car, and the only real lead he got on a cream-colored Buick with similar tags turned out to be a vehicle that had been reported stolen. The three would-be killers were clearly professionals, far too clever to do their misdeeds in a car that could be traced to them. And Shelby had gotten no information on Miles out on the streets. He did agree to keep trying with the information they'd just gotten.

Mallory's house seemed eerily silent when they went inside. And the overturned and dismantled furniture left by the searchers was a grim reminder of the danger they and Emily were in. Mallory tossed Mac's sack of mail on the table in the breakfast nook and, driven by hunger she could no longer ignore, stepped to the refrigerator. She needed her strength.

She withdrew a container of yogurt. "Want something?" Mallory asked.

"Two of those for me," Mac replied, pointing to Mallory's yogurt.

They ate standing, backs to the counter, their gazes locked on nothing, eyes glazed with exhaustion. Mallory was trying desperately to be optimistic. Mac had to be right. Lucetti *would* give them more time. She either had to believe in that or lose her mind.

When the containers of yogurt were scooped clean, they gravitated upstairs to reassemble Mallory's bed. It would accommodate two bodies. Both of them were too tired to wade through the shambles in another bedroom to fix a second bed, and Mac seemed inclined to sleep near her. She supposed he was uneasy because of the attempts on their lives that day. She could understand that and appreciate it. She needed to stay alive until Em was home safe. But it seemed an unnecessary precaution; every window and door had a safety latch. Then she remembered Lucetti's men had already gotten into the house, and how easily Mac had broken in. Maybe it was a sensible precaution.

Mac stripped off his jacket, holster, shirt and wristbands, discarding them in a pile on the rug. Then he toppled onto the bed on his back. Slanting an arm across his eyes, he yawned and groaned. Mallory stared at him, convinced the breadth of his shoulders took up more than half the space. Her gaze lowered to his bronzed chest and her throat tightened. She had never seen male flesh contoured into so many rock-hard bulges and ridges.

"I'm so tired, I'm dead," he murmured on the crest of a sigh.

He looked amazingly vital to Mallory. Suddenly she needed a little distance. "I'm going to wash off and put on my nightclothes. That is, if you don't mind. I have a flannel gown that's—"

"Honey, you can come back in nothing and I won't notice," he cut in gently. "Just do whatever you have to and come to bed so you can get some rest. There's nothing more we can do tonight."

Closeted in the bathroom, Mallory washed her face, applied night cream, brushed her teeth and wriggled out of her clothes. The clean flannel gown felt like heaven. She supposed she should sleep dressed since there was a man in her bed, but she was too sore. She had chosen her primmest gown. Stepping back into the bedroom, she felt suddenly shy and doused the light. As she moved toward the bed, a rumbling sound made her leap. She peered through the darkness. There it came again. Mac was snoring. The sound was comforting, made her feel less alone. She lay down, trying not to wiggle the mattress, and hugged her side to keep space between them.

Mac muttered something and rolled toward her, slinging a heavy arm across her waist. He pulled her close and nuzzled his face into her hair. Just when she was about to protest, he let loose with another rumbling snore that fluttered the hair at her nape. The stiffness left Mallory's body. If this was a sly pass, he was a master and his embrace was comforting.

She leaned back against the broad, cushioned wall of his chest. It had been so long since a man had held her that she had forgotten how good it felt. Surely it couldn't hurt…just for a while. He was asleep, after all. And— as she often told Em—everyone needed a hug now and again, even mommies. His arm was heavy, but not too heavy, the bone and sinew overlaid with a thick layer of muscle and smooth flesh. Wonderfully warm. Lying close to him made her feel confident that everything would indeed be okay. If needing that kind of reassurance was wrong, if it was weak of her, then it would be her secret.

In just a few minutes, she would pull away. He would never know. She closed her eyes, absorbing his heat, finding solace, however meager, for this little while. Her last thoughts were of Emily as she plummeted into a black void of exhaustion.

Sometime later—Mallory had no idea how long—she awoke with a start, her heart slamming as she clawed her way up from a nightmare. She had been standing on a city sidewalk, looking up at the grimy window of an apartment. Emily's face was on the other side of the glass. Creeping up behind her was a horrible man with a switchblade, his mouth twisted in an evil grin. Running frantically back and forth in front of the building, Mallory sought a door. Above her, she heard Emily screaming. There was no way inside the building, no way to reach her. She was going to be killed, and Mallory couldn't save her.... Drenched in sweat, Mallory had jerked awake, her hands clawing the mattress.

For several moments, the dream still held her in its clutches, so real she could hear Em crying, "Mommy, Mommy, save me, save me!" Not wishing to wake Mac, Mallory slipped out of the bed. The residual horror of the nightmare drove her into the hall. She went to Em's room and flipped on the light. After staring at the mess for several minutes, she began putting Em's clothes back into her drawers. When that was done, she dragged the mattress into place and remade the bed. One chore led to another, and before she knew it, she was putting the whole room back together, feverish in her need to have everything as it had been before.

She worked until she was limp with exhaustion. Then she found Ragsdale. The little dog had been gutted, his stuffing tossed all over the floor. A cry tore from her throat and she began to shake. She fled the room, hugging the destroyed toy to her breast. She walked aimlessly through the house, stumbling sometimes on out-of-place cushions and lamps. Tears flowed down her cheeks and soaked Ragsdale's floppy ears. When her sobs became so ragged that they sapped her remaining strength, she sank to her knees and leaned against the dining-room wall. She had no idea how long she cried, only that she at last cried herself empty. No more tears, no more anything. Just a great aching hole where her heart had once been.

That was how Mac found her. He had missed her in his sleep and jerked awake to go find her. In the moonlight, she looked like a little girl, huddled on the floor in a trailing nightgown, hair tousled into a silken cloud. Dropping to one knee beside her, he touched Ragsdale and felt the wet fur.

"Mallory, sweetheart, what're you doing down here?"

"Just thinking."

"Thinking? You've got to get some sleep."

"I did. I slept. They tore Ragsdale apart, Mac."

He glanced down at the dog's flattened torso. There was a peculiar, hollow sound to her voice. He knew that she was somehow equating the destroyed dog with her daughter, imagining Em destroyed, as well. Mac settled for touching her hair, but what he really wanted was to gather her into his arms and soothe away her pain. If only he could. "Can you think in bed where you won't get chilled?"

"I didn't want to wake you." She turned her face toward him, "That Chapin man—he was a horrible person, wasn't he? Em may be dead, Mac. I have to face that."

He sighed. She had seen an ugliness tonight she had never glimpsed before. He wished there was something he could say to ease her mind, but there was nothing. The bald truth was, she was right. Em might be dead. And if she wasn't yet, she might be soon.

Gathering her into his arms, Mac rose to his feet, amazed that she weighed so little. As he shifted her so he could maneuver the stairs, Ragsdale's wet ears flopped against his bare chest. He felt her drop the dog onto her lap. The next instant, she looped her slender arms around his neck and pressed her face into the hollow of his throat, clinging to him as though he were a lifeline. She smelled like night cream and flannel, a sweet, clean scent that was far more arousing to him than expensive perfume. Some knight in shining armor he was, he thought with disgust.

When he crested the landing, he turned left down the hall to her room. When he lowered her onto the bed, she still held on to him. Warning bells rang in his head. He stretched out beside her. She pressed close, flattening her small breasts against his ribs, fitting her pelvis to the slope of his denim-clad hip. Her hair fanned across his chest like warm silk. He felt her lips, velvety against the hollow of his shoulder, her breath a mist of sweetness. He could feel her trembling.

"Mac…" Her voice drifted to him no louder than a whisper. "Would you—" She pressed even closer, clinging, almost frantic. "Would you love me?"

Mac wasn't sure where his stomach went, but from the feel of things, it was somewhere under the bed. His arm stiffened around her. It seemed to him that her small body turned molten, impressing itself into his skin like a searing brand. Would he love her? As if it would be some gigantic favor? He wanted her with aching intensity.

"You'd be sorry later."

"I don't care about later. Make the hurting stop. Make me stop thinking. Hold me. Oh, please, Mac, hold me."

Her voice broke on the last word. Mac's every instinct told him to go for it. Only a heel would turn a lady down when she said please, right? Wrong. Only a heel would take her up on it. For a long while, he lay there, battling with his hormones. At last she relaxed and nuzzled her cheek into his shoulder. It ignited his every nerve ending. He rolled toward her so he could come up on one elbow above her. Placing a hand on the curve of her narrow waist, he lowered his head and feathered kisses across her forehead, ignoring the inviting curve of her tear-swollen mouth.

"You're not yourself right now, Mallory. You're frightened and exhausted and vulnerable. Ask me when Em's safe and sound, and I'll take you up on it, fast." As if she would. This was a once in a lifetime chance and, idiot that he was, he was passing it up.

She said nothing. He imagined that she was lying there feeling humiliated, and he wanted to kick himself. Truth was, he wasn't well practiced in turning down gorgeous women. First off, not many had asked. Secondly, he was no monk. Mallory, however, seemed different. Too sweet, too vulnerable, too precious to him. Her hip bone fit into his palm as if she had been molded especially for him. One of his knees had slipped between her thighs, stretching the flannel taut between their juncture so he could feel the white-hot softness of her. The fire in his loins intensified. Without realizing it, he trailed his mouth to her cheek, to the corner of her mouth. He felt his willpower slipping, imagined plunging into the honeyed slickness of her, imagined touching every satiny inch of her skin.

"Unless you're sure," he amended, hating himself for

being so completely conscienceless. "Do you promise not to hate me later?"

No answer.

"Mallory?"

He brushed his lips across hers. Her silken mouth was slack. His twisted into a reluctant grin. She had fallen into an exhausted sleep. He groaned and rolled off her, doing a face plant on the mattress. His body found no solace there. Nearly an hour later, he was still awake, his hands curled into loose fists. *Mac, would you love me?* The question replayed in his head a hundred—no, a thousand—times. When at last the ache of need released its hold on him, he was glad his answer had been no. Only desperation could have driven her to such a request. He had to find her child. It wasn't just a favor to Keith anymore, something he was involved in because he felt obligated. It was something more personal. *Mac, would you love me?* Heaven help him, yes. It went against everything he had believed in for fourteen years, but yes....

LUCETTI CALLED AT eight fifty-nine the next morning, which was a vast improvement on the waiting game they had endured the previous day. They had discussed strategy, so this time Mac answered the phone. Mac was afraid Lucetti might get nasty, and they thought Mac would be better able to withstand his threats. In an icy tone, he explained that Mallory had not yet been able to find the key.

"I told you twenty-four hours," Lucetti snarled.

Mac cocked his head. In the background, he could hear a church bell ringing out the hour. No horns, only an occasional hum of tires. Wherever Lucetti was, it was an extremely quiet neighborhood. "We did our best to come through. A key is hard to find. We've had some complications, namely some men trying to kill us at every turn. And they aren't in any way connected to me, I can guarantee that. Three men, wearing suits—"

"You're lying, Mac Phearson! I have my men shadowing you every minute of the day. If there had been an attempt on your lives, I would have been informed of it."

"Then it must be *your* men doing it. At least check out my story. Put a tail on them or something. We can't find a key while dodging bullets and car bombs."

"You're stalling. My men don't act without orders. That's how I operate and they know it."

"We need more time. Two extra days, at least."

"Forget it. Eight hours, Mac Phearson, then it's funeral time. You don't seem to understand. I'm holding the trump card, the kid."

Mac had hoped to avoid admitting that he and Mallory knew about Miles's murder, but Em's life was at stake and it was the only bargaining chip he had. "You hold *most* of the trump," he replied. "If you're a pinochle player, however, you know that's not enough. To shoot the moon, you need them all."

"Meaning?"

"I went slumming in downtown Seattle last night." Mac could only hope that by hinting around, he could imply that he knew a great deal more than he actually did. "Does the murder of Steven Miles jog any memories? And the death of a certain professional? If the wrong people get wind of that, things could become very uncomfortable for you."

The silence on the other end of the line stretched into infinity. "Leak it to the cops and the kid's dead."

Mac swallowed down an upsurge of anger. "I have no intention of leaking anything. We need more time. And to borrow your phrase, I'm playing my trump. Cooperation's the name of this game. Now do we get some leeway here, or not?"

"Another forty-eight hours. And that's it. If you don't come through by then, Mrs. Christiani will be the one who receives a package. A small one, to start. Would her daughter's little finger motivate her, do you think?"

Mac heard a whimper erupt from Mallory. Sweat popped out on his face. He wanted to shove the phone down Lucetti's throat. "Put the child on the phone. I stress this. If I don't talk to her, if I'm not completely satisfied that she's not only alive but in good spirits, I phone the cops. In short, you'd better treat that little girl like she's made of glass. Got it?"

"I'll call back."

The line went abruptly dead. Mac hung up and turned to look at Mallory. She stood near him, her face blanched pasty white, her eyes gigantic. She looked like she'd topple if he touched a finger to her forehead. Mac closed the distance between them and enfolded her in his arms even though he had sworn off any further physical contact with her. Four o'clock that morning seemed like a lifetime ago. She felt so small and insubstantial. He tightened his embrace, hunched his shoulders around her and buried his face in her hair.

"It's okay. Just threats. He won't really do it."

"H-her finger? Oh, Mac…" Her voice trailed off into a wail. She clutched his shirt so hard that he felt her nails dig into his skin. "What am I going to do?"

"Mallory, it's all right. Shh. Don't let him do this to you."

Unable to think of anything else to say, Mac simply held her, stroking her hair, swaying with her from side to side, keeping his arms cinched tight as if he could pour his strength into her. When the phone rang, he lowered her onto a chair.

"You want to talk to her?"

She covered her face with trembling hands and gave her head a vehement shake. "In a minute. I don't want to f-frighten her."

Mac stepped to the phone, lifted the receiver and said hello. A brief silence ensued. Then Em's hesitant voice came over the wire. "Where's my mommy? Do I have the wrong house?"

That voice reached right down inside Mac and wrapped itself around his heart. He closed his eyes and smiled. "This must be Em. I'm Mac, your mommy's friend."

Another silence. "A boyfriend?" she asked, clearly amazed.

Mac's smile widened. "Sort of."

"Do you have hair?"

That question took him aback for a moment. "Um— yeah, I have hair."

"Oh, good. Gerald didn't. I didn't want a new daddy who didn't have hair so Mommy stopped bringing him. Gramps said he was stuffy, anyway."

Good for Keith. "How are you, Emily? Are the people there treating you nice?"

"Yeah, but I still wish Gramps would get well so I could come home. The lady where I'm at brings me movies and ice cream, but it's not fun like it is with Mommy. I don't have my Pooh bag and I miss Ragsdale."

The child evidently still believed she was staying away from home because her grandfather was still in the hospital. "Your mommy's been really busy," Mac replied. "She couldn't get away to bring you Ragsdale."

"Is my Gramps real sick?"

"He's a little better, but still very weak."

"Can I say hi to my mommy, please?"

Mac glanced toward Mallory. She was so white, she looked as though she might faint, but she stood and came to take the phone. In a tremulous voice, she said, "Hi, princess. How's my favorite girl?"

"Fine. Do I get to see you today?"

Mallory closed her eyes. "Not today, darling, but soon."

"Tomorrow, then?" Em whispered something and the line crackled. "I have to go, Mommy. Would you bring me quarters when you come so I can talk a long time? I love you. Don't forget Ragsdale, okay? Bye."

"I love you, too, Em." Mallory tightened her grip on the phone. Mac heard more rustling noises coming over the wire. The next moment, Lucetti's voice rasped over the speaker. "Forty-eight hours, same place, same time of morning." Lucetti punctuated the order with a click of the phone. Mac sighed and cast a concerned glance at Mallory as she dropped the receiver into its cradle. She was still shaking.

"I want to try questioning Keith again," she said. "There m-must be a way to set up some s-sort of signal. There has to be. I'll call his physician and get special permission for you to enter the ICU."

"Are you sure you want to take that risk? If he realizes Em's been kidnapped, it might make him worse."

She nodded. "If something happens to her, he'll n-never forgive me for not at least trying."

Mac wasn't as concerned about Keith's feelings as he was about Mallory's. If questioning the older man caused a second stroke, she would spend the rest of her life blaming herself for it. On the other hand, if they didn't question Keith, and Emily was killed… Mac shuddered. Just talking to the child for a few minutes, he had completely lost his heart to her. And if he felt that strong a pull, what must Mallory be feeling?

THE MOMENT THEY STEPPED into the ICU, Keith's eyes filled with apprehension. Mallory caught her lower lip between her teeth and approached the bed. As before, Keith's hand felt cold when she grasped it. Was it her imagination, or was he thinner? The network of bones in his hand felt fragile. Mallory tried to smile and failed miserably. Keith's mouth drew down at one corner and he moaned, glancing pleadingly at Mac.

"Dad," Mallory began hesitantly. "I, um, want you to stay calm, okay? I have something to tell you—bad news, I'm afraid." She hesitated to let that sink in. "Em's been kidnapped."

Keith shrank into the mattress like a deflated doll, his eyes falling closed.

"She's safe. We spoke to her just a few minutes ago. They're giving her ice cream and showing her movies. She sounded fine." Mallory took a deep breath. "In exchange for her return, Lucetti is demanding a package. He believes it's in your safe-deposit box at the bank. We, um, are having some difficulty finding the box key."

Keith's eyes flew open. He looked imploringly at Mac. Leaning forward, Mac grasped his shoulder. "You can count on me, Keith. I'll get her home, safe and sound."

Mallory took another deep, bracing breath. "We're hoping to set up some kind of signal with you so that you can give us some hints as to where the key might be."

Keith kept his gaze glued to Mac and moaned. The sound was so pitiful that Mallory flinched.

"Anyway, I came up with an idea. I know that you can't control your eyelids enough to blink just once. We tried that last night. But if you could only blink when you mean yes and try your best not to let your eyelids close when your answer is no, maybe we can ask you enough questions to find the key. Do you think you could do that?"

Keith blinked in rapid succession. Mallory threw Mac a joyful glance. "Oh, Dad, that's great."

Mac drew up a chair and sat down. Mallory lifted Keith's hand to enfold it in hers. "Dad, it's crucial that you stay calm through this. We don't want to hurt you, you know. So before we start, I want to assure you that Emily will be fine. Mac dug up some dirt on Lucetti, so he doesn't harm her. If he does, he knows we'll have him arrested. So there's no reason to feel frightened for her, okay?"

Keith's eyelids fluttered and Mac smiled encouragement to Mallory. "Okay," she said, "if you get tired, just keep your eyes closed and we'll let you rest. First question. Is the package in your safe-deposit box?"

Keith blinked furiously.

"Okay, so all we have to do is find the key." Mallory glanced at Mac. "Is the key at the house?"

No blinking.

"Not at the house. Okay. Is it at your office?"

No.

"Is it in your car?"

No.

"Is it in Bellevue?"

No blinking. Mallory began to squirm. This yes and no questioning could only go so far. *Please, God.*

"Is it in Seattle?"

Keith's eyes went crazy and he moaned.

"Now, Dad, stay calm," she reminded him. "Don't become frustrated. Remember that every answer you give us eliminates a wild-goose chase and brings us one step closer to finding the key. Think of it positively, even if you can't tell us everything you'd like." A frown drew her brows together. "Is it in another safe-deposit box in Seattle?"

No.

"In a locker at the bus depot?"

No.

"At the airport?"

No.

Keith was breathing heavily now, his air rasping as it went down his throat. Mallory glanced at the monitor. His pulse had accelerated. "Mac, it's about time for him to rest," she warned.

Mac rose from his chair to place a staying hand on her shoulder, his gaze intent on Keith's. "Just one more question. Did you give it to a friend?"

Keith's eyelids fluttered wildly and his bottom lip twisted in a grotesque grin as he tried desperately to say something.

"Okay—okay, relax, Keith," Mac said soothingly. "It's with a friend. That's something for us to go on. The rest is elementary. We'll just get on the horn and start calling people. Did you tell this friend not to give the key to anyone?"

No.

"That's great," Mac said enthusiastically. "Now all we have to do is find the friend. There can't be that many people you trust that much."

Keith looked so tormented that Mallory wished they hadn't come. "Dad, you have to stay calm."

The ICU nurse came bustling in just then. Her blue eyes shot daggers at Mac as she came around the end of the bed. "He's going to have to rest now. I'll have to ask you to leave."

Mac leaned over Keith. "Trust me. I'll find it. We'll try to get word to you as soon as we have news. Meanwhile, remember one thing. When I needed you, you were there. This is my chance to pay you back. I'll come through for you. You've got my word on it. So don't worry, okay? Concentrate on getting well."

As THEY EXITED the hospital, Mallory glanced up and spied tears glistening in Mac's eyes. To her surprise, he made no effort to conceal them. When one escaped and trailed down his cheek, he wiped it away, throwing her a rueful smile.

"I love that old man," he muttered. "It kills me, seeing him like that. I hated upsetting him. Makes me feel like I ran the knife in deeper and gave it a twist."

"I know what you mean," she said in a tight voice.

"No. I don't think anyone can." He lifted one shoulder in a shrug. "He's—" He shook his head. "To me, he's the father I never had."

"What was the favor he did for you?"

He shoved his hands deep into his slacks pockets. "Put my life back together for me. Have you ever been completely alone?"

Mallory hadn't been, but she understood now what he meant, better than he knew. If not for Mac, she would have been alone since Em's abduction. Alone and desperate.

"So alone that there's no hope, no way out? I—" He took a ragged breath. "Someone I loved got killed. My brother. We'd had an argument. I was working to put him through school. He was throwing four years of my life away, his grades going to hell, his attitude disintegrating. I had put up with all I was going to. He left in a rage. Got drunk. Killed himself in a car. I blamed myself. Couldn't forget the ugly things I had said. I felt like I had driven him to it."

Randy. Mallory averted her face.

"I started drinking. I know that sounds weak, but I was young, confused—I think I wanted to die, too. I'd sit by his grave, me and my whiskey bottle, and stare at his name until I got so blasted I couldn't read it anymore. When my poor mother was at her wit's end, she called Keith Christiani. He found me. Took me to a hotel. Threw me in a cold shower. And made me so miserable I sobered up in self-defense. It took him a while, but he finally made me see that I wasn't to blame, that I couldn't have stopped what happened, even if I'd seen it coming."

"He's a wonderful man," Mallory whispered. "A loving man."

Mac sighed, a shaky, wet sound. "I never knew my biological father. Maybe it sounds corny, but Keith's the only person besides my mother who ever believed in me. Because he had been so fond of my brother and knew I had worked to put him through school, he saw something worthwhile in me that I had never been able to see. He stuck his neck out for me, not once but a dozen times. When I didn't have confidence, he had enough for both of us. If not for him, I'd be— You said once that I didn't owe him my life? I do, Mallory, I really do."

She at last found the courage to face him. "Add another person to that list."

"What list?"

"Of people who believe in you." She felt tears welling

in her own eyes. "Make that two people. I have a feeling Em will want to be on it one day."

When they reached the BMW, Mac checked the car over for explosives. When he found nothing, he waved Mallory in on her side, then climbed behind the wheel and cranked the engine. He didn't seem to want to talk about Keith anymore. She didn't, either. It could lead too easily into a discussion of Randy.

"Well, now where to?" he asked. "Your head seems to be operating better than mine, today. You choose."

"His office."

"But he said it wasn't there."

"Yes, but Trudy is. If anyone would know who Keith would have given something that important to, it'd be Trudy."

"WHY MAC, OF course," was Trudy's immediate response after she had pummeled them with questions about the gunfire yesterday. "Of all his friends, it would be Mac he'd call if he were in trouble. What kind of trouble was he in? I knew he was upset, but I didn't know why."

Mac ignored the question. "I was out of town. Who else, Trudy? Think hard. It's extremely important."

Trudy hesitated. "Well, he has dozens of friends, all of them loyal, I'm sure. Keith inspires that in people."

"Dozens?" Mac said faintly. "Do you have a list?"

"I can give you his Rolodex."

Mallory's heart sank. It would take the remainder of the day to call all the people in a Rolodex. "Would you, Trudy?"

Trudy disappeared into Keith's office and reappeared a moment later with the Rolodex, which she handed to Mac. Her green eyes filled with concern as she peered at Mallory over the tinted lenses of her glasses. "There's something terribly wrong, isn't there? Something's happened? Something other than Keith's stroke."

"I—I can't say," Mallory told her gently. "Just pray for us, Trudy. We need all the help we can get."

THEY DID THE PHONE CALLING in shifts. Late in the afternoon, while Mallory took her turn dialing and interrogating people, Mac cleaned up the kitchen, then foraged in the freezer and quick-thawed some sirloin for dinner. She wasn't sure how she was going to manage to eat. But she knew she must. To help Em, she needed to keep her strength up. That meant eating nutritious food and resting whenever an opportunity presented itself. It also meant she must have faith that everything would turn out all right. Otherwise, swallowing food would be an impossibility. And so would closing her eyes.

In less than an hour, Mac insisted she take a break from telephoning and eat the meal he'd prepared. She finished her conversation with a man from Seattle named Harry Reisling who claimed to be an old service buddy of Keith's. No, he hadn't seen Keith in months. No, he didn't have a key belonging to Keith. He was extremely sorry to hear that his friend had suffered a stroke. Mallory rang off with a promise that she would give her father-in-law Harry's best.

To her surprise, she was ravenously hungry and managed to make quite a dent in the food Mac had heaped on her plate. When she couldn't swallow another morsel, Mallory settled back in her chair and toyed with the handle of her coffee cup. Mac propped his elbows on the table and rested his chin on his fists. "Now," he said in a low voice, "how about a long, hot shower and an early night. You didn't get much rest last night."

Despite the fact that she had only just lectured herself on the importance of getting rest, Mallory found it difficult to follow through. Em was out there somewhere. Her life was in danger. She glanced at the Rolodex. "I'm not finished."

"I'll finish. We have an entire day left." Not a lot of time, he thought, but he wasn't about to say so. "You can afford to rest and recoup your strength."

As tired as she was, Mallory hated to leave him with all the work. "Only if I clean up the kitchen first."

"A deal. I hate dishes."

They finished their coffee in silence, the first real lull they'd had all day. Mallory avoided looking at him, afraid of what she might read in his eyes. Had she really asked him to make love to her last night? Or had she dreamed it? It was a question that had plagued her all day. An unanswerable question because her memories of it were so jumbled and vague. She remembered feeling frantic, clinging to him, wanting him to make the pain go away. And then...nothing. Had she fallen asleep in his arms? What had he said? When she had awakened beside him this morning, both of them were still clothed. Clearly Mac had declined her offer if she had made one.

Rising from the table, she gathered the plates and scraped the food off them into the disposal. Mac stationed himself on the other side of the counter and began phoning the *S* section in the Rolodex, hitting every Seattle address. He had finished and begun the *T* section by the time she wiped the last trace of their meal from the counters and table.

Folding the dishcloth and laying it across the sink divider, Mallory waited for him to end a conversation, then said, "I'll take Em's room. You'll be more comfortable in the larger bed."

His gray eyes lifted. Mallory glanced uneasily away, unable to meet his gaze. Heat flamed to her cheeks.

"You sure? I hate to run you out of your own room."

"Her bed is perfectly comfortable. And I'll feel closer to her in there. Really, I don't mind."

Escaping the kitchen, Mallory took the stairs at a near run. After gathering her night things, she showered in the main bath just in case Mac finished up the Rolodex and wanted a shower himself. The hot water felt wonderfully soothing on her bruised body. After soaping down and shampooing her hair, she stood under the spray for several minutes, making her mind completely blank. No thoughts of Em. Of Keith. Of his many friends in Seattle. Of anything. She had to relax if she intended to sleep. And she *needed* sleep. Exhaustion was weighing on her, making her feel rubbery all over.

After blowing her hair dry, she tugged on her gown, straightened up the bathroom and went across the hall to Em's room. The bed felt like a mother's arms as she stretched out between the sheets and pulled the pink down comforter to her chin. Now if only she could sleep. A picture flashed in her head of Em's finger lying inside a small box and she rolled onto her stomach to bury her face. The tears that she had held at bay all day flooded from her eyes, accompanied by muffled sobs. She cried until she was empty and numb again, then just lay there, her eyes squeezed closed, her hands knotted into fists.

It wouldn't happen, she promised herself. She and Mac were going to find the key. They had to. If they didn't,

Mallory didn't want to live. That was her last thought. Like a blown bulb, her lights went out. Blackness swooped over her.

RUFFLES AND LACE and Mallory Christiani…a heady combination. Mac leaned a shoulder against the bedpost and studied the sleeping woman before him, his mouth curved into a wry smile. He toyed with his tie, rasping his fingertips across the silk, imagining silken skin instead. *Mac, would you love me?* An ache of longing had centered itself in his chest last night and hadn't eased up all day. Not a sexual longing, just need, raw and elemental and completely baffling. He wanted inside her skin, to drown in the sensation of simply holding her. Dangerous feelings. Not even thoughts of Randy seemed to douse the fire.

She had been crying. Even in the shadows, he could see the puffy blueness of her eyelids, the swollen vulnerability of her lips, the streaks on her cheeks. All day long, she had held it in. He wished she hadn't, that she could let herself go, but at the same time, he had to admire her grit.

Mac sighed and turned away. The last of the Rolodex file hadn't turned up the possessor of the key. No key, no kid. Simple as that. He strode to Mallory's room and flung open the door. As he stepped across the threshold, memories of the previous night washed over him. He approached the bed and stared down at the destroyed toy dog. Good old Ragsdale. Ripped apart. Just like Mac would be if he didn't get a handle on his emotions. His and Mallory's worlds were so far apart. When this was over, he'd go his way, she'd go hers. He would probably see her only rarely, from a distance, just as before. Which was as it should be.

He glanced at the beautiful bedroom. It had taken a great deal of money to decorate it. More money than he had to spare in a year, probably. Even if Mallory fell in love with him, which was hoping for the moon, she'd soon grow unhappy when she found out he couldn't afford the lifestyle she was used to. Not for her. Not for her daughter. There'd be no fancy canopy beds. No Mercedes. No tailored suits. No salons.

He flopped onto his back and closed his eyes, determined to banish foolish thoughts about Mallory and any kind of future with her from his mind. He was just a poor kid from Seattle. That was all he had ever been, all he would ever be. He'd best remember it and keep his mind on the job.

CHAPTER TWELVE

TWO-THIRTY. MALLORY STARED at the luminous dials on Em's Snoopy alarm clock, wondering what had disturbed her. She had been asleep for several hours. Too long, from the feel of things. She was wide-awake, her mind clamoring with thoughts of Em and the elusive key. In some nether region of her mind, she heard a continuous whisper, *time is running out, time is running out.* It filled her with panic.

Throwing her legs over the edge of the bed, she sat up and stretched. Some of the soreness had left her body. She reached for her robe with trembling hands, donned it and left the bedroom. Up the hall, she could hear the uneven sputter of Mac's breathing. The sound beckoned, and for a moment, she thought about sneaking in to be near him. He soothed her, somehow. But after last night, if he woke up and caught her, he'd think she was throwing herself at him. A man, especially a childless man, would never understand the hysteria that nipped constantly at her heels. Only a mother could know how she felt, how her body ached to hold her daughter. She turned in the opposite direction and headed for the stair landing.

She didn't turn on lights for fear of waking Mac. A cup of herb tea sounded good, but there was no point in him losing sleep while she had one. She would wait and turn on lights when she reached the kitchen. The layout of the house was so familiar to her, she could walk it blind, anyway.

The front half of the entry reached two stories high to the skylight in the vaulted ceiling. Moonlight illuminated the hall, throwing everything into eerie shadow. Her pink robe looked blue. The tile felt cold on her bare feet and made her wish she had worn her slippers. She stepped into the kitchen and reached for the light switch. Just as her fingers touched the plastic, she heard a sound out on the patio that made her hesitate. Not overly alarmed because she knew the sliding doors had safety locks, she tiptoed to the adjoining dining room. As she approached the glass doors to peer outside, she saw the silhouette of a man standing beside the patio umbrella table. From his sudden stillness, she guessed he had spotted her.

For a moment, Mallory stood frozen in her tracks and stared. Then she saw the man lift his hand, saw moonlight glint off blue-black metal. Orange flame licked the air. *Tatta-tat-tat.* The glass in the doors erupted toward her. She threw up her arm and staggered backward, using the hutch as a shield, horrified as the night and the room around her shattered into a million exploding fragments.

Tatta-tat-tat. Tatta-tat-tat. Mallory's ears rang as the guttural burping of the gun surrounded her. Instinctively she dropped to the floor, slamming the air out of her lungs upon impact. The carpet beneath her was peppered with glass fragments. Bits of flying plaster splattered her face, sharp and stinging. Above her, bullets found the ornate, gilt-framed mirror. Its moon-silvered surface erupted and rained shimmering shards, their musical tinkling filling her ears as they pelted her body. She tried to move. Couldn't. She tried to scream. No sound would come out. All she could do was stare. At the man. At the glinting gun. He was stepping through the door frame—into the room with her.

Panting, Mallory scrambled on her belly into the kitchen. As she clawed for purchase on the tiles, she heard footsteps behind her. Her heart slammed like a kettle-drum. *The breakfast nook. I have to reach the breakfast nook.* Upstairs, she heard a thump. Tearing her nails as she fought for handholds on the smooth floor, she reached the table and crawled beneath it, praying the moonlight wasn't so bright she could be seen.

Tatta-tat-tat. Tatta-tat-tat. The kitchen burst into a gro-tesque symphony of sound. Bullets thudded into the oak cupboards, rang out against pots, *kerplunked* on tile. She heard a sudden gush of water cascading onto the floor. A water pipe? The faucet? Throwing a glance toward the day room, she wondered if she could make it across the floor without being seen. Mac, where was Mac? Another burst of gunfire. Zigzagging streaks of blue light flared in the kitchen. In the explosions of illumination, she saw that the automatic coffeemaker's cord had been severed close to its base. Still plugged into the wall socket, the cord was live, dancing and whipping like a snake, spurt-ing tongues of electricity. She no sooner ascertained the source of light than she realized the man entering the kitchen might be able to see her.

"Mallory!" Mac roared.

His footsteps thumped above her and came down the long upstairs hall. A moment later, the stairs creaked. Terror paralyzed her throat. If Mac ran into the kitchen, he would be killed. If she dared call out to warn him, she would be. Footsteps, running. Closer, closer. The man in the kitchen pressed his back to the cupboards, his gun raised.

"Mac, no!" she screamed. "The kitchen, he's in the kitchen!"

Splat—Splat—Splat. The table did a tap dance around her. Slugs from the Uzi buried themselves in the wood above her head. Mac's sack of mail fell to the tile. Diving, Mallory rolled across the floor to the archway that opened into the day room, every nerve in her body raw with expectancy as she anticipated a bullet. She thudded over the step-down and scrambled for cover behind the sofa.

Silence swooped over her, broken only by the spurting hisses of electricity frying water. Blue-white light flashed as she peeked over the cushions. Mac, where was he? She held her breath, listening, glancing first toward the kitchen, then toward the door that opened into the entry hall. Had he heard her?

"Mac! He's in the kitchen!" she screamed again.

A shadow moved in the entry. Mallory peered out and saw Mac, gun uplifted before him, easing along the hallway wall. She threw an anxious glance toward the bluewhite bursts of light. She thought she detected a stealthy footstep in the kitchen. Another. She dug her fingers into the sofa upholstery and held her breath.

"Ar-rr-gh!"

The cry ripped through the semidarkness, shrill agony tearing up from a masculine throat. Coldness washed over her. She stared at the intruder's silhouette, thrown upon the breakfast room wall by moonlight and electric blue. Jerking, twisting. A grotesque dance of death. A ceaseless spatting of bullets rent the air as the intruder's finger convulsed on the Uzi's trigger.

"Mac?"

"Stay down!" he growled from somewhere nearby.

She couldn't drag her eyes from the silhouette. A sickening smell drifted to her. Bile rose in her throat along with an upsurge of horror. She felt Mac crawling up beside her. He, too, stared at the breakfast room wall, his face taut in the play of blue-white light, his muscles twitching each time the other man's gun spat bullets.

"Electrocuted, he's being electrocuted," she cried. "The coffeemaker cord. A pipe broke." Disbelief mushroomed inside her. "M-Mac? He'll die if we don't do something."

His only reply was to grab her arm and jerk her to her feet. Dragging her in his wake, he sprinted across the day room, out into the hall, his destination the front door. Throwing it open, he leaped out onto the porch and hunkered down to avoid being seen. Mallory followed his example. They jumped off the end of the porch into the shrubs. She didn't even feel the branches scratching her legs, she was so scared. Off across the lawn. Through the shrubs that divided their yard from the neighbors. They zigzagged back and forth, keeping close to the ground. Porch lights along the street were coming on.

"Other men," he panted. "Back at the house. Keep low."

This isn't happening. Mallory kept thinking that as Mac hauled her relentlessly through one yard, then another. His pace never let up, not even when they hit pea gravel in their bare feet. At the end of the cul-de-sac, they took to the sidewalk. One block, two. He turned right. They ran another block. Another. Mallory feared she might collapse. The only sound in her head was the laboring rasp of her own breathing. She fell back slightly. Mac's arm was stretched out behind him to keep a hold on her hand. She forced her legs to keep pumping. Another block. Another. Her lungs began to whine.

At last, Mac drew up beside a black Cadillac. Relief

washed through Mallory when Mac tried the door and
it wasn't locked. He threw his gun on the seat and bent
to locate the ignition wires under the dash. Within seconds, the engine sputtered, kicked over and roared to life.
"Let's go!" he cried.

Mallory leaped in on the passenger side, slammed her
door and put on her seat belt. Glancing over at Mac, she
clamped a hand to her chest and gulped for air. He ran his
palms over her, feeling for blood. "You okay?"

"Fine."

He jerked the shift into Drive and peeled the tires in a
U-turn, throwing her sideways in the seat. As the car sped
down the street, she leaned her head against the rest and
struggled for air, her mouth slack, eyes closed, body slick
with sweat. They were safe—at least for now. It didn't
matter that they were in a stolen car. It didn't matter that
there was a dead man in her kitchen. It didn't matter that
her house was shot apart, bullets embedded everywhere.
They were safe.... She didn't know how she would ever
explain this to the police, and for the moment, she didn't
have the energy to worry about it.

MAC DROVE NORTH to a seedy motel on Highway 99 on the
outskirts of Everett. Mallory sat in the stolen car while
he rousted the motel manager out of his bed and rented
a room. At any moment, she expected him to come back
to the car and say he had been turned away, but evidently run-down motels with white paint and hot-pink
trim weren't all that particular about their patrons. Shirt-
less and barefoot, Mac looked none too respectable, nice
car or not. Thank goodness he hadn't emptied his pants
pockets earlier tonight before crawling into bed. He had
his charge cards with him.

"Room eleven, my lucky number," he said as he climbed back into the Caddy. His voice sounded oddly tight. He pulled into a parking space only a short distance from the office and cut the car engine. Picking up his gun, he wedged it under his waistband. "I'm afraid this isn't the Ritz. The big advertised feature is a vibrating bed."

Mallory hugged her robe to her breasts and climbed from the car, glancing nervously around the dark parking lot before she closed the door. The manager peered out the lobby window at her and shook his gray head, clearly bewildered. She supposed it wasn't often that women arrived here in their nightclothes. It was putting the cart before the horse, she had to admit. Just so long as he didn't think they looked so suspicious that he called the police. That was all that mattered.

Horrid wasn't the word to describe their room, but close. The hot-pink walls had faded and gathered grime until they were more gray than pink. The pink chenille bedspread was missing sections of fringe. The scarlet rug was worn bare in places. Mac jerked the bedding back. "Sheets are fresh." He stepped into the bathroom and flipped on the fan light. A loud rattle began in the ceiling. He quickly hit the switch again to turn it off. "Clean towels and a sanitary guard on the toilet. I guess it'll do until daylight. Sorry, Mallory, but places like this don't ask questions or call in to check license plates."

With that, he put his gun on the dresser and sank into a frayed red easy chair, propping his elbows on his knees and burying his face in his hands. Mallory stared at him. He was shaking. She had seen him walk away from a switchblade fight and an exploding car without any outward sign of fear. Had he been shot and not told her? She scanned him for any trace of blood.

"Mac?" She took a halting step toward him. "Mac, you aren't hurt?" He didn't answer. She ran to him and began searching frantically for a wound. "Mac?"

With no warning, he snaked an arm around her waist, fell back in the chair and swept her onto his lap. A strange sound erupted from his chest as his arms tightened their hold. His body trembled violently. He buried his face in the curve of her neck and clung to her. She felt wetness trickle past the collar of her gown and realized, with a shock, that he was crying.

"I—I thought they'd killed you," he croaked. "I woke up to the gunfire, and I thought they'd killed you."

"Oh, Mac... I'm all right." She ran her hands into his hair and closed her eyes. "I'm fine. Nothing happened."

For an endless time, he clung to her. Then he rubbed his cheeks dry on her robe and whispered, "I've never felt this way before. Not about anyone."

She knew he was referring to the crazy, irrational attachment they were developing for each other. How long had she known him now? She tried to count the days, but they stretched into eternity in her mind. Mac had always been there, always would be.

"Mallory...?"

There was a weak note of warning in his voice. He loosened his hold on her and moved back to capture her face between his hands. His eyes searched hers, aching with confusion and need. For a moment, she thought he might kiss her. But at the last second, he cursed under his breath and averted his face.

"This is insane," he said with ragged intensity. His hands dropped to his lap and he gave her a little nudge to move her. The moment she stood, he sprang from the chair, took a step and sprawled on the bed, rolling onto his back. He grabbed the pillow lying above his head and plopped it down in the middle of the mattress. "I don't know about you, but I'm getting some sleep before I do something we'll both regret. And, please, no cracks about a pillow not being enough to keep me away from you. It's better than nothing."

With that, he turned onto his side, his broad back to the pillow, his head resting on his folded arm. For a moment, Mallory stared at the pitifully inadequate barrier he had erected, then she stepped to the door and touched the light switch. The room was plunged into an eerie blackness that was soon streaked by muted pink rays of light that shone through the red drapes. The silence dripped tension, suffocating and electrical. She pressed her back to the wall.

"Come lie down," he whispered. "You can't stand there all night."

Mallory peeled off her robe, slung it on the floor and circled him to climb into the bed, careful to stay on her side. The pillow was soft against her hip as she stretched out on her back. His breathing was tense and measured. She found herself wishing he would fall asleep and begin to snore. It was a comfortable sound, and she had grown accustomed to hearing it.

For what seemed like forever, she lay there, rigid and uncertain. She had already slept several hours and, tired as she was from running, it wasn't a drowsy tired, just bone-deep weariness. Then, at last, he started snoring and her eyelids grew heavy. She slipped into slumber without realizing it. At first she dreamed of men chasing them with guns.

Then the scene changed abruptly, and Mallory found herself in a room filled with small white gift boxes, lids decorated with shimmering ribbons. For some reason, the sight of them struck terror into her. She didn't want to open them, didn't want to see what they held, but there were so many on the floor that she couldn't take a step without bumping one. Her skin began to prickle with panic. A scream slid up the back of her throat. She whirled to run and overturned a box. A fluff of tissue paper spilled out and began to unfurl. Within its folds was a child's hand. Mallory stared down at it. *Emily.* She began to whimper. All the boxes began to tip sideways. She knew what they held. She heard Darren's voice pleading with her. *Do something. Don't just stand there and let us die. Not again. Save us.* Cruel laughter began to echo off the walls....

Mac jerked awake, his muscles knotted, every nerve ending alert. He wasn't sure what had disturbed him. Then he heard it, a strangled whimpering sound. Rolling over, he rose on an elbow. In the shafts of pink light, he could see Mallory thrashing in her sleep. He grasped her shoulder to waken her. Her flannel gown was sopped with sweat. "Mallory? Sweetheart, wake up."

She woke up, all right, swinging at him and screaming, the sounds shrill and piercing. Acutely aware of how thin the walls probably were, Mac clamped a hand over her mouth and scrambled over the pillow lying between them. He felt her teeth sinking into his palm. He used his body to pin her thrashing limbs.

"Mallory—honey, it's me, it's only me. It's a nightmare, just a nightmare."

Her teeth worried the leather skin that padded his knuckles. Her breath whined through her nose. Her eyes were huge above his hand, still glazed with terror. Then, with a muffled sob, she went limp and began to cry, an awful, tearing sound. His stomach knotted. He drew his hand from her mouth and enfolded her in his arms, pulling her close and slinging his leg over hers.

"Boxes," she sobbed. "Everywhere. He did it, Mac, he did it. Her hand... He sent her home to me in pieces."

Nausea rolled through him in waves. "Oh, Mallory...."

The violent shaking of her body reminded him of that first night when he had found her rocking Ragsdale. Only this time, he didn't have to ask her to come to him. She was wrapped around him like a sarong. He could feel her heart slamming, her skin pulsating and growing hot as her blood sluiced through her veins. Her slender arms were cinched around his neck, rigid in their hold, her face pressed against his shoulder.

Mac feathered kisses from her temple to her brow and whispered softly, not sure what he was saying, responding instinctively to her need. Running his hands over her, he kneaded her tortured muscles, forcing out the kinks, his one thought being to comfort her. *Damn Lucetti for doing this to her.*

He wasn't sure when his motives changed. Desire flared inside him with a suddenness that blinded him, red and searing. His own heart accelerated its beat to match hers. He wanted her, had to have her. It wasn't a thought or even a decision, just an instinctive taking that erupted from a dark, conscienceless place within him.

As overwhelming as the impulse was, Mac would have stopped if Mallory had seemed hesitant. But when he kissed her, she sobbed into his mouth and pressed closer, the urgency in her body matching his own. He had imagined loving her...sweetly, gently, languorously, coaxing her not to be shy. This was nothing like that. It was hunger that left no room for gentle coaxing, too elemental to be sweet.

In the nether regions of his mind, he was vaguely aware that he was peeling off her gown as though it were the skin on a succulent fruit and he was a starving man. As the flannel hem skidded up her torso, he followed in its wake with his mouth, devouring the taste of her skin, nibbling with his lips, then with his teeth, his senses electrified by her cries as he grazed each of her ribs. Like a moth drawn to flame, he found her breast, drawing its sensitive peak into his mouth to lave it with wet heat. She whimpered and arched her body up to him, her muscles quivering and jerking with each relentless pull. Little warning bells went off inside his head. She was a small woman with skin as soft as velvet. He didn't want to hurt her. But the moment he started to surface to a more reasoning plane of consciousness, she moaned and clung, dragging him back down with her into a kaleidoscopic world where sensation ruled.

Mallory. She was rose petals and honey, berry froth and cream, an elusive, silken temptress who entwined herself in a pink mist around him. Or was it the pink shimmering shafts of light that angled across the bed? When he slitted his eyes, he saw only her, felt only her. A delectable confection that melted against him. Beautiful, precious, unattainable Mallory.

With feverish urgency, he trailed his hungry lips down her belly to her navel and the satiny skin below, his tongue finding the tiny white ridges left there by her pregnancy with Em. Oddly enough, each mark made her all the more beautiful to him. When he started to move lower to find the throbbing sweetness of her womanhood, he felt her stiffen, heard her call his name in a tremulous whisper.

He murmured a husky protest, but forced himself to stop. He could tell by the way she had said his name that she was shocked right down to her prim little manicured toenails. Trailing kisses back up her body, he once again found her mouth, claiming it with masterful thrusts of his tongue that soon made her forget her momentary shyness. When he felt her melting against him, he slid his hand to the juncture of her thighs, found her moistness and contented himself with gently stroking her. The first sweep of his fingers made her gasp. He felt her lashes brush his cheek as her eyes flew open. Perplexed, he deepened their kiss. She grabbed his wrist and tried to pull his hand away. It was his turn to feel shocked. Maybe wealthy fellows didn't make love the same way poor boys did.

Freeing her mouth, he feathered kisses to her ear, keeping his hand insinuated between her thighs. "Trust me, Mallory."

"I—" Her breath caught and she shuddered. "I'm sorry."

He drew back slightly to see her. "Sorry?"

"It's been—since Darren—no one else—ever." Her eyes widened and her facial muscles tightened as his fingers found with unerring accuracy the supersensitive flesh they had been seeking.

He couldn't resist kissing the quivering corners of her mouth even though part of him wanted nothing more than to watch her small face while he explored her sensitive flesh and made her passions peak. "Don't hold back. Trust me." He felt her legs relaxing, parting ever so slightly. Her hips instinctively lifted toward his hand and he watched as her pupils dilated and her lashes drifted halfway closed. A tremor ran the length of her, slight but unmistakable. He read her expressions and knew the exact moment when she felt herself slipping over the edge. "Ah, Mallory, let go, let it happen."

A whimper worked its way up her throat and her eyes drifted completely closed. With arms that were suddenly aquiver, she hugged his neck and arched toward his hand with mindless abandon, a cry tearing up from her throat as he brought her to climax. Afterward, he cradled her shuddering form against him, pressing kisses to her closed eyelids. When at last the aftershocks left her body, he peeled off his slacks and rose over her.

She showed no hesitation as he entered her. She was honey and silk and fire, all rolled into one small perfectly shaped woman who clung to him and met him thrust for thrust. So sweet. He couldn't believe how good she felt, how good she made *him* feel.

When he had spent himself, Mac didn't want to release her. It was over, yet it wasn't. He realized as he gathered her close in his arms that with Mallory it would never be over, never be something he could walk away from and forget the moment his tie was straightened. He doubted that he'd ever get all of her that he wanted.

A smile curved his mouth. He buried his face in her hair and inhaled the sweet smell of her. When had her scent become so familiar and so dear to him? *Mallory.* How had he let himself fall for her like this? Was he out of his mind? Had Randy's death taught him nothing? He closed his eyes and drew her closer. Later, he'd worry about it later....

Time drifted by like mist on a windless night. Mallory had no idea how long she lay there in Mac's arms. He was long since asleep, his arms locked tightly around her, his face buried in her hair, clinging to her as if to assure himself, even in slumber, that she was there and safe. She pressed closer to him. He had been her one and only constant since this had begun. Warm, solid, her only security. She stared into the shadows, afraid to close her eyes. The nightmare she was living was terrifying enough. She couldn't bear to face it in her sleep, where she was completely helpless against it.

COME DAYLIGHT, THE room looked even dingier than it had last night. Mac woke slowly, deliciously aware of the silken body he held clamped in his arms, of the soft curve of buttock pressed against his awakening manhood. He had a small breast cupped in one hand. Desire shot through him like an electrical charge. Instinctively he started to disentangle himself, then hesitated. Sudden movement would wake Mallory, and she needed rest.

He closed his eyes on a wave of guilt. What had he been thinking last night? That was exactly the problem. He hadn't been thinking, period. He had woken up out of a sound sleep and done what came naturally, the devil take tomorrow. She wasn't the kind of woman to have sex with just anyone. And what could he offer her? He had seen the look on her face the night before last when she had first seen him in his street clothes. Shock, apprehension, uncertainty as to what to expect from him. And later, on the streets, she had been completely out of her element.

She was the daughter of an ex-congressman. She had grown up eating her cereal out of a crystal bowl. She thought poor meant driving a Caddy instead of a Mercedes. Mac could show her what *poor* really was. He had lived poverty, breathed it, clawed his way up from it. They had nothing in common, nothing. If they ever once got into a deep conversation, she would immediately realize how little education he had. And it would tear him apart to lose her once he let himself start to love her.

Once he let himself? What a joke that was. He was already in over his head and floundering. Gently he disengaged himself from her sweet softness and slid from the bed, dragging on his slacks. She murmured something and rolled over, reaching for him. He stared over his shoulder at the bruise on her face, at the cut on her collarbone. *Fragile.* If he had even a grain of decency, he'd end this now. For her sake. And for his own.

"Mac?"

"I'm here." His throat tightened as her thick lashes lifted and her deep brown eyes sought his. How could he be brusque with her? Or hold her at arm's length? She needed someone to lean on, someone to hold her, comfort her and care. And like it or not, he was the only someone available. With a silent groan, he sat down and enfolded her hand in his. "I'm here, honey."

She clung to his fingers. "I thought you'd left."

"I won't leave. You know that." His problem was that he liked being there for her all too well.

She started to sit up, then remembered she was naked. Her cheeks flushed a delicate pink as she scrambled for the sheet and covered herself. Momentary confusion played upon her face. He could almost read her thoughts as she slowly cataloged the room around her and remembered exactly what had transpired between them a few hours before. Guilt roiled within him. He should have maintained control. Her blush deepened to crimson as her gaze slid to his back. Slowly her eyes climbed the ladder of his ribs to meet his gaze. There was a question in the look. *Are you sorry?*

He jerked his hand from hers, stood and buckled his

belt. Damned right, he was sorry. To distract her and himself, he strode to the window and glanced out, pretending he thought there might be someone out there. He didn't, but any ruse that worked wasn't beneath him. "You know, I just can't figure it out. We've both agreed that it can't be Lucetti trying to kill you. But if it's not Lucetti, who?"

Relief washed over him as he turned from the window. She was not only distracted, but deep in thought if her frown was any indication. He wasn't ready to deal with what was happening between them. How could he verbalize feelings he couldn't yet understand himself? He needed time—time to sort things out, time to come to grips with his involvement with her, time to rationalize it all into something he could deal with. If they discussed it now, his uncertainty would only hurt her. And he couldn't bear the thought of that.

"They're smart, I'll say that for them," he went on. "Amateurs wouldn't let up, but these guys back off, let us relax a little, then hit when we least expect it. I tell you, they work like Lucetti does. That bomb in my car was made by an expert or it would have demolished half a block. It was also timed in hopes that we'd leave the congested parking lot before it went off. Less risk of bystanders getting hurt that way. Those fellows have been around and know exactly what they're doing, no guesswork. If I didn't know better, I'd swear they were following Lucetti's orders."

"Which makes no sense."

"No, none at all. Which convinces me we were right all along, that they're Lucetti's men, acting on their own."

"They don't want me giving him that package." Mallory leaned back against the headboard. "And what's the best way to make sure I don't?" She snapped her fingers.

"Waste me. It makes sense. Unless he finds that key on his own, which is unlikely, Lucetti doesn't have a prayer of getting into that deposit box without me."

Mac nearly smiled at how quickly she had picked up on the lingo she had heard downtown. He was willing to bet that until the night before last, the only "waste" Mallory had known about was the kind that went down her garbage disposal. "It's something in that package that they don't want Lucetti to see. But what?"

"Ledgers equal embezzlement," she said with certainty. "What else could it be? Embezzlement or proof somehow that they had cheated him."

Mac dropped into the red chair, his mind racing. After a moment, he shook his head. "To embezzle, they'd have to be bookkeepers. No way. Bookkeepers aren't that friendly with guns and explosives." He lifted an eyebrow. "Maybe they aren't bookkeepers. What if they're collectors? Like Chapin said?"

"Collectors?"

"Yeah, the money boys." Mac's eyes began to gleam with excitement. "Mallory, you're a genius. They've been skimming! Miles's ledgers must implicate them somehow." Leaping up, he began to pace. "If Lucetti sees the books and discovers his collectors have betrayed him, they're as good as dead. Perfect motivation! No wonder they're trying to rub you out. It's you or them."

"What a comforting thought," she said in a faint voice.

He flashed her a grin. "Hey, so far, we've outsmarted them."

"Correction. *You* have."

"Well, I'd say luck has bailed us out more times than not. And it's your luck as much as mine. Those guys are good at what they do, damned good." He settled back in the chair.

She managed a wry smile. "You can't say it's all been luck, Mac. Your driving skills saved us the first time, your quick thinking, the second. If not for you, I'd be wearing a toe tag by now."

That grim thought brought silence swooping over them for a moment.

"So…" He lifted his hands. "What next, Einstein? Any ideas?" He leaned forward and draped his arms on his knees. "So far, I haven't got any leads on Lucetti unless I want to wait till the weekend and go to the racetrack to find Andrews. But we don't have time for that. We don't have an ID as yet on the three thugs, just the one possible name Shelby's checking out. And no clue what friend it was that Keith gave the key to. I'm fresh out of ideas."

"You know what's weird?" Mallory said. "Lucetti doesn't *know* what friend Keith gave it to. He wanted those ledgers so badly, he admitted he'd had Keith followed— to be sure he mailed the package. And he was having *me* followed, too, after all, or he wouldn't have known where Em was. You'd think he'd know everywhere Keith went, everyone he came in contact with."

Mac shook his head. "You're forgetting the mail."

"True. I don't suppose Lucetti could have monitored all the mail that left the law firm, even if he tried." Mallory stared at Mac, the germ of an idea taking root. The mail? She remembered a plot twist in a mystery novel she had read some time ago. *Evidence found on a type-writer ribbon.* "Mac?" she squeaked. "Oh, good grief! Why didn't we think of it?"

She leaped from the bed and fumbled for her night-gown. Mac stared at her. "Come again?"

"The typewriter. Don't you see? If Keith sent the key to someone, he would have typed an accompanying letter. If he was being secretive, he wouldn't have had Trudy do it. We can get the name off his ribbon. He uses a film cartridge on the typewriter. And a film ribbon is one-strike. You simply reverse your ribbon, find the section of film you want and transcribe the letters in the proper order to see what was written."

"Why would he bother to type a letter? It would be quicker to do it longhand."

"Keith's handwriting is awful, he never writes by hand."

Mac rose slowly from the chair. His mind whirled as he tried to remember whether or not the typewriter, like everything else in Keith's office, had been torn apart. "Don't get too excited. That ribbon could have been tossed when Trudy cleaned up the mess in his office."

She threw him a glare as she shoved her arms into the sleeves of her robe. "Don't even *think* that way."

CHAPTER THIRTEEN

IT WAS OVER two hours before Mac and Mallory could get to Keith's firm. First, they had to be decently attired. When they drove by Mallory's to get clothes, they saw that the doors and windows of the house had been sealed with tape, the yard cordoned off. Evidently the police had been called by neighbors who reported the shooting, and the electrocuted body of the intruder had been discovered. Mac and Mallory didn't dare enter the house. As it was, they needed to ditch the stolen Cadillac as quickly as they could before the police made a connection between the missing car and the shooting incident.

They were left with no choice but to stop someplace and buy Mallory clothing. After going to Mac's apartment so he could dress, they drove to Bellevue Square. Mac took a list of Mallory's sizes and went inside to buy her a new set of clothes and shoes. She had to dress in the rest room of an Exxon station across the street.

"Not bad," Mac commented when she emerged from the ladies room and climbed back into the Cadillac. "Jeans and sneakers do something for you. Or maybe it's the other way around, you do something for jeans and sneakers."

She brushed her hair with her fingers, flashing him a smile. "It's just your great taste."

Giving her another once-over, Mac had to agree. The

pale blue knit top he had chosen hugged her sleek lines like a second skin. *Choice,* as Danno would say. The question was, could Mac afford her? She didn't seem to mind blue jeans and tennies, but he wasn't offering them to her as a steady diet, either. Not that he wouldn't buy her nice clothing if dressing her ever became his responsibility. He simply couldn't compete with her father. Never would be able to, for that matter.

"Well, this is where we leave the Caddy." Mac pulled out his wallet and cast a gloomy glance at his quickly dwindling money supply. "I wish we could leave them something to compensate for all the trouble we've caused them."

Mallory took off her diamond solitaire earrings and stuck them in an old registration envelope she found in the glove box. Laying the offering on the seat, she threw Mac a smile. "No great sentimental value. A gift from my father."

"Mallory, diamonds from your father? If they didn't mean a lot, you wouldn't be wearing them."

She threw open her door. "The only reason I wear them is that he has a fit if I don't."

He climbed out on his side and shut his door, eyeing her over the shiny black roof. "Fifteen hundred dollars of ice?"

"Ice—exactly—not love or a hug."

The fleeting sadness that touched her face made Mac's heart catch. She skirted the car, walking with a new jauntiness in the comfortable sneakers. His gaze dropped to the swing of her hips. She definitely added new dimensions to denim. Dropping an arm around her shoulders, he gave her that hug her father had failed to give her as he fell into step with her. As they crossed the parking lot, he was achingly aware that he wanted to do a whole lot more than just hug her. And he wanted a whole lot longer than a day in which to do it.

They walked to the law firm, which was several blocks away. Mallory looked so different in her new outfit that Mac didn't think anyone was likely to recognize her. Trudy proved him right when they entered the firm's lobby. She cast a vague glance at Mallory, zeroed in on Mac and then did a double take.

"Mallory?"

"It's my new look. Uh, Trudy, can we slip into Keith's office for a moment? There's something I need to check on."

"Certainly, help yourself. I know Keith wouldn't mind."

Mallory spun toward the office. Mac, much to his consternation, found that he couldn't take his eyes off her jeans as he fell in behind her. Though he lectured himself that this was no time to be thinking about making love to her, another part of him kept arguing that it might very well be the *only* time he ever could.

Mallory whooped with delight when she found the IBM still had a ribbon cartridge inside it. She flipped the lock lever and pulled the cartridge free from its base. After carrying it to Keith's desk, she bent over it and began turning the right-hand knob counterclockwise until a fair amount of black ribbon was unwound. She gave a section of it a close study and smiled.

"We're in luck, Mac. Grab a pad and pen. I'll call off the letters."

He hovered beside her, pen at the ready. The first string of letters she called off were part of a dated memo. No luck there. She skipped a section of tape. "*O—N—*an apostrophe, I think—*T—C—A—L—L—T—H—E—P—O—L*...." She heaved a disgusted sigh. "Is it making any sense at all yet?"

"Keep reading," he ordered in a tense voice.

"I—C—E—U—N—T—I—L—" She leaned over to see what he had written thus far and her eyes widened. "Don't call the police? Oh, Mac! This is it—part of the letter he sent with the key." Her hands began to shake as she bent back over the tape. "I *knew* it!"

"Calm down! You'll tear the film."

She closed her eyes for an instant and took a deep breath. "Right. I have to stay calm. Okay. Ready?"

He grunted, hardly able to contain himself as he jotted letters down and tried to make sense of them.

"D—O—N—another apostrophe, maybe a comma—*T—T—R—U—S—T—A—N—Y—O—N—E*—another itsy mark, an apostrophe or period—a period, I think—*I—A—M—C—O—U—N—T—I—N—G—O—N—Y—O—U*—a period—*K—E—I—T—H.*"

"Stop a sec." Mac frowned and went back over the last string of letters. "Don't trust anyone! I'm counting—yeah—I'm counting on you. Then he signed off. The rest, Mallory. The address should be coming up. Hurry, sweetheart."

"Um…" She squinted at the film and slowly began calling off letters again, unable to make words from them because she was too intent on deciphering the indistinct type. *"B—U—D—M—A—C—P—H—"*

Mac threw the pen down and grabbed her by the arm, nearly jerking her off her feet. As he hauled her with him across the room, he cried, "How could I be so stupid! He mailed it! That's why he looked at me that way!"

"What did it say?"

"He mailed it to *me!* Trudy was right. If he was in a jam, I'd be the one he'd call! I wasn't in town, so he mailed it to me. *I've* got the key, Mallory. I've had it the whole damned time and just didn't know it."

Trudy's eyes widened when they burst into the lobby. Mac dropped Mallory's arm and ran to the older woman's desk. "Trudy, I need to borrow your car."

"My car?" She leaned sideways to grab her purse off the shelf and get her keys. As she handed them to Mac, she said, "Why do you need my car?"

"Mine was blown up." Mac snagged the keys, blew her a kiss and grabbed Mallory's arm again. "Thanks, Trudy. You're an angel. Take a cab if I don't bring it back before you get off work. I'll pick up your tab later."

"But—blown up? Oh, my, what on earth is—"

They never heard the rest of what Trudy was going to say. Mac slammed the door behind them and took off down the hall at a run, hauling Mallory in his wake. When they reached the parking lot, he staggered to a stop. "Which car does she drive, anyway?"

"That Honda." The words were no sooner out than Mac was off and running again, towing her along. "If he mailed it to y—"

"He did. Trust me." He parted company with her at the fender of the car, ran around to the driver's side, unlocked the door and leaped in. For a moment, Mallory thought he might drive off without her, but he remembered her and unlocked her side. She climbed in and threw him a worried look. He didn't even notice, just kept talking nonstop. "We drive to my place, get my mail. Go to the bank, get the package. Spend the night at a motel. Wait for Lucetti's call in the morning at your place. It'll be a little risky getting inside your house. Might have to go before daylight so no one sees us and calls the cops, but—"

"Mac!"

He at last focused on her. "What?"

"The mail. *Your* mail?"

"What about it?"

"I gathered it up in that sack. It's *inside* my house. At least I hope it is. What if the police took it?"

For a moment, he stared at her. Then he swore—not under his breath this time—and began to pound his fists on the steering wheel. Mallory watched anxiously. At last, he leaned his head against the rest and closed his eyes, his teeth clenched.

"I—" She licked her lips. "I guess I really messed up. Oh, Mac, why didn't I *look* at the mail when I was gathering it."

"You were upset. It's not your fault. I didn't take time to *read* it. I can't believe I was so dense."

"Mac, we've scarcely had time to eat."

"But I've had it all this time! We've been running around like a couple of fools—" He broke off and groaned. "I hope the cops didn't take that sack as evidence. If they did, how will we ever get that key?"

THERE WAS NO SACK OF MAIL in the breakfast nook. Mac searched the kitchen, the day room, then the entire downstairs, dreading the moment when he'd have to tell Mallory. Either the killers had taken it, or the police had. Either way, they were in big trouble. He crept upstairs to grab Mallory's purse in case she needed it later, then left the house and snuck through the backyard, cutting across an adjoining property to reach Mallory where she waited in the Honda over on the next block. They hadn't been able to park nearby, for fear someone would spot them.

"Well?" she demanded when he climbed into the car. "Did you get it?"

He shook his head. "Don't panic, though. If the cops took it, we might still be in business."

"How so?"

"Remember that first night up at Lake Tuck? I told you one of my best buddies worked for the department? Well, I think he'll get me the key if I level with him."

"But the grapevine. You said we didn't dare tell any police."

"Not to have them do an investigation. Several policemen would have known about it then, and one of them could have leaked it to the wrong fellow. This is different. Scotty won't tell anyone."

"You're sure?"

He locked gazes with her. "Mallory, let's put it this way. We don't have any other options. I have to call him."

FIFTEEN MINUTES LATER, Mac was on hold, waiting to be put through to his friend, Scotty Herman, a King County detective. The moment Scotty heard Mac's voice, he began yelling so loudly that the sound reverberated inside the phone booth.

"What in hell are you up to, Mac? Do you know how disconcerting it is to be investigating a case and suddenly find out a friend is somehow involved? First the Volvo. Then a fried goon. Then a stolen car? We found your prints, you know."

Mac waited for Scotty to wind down, then explained the situation. "I'm counting on you to keep your lip zipped on this. You don't dare tell anyone. The kid could end up dead."

"Mac, you ever heard the cardinal rule? Call your local police? Who do you think you are, Superman? And now you want me to—" He broke off, cleared his throat and continued in a whisper. "You want me to steal evidence gathered from a homicide scene? Have you lost your mind? They itemize that stuff. I could lose my job."

"Just one little envelope, the one from Keith. Come on, Scotty. You can fix it so no one realizes anything's missing."

"You're asking me to put my career on the line."

"It's a kid's *life* on the line. Will you do it?"

Long silence. "Yeah, yeah, I'll do it. I'll meet you in two hours at the Denny's on 116th. We're even after this one, though. Consider me paid up in full."

"Scotty, I've never kept score. Two hours? I still have to get some fake ID made so I can get into Christiani's safe-deposit box sometime today."

"I didn't hear that." Scotty groaned. "Mac, breaking the law is one thing, but do you have to outline your itinerary to me before you go do it?"

"So throw me in jail. What should I do, let him kill her? What would *you* do, Scotty. I wanna hear this."

"Oh, shut up. Two hours, take it or leave it. I gotta go through channels, you know."

SCOTTY WAS A TALL, dark-haired man in a gray suit and a perfectly awful blue-gray tie with turquoise polka dots. Mac met him at the entrance of Denny's. Scotty seemed none too thrilled about standing around with Mac, so he passed the envelope with all speed, lifted a hand to acknowledge Mallory, who had stayed in the car, and left as quickly as he had come.

Mac hurried back to the car, ripped open the envelope, and whooped triumphantly when the key fell out in his hand. Mallory felt tears welling in her eyes and had to look away for a moment. Mac would have none of that. He placed a hand behind her head and pulled her toward him. "Home free, Mallory. We've got it."

She clung to him.

"Tomorrow, honey, and she'll be home. I'll set up the exchange with Lucetti when he calls in the morning." Bending his head, he kissed the tears from her cheeks. "What do you say we call the hospital and have the nurse tell Keith the good news, hmm? We'll have to watch what we say, but we should be able to get the message across. Then we'll run over to Seattle."

"Why do we need to go to Seattle?"

"I'll need authentic looking ID when I go to the bank. I know a guy downtown who can take Keith's identification, put my picture on it, alter the dates with transfer lettering, laminate it and no one will ever know it isn't mine."

Mallory's stomach clenched. She had completely forgotten that Mac would have to forge Keith's signature to get into the box. "Oh, Mac, what if it doesn't work?"

He caught her face between his hands and pressed a kiss on the tip of her nose. "Have I let you down yet?"

"No."

"Then trust me. I'll get that package if I have to rob the place."

He said it in a teasing tone, but when Mallory glanced over at him, there was a determined glint in his eye that made her wonder. She believed he would do it if it came to that, risk his whole future for a little girl he had never met. Her little girl. She stared straight ahead as he backed the Honda out of the parking space. Memories of last night drifted through her mind. She regretted nothing. She had fallen head over heels in love with this man. Sneaking another look at him, she decided that most women would. Big, rugged and handsome, with a heart like a marshmallow, that was Mac. One in a million.

MAC'S HANDWRITING WAS *worse* than Keith's—if that was possible. Mallory stared at his last attempt at duplicating Keith's signature, then cast a worried frown at the bank. "Mac, I'm afraid this won't work."

He held up his bandaged right hand. It looked as though it had been wrapped by a professional, which of course it should, since Mallory had done it. "A guy can't be expected to write too well when his hand is bunged up. Relax, Mallory. They don't know the life history of every customer. For the next ten minutes, I *am* Keith Christiani."

"If you get someone who knows him, you're sunk."

Mac jabbed a thumb skyward. "*He* has to take care of that part. Where's your faith? I'll be back before you know it."

Five minutes dragged by. Mallory tried not to look at her watch, but she couldn't help it. *Ten minutes.* How long could it take to open a safe-deposit box? Panic tightened her throat. She wasn't worried about Mac getting into trouble. She not only knew the best defense attorneys in the state, but she could also afford their fees. But Em… If Mac couldn't get that package, Mallory would have to get a court order to have the box opened. To do that, she would have to tell the authorities why. And if she did that Lucetti would kill her daughter.

Just when she was about to go inside to see what on earth was taking so long, Mac rounded the corner and came striding down the sidewalk toward the car. Tucked under one arm, he carried a large manila envelope. He was grinning from ear to ear, his eyes dancing with triumphant laughter.

CHAPTER FOURTEEN

ONCE THEY WERE certain they hadn't been followed from the bank, they went back to the same motel they had stayed in last night. They both sat on the bed, the ledgers and several of Steven Miles's letters spread before them. Mallory, sitting cross-legged, propped her elbows on her knees and covered her face with her hands. "This is a nightmare. Darren was murdered? It wasn't an accident?"

Her voice shook so badly that Mac put a hand on her shoulder to steady her. He knew how frightened she must feel. She'd just found out her daughter was being held by the same man who had slain her husband. "We knew Lucetti was slime. This just proves it."

"Worse than slime, a monster." Her eyes sought his, aching with questions. "Darren was a good person. Why kill him? And why inject him with an anticoagulant? All this time, I thought that—" She shook her head. "Why, Mac?"

"He knew too much. As for the anticoagulant, they probably wanted to be sure the wound would be fatal. It sounds like Lucetti's MO. No loose ends. He has a reputation for it."

A sick knot settled in Mac's stomach. He was as floored by the contents of the package as Mallory. Pete Lucetti didn't really exist? The identity was a front for a prominent Seattle businessman named John Carmichael?

The man was almost legend, the owner of two perfectly respectable and highly successful corporations. He had even run for mayor, and indications were that he'd win the next election. The more Mac read, the more it all made sense. Small wonder the cops could never nail Lucetti. He was a fanatic about never leaving evidence because Carmichael had too much to lose if any of his criminal activities were ever traced back to him. Mac remembered thinking that Lucetti's speech patterns were odd for a Seattle lowlife. He also remembered the lack of noise on the phone when Carmichael had called. The clues to Lucetti's true identity had been there all the time, but he had failed to see them.

"Keith was trying to make sure Darren's murderer was sent to prison. That's what got us into this whole mess, revenge?"

"You can't blame Keith, Mallory. Rather than turn the evidence over to Darren's killer, he tried to outsmart him. I'm sure he must have thought he could protect you. Things got out of hand. He had the stroke. It wasn't how he planned it."

She sighed and looked down at the letters Steven Miles had written. "Talk about a domino effect. Two girls come into Seattle, start working Carmichael's turf without paying him a percentage, and my little girl ends up paying for it."

"It's not quite that simple. It started with the two prostitutes, all right, but then it mushroomed, and finally involved Keith. Em is peripheral. Remember when I told you my friend, Corrine, was a decent sort, that she hated Lucetti? The reason is that he plays so dirty. Girls don't work his turf without giving him a cut—a big one. They end up with only a fraction of what they earn. If they complain, he has them roughed up. If they try to run out on him, he gets rougher. Once they go to work for him, there is no escape."

"And meanwhile he gets rich?"

"Exactly. And if they defy him like these two girls did?" He made a slashing motion across his throat. "Angela and Vicki and several other girls were skimming. Carmichael chose Vicki to take the fall."

"And Angela decided to avenge her by putting Carmichael in prison? She must have realized he would suspect she was gathering evidence against him and have her killed."

"Without a doubt. Carmichael runs a tight organization. He wouldn't have someone killed, then fail to monitor the movements of the victim's best friend. Angela knew that. He *did* overlook one thing, though. The dead girl and his accountant, Miles, had been having an affair."

"And Miles was in love with her?"

"He risked everything to avenge her murder."

Mallory closed her eyes for a moment, her head swimming. It was like reading a disjointed, convoluted mystery novel. She desperately needed to put it all in order. Right now, only one thing seemed clear, that Em was being held by a killer. The rest seemed like a nightmare of craziness.

Aloud, she went through it one more time. "So...two prostitutes named Vicki and Angela came into Seattle and were coerced into working for Lucetti—whom we now know is actually John Carmichael. Vicki became disillusioned and despite warnings from Angela and her lover, Steven Miles, she began holding out on Carmichael. Carmichael discovered she was cheating him and had her killed. Angela couldn't bear for Vicki's murder to go unpunished, even though she knew she could end up dead herself, and began compiling evidence to put Carmichael away."

"Right. And after about a year, when she had enough to send Carmichael up, she confided her plan to Steven Miles, gave him duplicates of the evidence, just in case something happened to her, and called your husband, the do-gooder lawyer, to see if he would help her. She would have been afraid of going to the police, remember, because she'd found out two men on the force had been bought."

Tears gathered in Mallory's eyes. "And of course, Darren agreed to take the evidence to the right people."

"So Angela arranged to bring it to him the next day."

"Only she was murdered before she could?"

"Probably within hours. I'm sure Darren didn't realize his own life was in danger."

"After Angela's call, Carmichael knew Darren might know who Pete Lucetti really was, so Darren had to be silenced. Within forty-eight hours, Darren was dead, his death made to look like an accident." Mallory sighed shakily. "So Miles was left holding the bag."

Mac nodded. "And plenty scared. Three people were dead. He assessed the situation and decided to wait to make his move until Carmichael's guard was down. Miles was an accountant—a man who spent most of his waking moments recording stuff. For years, he had been the head accountant for Carmichael, laundering his ill-gotten gains, so to speak, by making it all look legal on paper. After Vicki and Angela were killed, he decided to start a second set of records, a truthful set, documenting every criminal activity Carmichael's organization was involved in."

"An exposé."

"Exactly. The stuff Angela had dug up on Carmichael was probably child's play by comparison. If Miles was going to blow the whistle, he decided to go foghorn-style, tattling on everybody involved, the cops on the take, the pimps, the working girls, the bookies, everybody. When he got done, there would be no organization left."

"What a boon for Seattle that would have been."

Mac nodded. "While he waited, building up his evidence, he formed an alliance with—" Mac tapped a finger on one of the ledgers "—Paisley, Fields and Godbey, the murderous trio who've been chasing us—they skimmed the money, he doctored the books so Carmichael couldn't tell. The profits were divided four ways."

"And Miles slowly transferred his share to foreign banks?" Mallory asked.

"With enough money, a man can begin a new life anywhere. While Carmichael rotted in prison, Miles wanted to be lounging on a sunny beach someplace."

"But he needed someone he could trust to deliver the package to the D.A."

"And who better than Keith Christiani?" Mac looked resigned. "Keith was knowledgeable about the law, knew which authorities to contact, and he would be well motivated to want Carmichael behind bars once he received evidence Darren had been murdered."

"So Miles sent Keith a copy of the exposé accompanied by lengthy letters of explanation, asking him to help get the package to the D.A.'s office."

"My guess is that Miles called Keith to be certain he had received the evidence in the mail."

Mallory licked her lips. "Which was probably his mistake. Carmichael, typically paranoid, must have become suspicious of Miles for some reason and had his phone tapped."

"And Miles was killed. Then, of course, the threats against Keith started. He was told to return the package to Carmichael, or else."

"But instead Keith tried to trick him?"

"Carmichael said Keith mailed him a dummy package and must have put the real one in his safe-deposit box. He probably planned to get you and Em out of town before Carmichael received the package, and have me deliver the key to the district attorney after you were safe. Then something went haywire. He called me and was leaving me a message when he collapsed. The rest, we know."

Mallory shoved the papers away as if the sight of them sickened her. Dropping her forehead to rest against her palm, she whispered, "One thing doesn't make sense. Those three men, how did they know that Miles had exposed their skimming activities?"

A grim smile curved his mouth. "Remember when I was questioning Chapin down in Seattle the other night? He said Carmichael had sicced three goons on Miles, one named Fields?"

Mallory leafed quickly through the papers. "Fields! One of the men who had skimmed with Miles!"

"Exactly. This is only conjecture, but my guess is that after hearing that telltale phone conversation between Keith and Miles, Carmichael sent his not-so-trustworthy employees to eliminate Miles and get the ledgers. They probably caught Miles by surprise, and saw his copy of the exposé. When they realized exactly what was in it, they knew they would wind up dead if Carmichael ever saw it."

"So they destroyed the set Miles had and started trying to get their hands on the set Carmichael had told them Miles had sent to Keith?"

"And so began the frantic search for the safe-deposit-box key. When they couldn't find it, they had one other option."

"To take me out of the picture? So the entire time Carmichael has been trying to make me cough up the evidence, those three have been trying to keep me from it?"

"Exactly. They're probably terrified. Carmichael doesn't slap hands. They were racing against time. They needed you out of the way. I'm sure Keith would have been next. Eventually someone would have been awarded the contents of the safe-deposit box. Once that person had the package, they would have stolen it."

"And killed anyone who got in their way."

"Their lives are on the line, Mallory. These fellows have killed for less."

Mallory groaned. "Poor Keith. It must have been awful for him when he realized he wasn't going to be able to pull things off." Her voice rang hollow. "His only hope was to reach you. He must have thought you were due back that day."

"I *was* due back that day. Something came up, and I came home a day late, which was why I went directly to the baseball field after I landed at Sea-Tac." Mac sighed. "No wonder poor Keith had the stroke. He was under incredible pressure."

"Not to mention the shock it must have been to learn Darren had been murdered. I wish he had confided in me. But I guess he thought the less I knew, the safer I was." Mallory lifted her head. Her mouth trembled. "I still can't believe Darren was murdered. He was a gun collector, you know, antique weapons." She made a feeble little gesture with her hands. "It looked as if he had been cleaning one of the weapons and it had accidentally discharged. It—under the chin—and he was bleeding everywhere. I had taken Em shopping. When we came home, we found him in the den."

"Oh, Mallory, I never knew you were the one who found him."

Her eyes widened. "Why did you think I quit nursing?"

"I figured you got bored with it. With your money, you don't have to work."

She leaped off the bed, pacing back and forth as the full implication of what he had just said sank in. "Bored with it? Nursing was the most important thing in my life except for my husband and child." She whirled and held out her hands, her eyes flashing with anger. "Oh, Mac, why can't you look beyond my father's money to the person I am? Do you think it's fun being raised in a wealthy family? Do you think I wasn't aware of the Third World? Of all the sick and homeless?"

"I guess I never thought about it."

"Yes, you did. You just assumed I didn't care."

It was an undeniable truth, so Mac made no reply.

"When I was young I wanted to join the Peace Corps. Did you know that?"

"Why didn't you?"

"My folks came unglued. They wanted me to fulfill *their* dream, which was to marry into the *right* family and drive around in one of those fifty-thousand-dollar cars you hate so much. I was young—easily intimidated—my father is a master at intimidation. I finally compromised and went into nursing. They weren't thrilled, but it was better than my being a missionary."

She shoved her hands into her back pockets and smiled

wistfully. "I met Darren in college. Miracle of miracles, he was from an *acceptable* family. We were going to make a difference, he and I, he with his law practice and me with my nursing. He and Randy planned to open a law office in Seattle, a place that would volunteer legal services to the poor. They both planned to work there in addition to jobs at a regular law firm. I worked for nothing at a low-income clinic." A bitter twist replaced the smile on her lips. "Like you said, I didn't *need* the money."

The mention of Randy made Mac glance away.

"Oh, yes, I know who you are," she blurted out. "I've known since I saw Randy's photograph at your apartment."

"Why didn't you say something?"

She hesitated before answering. "I was afraid you might walk out on me."

"Mallory…" He lifted an eyebrow. "And now?"

"Now I know you never would, no matter how badly you might hate me. You'd stay for Em. And for Keith. I didn't have enough faith in you. I apologize for that. But I was scared."

"Mallory, I don't hate you." He raked a hand through his hair. "At least not anymore."

"But you did. For years. Admit it, Mac. The very least we owe each other is the truth."

He avoided meeting her eyes. "I was wrong to blame you. It was Bettina Rawlins who hurt Randy, not you."

The fact that he couldn't look at her when he admitted it didn't make Mallory feel too hot. With a shock, she realized that he hadn't completely vindicated her yet. That hurt. Especially when she recalled their lovemaking. *Trust me, Mallory. Don't hold back.* The memories humiliated her.

"Mac…you don't *still* blame me, do you?"

"No—not—oh, hell, I don't know." He sighed. "I know now that I was wrong. But there's still this—"

"Doubt?" she supplied shrilly.

"Not doubt, exactly, just a lingering…distaste." He stared at the rug, scraping a bare spot in the nap with his toe. "I've spent fourteen years of my life hating the kind of woman you are. Bettina Rawlins destroyed my brother. He had such big dreams before meeting her. And by the time she was done with him, he was sure he wasn't good enough to be a shoe-shine boy. I had to watch his life disintegrate. All because of a no good, self-centered little piece of fluff who led him on. It's not easy to do an about-face after that. Give me some time."

"Exactly what *kind* of woman do you think I am?"

He looked distinctly uncomfortable and still avoided eye contact with her. "I always believed you were spoiled and empty-headed and selfish, like Bettina." The electrical silence that punctuated that admission spurred him to add, "You *did* ask for the truth. I'm not saying that's what you *are,* only that I perceived you that way."

Mallory fought to maintain her self-control. She had been under a lot of pressure these past few days. She knew her nerves were probably shot, and Mac's probably were, as well. If they lost their tempers… She ground her teeth. Spoiled, empty-headed and selfish, was she? With biting sarcasm, she said, "What's that saying Marines have about women? If she's ugly, put a flag over her head and do it for the glory? You've got your own version for shallow, spoiled rich women. Turn off the lights and do it for the heck of it!"

His eyes flew to hers, filled with shock. "Mallory!"

The censure in his tone galled her. "Don't Mallory me.

How can you make love to me and then, only a few hours later, use the word *distaste* when you're referring to me?"

He stared at her, saying nothing.

"What was it? I was convenient? The pillow wasn't big enough? You wanted revenge? What?"

"I don't think that deserves an answer."

All the stress Mallory had been under these past few days began to roil within her and surged up her throat in a wave of irrational rage. "Do you remember when you accused *me* of using you? I think maybe it was the other way around." Even as she spoke, her throat tightened around the words. "What was it, your way of avenging Randy? Daddy's little rich girl finally gets her just deserts?"

He said nothing to defend himself, which only fueled her anger.

"Randy *was* twenty-three, old enough to make his own decisions. If he fell for Bettina's lines, how can you possibly hold me accountable for it? Do you really think Darren and I didn't try to warn him? Blame me, by all means, if it makes you feel better. Blame everyone in Bellevue. I can understand your resenting me, truly I can. Especially when you didn't know me. But I think it's gone beyond resentment when you *use* someone who cares for you for some sick sort of revenge."

Mac leaned forward. He knew he wasn't himself right now and that he should keep his mouth shut. His nerves were raw. He was exhausted. It was no time to engage in this kind of fight. Tongues could draw blood, and when he got mad, his could be razor sharp. He didn't want to hurt Mallory. He had hurt her enough already. But after everything he had tried to do, all the risks he had taken, how could she accuse him of using her? "Don't sling garbage unless you want it slung back. I didn't *use* you, lady. You were panting for it, *begging* for it. I turned you down once. What do you think I'm made of, rock? *Love me, Mac.* Isn't that what you said? Not to mention the fact that you were *crawling* all over me. *Used* you? Don't make me laugh. As for Randy, let's leave him out of this, shall we? Without me, where will you and Em be? Up the creek, that's where."

Mallory's legs were shaking so badly that she thought she might fall. She looked at him beseechingly, unwilling to believe he really meant what he'd just said.

Mac cradled his head in his hands. After a long while, he said, "I didn't mean that. I couldn't walk out on you and Em."

She wrapped her arms around herself. "I know that," she said softly. "Do you think I would sleep with a man I thought was heartless?"

He shot her a glare. "You must think I'm pretty heartless if you think last night was my way of getting back at you."

"What was it, then? If you still blame me, you can't *like* me, let alone have any deeper feelings. What is sex without feeling? What did last night mean to you? Anything?"

That did it. Mac shot up off the bed. "You tell me! You're so good at analysis. I suppose you studied it in school."

"Another count against me, hmm? A college education. I think you're so confused, you don't know what you think. Guilt has a way of doing that to you."

"And what would you know about guilt? Give me a break."

"I know plenty. I quit nursing, didn't I?"

"What's that mean?"

"It means—" Her voice broke. "It means I thought it was partly my fault Darren died."

He froze midstride.

"Don't look at me like that. Do you think you're the only person who lost someone and blamed himself? I not only wasn't there when he needed me, but I couldn't help him when I finally got there. I couldn't stop the bleeding. And I was a *trained* nurse."

"He was pumped full of anticoagulant."

"I didn't know that!" She turned away from him. "My first thought was to slow the bleeding before I called an ambulance. I wasted precious time. I thought I knew what to do, that *I* could take the preliminary steps to help save him. And he died."

Mac touched her shoulder, and she jerked away.

"He bled to death in my arms. After that, I thought of all the things I *should* have done. Sound familiar? I started to lose confidence in my abilities. I felt panicky when I was left alone with an injured patient. Finally one afternoon after a man was brought into the clinic after a car wreck, I quit. Threw my hat and pin into the trash and just walked out. I didn't want another life on my conscience." She passed a hand over her eyes. "I was afraid. Afraid that I wasn't good enough. And so are you."

Mac chose to ignore that comment. "So you quit doing what you loved. I saw you in action with Mark, remember. You're a natural, an excellent nurse."

"I thought I was once." She dashed tears from her cheeks. "Who knows. Maybe now, I can try again."

"Maybe?"

"You think *I* should do an about-face more easily than you did?"

He rolled his eyes. "Mallory, you don't fight fair."

"And you don't judge fairly. I'd say that makes us even."

"I never meant to judge you. And that crack about distaste, I didn't mean it the way it sounded. It's just that—"

"Yes?"

"The money gets in my way."

"It didn't last night."

His eyes narrowed. "Last night, the last thing on my mind was how much money you had. You were terrified for your daughter. You needed me."

Her daughter. A wave of guilt washed over Mallory. Nothing should matter to her right now but Emily. Confused by the myriad emotions washing over her, she couldn't make sense of anything. She only knew that Mac had insinuated himself into her world and become as important to her as the air she breathed. That feeling in no way distracted her from her concerns about Emily. Somehow, Mac wasn't peripheral to her love for her daughter anymore but, inexplicably, a part of it. "I can get rid of the money, you know. Or only use it for helping people."

The plea in her eyes was unmistakable. Mac longed to take her in his arms, but to do so would have been dishonest. If he and Mallory were to have a future together, and his mind emphasized the *if*, then they'd have to find equal ground to build it on. He couldn't let her throw her money away because of him, but he couldn't accept the fact that she had it. It seemed an insurmountable obstacle, especially now, when both of them were so consumed with finding her daughter. There wasn't time to worry about their relationship right now, to sort it out, to make sense of it. And until there was time, it was better to say nothing.

"I'm already using it to help people," she told him, her gaze still clinging to his. "Remember the office Darren and Randy planned to open, the legal-aid center for the poor? Darren opened it after he passed the bar. I've funded it since his death so it wouldn't close down. *Christiani and Watts,* after Darren and Randy. That's where I told Danno he could get on-the-job training."

Mac could only stare at her for what seemed endless minutes. "Darren opened a firm and named it after my brother? Why didn't Keith ever tell me?"

Mac averted his face. He knew why Keith had never told him. Keith had wanted him to work his way through the bitterness on his own. To find his own truth, however long it took, however painful the healing might be. In the end, it had taken the kidnapping of a child to get through to him; and, of course, getting to know Mallory. Seeing how desperately she loved her daughter. Sharing in her pain. Tasting her panic.

If only things were as simple as they looked on the surface. Was Mallory right? Was he afraid he wasn't good enough? *Yes.* Not good enough for her and not good enough to be a parent to her child. Until he ironed out his feelings, how could he and Mallory continue in a relationship? Every time he looked at her, he saw something to remind him of how inadequate he was and remembered Randy's heartbreak.

"What do you say we let things ride until this is over? We're both exhausted. We have a lot of planning to do. What's between us will still be there later."

"Unfortunately." Mallory swallowed back any further retort. He was right about putting everything on hold. They had Em to think of. Their relationship, whatever remained of it, could be examined later.

They left it at that, but the unspoken was still there between them. Mac sat back down on the bed and began studying the documents again. "You name it, Carmichael has a finger in it. Illegal betting, stolen merchandise, collecting protection money. Murder. Pimping."

"What should we do about the two men still after us?"

"See they get their comeuppance. What else?" A lazy smile curved his mouth. "Sit down, Mallory. What do you think of this plan?"

Mallory lowered herself into the chair, acutely aware that he was still avoiding eye contact with her. The tension between them left her feeling shattered. She had grown so dependent upon his strength. Now she felt as though he had withdrawn his support. Just when she needed him the most—when the situation with Em was finally reaching a critical point.

"I'm going to take the package to my office and put it in my combination safe. Then we'll slip back into your house in the morning to wait for Carmichael's call, just as we planned. I'll arrange a meeting with him, to exchange the package for Emily, at the Seattle City Center, by that big round fountain."

She knew the place. "How can you do that if the package is in your safe?"

"Just listen. I'll be the go-between and carry the package to Carmichael. While Em walks to you around one side of the fountain, I'll walk to him around the other. When I reach him, I'll tell him I'm carrying a dummy package, that only I know where the real package is. I'll take Em's place as hostage. You run with Em into the crowd. Carmichael won't dare shoot in the crowd, and he won't want to kill me until he gets that package, right? I'll tell him it might fall into the wrong hands if something should happen to me. That will ensure that you and Em can get out of there safely. I'll make arrangements with

Shelby to get you both out of town before I agree to take Carmichael to the package, and Shelby will keep you safe until everything is over."

"No!" Mallory shot up from her chair. "You'll end up dead. No way, Mac."

"I already have an escape plan. And once I'm away from Carmichael, I'll go to my office, get the evidence and take it to the authorities. Happy ending."

"It's too risky. What if you can't escape?"

"I've been in tighter spots. I'll get away. And if I can't find a way out, I can always take him to the safe and give him the package, Mallory. That would mean you and I would have to take Em and go into hiding, but it would be better than dying. Trust me, I don't have a death wish." At last he looked deeply into her eyes. "Mallory, use your head. You have Em's safety to think of. Carmichael will be more willing to go along if I'm the hostage. I'm a professional. I'm more of a threat to him than you are. He'll figure you'll do as you're told, no questions. I might play the hero, make trouble."

"She's *my* daughter." Mallory doubled her hands into fists. She knew he couldn't really have an escape plan. There were too many variables. "I'll be the go-between."

"No," Mac replied stubbornly. "Em needs you. So, we either do it my way, or we don't do it at all."

She knew arguing with him wouldn't do any good. His pride would never let him stand aside while she went to Carmichael. As noble a gesture as it was, there was no way she could just let him do it. There had to be something she could do to help him get away once Em was safe.

Mac stood and reached for his jacket where it was draped over the back of the chair. After slipping it on, he began gathering the papers on the bed.

"Where do you think you're going?"

"To put this in my safe."

"Not without me, you aren't."

He groaned. "Mallory, I'd like to keep you out of this for now. The less you know, the safer you are."

"You can't keep me out of it. I'm already in up to my neck. Em's *my* daughter, not yours."

"Do you realize how dangerous this could be?" he asked. "Just getting to my office will be a feat in itself. We're not only going to have to make certain we're not tailed, but after we get there, we have to be sure no one's staking out the building."

"Then I'll come in handy, won't I? You'll be needing a second pair of eyes. As for anyone who might be watching the building? If we see someone we'll just call the police and report a nutcase in the building who's wearing nothing but a raincoat who's hiding and leaping out at women. Not even Lucetti's goons would be stupid enough to make a move on us when the place is crawling with cops."

Mac couldn't keep from grinning. "You have a devious streak, don't you?"

"You're just now realizing that? Either you're slow, Mac, or I haven't been performing up to my usual standards since we've been hanging around together."

A HALF HOUR LATER, Mac was sitting at his desk, addressing a large manila envelope to Scotty Herman. Inside were copies of the ledgers, which Mallory had helped make, and all of Miles's correspondence to Keith, which was self-explanatory. Mac knew he could count on Scotty to get the evidence into the right hands. And with mail time delaying things, Scotty wouldn't receive it until well after Em and Mallory were safely away. There was no risk this way of cops on the take reporting back to Carmichael and endangering either of them.

Mac tossed his pen on his desk and rose from his chair. He had sent Mallory up the hall to a pop machine so he could fill out the address on the envelope while she was out of the room. She'd be back soon. Picking up the package, he hurried out into the hall and dropped the envelope into the mail drop. Because Mallory had insisted on coming, Mac had had no choice but to let her know he had made copies, but he didn't dare tell her who he was sending them to. Number one, she'd be upset, fearing the wrong people in the precinct would get hold of them. And he also had to think of Scotty's safety. If something went wrong and Mallory didn't escape with Em, Carmichael was probably an expert at making people talk. As long as Mallory didn't know who would receive the copies, Scotty wouldn't be endangered.

Returning to the office, Mac gave the room a long, slow study, committing it to memory. This might be the last time he ever stood in here. He had a lot of good memories. His gaze drifted to the clutter on top of his desk. If he had time, he would clean it up. Less mess for someone else to sort through. A grin tilted his mouth. Might as well go out like he had lived. Why disappoint everybody?

He sighed and glanced at the telephone. It reminded him he still had to get to a pay phone and call Shelby. He was the one person Mac trusted enough to take care of Em and Mallory.

"ANY PROBLEMS?" MALLORY stepped into the room just as Mac glanced away from the phone. She popped the seal on a can of Coke and set it on the desk for him.

Mac avoided looking at her. He had never been good

at deceptions. "None. One package is in the mail. The other is in the safe. All I have left to do is make arrangements with Shelby."

"Who did you send the copies to?"

Mac smiled ruefully. Count on Mallory to ask the one question he had hoped she wouldn't. "I can't tell you that."

He expected an argument, but to his surprise, Mallory nodded. "Good precaution. What I don't know, I can't repeat." Catching the surprise in his expression, she added, "I want to help, Mac. And I want to know what's going on. But not when it serves no good purpose or jeopardizes someone's safety. What sort of arrangements are you making with Shelby?"

He handed her a piece of paper. "That's his address. I'll make sure he'll be there waiting for you and Em tomorrow. I don't want him anywhere near the center, just in case Carmichael or his goons spotted him. When you arrive at Shelby's, he'll take you out of Seattle to that mountain cabin I told you about. After you're both safe, he'll call my answering machine at the office and leave the number of a phone booth near the hideout so I'll be able to contact him later. Carmichael will have to let me call if I tell him that's the only way he'll get the package. I can call my answering machine and get the number after the twenty-four hours are up. That way I'll know you're safe before I make my break. Once I'm free I'll call Shelby. We'll set a time for him to be waiting at his end."

Mallory felt slightly sick. Mac's plan was nearly in motion, and it looked as if it could work. But what if it backfired?

"We'll arrange the exchange in the late afternoon so the Seattle City Center will be packed with people. This time of year, there should be crowds of vacationers. Carmichael won't want any trouble if he's afoot. And I'm going to demand he come himself."

"But then he'll know that we know his true identity."

"He already does. We've seen the ledgers, remember? He's got to know that. I want the weasel there, Mallory, so there won't be any surprises. He'll be too worried about his own skin to play any tricks."

"Oh, Mac." Despite their recent argument, Mallory set her can of pop down and hurried around the desk to him.

To her surprise, he enfolded her in his arms without hesitation. "Nothing'll happen. Think about you and Em and Keith all being together again."

How could she make him see that for her the picture no longer seemed idyllic without him being included?

CHAPTER FIFTEEN

THE NEXT NINE hours passed as slowly for Mallory as cold molasses dripping through a pinhole. Mac, being the kind man he was, tried to set their differences aside and be supportive of her, but nothing could really lessen her anguish. She spent the night sitting up in bed, a slat in the headboard crushing her spine, her gaze fastened on shadows as she thought about Emily and all the things that could go wrong during the exchange. She was also trying desperately to come up with a plan to rescue Mac once *he* became Carmichael's hostage. Mac lay beside her, awake most of the time, her hand cradled in his, his thumb making circles on her skin.

Long before dawn, they drove to her place. As he had once before, Mac drove up and down the side streets near her house looking for watchers before pulling into the cul-de-sac. Mallory scanned the neighborhood for any suspicious movements in the shrubs while Mac searched for strange cars. They saw nothing. They broke the police seals on her garage door to sneak inside the house to await Carmichael's phone call. Since they couldn't afford to be seen, they had to sit there in the semidarkness for hours.

When it grew light enough, Mac passed some of the time showing her how to use his gun, a Smith & Wesson .38 Chief's Special. Mallory swallowed down her aversion to firearms. If her becoming proficient with a gun would increase Emily's chances, then Mallory was determined to cooperate. She did exactly as Mac instructed: loading, snapping the cylinder into place and taking a firing stance to grip the gun with both hands to aim. When she sighted down the barrel, she imagined Carmichael's face as a target. Could she kill someone? Sweat trickled down her spine. For Emily's sake, Mallory knew she could do almost anything.

They repeated the procedure with the gun until Mallory could do it by rote. When they were finished, Mac gave her six extra cartridges to carry in her jeans pocket. She didn't ask why. She didn't want to know. After the gun lesson, they went over their plans again, step by step, so she would know exactly how to reach Shelby once the exchange had taken place. She could tell by the expression in Mac's eyes that he didn't expect to meet her at the hiding place in two days as he claimed he would. Fear coiled within her like a poisonous snake and seeped its venom into her system. She wouldn't let him die. Not after all he'd done for her and Emily. She *wouldn't*.

When the phone finally rang, she was shaking. Until now, Carmichael had called most of the shots. Now she and Mac were going to make demands. There was no way they could anticipate Carmichael's reaction, whether it would be angry or retaliatory. Mallory couldn't help but be frightened. It wasn't her own life she was gambling with, but her daughter's.

Mac stood beside her while she answered the phone. Mallory took a deep breath, sent up a prayer and then said, "Hello?"

"You have it?"

"Yes, Mr. Carmichael, I have it." There was complete silence after she said his name. Licking her lips, Mallory rushed on. "I'll meet you by the fountain at the Seattle City Center, one o'clock. You, Mr. Carmichael, not a stand-in. You may bring one man with you, no more. If you send someone in your place or if I see you've brought more than one man, I'll leave. I'll stand on the west side of the fountain, you on the east."

To her surprise, Carmichael didn't argue. "You'll come alone, no police."

"I'm bringing Mr. Mac Phearson. He's going to be the go-between. As he walks toward you around one side of the fountain with the package, I want my daughter walking alone toward me around the other side."

"That sounds fair. If Mac Phearson's going to be there, I want him in plain view so I can keep an eye on him."

"So it's agreed? One o'clock this afternoon?"

"Agreed."

Mac grabbed the phone from Mallory's hands. "Carmichael? One more thing. If you expect this exchange to go off without a hitch, you'd better call off your goons, Paisley, Fields and Godbey, whichever two of them are still alive. After going through Miles's correspondence last night, we have reason to believe they're the men who have been trying to kill Mrs. Christiani. The one who died, in fact, was electrocuted the night before last after breaking into her house. They don't want you seeing those ledgers because the evidence Miles recorded incriminates them. They worked with Miles, skimming your profits. Miles doctored your books so you wouldn't suspect."

Another long silence ensued on Carmichael's end. "Rest assured, they won't be bothering Mrs. Christiani anymore."

Mac nodded. "And now the child? I'd like to speak with her."

"I anticipated that."

Mac heard a rustling sound, then Em said, "Mommy?" Mac smiled and handed the phone over to Mallory. The glow that washed over her face upon hearing her daughter's voice made Mac's heart catch. Love like that, so perfect, so selfless, was rare. Mac had never been self-sacrificing and he certainly harbored no suicidal tendencies, but bringing Emily home to her mother was something he was willing to risk his life for. Even though the odds were stacked against him.

TWELVE FIFTY-THREE. MALLORY glanced from her watch to the opposite side of the fountain, her heart slamming like a sledgehammer as she scanned the milling crowd. *Emily.* It seemed like years since she had seen her, held her in her arms. Seven more minutes. What if Carmichael didn't come? What if he planned a double cross? What if he had planned one all along? What if Em was already dead? Mallory's legs began to shake. She had a sudden, painful urge to go to the ladies' room. When she tried to pray, the words jumbled in her head.

"Here they come," Mac whispered.

Mallory was suddenly conscious of the pistol Mac had given her that was stuck in her waistband. She pulled her sweater to be sure it was covered, and turned to gaze across the expanse of water. Coming in the entrance gate, she saw Carmichael. She recognized him immediately from pictures she had seen of him in newspapers. He was a tall, attractive man with brown hair, very refined looking and well dressed, not at all what one would expect. Beside him walked a shorter, gray-haired man, also dressed in a suit. Criminals? Killers? Kidnappers? It didn't seem possible. Her gaze dropped to the amber-

haired child in a red-plaid school jumper who walked between them. Tears rushed to Mallory's eyes. Em, alive
and well. *Thank you, God.*

Mac turned slightly and placed a hand on her shoulder.
When she looked up, she found his eyes intent on her face.
"Mallory, just in case…once they get here, I may not have
another chance to tell you that…" His voice trailed off
and he cleared his throat. "I just want you to know…" His
expression became taut. Very quickly, he bent his head
and brushed his lips across hers. "I'll never forget. I'll
treasure the memory of being with you as long as I live."

She caught his sleeve before he could turn away. Tears
rolled down her cheeks, leaving cold trails on her skin.
She felt her face contorting, her mouth twisting. "Thank
you. For bringing her back to me. Thank you so much."

He cupped her cheek in his hand. "When you get to
Shelby's, would you do something for me? Tell him this
one is a ringer. He'll know what it means."

She dashed the wetness from her cheeks. "A ringer.
Yes, I'll tell him."

Mac repositioned the manila envelope under his arm
and turned to watch Carmichael's approach. Taking a
deep breath, he steeled himself to start around the fountain. A few more steps and Carmichael would reach his
destination. Mac lowered his gaze to the child and feasted
his eyes on her for a moment. A miniature of Mallory.
Even at this distance, her eyes looked as big as dinner
plates in her elfin face.

Carmichael looked nervous as he drew to a stop. He
checked Mac over to be sure he had the package. Mac
lifted his jacket to show that he wasn't armed. Carmichael nodded and scanned the surrounding area for any
sign of police. When at last he seemed satisfied, he gave

another nod and released his hold on Em's hand. Mac started walking. For a moment the child just stood there, seemingly unaware that her mother was nearby. She had her head tipped back to study the Space Needle, the tallest structure in the city center. Carmichael said something to her and pointed. Em leaned sideways to see around the spiral of orange metal in the center of the fountain, her gaze following the direction of Carmichael's finger. The next instant, her small face lit up with delight. "Mommy!"

Before Carmichael could react, Em bolted in the wrong direction and came around the south side of the fountain toward Mac. Mac's guts coiled into icy knots.

"Freeze, Mac Phearson!" Carmichael yelled.

Mac stepped away from the fountain and held his arms out from his sides. *Please, God, don't let him panic.* Carmichael reached under his jacket, his attention riveted on the fleeing child. *Don't let him shoot. Please, not at the kid.* Mac tensed, ready to knock Em to the ground as she passed if Carmichael drew his weapon. The little girl sped by, so close Mac could have touched her, her big brown eyes riveted on her mother, her face aglow with anticipation. "Mommy?"

"Em," Mallory cried. "Oh, Em!"

Standing where he was, Mac was afforded a view of Mallory as she caught her daughter up in her arms. It was a moment he was glad he hadn't missed. Mallory sobbing, Em chattering like a magpie, every few words interrupted by a giggle. For just an instant, Mac allowed himself to drink in the sight of them, amber heads glinting in the sunshine, their faces shimmering. Then he forced himself to turn and start walking. When next he glanced back, Mallory and her child had disappeared into the crowd.

MALLORY'S HANDS SHOOK as she shoved the key into the ignition of the Honda. She had checked for explosives before getting into the car, but that didn't mean there was no one nearby, sighting on them with a rifle. She was so panicked that she forgot to depress the clutch and the car lurched when she started the engine. Em, perched on the passenger seat, fastened wide eyes on her.

"Mommy, why did you lay on the ground before we got in? You're shivering. This isn't our car. Did you buy a new one? Is Gramps okay?"

Mallory got the car started. A thick line of traffic had her momentarily boxed in. Keeping the clutch depressed, she leaned sideways and gave her daughter another swift hug, afraid to linger for fear Carmichael might have set a trap. Em clung to her like a little octopus, her plump arms squeezing Mallory's neck. Prying her loose, Mallory smoothed her hair and flashed what she knew was an unconvincing smile. "Oh, darling, yes, Gramps is okay. I'm just in a hurry, that's all. We're going to meet a new friend. His name is Shelby, and he's expecting us. If we're late, he may worry."

"I thought your new friend was named Mac."

"Yes. Shelby is another new friend. We can have more than one new friend, can't we? How are you, princess? Did those people treat you nice? They weren't—" Mallory tightened her hold on the steering wheel. "Were they cross or anything?"

There was still no break in the line of traffic. Mallory watched her rearview mirror.

"No. They were nice. There was a cat named Peaches and a parakeet. Can we have a parakeet? They can learn to talk, you know. I watched lots of movies. Ruthie, the lady, rented some dumb ones, though."

"But she was nice to you?"

"Yes, except for when I let the bird loose and Peaches tried to eat him." Em's small face puckered in a frown. "Mommy, why did you leave me there if you thought Ruthie wouldn't treat me nice? I liked it better at Beth's house."

"I didn't—" Mallory flashed her daughter a too-bright smile. "It's been a busy week. I'm glad Ruthie was nice. Peaches didn't hurt the bird, I hope."

Em grinned. "Nope, but he made snags in the curtains climbing up them. Ruthie's face turned purple and her eyes bugged at me. I thought she might spank me, but she didn't."

Mallory swerved out when a break in traffic gave her the opportunity. Then she forced herself to concentrate on driving. Em was safe. At least, she soon would be. *Think, Mallory.* She checked her mirrors, glanced out the side windows. *No tail.* Without signaling, she swung across two lanes and took a sharp left turn. After being around Mac, she knew better than to drive directly to Shelby's. No way. If Carmichael had someone following her, she'd give them a merry chase or die trying.

"Mommy, you just went on a red light."

Mallory laughed softly and nodded. "I did, didn't I? Wonders never cease. Are you buckled in? Good girl. If I tell you to, Em, you undo your belt and get on the floorboard, okay? We're going to play *running from bad guys.* Sound fun?"

"Not very."

"Well, fun or not, humor me."

"Okay. What kind of bad guys?"

"The kind we don't want to catch us. *Bad* bad guys."

"Are we going to play it until we get to Shelby's?"

"Yes, darling, until we get to Shelby's."

SHELBY LIVED IN a new high rise on the west side. Mallory parked on the street and glanced at the paper she'd pulled from her pocket. His was apartment 1410. She climbed out of the car and tipped her head back to look up at the building. Would he welcome them? Be hostile? Recalling the conversation she had overheard between him and Mac, she fought off apprehension. Mac trusted Shelby. He had extracted her promise that she would come here. It was too late to change arrangements at this point.

Mallory helped her daughter from the car and then drew her toward the high-rise entrance, holding tightly to her small hand. *Please, let him be nice.* If he was unpleasant—if he so much as *seemed* reluctant to help them—how could she possibly leave Em with him?

"Mommy, is Shelby nice?"

"Mmm, yes, very nice." Mallory wasn't sure who she was trying to convince, Em or herself. She pressed the elevator button. "He's Mac's best friend, so he has to be a nice man."

"Do you like Mac a lot?"

Mallory had forgotten how many questions Emily could ask. She smiled as she pulled her into the elevator. "I like him very much."

The elevator jerked and then began its ascent. Em grasped the handrail. "Very *very* much?"

Dropping to her knees, Mallory wrapped both arms around her daughter. This was the first opportunity she had had to simply hold her, to *absorb* the fact that she was actually here and in one piece. Unshed tears ached behind her eyes. Em, of course, didn't realize how close

she had come to dying so Mallory had to play down her
own relief to avoid frightening her. This wasn't the first
time that she and Mallory had been separated, so Em
couldn't see what the big deal was. Mallory was grateful
to Carmichael for that. The man had *some* good in him.

"Yes, Em, I like Mac very very much. But not as much
as you."

"Silly, you *love* me."

The elevator doors slid open. Mallory took Emily's
hand in hers again. Together, they exited into a plushly
carpeted hall. Arrows indicated that Shelby's apartment
was to her right. Mallory turned, tugging Em along beside her. Apartment 1410 was only a few doors down.
Mallory halted before the door and took a deep, bracing breath. Here went nothing. She rapped softly. Seconds later, she heard a chain rasp and the portal opened
a crack. A tall black man with a mustache and dimples
peered out. There was a hard, rough edge to his features,
but he had twinkling eyes that glowed warm and friendly
from his brown face.

"Are you Shelby?"

"That's my name. You must be Mallory." The door
swung wide. "And *you* must be—Ellen? Or was it Etta?
Esther? Emma?"

Emily giggled as she and Mallory stepped across the
threshold. "You're getting warmer. I'm—"

Shelby held up a hand. "No, no, don't give it away! If I
can't get it right, I have to pay off with a banana split from
the Dairy Queen. House rule around here if you forget
somebody's name. You *do* like banana splits?"

"Yummy. My favorite."

"Oh, that's good. We wouldn't have hit it off at all if
you didn't." Shelby shut the door and fastened the chain.

Meeting Mallory's gaze over the top of Em's head, his expression grew suddenly serious. "Did everything go all right?"

What could she say? Yes, it went fine? A lump rose in Mallory's throat. "He—um—yes, well enough. He gave me a message for you. He said to tell you this one was a ringer."

Shelby smiled slowly. He ran his gaze over her and lifted a quizzical eyebrow. "Oh, he did, did he?" His smile dimpled his cheeks. "Well, now, isn't that a mind-blowing development?"

Mallory wasn't quite sure what that meant. Since Shelby seemed to find it amusing, she relaxed a bit. "It's not bad news, then?"

"It depends on how you look at it, I guess. Is your name Erica?" Shelby hunkered down in front of Em. "Evelyn? None of those, hmm? I can't believe this. I'm usually very good at remembering names. Especially when the owner is so pretty. Erin?" He heaved a theatrical sigh. "Egghead?"

Emily was clearly disarmed by Shelby's teasing grin. "Shall I tell you? I'm afraid you aren't going to guess."

"Well, it means I'm out the money for a trip to the Dairy Queen, but I reckon I have to give up. Tell me."

"Emily."

Shelby clapped his hand to his forehead. "Emily! Of course. I remember now. I came close with Emma. I think we should *share* a banana split."

"Oh, no. You didn't guess it! And it's *your* rule."

"True," Shelby conceded. "Close is only good in horse-shoes. How about I let you eat three-fourths?"

"Nope, you owe me a whole one."

Shelby cupped the child's chin in his hand. "My goodness! I never saw so many freckles on one little nose in all my life. How do you do it? I can stay out in the sun until I'm cooked to the bone and I can't get a single one."

Emily found that hilarious and giggled with delight. "*You* can't get freckles."

"I can't?"

"Nope. But don't feel sad. You'd hate them once you had some. They won't wash off, you know."

"They're too pretty to wash off. If I can guess how many freckles you've got, will you call us even?"

"Nope. I want my banana split. Besides, I'd starve by the time you got all *my* freckles counted. I've got 'em all over."

Mallory had to look away because her eyes were filling with tears. She should have known Shelby would be wonderful. He was Mac's best friend, so he had to be. He clearly loved children. Em would not only be safe with him, but as happy as a bug. Now all that remained for her to do was be certain Shelby's plan of escape was fail-safe and then to inform him of her own plans. Glancing at her watch, she did some quick calculations. Mac planned to stall Carmichael for twenty-four hours before taking him to the safe at his office and giving him the package. That didn't give her much time. She hoped Shelby didn't decide to be difficult.

TWO HOURS LATER, after Mallory had grilled Shelby mercilessly to satisfy herself that he was capable and that his plans for fleeing Seattle had no holes in them that might endanger her daughter, she told him her intentions.

"You're gonna *what?*"

Until this moment, she had thought Shelby had very nice eyes. Now, however, they looked a little wild. "I'm going to bargain for Mac's release," she repeated, peeking into the living room to be sure Em was still happily absorbed in the movie they had been watching on Shelby's VCR. Shelby wasn't exactly whispering. "Please don't be difficult, Shelby. I'm going to do it no matter what you say, and you'll only waste precious time."

"Oh, no, you ain't!"

She pursed her lips. Shelby's grammar became nonexistent when he got upset. "I'm perfectly capable, you know. I've got it all planned out. And when it boils right down to it, you haven't got much to say about it."

"Once you get to know me better, you'll find out I always got plenty to say about everything. No. That's *N-O,* as in absolutely not. Mac sent you here for me to watch out for you. Soon as it's dark, we're gonna get in my car and head east over the mountains to that cabin where nobody can find us. If I let you do otherwise, when he finds out, I'll think I'm grass and he's a lawn mower. No way. It'd be different if I could go with you, but I can't. So just put it out of your pretty little head."

Mallory felt her temper rising. Her pretty little head? She planted her hands on her hips. "Look into my eyes. Do you see a vacancy sign? Don't talk to me like I have feathers between my ears."

He jutted his chin at her. "Feathers? I think all you got up there is air. Those boys don't play nice. Do you understand what I'm saying? They pack weapons that fire *real* bullets." He motioned toward the living room with his thumb. "I'm taking you and sweet thing to eastern Washington. That's it. No arguments."

"Shelby, I love him. Can't you understand? If he dies, how will I live with it? Now that I know Em will be okay,

I have to do something. When Mac calls you tomorrow, just tell him I'm with you."

He groaned, rolled his eyes and did a half turn away from her. "I'm not lyin' to him. No way. Forget that idea."

"You'll have to. Otherwise, he'll do something foolish before I can make my move. You don't want him dead, do you?"

"Mac's no dummy. He'll get himself out of it. He told me over the phone that he had a plan."

"He lied. His only plan was to exchange himself for Em. Don't you see? Look at her, Shelby. Could you let her die? He decided to take her place. He *lied* to you."

Shelby groaned. "It was his choice. I promised him, Mallory. You know that message he sent me? About the ringer? *You're* the ringer. It's a name we came up with years ago. Over in Nam. I was engaged to be married, and Mac called my girl a ringer because of the engagement ring I bought her. I got hurt over there—bad hurt—and he promised me if I didn't make it, he'd take care of her. You understand? He sent that message in case he didn't come back. He wanted me to look out for you."

Mallory's throat tightened. *Oh, Mac.* "You'll be taking care of Em. That's the most important thing. As soon as it's dark, you'll leave and head east over the mountains. She'll be safe over there. Carmichael won't be able to find her. Day after tomorrow, Mac and I will join you."

"And what if something goes wrong? What happens to her?"

"My parents will raise her if Keith isn't able. Believe me, the thought of that is enough to keep me on my toes. Trust me, Shelby. I've been planning this since last night. I won't leave room for mistakes."

She could see that Shelby was weakening. She spoke

to him quietly for several minutes then showed him the note she'd composed and planned to leave for Carmichael.

He read it carefully then nodded once, convinced. She smiled tremulously and turned toward the living room to say goodbye to Em. Leaving her daughter was going to be the hardest thing she had ever done in her life.

Em reacted to Mallory's announcement that she was leaving with only momentary sadness. "I get to go camping with Shelby? And pretty soon you and Mac are coming? That'll be radical."

Mallory scooped the child into her arms and clung to her, fighting back a deluge of tears. "Oh, Em, I love you so much, darling. Do you have any idea how I've missed you?"

Em squeezed her back and craned her neck to see what Spock was doing. Mallory had clearly interrupted her during a suspenseful moment in the movie. "I missed you, too, Mommy. Shelby! Come and watch! Spock's going to get killed."

Shelby, clearly reluctant to hone in on such an emotion-packed farewell, obliged the child, throwing Mallory an apologetic glance. Mallory forced herself to release her hold on her daughter, trying to comfort herself with the realization that this was a difficult parting only for her.

Rising to her feet, she swiped at a stray tear on her cheek. Shelby smiled and gripped her shoulder. "You take care. Don't go gettin' yourself hurt. He'll never forgive me." His face tightened. "And now that I know you, I'm afraid I'd never forgive myself, either."

CHAPTER SIXTEEN

MALLORY LEFT SHELBY'S apartment and drove directly to Mac's office building. Breaking and entering in broad daylight wasn't her idea of fun, especially when she had never in her life broken in anywhere. But she didn't dare wait until dark. Just in case Carmichael somehow managed to make Mac reveal the whereabouts of the package sooner than planned, she wanted that safe to be empty. Except, of course, for the note she'd shown Shelby.

Mac's office door had a window in the top half. That helped. All she had to do was break the glass. No need to pick the lock, thank goodness. The only trick would be to break the glass so quietly that no one called the police. She had watched enough television to know she needed tape. Going to a store for it would waste time. She cast a dubious glance at her attire. Maybe, just maybe, since Mac was so haphazard about everything else, someone in a neighboring office would believe his new secretary came to work dressed in jeans and athletic shoes.

Repositioning the shoulder strap of her purse, Mallory took off down the hall. Several offices away, she looked through a door window similar to Mac's and saw a woman bent over an adding machine. Mallory pasted on a smile and stepped inside. "Hi, there. I'm Mallory, the new secretary up the hall. I work for Bud Mac Phearson. Could you save the day and lend me a roll of tape for about five minutes? I forgot to get some, and I'd really rather not be fired my second day on the job."

"Oh, sure, no problem. As if Mac ever fired anyone." She threw Mallory a conspiratorial smile. "He just drives people crazy until they quit. He's having a good day if he comes in wearing socks that match." She shoved the tape dispenser forward, her eyes alight with laughter. "You aren't going to do anything foolish, like straighten his desk, are you? It completely throws him off stride. Believe it or not, he knows where everything is in that jungle he calls an office."

Mallory remembered the condition of Mac's Volvo and chuckled. "What the man needs is a wife."

The other woman rolled her eyes. "Isn't he a doll? I wouldn't kick him out of bed for eating crackers, that's for sure. Hang in there, kiddo. If I wasn't already married…"

Mallory picked up the tape. "Thanks. I'll be right back."

Her heart slammed all the way back up the hall. She quickly crisscrossed Mac's door window with tape, then used the tape dispenser to whack it. Glass splintered in both directions, and not very quietly. She winced and wiggled one foot to dislodge several errant slivers from her shoe. Nothing ever worked the way it did on television. After returning the tape with a cheerful thank-you, she raced back to Mac's office. *Hurry, hurry.* Reaching through the broken window, she unlocked the door, shoved it inward and then kicked the scattered glass across the threshold so nobody would see it.

Mac's filing system, if there was one, left much to be desired. How did he ever find anything in all these piles of papers? She focused on the safe, which sat in one corner of the room, serving as the stand for a drip coffeemaker.

As she stepped across the room, she reached in her purse for the note she had already composed. Grabbing the safe dial, she worked the combination, which she had committed to memory when she had seen Mac open it earlier. To her relief, the door swung open after her first try. She removed the familiar manila envelope. Very quickly, she scanned the note one more time to be sure she hadn't left anything out. Carmichael should get it tomorrow, when Mac brought him to pick up the package.

Mr. Carmichael:
If you want your precious package, meet me tonight at the Mukilteo ferry at 12:55 a.m. If you're late, I will take your package directly to the police and it will be in their hands by 1:30 a.m. I want you, no one else, to walk to the ferry ramp with Mr. Mac Phearson. I will be waiting for you there. As Mac Phearson steps onto the ferry, I will hand you the package. You will return to your men; I and Mr. Mac Phearson will depart on the ferry to Whidbey Island. No tricks. Keep Mac Phearson in good health if you value your freedom.

She had signed it with her full name.

Mallory's hands shook as she laid the note on the floor of the safe and closed the door. She was trusting Mac's assessment of Carmichael's character. If he was right, she knew that the moment Carmichael read her note, he would fly into a rage. She wanted him angry—so angry that he became careless. A lone woman, and a not very astute one at that, against his army of trained professionals? Carmichael would believe that getting the package from her would be as simple as taking candy from a baby.

Mallory had news for him. She would be the first to admit that she had been out of her element these past few days. She wasn't much good at playing duck in a shooting gallery. And threats against her daughter's life reduced her to sniveling terror. But Em was safe now. No more mindless panic. No more feeling powerless. Carmichael was about to learn a very bitter lesson, that muscle could never take the place of brains.

Mallory had planned carefully. The hardest part had been to forget what Mallory Christiani might do and start thinking like Carmichael would. Last night, when she had first conceived this idea, she had tried to put herself inside his skin and anticipate his every move. It hadn't been too difficult once she started getting the hang of it. For instance, the very first thing she had imagined him doing was to assess the situation from all angles and study the layout of the area that she had chosen for the exchange. He would instantly realize that an island like Whidbey could become a death trap. The last ferry run was at 1:00 a.m., so once she and Mac went over to Clinton Landing and disembarked, they would have only one escape route off Whidbey, the Deception Pass Bridge, which connected into the mainland at the north end. Carmichael would be ecstatic when he realized that. Because it would be dark, he wouldn't even have to worry about witnesses identifying him.

To saturate him with false security, that was her aim. She had deliberately chosen a place where he could close off every avenue of escape. He would station snipers at strategic spots around both ferry landings. If his men couldn't nail her and Mac at the ferry dock on the mainland, they would try again after she and Mac disembarked at Clinton Landing over on the island. And, just in case that failed, Carmichael would have both ends of the Deception Pass Bridge covered. Oh, yes, he would think of everything. And feel utterly confident that she was a stupid little broad who was playing right into his hands. Which was exactly what she wanted him to think. That he was shrewd, that she was as good as had, that it was only a matter of time. Oh, yes…let him feel cocky. He would never expect her to pull a switchback like this, to outsmart him at his own game. Let him forget that she came from the upper crust world of politics and wheeler-dealer big business. She had grown up watching her father grind much better men than Carmichael under his heel.

"A piece of cake," she whispered, thinking of Mac as she shut the safe with an ominous little click. He had been her rock for days, watching out for her, taking care of her, lending her his strength, thinking for her when she couldn't think for herself. Well, now it was her turn to carry the ball.

Striding to the desk, Mallory picked up the phone and dialed her bank. A woman named Sarah answered. "Yes, Sarah, this is Mallory Christiani." Mallory recited her account numbers. "I'd like to arrange for withdrawal of my funds by morning."

Sarah hesitated. "All of them? Less than twenty-four hours isn't much time to give us."

"I'm sorry. It's an emergency."

"Have you become dissatisfied with our service?"

"Not at all. I simply need a lot of cash."

"If we liquidate your market bonds, you'll lose large sums of money."

"I don't care. I want the cash—three thousand in small bills, the remainder in large denominations, so it will be easier to carry. See to it, please?"

Mallory hung up and pulled her list of things to do from her pocket. She only had until tomorrow night, so every second had to count. Some of this stuff simply couldn't be done today, though. Not until she had withdrawn all her funds from the bank. She sighed and ran a hand over her eyes. If she forgot one minor detail, she and Mac might pay for it with their lives. The first thing tomorrow morning, before banking hours, she would have to drive to the hospital and exchange Trudy's Honda for her Mercedes. Then she'd park her Mercedes at the Mukilteo ferry landing and take a cab into Everett to rent a dark-colored car, preferably one with plenty of horse-power, in case she needed speed.

Tomorrow afternoon after withdrawing her money from the bank, she would put the cash in the trunk of the rental car and take the vehicle over to Whidbey Island on the ferry, park it up the road from the landing where it wouldn't be conspicuous, and then return to the main-land as a walk-on ferry passenger. Once that was done, she would drive her Mercedes down to Tacoma and rent still another car, which she would leave parked near the marina slips there. Today, all she had left to do was some shopping. She needed a box of large heavy-duty freezer bags, a sturdy leather belt, an extra key chain and a suit-case in which to carry the cash.

It was going to be the slowest day and night of her life waiting for tomorrow night to finally arrive. Mallory picked up the phone and dialed the hospital to get the good news about Em to Keith. No sense in both of them waiting in agony. She wanted to make sure he knew Em was safe.

TWENTY-EIGHT HOURS LATER, the longest hours of Mac's whole life, he hung up the phone after speaking to Shelby.

He'd been all too aware of Carmichael, who was squeezed into the phone booth behind him, jabbing him in the back with a gun. Mac figured he might survive the loss of one kidney, but he wasn't too sure what else a bullet there might blow away. He'd have to wait for a better opportunity to make an escape attempt. At least now that he had spoken to Shelby, he knew Em and Mallory were safe in eastern Washington. From here on in, all he had to worry about was himself.

"Satisfied?" Carmichael snarled.

Mac turned slightly. "Yes."

"Then take me to the package. And no tricks."

"No tricks. It's hidden in my office building."

Carmichael backed out of the phone booth, keeping the gun trained on Mac.

MAC KNEW SOMETHING was wrong the moment he approached the door of his office. The window had been broken. A chill of apprehension inched up his spine. Wouldn't it be just his luck if vandals had stripped the place? The first thing they would steal was a safe. He unlocked the door, put his hand on the knob, gave it a twist, stepped inside. *Relief.* The safe was still in the corner. He looked over his shoulder at the three armed men behind him. He wasn't going to get out of this one. Carmichael was going to plant a slug between his eyes the minute he got his hands on that package. The building was empty at this time of night, so no one would hear the shot.

Mac cast a panicked glance around him. No place to hide. nowhere to run. This was it. He tried to pray as he walked to the safe, but the only prayer he could remember was a dinner blessing he had learned as a child— *bless us, oh, Lord, and these, Thy gifts.* Somehow it didn't seem fitting. So as he grasped the safe dial, he resorted to the basics, a straight-from the heart plea. *Please, God.* He didn't know for sure what he was requesting. Rescue would be nice. A bolt of lightning that struck everyone in the room but him, maybe? Salvation was less appealing, but it was certainly a thought, given the fact that he was about to meet the Grim Reaper.

"Hurry it up!" Carmichael shoved the barrel of his gun against Mac's temple. "You're stalling."

One more number. Mac heard a click. The safe door swung open. His legs wobbled a bit. Sweat was running down his face. *Come on, Mac, where's your pride?* He took a deep breath and tensed, trying to prepare himself for the explosion of noise, for the sudden pain that would surely come, even if only for an instant. In his mind's eye, he pictured Mallory's face, then Em's. Knowing they were together made everything worthwhile, all of it, even dying.

"What the hell? Where is it? I told you, no tricks!"

Mac focused on the inside of the safe. His guts clenched. *No package?* He stared at the small piece of white paper lying there, unable to believe his eyes. "It isn't a trick. I left it here, I swear it." He had an insane urge to laugh.

Carmichael snatched up the paper to read what was written on it. Mac swiped at his upper lip, relieved that the gun was no longer pointed at his skull.

"That stupid little—" Carmichael butted the safe door with the heel of his hand and whirled to glare at his men. "The Christiani woman has taken the package. Can you believe it? The naive little twit thinks she can play power games with me?"

Now Mac's legs felt *really* wobbly. Mallory? She was

supposed to be in eastern Washington. Less than thirty minutes ago, Shelby had said, "Don't worry, Mac. Em and Mallory are both okay." Shelby had never lied to him. Well, maybe *never* was too strong a word, but he certainly didn't make a habit of it. Surely he wouldn't have started now. Or would he? A wave of nausea rolled over him. *Damn.* Mallory had stayed in Seattle? Like an idiot, he had brought her to the office and let her see him open the safe. She must have memorized the combination and come here to take the package, probably to try to bargain for his release. He couldn't bear the thought that she might end up getting herself killed for him.

Carmichael started roaring orders. "We have to meet her down at the Mukilteo ferry at twelve fifty-five. There isn't much time. I want every available man on this."

THE FORLORN CRIES of the gulls drifted on the night breeze, a lonely, spine-chilling sound. Mac climbed from the brown sedan and gazed toward the *Kitsap,* which was already docked. He ignored the bulge of the gun under Carmichael's jacket. At this point, Mac sincerely wished it had all ended back there in the office with a bullet between his eyes. He couldn't see any way Mallory could pull this off, not against a pro like Carmichael. The man had every base covered. There were men here, men across the sound at Clinton Landing, men at the north end of the island on the Deception Pass Bridge. She was trapped with no way out.

"It's time," Carmichael hissed. "Start walking. No funny stuff. Think of it this way. If you behave yourself until we get to her, she can die in your arms. Touching, don't you agree? Lovers forevermore."

Mac yearned to bash the creep's face in. He set off

walking, the parking lot a blur around him, only the ferry in focus. Mallory, where was she? Didn't she know there were a half-dozen high-powered scopes trained on him? The moment she showed herself to give Carmichael the package, they would mow her down. Never in all his life had Mac been so scared. *The little fool.* He loved her so much. And now she was going to die.

As they drew near the ferry ramp, Mac spotted the red Mercedes's gleaming rear fenders, the last car in the far right parking lane. No sign of Mallory. Carmichael swore under his breath. Mac sent up a silent prayer of thanks. Closer, closer. His heart began to slam. His throat constricted until he could scarcely breathe. She was here someplace, but where? *Stay hidden, sweetheart. Change your mind. Don't take a stupid chance like this. I'm not worth it.*

"Stop walking, Carmichael!" Mallory's voice rang out from somewhere in front of the car. "No sudden moves."

Carmichael froze. Mac stopped beside him. His stomach flipped and plummeted to the region of his knees. The loading lanes inside the ferry were lit up. If she showed herself, even for a second, one of the snipers would pick her off. He glimpsed amber hair, just a flash, behind the left front fender of the car. At least she was keeping out of sight. To his utter amazement, his Smith & Wesson, gripped by a small, white hand, appeared.

"Toss your weapon, Carmichael! Hurry it up. Into the water."

Carmichael did as he was told, then turned back, his expression grim.

"Signal your men not to shoot. I mean it, Carmichael. And you'd better make it convincing. Don't make the mistake of thinking I can't hit you before they get me.

Remember that gun collection of my husband's? I'm an ace shot."

Carmichael pivoted and waved his arms, then spun back. "I want that package. You can't run far enough, I promise you that. I'll find you."

Mallory's head inched up. "You'll get your package. Put your hands up and start walking, very slowly. Hurry, before the ferry attendants come forward to put up the guard lines."

Mac's legs shook with each step. He and Carmichael reached the ferry and stopped.

"Okay, Mac, come aboard," Mallory called.

Mac stepped on board. As he did, a manila envelope arced through the air and plopped, then skidded, up to Carmichael's feet.

"Don't move! Keep those hands up or I'll shoot!" Mallory's voice dripped such venom that Mac scarcely recognized it. "Hurry, Mac, dive for cover."

Mac didn't have to be told twice. He ran in a crouch to join her at the front of the car.

"Okay, Carmichael, you stand right there. Understand? Until the ferry is well away from the dock. Don't move. Don't even breathe. I'll have this gun trained on you every second."

Two ferry operators were coming forward to tie off the safety ropes. When they saw Mallory, they stopped walking.

"It's all right. Go on about your business," she instructed them.

Since she was holding a gun, they hastened to comply, giving the Mercedes a wide berth. Mac figured they'd hightail it to the bridge and radio for the authorities the first chance they got. The ferry engines began to roar. He felt the vessel begin to move. Mallory didn't take her eyes off Carmichael until the ferry had moved a safe distance away from the dock. Then she let out a rush of pent-up air and turned to throw her arms around his neck. It was testimony to how scared he was that he didn't even flinch when he felt the barrel of his .38 bang against the back of his head. If he had to die, he couldn't think of a better way to do it than with Mallory in his arms.

"Mallory, you sweet, wonderful little idiot."

She laughed almost hysterically. "Oh, Mac, you're all right. I *did* it! I did it!"

He hated to burst her bubble. "Honey, we're not going to make it! Clinton Landing is crawling with his men. And even if we make it past them, he's got the bridge covered. We'll never get off the island, probably not even off the ferry. Why did you do this? Why? I thought we agreed the most important thing was getting Em to safety?" He tightened his arms around her, wishing he could hold her like that forever, protect her, but he knew he couldn't. If only she had stayed with Shelby. "Didn't you know he'd cover all the escape routes? I could wring your neck, dammit. How *could* you do something so totally—"

"Em is fine. Shelby called me this morning at my motel to let me know they had arrived safely." She rained kisses on his face, then pulled away. "I have it all figured out. Trust me." She plucked a large freezer bag off the floor, three layers thick, two bags inserted inside the exterior one. She put the gun into the plastic and sealed it, grinning brightly as she handed it over. "Watertight. If you aren't a good swimmer, I can carry it."

"A good *what?* Mallory, we can't swim across the sound."

"We aren't going to swim *across* it, just partway. Trust

me, Mac." She stood and offered him a hand. "Come on, we have to hurry. I can't explain it all now."

He rose to his feet and zigzagged through cars with her to the other side of the ferry. When they reached the rail, she began unlacing her shoes. "Hurry up. We don't have much time. You'd better shed that jacket. You *can* swim, I hope. I've done some lifeguarding, but it'll be quite a distance to haul you."

"You do realize these are orca waters?"

"Oh, come on, Mac. Have you ever heard of a killer whale attack in this area? Hurry! We have to be ready to jump at just the right moment."

He kicked off a shoe and shot a leery glance over the side into the inky black water. Unreasoning anger roiled within him. She was going to end up dead, and there was nothing he could do to save her this time. "I hope you know what you're getting us into."

"Out of. I'm getting us out of trouble. Home free, Mac. We'll pick up Em tomorrow and then we're off."

"To where?"

"To anywhere. The Bahamas. Hawaii, maybe? Florida? Mexico would be fun. What suits you?" She peeled off her socks and braced her hands on the rail to look over. "Oh, my, it's a long way down, isn't it?"

She sounded a little shaky. He curled his toes to keep them off the cold cement. "You just noticed? How's *Atlantis* strike you? Need I mention that the ferry engines could suck us up? I've never seen a ferry engine, mind you, but if they have propellers, we'll be minced into orca appetizers."

"We'll just have to swim like the devil, that's all." Her voice sounded tight. She looked toward the dark hulking outline of Whidbey. The scattered lights twinkled like diamonds. "It won't be too long now."

With a sinking feeling, Mac seconded that. It wouldn't be long. Fifteen minutes, max. He had wanted so desperately to keep her safe. The thought of what awaited them made him feel sick. Even if they swam to shore and managed to elude Carmichael's men for a while, they couldn't do it for long. Whidbey wasn't that big. He threw a worried glance over his shoulder to make sure no one was approaching, then stuffed the plastic-wrapped gun into his shoulder holster and snaked an arm around her waist to haul her against him. Giving her a fierce hug, he bent his head and buried his face in his favorite spot, the sweet curve of her neck. It was as good a way to pass the time as any—the best way. Minutes slipped past.

She was trembling, the only outward sign of how truly frightened she was. With a stab of remorse, he realized how much it had cost her to pull this harebrained stunt. And here he was, making cracks. Why? Because he had tried to protect her, and she had muffed it up trying to do the same for him. He hugged her more tightly. He couldn't stand the thought of her dying.

But it was done. She had risked everything for him, and the least he could do was make the best of it. Maybe, just maybe, they could squeak through alive. He lifted his head and watched the black outline of Whidbey coming closer. She stiffened in his arms.

"It's about time, don't you think?" She craned her neck to see his face. "See that light just to the left of the landing? Head toward it. That's where I parked the rental car."

Mac stifled a groan. There was no way to *drive* off the island. "Okay, I'm ready." He gave her a quick kiss. "If something happens and I sink, this may be my last chance to tell you that you're quite some lady. Words don't seem enough."

She turned and looped her arms around his neck. "Oh, Mac, if I did this a hundred times over, it'd never make us even. My little girl is safe and happy. I'm the one who doesn't know how to express my gratitude. Shelby was so wonderful. Em didn't even care when I left her with him."

"Yeah, that's Shelby for you." Mac was going to take him apart if he ever got his hands on him. "He's a great guy. Loves kids. Well, it's time to jump."

He set her away from him to peel off his jacket. They climbed up on the rail together, tensing for the dive. Mac looked over at her, and suddenly, he knew he couldn't push off without telling her one more thing. Not even his memories of Randy could stop the words from coming. "I love you, Mallory."

There were tears sparkling on her cheeks. "I know you do."

The next instant, she dived off into the blackness. Panic filled Mac when he lost sight of her. He launched himself into the air. Ice-cold water enveloped him, dragging him down to what seemed like fathomless depths. He fought to reach the surface, but the current dragged him back. *Mallory*. She was so small. She'd never have the strength— His chest felt as though it might explode. Then, like a cork, he bobbed to the top, shooting from the water to spew and gasp. *No Mallory*.

He spun in the water, horribly aware of how close the ferry was. He could feel the current sucking at him, trying to drag him under the broad underside of the vessel. "Mallory!" he screamed. "Mallory, answer me!"

CHAPTER SEVENTEEN

ONLY THE SURGING of the water and the roar of the huge engines answered him. Mac thrashed his arms, swimming first one direction, then another. Where was she? *Oh, please, God, please.* He couldn't see far. He thought he heard something and struck off swimming. Blackness. Nothingness. He was swimming away from land.

"Mallory!" he yelled. "Mallory!"

Suddenly the water seemed like a living thing, bottomless, monstrous, an overwhelming enemy. And it had literally swallowed up the woman he loved. His breath whined in his lungs. The cold made him feel numb. Frantic, he thought about diving to find her, but he knew there was too large an area and the water was far too deep. He was already tired. The ferry was pulling farther away. If he didn't head inland soon, he'd never make it.

"Mallory!" A sob tore up his throat. He couldn't swim away. He wouldn't. He'd rather drown with her than leave her. "Mallory! Mallory, answer me!" He was screaming and the ferry engines were no longer nearby to drown out the noise. His voice would carry across the water. Let them hear him. He didn't care. He had to find her. "Mallory!"

"Mac! Over here!"

Joy ripped through him. He flailed in the water, choking, blinking, trying to see her. "Where are you?"

"Here!"

He saw the black outline of her arm waving and struck off toward her. When he reached her, they clung to each other, almost sinking. He started to laugh. "You scared the living hell out of me, lady."

"*I* scared *you?*" She pulled away and started doing a breast stroke. "Come on before you become whale feed."

They swam in tandem. It was a long way to shore. When they could finally touch bottom, they were both so exhausted they staggered from the water, their clothes pouring water. Up by the landing, Mac could see Carmichael's men swarming forward on the ferry dock, waiting for the boat. Mallory took his hand and led him up a steep bank. They had to fight their way through underbrush. When at last they broke through to the road, they had to walk quite a distance to reach the car. She unfastened a key chain from her belt and unlocked the doors.

"I'll drive. I know where we're heading."

Mac nearly protested, but stopped himself. She had brought them this far. He climbed in and fastened his seat belt. She drove toward the south end of the island and pulled into a winding, overgrown driveway that twisted down to a beach house.

"It belongs to friends. I called them and they said we could borrow the boat. They keep it gassed up. They left the keys hidden on deck. We'll have plenty of fuel to reach the Tacoma marina. I have a rental car waiting for us there."

A boat? A boat! Of course, a boat. It was perfect. Carmichael would never have thought of them finding a pleasure craft this swiftly. He climbed from the car, feeling suddenly elated. A boat! She had planned this right down to the last detail. He watched her run around to the trunk. Throwing it open, she dragged out a suitcase.

"Money," she explained as she led the way down to the boat house. "Enough to take us anywhere."

"How much is that?"

"Give or take a few thousand, a little over eight."

Mac nodded. They could hide out a few weeks on that. Then it hit him what she had said. When speaking of less than ten grand, one didn't say "give or take a few thousand." He stopped dead in the path. "Not eight *hundred* thousand?"

Mallory giggled. "Isn't that enough?"

Eight hundred thousand. Mac knew he should be pleased, but instead he just felt shocked. He had roughly twelve hundred in savings after paying last quarter's tuition for Danno and Mark. He followed on her heels, saying nothing. And then she opened a boat house the size of a barn and he found himself staring up at the biggest monstrosity of a yacht he had ever seen in his life. "Mallory, honey, this is *not* a boat. This is a *ship.*"

She was already scaling the ladder. "A beauty, isn't she?"

"I can't drive this." His voice rang like a death knell and bounced off the aluminum walls.

"You don't *drive* it, you navigate it. Throw open the doors for me, would you?"

He shook his head. "I can't *navigate* it, then. I'm serious, Mallory. Hold up. Isn't there a *little* boat around here?"

Her wet head appeared over the side. "Mac, I can handle the boat. Just open the doors."

"Ship."

"Ship, then. Open the doors and loosen the ties."

Dubious, he slid the doors wide, struggled to unfasten simple-looking knots that managed to become intricate under his clumsy touch, then climbed aboard, convinced that she wasn't *big* enough to handle something so gigantic. To his surprise, she backed it out of the slip like a pro and before he knew it, they were gliding through the black waters of Puget Sound toward Tacoma. Several minutes later, after taking a tour of the *ship,* which had more rooms than his apartment, he stood beside her at the helm, looking out the cabin windows at the city lights of Seattle twinkling along the coastline.

"Home free," she said softly.

Mac wanted nothing more than to take her into his arms, but seeing her at the wheel of such an expensive craft brought it home to him how impossibly distanced their two worlds were. She came to him all wrapped up in a bow with eight *hundred* thousand dollars resting at her feet, and probably more where that came from.

"I have one question. Who received the package? Will he get it to the police so Carmichael will go to prison for killing Darren? If not, we'll never be able to return to Seattle. We know who he really is."

Mac quickly relieved her of that notion.

"You mean you sent it to Scotty? So we can just stay in the mountains for a while and wait until everyone involved is arrested?"

"Yeah. No trip to the Bahamas or Florida or Mexico. All you get is a dirty old cabin."

Her eyes lit up with happiness. "Oh, Mac!" With a cry of delight, she flipped a switch on the control panel and turned loose of the wheel to launch herself into his arms. "Oh, Mac, I love you! That was brilliant, sending Scotty copies."

"Mallory…" He pressed his face into her hair. With all his heart, he wished he could hold her forever.

Something in his voice made Mallory draw back. Looking up at him, she felt a sinking sensation. His eyes were dark with emotion, and it wasn't happiness. "Mac? What is it?"

"Just that I let myself fall in love with you. But there's no future for us, Mallory."

She stiffened. "After everything I've done, you still—" She licked her lips. "What do you mean, Mac?"

He glanced around the cabin. "*This!* We're nothing alike. I could never measure up." He raked a hand through his hair and moved farther away from her. "I could *never* make enough money. You'd hate me within a year. You don't want that for Em. You want to stick her in a middle-income apartment and give her a dad who can't spell *elaborate?* Give me a break."

"Mac…I'm sure you can spell elaborate."

"If I can, there's something else I *can't* spell." He turned and flashed her a grin exactly like Danno's. It was a grin that told her more than a thousand words might have. A vulnerable grin, calculated to hide his feelings. He lifted an eyebrow. "Imagine taking me home to your mother? Or the two of us going to one of your charity shindigs. I didn't even make it through my sophomore year of high school. I lied about my age and joined the Marines at fifteen. I'd embarrass you. I'd embarrass your daughter as soon as she got old enough to realize what I really am. And after a month or so, I'd bore you to tears, too. You need a man who can stimulate you."

"I found you wonderfully stimulating."

He rolled his eyes. "You need someone to share your interests, to *talk* to you on your own level."

"Is it because of Randy?" she asked hollowly.

He groaned. "No. I realize how wrong I was about that."

"Oh, really? But now you'll turn your back on me because I'm the little rich girl from Bellevue? Why can't you open your eyes and see me for what I am? I love you. Sell the Mercedes. Give me a red Volkswagen and I'll be happy. I don't care if you can spell *elaborate!* I don't care if you can spell *I love you,* just as long as you can say it."

"It'd never work."

"So you say. Well, let me tell you something. *I* was the one born to money, not Em. And I hated it. My father could never show me affection, so he bought me expensive cars and pretty clothes and sent me to schools I hated. And all my mother cared about was making me into the perfect little lady. I want better than that for my daughter. My life was miserable. And now *you're* going to toss me back because you don't think *you* measure up? If I could give my daughter a father like you who would hug her and hold her when she cried, that would matter. Not what he could buy her! It's *what* a parent says to a child, not how *well* he says it." She grabbed up the suitcase. "I'll show you what I think of my dad's money, anybody's money."

"What—Mallory!" Mac raced out the cabin door after her and caught the suitcase in midair, barely saving it from a one-way trip into the sound. He nearly collapsed on the deck when he had it safely in his arms. He put it down behind himself and stared at her. "Are you out of your mind?"

"No, I'm furious!"

"Raving mad, more like. Do you know how many kids this would put through college?"

"Fine, put kids through college with it! Just don't

throw it in my face. I've had it thrown in my face for thirty-four years. Take it! I don't need it. I don't *want* it. It was an escape route for us, nothing more. Why do you think there's so much of it? Because I never *spent* it." She brushed angrily at the tears streaming down her cheeks. "Put *yourself* through college with it. Go learn how to spell *elaborate* if it will make you feel better. I can work as a nurse and buy my own red Volkswagen."

Mac sighed. There was no doubt at all, she was right. Now he had to find a way to let her know he was convinced. "Mallory, shouldn't one of us be driving the boat? We might crash."

"Who cares?"

"I do. If I plan to marry you, I have to survive the trip."

"It's on automatic pilot." She took one last swipe at her nose and blinked. "What did you say?"

"You heard me." He caught her up in his arms. Leaning back, he studied her, his eyes glistening in the moonlight. "Are you sure? We *could* date for a while, you know, try each other out for size. You have no idea what a slob I am."

She grinned. "Nobody's perfect. As for trying you on for size, I already have. And you, sir, are a perfect fit."

"Will you marry me?"

"I thought you'd never ask."

He chuckled. "You won't want an *elaborate* wedding, I hope?" She encircled his neck with her arms and hung on tight. He buried his face in the curve of her neck and rocked her to and fro. His foot bumped the suitcase and he smiled. "One nice thing, if it doesn't work out, I can sue you for alimony."

She nipped his earlobe. "No way. Keith would keep you tied up in court for years. They told me yesterday that he's improving, and I have a hunch he'll like having you in the family so well that he won't let you get away without a fight."

He groaned happily. "I guess I'm stuck with you forever, then."

"And don't you ever forget it."

* * * * *

CRY OF THE WILD

In memory of Barton Eugene Gatewood.
With special thanks to Gerald Christean.

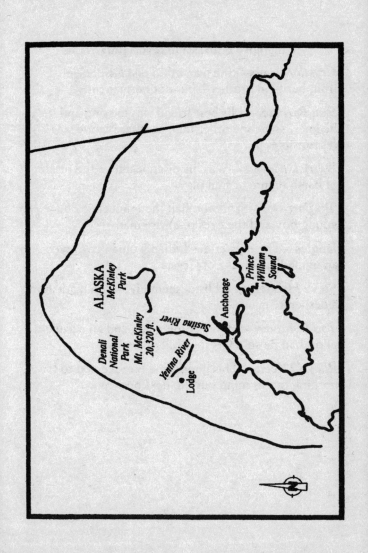

CAST OF CHARACTERS

Crysta Meyers—She wanted to distance herself from her twin brother—but not permanently.

Sam Barrister—His best friend was missing and he knew someone other than Mother Nature was responsible.

Derrick Meyers—Was his disappearance the result of harsh nature or foul play?

Tip Barrister—Sam's son had the innocence of a young boy and the eyes of a wise man.

Jangles—The mysterious Indian woman conveyed an immediate dislike of Crysta.

Steve Henderson—His desperately ill son made him a desperate man.

Todd Shriver—An incorrigible flirt and an excellent pilot, had he sold Crysta a bill of goods?

Riley O'Keefe—This good-time boy seemed to have nothing on his mind but the next beer run.

CHAPTER ONE

A MIDNIGHT-BLACK WIND *swirled around Crysta Meyers, drawing her toward a point of light that grew steadily larger. When she reached it, she found herself walking along a brightly lit corridor. Alarmed without knowing why, she examined the walls and saw that they were actually tall stacks of sturdy packing boxes, each about two feet long and over a foot deep. A storage building of some kind? Dust particles stung her nostrils. Fluorescent light fixtures, blue-white and eerie, hung from lofty steel ceiling beams.*

Her boots echoed on the concrete floor as she moved along the narrow aisle. She paused to make a quick inventory of the boxes and came up with over a hundred. What was inside them? And why this sense of urgency?

She took another step, then glanced down at herself. The top three buttons of her blue chambray shirt were unfastened, the neckline gaping. Each time she moved, corded muscle flexed in her thighs beneath the faded denim of her jeans. She wore a wide leather belt with a large silver-dollar buckle. She studied the buckle a moment and then realized it was her twin brother Derrick's, personalized with his initials. She had had it made for him five years ago as a twenty-fifth-birthday gift.

Crysta turned a corner and found herself in still another aisle. Something sticky swept across her face. A cobweb. She sputtered and wiped her lips. Ahead of her, she saw a row of wooden crates. Diablo Building Supplies, Inc. was printed in black on the side of each. She wanted to hurry forward to see what was inside them, but her body froze midstride. She could hear her heart slamming, feel sweat popping out on her forehead. Fear.

Was someone coming? Yes, she heard them now, men talking, somewhere off to the left. She shrank back and immediately wondered what had prompted her to hide. Who were the men? And why did they frighten her so?

Crysta heard the men drawing closer. The more distinct their voices became, the more frightened she felt. A shadow shifted in the aisle up ahead. Crysta stared, then whirled and ran. Up one aisle, down another, left, then right, like a terrified mouse in a maze. The jogging loosened her belt. She heard a clatter. She whirled and spied Derrick's buckle lying on the floor several feet behind her. The silver dollar had been jarred loose and was rolling to disappear beneath a wooden pallet. She shouldn't leave it behind, not with Derrick's initials on it. Before she could go back for it, though, the shadow ahead took on the distinct outline of a man.

Hurry, hurry, before he sees you. *She had no idea who the man might be, but her sense of urgency to escape undetected was too strong to be ignored. She threw a wild glance around her, looking for anything that would earmark this aisle so she could come back for the buckle later. On the floor, near the pallet, she saw a splotch of green paint. Satisfied, she turned to flee.*

Suddenly, inexplicably, Crysta's surroundings changed. Momentarily disoriented, she faltered, a different kind of fear swamping her as she tried to recognize where she was and figure out how she had gotten there.

Cottonwood trees stood all around her, their billowy tops silhouetted against a powder-blue sky. Numbing coldness shot up her legs. She looked down and saw she was no longer on concrete but slogging through ankle-deep water in the shallows of a river. She could hear the stream rushing, the wind whistling.

The shirt she now wore was red flannel, Western-style with pearl snaps. Icy water seeped through her jeans and heavy boots. She wore a different belt now, narrow with an ordinary prong buckle. Exhaustion made her legs quiver. Tired, so tired.

Sunshine glinted off the water. By the weariness in her legs, she knew she had been running a long while. To her right, up on the riverbank, was a stunted spruce, its trunk wind-twisted from years of harsh exposure.

Crysta's lungs whined for breath. Defeat and exhaustion dragged her feet to a stop. There was a thrashing sound in the water behind her, then low curses. Apprehension tingled up her spine. She was afraid to turn around.

"You can't get away, Meyers!"

The voice rent the air, deep and booming. Was it one of the voices she had heard inside the storage building? She couldn't be certain. Something silver arced over her shoulder and splashed at her feet. Through the distortion of the ripples, she recognized Derrick's personalized belt buckle, minus the silver dollar, the one she had lost in the storage building.

Another man spoke. "You dropped that the other night. We thought you might like it back. Pretty expensive mistake, leaving it behind. Sorry, chum, but the game's up."

Her movements sluggish, Crysta stooped and picked up the buckle. As she dropped it into her left breast pocket, her arm trembled. Still gasping for breath, she

*managed to reply, in a voice that sounded unlike her own,
"Don't be worse fools than you already are. I've passed
on the information."*

"You're bluffing. Who could you have told?"

*"Any number of people. For all you know, I could have
used your mobile phone to call the police in Anchorage."*

*From the corner of her eye, Crysta spotted one man's
rubber boots, military-green with yellow bands at the tops
and soles. A quick movement flashed. Pain exploded inside her head. She reeled, unable to see. The next instant,
she sprawled in the water. She willed herself to move, to
run, but was too dazed.*

*The shocking coldness of the water soaked her shirt
and lapped against her jaw, perilously close to her mouth
and nose. A metallic taste shriveled her tongue. Blood.
She stirred and moaned. When she opened her eyes, the
world spun. Disoriented, she stared at her outflung hand.
Her little finger came into focus, familiar yet somehow
not. A sickening smell wafted to her, thick and rotten,
like spoiled fish.*

"You idiot! Why did you hit him?" someone cried.

*"You heard what he said. Someone else knows. We
have to get rid of him. We don't have a choice."*

*"No! Are you crazy? What do you mean, get rid of
him?"*

*A funnel cloud sucked at Crysta, ink-black and swirl-
ing. She clung desperately to the shrinking microcosm
of reality, struggling to make sense of the words rico-
cheting around her. Him? Rolling weakly onto her side,
she tried to focus on the men's faces, but her vision was
badly blurred. Something gleamed in the sunlight. She
guessed what it was and tried to scream. She felt herself*

doing a free fall through blackness, the men's voices fading decibels a second.

"You can't kill him!"

"Watch me."

She heard an ominous little click. The next instant, an explosive noise rent the air.

CRYSTA JERKED AWAKE, eyes bulging, the sound of gunfire still ringing in her ears, her chest banded by a crushing pain. She didn't know where she was. Someone or something was holding her down. With a quick glance, she saw that the sheet and blankets were entwined around her. She must have been thrashing in her sleep.

A parched sob tore up her throat. Her head ached fiercely. She worked one arm loose from the sweat-soaked sheets and ran her fingers along her temple, half expecting to feel swelling. Nothing. She stared at her little finger, so similar to the one she had studied in her dream. She knew of only one person with hands so much like her own: her twin, Derrick.

With that realization came a surge of panic. Crysta rolled from the bed and onto her feet, so dizzy she could scarcely stand, fear washing over her in icy waves. "Derrick?"

The sound of her voice bounced off the walls, quavery and raw with emotion. She swallowed and turned a half circle.

"Derrick?"

There was no answer, just a resounding silence broken only by the wild thrumming of her heart. Crysta stopped breathing so she might hear better, her pulse accelerating with each passing second. Within her, for the very first time in her life, she heard only silence…an awful silence.

The horrible smell of rotting fish still clung to her. Her stomach plunged. Sick—she was going to be sick. She spun and headed for the bathroom. Minutes later, she clung to the porcelain toilet bowl, limbs trembling. The silence inside her head had magnified.

She just had the flu, she assured herself. Yes, that was all it was, a simple case of the flu. And a bad dream.

Her nightgown skimmed her body like wet gauze. Cinnamon-colored strands of hair hung in a curtain around her face, sticky with sweat and hair spray. She must have had a fever, and it had broken in her sleep. No wonder she had dreamed something so crazy. Delirium. So real, it had seemed so real.

Pressing a hand to her chest, she rested a few more minutes, trying to ignore the feeling of impending doom that still hovered around her. Struggling to get herself back on track, she shifted her gaze to the everyday things around her: the crimson dish of scented soap on the sink, her ratty pink slippers by the tub, her terry robe on the door hook, the rack of magazines by the toilet. Derrick. She couldn't rid herself of the feeling that something was wrong. She didn't have dreams like this about him unless he needed her.

Tempted to call Blanchette Construction to find out where Derrick was working this week, she glanced at her clock. 6:00 a.m. Derrick's boss wouldn't appreciate a phone call this early in the morning, and neither would Derrick. Besides, what would she say? Sorry for bothering you, brother dear, but I dreamed you were in trouble? She couldn't start making frantic phone calls. She wouldn't allow herself to. After three years of weekly therapy to distance herself from Derrick, she should be well equipped to handle a frightening dream about him without panicking. If she couldn't, then she had spent all that time and money for nothing.

Remembering her analyst's advice, Crysta closed her eyes and took a deep breath, repeating one sentence over and over in her mind. *It was only a dream.* She tried desperately to believe the words, but it wasn't that easy, not when her past was littered with dozens of similar dreams that had proven almost prophetic in their accuracy.

Childhood memories pelted Crysta. The time Derrick had been stricken with appendicitis while he was away at summer camp, and she had awakened in the dead of night screaming with abdominal pain. The time Derrick had been hit in the temple with a bat at baseball practice, and Crysta, miles away, had fallen to her knees, momentarily blinded with pain. Coincidences, the family physician had insisted, but Crysta and Derrick had known better. Over the years, Derrick had been treated to similar experiences, aware that Crysta was in trouble or ill when they were physically separated. In some indefinable, inexplicable way that even they couldn't understand, they were connected, emotionally and mentally, as other people were not.

As it always did after one of her dreams, a feeling of urgency filled Crysta, a compulsive need to find Derrick and assure herself he was okay. It was a compulsion she refused to gratify, for her sake and Derrick's.

Crysta forced herself to stand up, continuing to deep breathe. Only a dream, only a dream. It wasn't real. The litany provided little comfort. Even so, Crysta embraced the thought, determined not to let her dreams control her.

Not this time.

She would get started with her day and keep busy, just as her analyst had told her she should, until the dream lost its hold on her. It was what Derrick would insist she do if he were here. He was a grown man and perfectly capable of taking care of himself. If he was in trouble, he'd find a way to extricate himself from it.

A cup of tea would help settle her stomach, soothe her nerves and clear her mind. Groping her way from the bathroom, Crysta grabbed her robe from the hook and draped it around her shoulders. Still unsteady on her feet, she made her way through the living room and into the adjoining kitchen. After putting some water on to boil, she sat at the breakfast bar and dropped her head into her hands, fighting off another wave of nausea. Only a dream. She had to believe that.

FOUR HOURS LATER, Crysta still had a nagging sense of unease but otherwise felt fine. Her dream that morning had been just that: a scary dream.

She sat at her desk in the back room of her dress shop, tallying yesterday's receipts, the adding-machine keys clacking rhythmically beneath her quick fingers. The height of her spike heels prevented her from crossing her legs without colliding with the underside of the desk, and an ache inched up her thigh from sitting so long in the same position. She squirmed, tugging on her white skirt so it wouldn't be hopelessly crunched and wrinkled beneath her.

The boutique's entrance bell chimed. Crysta glanced out the office doorway at Rosanne, her partner, who was restocking the cashier stand with mauve shopping bags. "Is that Mrs. Grimes?"

"No, just a browser." Rosanne straightened the last stack of bags, then looked over her shoulder and grinned. "Since when did old Grimy ever come on time? Maybe something wonderful will happen and she won't show for her appointment. You don't look quite up to her today. What's her fantasy this month? To look like Twiggy?"

"No, Farrah, I think. She's gone blond."

Rosanne groaned. "Give me a break. Who does she think we are, miracle workers? That woman's built like a sumo wrestler."

Crysta bit back a grin. It was, after all, her business to design dresses to camouflage the problem figure. Mrs. Grimes just happened to have more problems than most—about a hundred of them, if Crysta was any judge of poundage. "I'll think of something."

"What, a tent dress? Or maybe a starvation diet?"

"Bite your tongue."

"Hey, I hate diets, too, but I detest fat more."

Crysta scanned Rosanne's stringy figure, quite certain the other woman had never dieted a day in her life. "The imperfect figure is what keeps us in business."

"Is that my cue to say thank goodness for Mrs. Grimes?"

"At least she makes a constant effort to look her best. She's very stylish, always does her hair and wears make—" A sudden pain in Crysta's chest made her break off and clamp a hand over her heart. She jackknifed forward over her desk, her head swimming with dizziness. "Oh…"

"Crysta!" Rosanne came running, her eyes round with concern. "What is it? What's wrong? Crysta, for heaven's sake, answer me."

A picture of treetops and blue sky flashed through Crysta's head. Then a horrifying sensation of falling came over her. She grabbed the desk, completely disoriented. When at last she got her bearings again, the pain had abated.

"Oh, God, do you think it's your heart? It happens sometimes, you know, even at our age."

"No—no, I'm fine," Crysta whispered shakily. "I'm fine. It was probably just a gas pain or something. It's gone now."

"You're sure? You look awfully pale. You shouldn't ignore chest pain. Maybe you should take the afternoon off and drop by the doctor's office. I can reschedule Grimy for another day."

The idea of an afternoon off appealed to Crysta, though she had absolutely no intention of using the time to see her doctor. Therapy or no, she was frightened now. Really frightened. "Do you really think you can handle everything alone? We've got a busy day scheduled."

"With my eyes closed."

CRYSTA LEANED BACK on her kitchen bar stool and tapped her fingernails on the Formica countertop, gazing at the wall phone. After an hour and a half of placing phone calls, one to Derrick's boss, one to Aunt Eva and several others to his friends, she had no more idea where her brother was than when she had begun. Derrick was on vacation, his boss had said, but he didn't know where. Her aunt and Derrick's friends had said the same.

Given the fact that Crysta and Derrick had been trying to wean themselves from one another, it didn't strike Crysta as odd that her brother had taken a vacation without notifying her. But it did seem odd that he hadn't specified where he was going. With their mother's heart the way it was, both Crysta and Derrick made it a point to be accessible by phone whenever possible. Even when Derrick went on his wilderness treks, he left word at his departure point of what area he expected to be in on any given day.

Crysta resisted the temptation to call her mother. Her mom might know where Derrick was, and then again, she might not. The only certainty was that Ellen Meyers would become alarmed if Crysta revealed that she was trying to locate Derrick. After several years of watching her children deliberately drift apart, Ellen would sense something was wrong. And Crysta couldn't risk that. Not over a dream that might or might not have had special meaning.

With another weary sigh, Crysta glanced at her watch, disgusted with herself for regressing to the point that she had taken off work in the middle of the day to stare at her telephone. Normal people didn't do things like this, and above all else, Crysta longed for normalcy.

"I can't go on like this," she whispered.

The words echoed in her mind long after they were spoken. During the long evening, Crysta repeated them many times, until they took on the solemnity of a vow. Would she never learn? She had to get Derrick out of her head, once and for all, or live the remainder of her life alone. That discouraging thought accompanied Crysta to bed and followed her into a restless sleep.

Two MORNINGS LATER, shortly after dawn, Crysta's ringing telephone jarred her from the depths of slumber. She shoved herself to a sitting position, threw a glance at the anemic light spilling in her bedroom window and reached for the receiver. Who would be calling at this hour? That question was answered when Crysta heard her mother babbling over the wire.

"Mom, what's wrong? Whoa, slow down. Derrick's what?"

"The police just called. He's missing!"

For an instant, Crysta felt as if the bed had dropped out from under her. "Missing?"

"Lost along the river. I knew he shouldn't go trekking off alone in that godawful country."

Crysta's head spun. She braced an arm behind her to keep her balance, trying to make sense of what her mother was saying. Derrick's job in quality control for Blanchette Construction took him up and down the West Coast doing random inspections at building sites. He could have chosen almost anywhere to spend his vacation. Godawful country, according to Ellen Meyers, was anyplace outside the reaches of Los Angeles.

"Mom, can you start at the beginning? Where was Derrick last seen?"

A little hard of hearing, especially when rattled, her mom rushed on. "Oh, Crysta, there are grizzlies in that place. And thousands of miles of wilderness. You have to go up there! You'd be able to find him. I just know it."

"So he was in Alaska?"

"Of course. People don't drop off the face of the earth here in the States."

"Mother, Alaska *is* a state. Try to calm down. I know you must be frightened, but getting so upset isn't good for you."

"But if he isn't found soon, he could die of exposure."

"Don't think the worst. I'm sure that won't happen."

Crysta wished she was as certain of that as she sounded. Her gaze flew to a snapshot on the nightstand. In it Derrick had an arm slung over her shoulders, head bent to press his cheek against hers. Reddish-brown hair, wide-set hazel eyes, fine features. They were a matched set except for gender. She couldn't imagine life without him.

Licking her lips, Crysta said, "Derrick's a competent woodsman. He'll find shelter. Have you called that Sam Barrister, the lodge owner? He and Derrick spend so much time together, he might know where Derrick went."

"I called him right away. He kept trying to reassure me, but I could tell he was worried. Derrick was staying at his lodge, like he always does when he goes up that way. He called from the lodge to check on me last week, in fact, right before he went on the hike. He disappeared along the Yentna River."

"How long has he been missing?"

"They can't be sure. It's been a whole day since he was due back, but he could have been lost earlier and no one would have known. When he didn't come back, Sam Barrister formed a search party. After they found Derrick's gear, he notified the authorities. He said that he tried to contact you, but he couldn't get your number through information."

"I see." Crysta's clammy skin turned icy. Images from her dream swept through her mind. Did the Yentna River have a wind-twisted spruce somewhere along its banks? And lots of cottonwood? *Stop it, Crysta. Stop it. You can't let yourself begin believing in the dreams again, not if you value your sanity.*

Wrapping the phone cord around her index finger, she watched her fingernail turn purple, then took a deep breath and exhaled very slowly. "Are they still searching for him?"

A jagged sob came over the line. "Yes, but for how long? After a certain period, they're bound to give up.

Crysta, you can take a few days off. That woman—what's her name?—she can run the shop."

"Oh, Mom…" Crysta wished she was with her mother so she could comfort her. Being upset like this was bad for her health. "Derrick's all right. I'm certain of it. Don't cry, please."

After a moment, Ellen seemed to regain control. She heaved a teary sigh. "Crysta, you haven't, um, been in touch with Derrick or anything, have you?"

"Mother, of course not. Don't you think I'd tell you?"

"No, I don't mean like that—not a phone call or anything. I mean the other way. When you said you were certain he was all right, I thought—I know you two have been trying to distance yourselves from each other, but…" Ellen's voice trailed off. "I knew no good would come from all that counseling. Look what's happened. You're brother's in trouble, and you haven't sensed a thing! This is the first time, the first time, Crysta. What does that tell you?"

Crysta closed her eyes and wondered if a person's head could actually explode from tension. She must guard her every word, her every inflection, or her mother would guess the truth: that she had dreamed of Derrick, over two days ago. Ellen was already far more upset than was good for her, and Crysta knew from experience that her mother would believe the dream had significance.

"Are you still there?"

"Yes. I'm getting a terrific headache, and it's hard to concentrate, that's all."

Ellen's voice became sharp. "Is it coming on suddenly? Oh, Crysta, you have to go up there. I know this thing between you and Derrick has been a source of heartache for you, but, darling, he may need you."

While talking with her mother, Crysta knew better than to deny her telepathic link with her twin. Ellen would only become more agitated. "I understand that, Mom. I haven't turned my back on Derrick—you know that. He and I have just been trying to get things into perspective."

"Then you'll go? The closer you are, the better chance you have of contacting him! You know—sensing where he is."

Crysta yearned to scream or hang up the phone, neither of which was an acceptable course of action. It wasn't that she didn't care. She cared far too much. The dreams were bunk; she had to believe that. And yet…

"Listen, Mom, why don't I call Barrister and the police, then get back to you? Let me see what I can find out. What's the name of Sam's lodge? I've forgotten it."

"Cottonwood Bend."

With a trembling hand, Crysta quickly jotted down the name, the report of a gun echoing in her mind. What if something had happened to Derrick, something terrible, and she had wasted precious time? "I'll call you right back, okay? Try to stay calm."

"Crysta, don't hang up! You will fly up there, won't you? I'll pay for your ticket. Promise me you'll go."

"Of course I'll go. And I'll pay for my own ticket. I love Derrick, Mom. I know it may not seem that way sometimes, but I do love him, just as much as ever."

As soon as she broke the connection, Crysta flopped back onto her pillow. Cottonwood Bend? Then there *were* cottonwoods along the Yentna. Uncertainty swamped her. Two entire days had passed since her dream. What if, against all the laws of logic, Derrick had been trying to send her a distress signal?

Sitting up, she quickly dialed her aunt Eva, not caring if she rousted the older woman from bed at so early an hour.

"Mom just phoned," Crysta explained hastily when her aunt finally answered. "The authorities in Alaska contacted her. Derrick's missing."

"Oh, dear God."

"I was wondering if you could go stay with her, Aunt Eva. She's awfully upset."

"You're not going up there, are you?" Eva's gravelly voice went taut. "Crysta, you've no idea what most of Alaska's like. Those lodges aren't located next door to shopping malls and bus stops. I went up there once with your uncle Fred, remember, and I know what I'm talking about. You love your brother, and I understand that, but in this instance, letting the authorities handle it would be the wiser choice."

Crysta glanced at her brother's photograph. As competent as the Alaskan authorities probably were, they didn't know and love Derrick the way she did. "I really feel that I should."

"Your mother?"

Crysta ran a hand into her hair. She could always count on Aunt Eva to understand. "She's terribly upset. If my being up there eases her mind, it's a small thing to do."

"Flying to Frisco, maybe. But Alaska? A woman, all alone?"

"I'm pretty adaptable, Aunt Eva. Besides, Derrick's best friend, Sam, owns the lodge. He'll watch out for me. I have to look at this practically. Staying here, I won't be much comfort to Mom. She'll feel better if she knows I've gone up there. And I'll feel better, too. At least that way I can assure myself that everything possible is being done to find Derrick." Crysta reached for the phone book.

"I need to make some calls and try to find out all I can. Meanwhile, Mom shouldn't be alone, not when she's so upset."

"I'll go right over."

"Try to calm her down, Aunt Eva. Stress the fact that Derrick's familiar with the area and a good woodsman. Remind her of who has been organizing the search. Derrick told me there's no better guide in all Alaska than Sam Barrister. I'll contact the authorities up there and divert their calls to me—either here or up there at Barrister's lodge. I'll get back to you with any news."

The moment Crysta hung up, she opened the phone book. After finding the area code for Alaska, which she could never seem to remember, she dialed information for the number to Cottonwood Bend and then placed a call to its owner. Seconds later, Barrister's deep voice crackled over the line. Was it similar to one of those she had heard in her dream? No, that was crazy.

She quickly introduced herself. "Are you having a storm up there, Mr. Barrister? We have a terrible connection."

"It's the mobile phone. I took it in for repairs, but it's still on the fritz. I'm trying to limp by with it until the end of the season."

The nape of Crysta's neck prickled. So the lodge wasn't serviced with phone lines. *"Your mobile phone,"* Derrick had said in her dream. Sam Barrister's?

"I'm thinking of coming up to help search for my brother, Mr. Barrister. I understand Derrick disappeared on a hiking trip in your vicinity."

"That's right.'

"And he's been missing a day?"

"Two, actually."

"Two! Why on earth did you wait so long to get a search started?"

"I wanted to give him the chance to make it back on his own. He came back a day late once before, so I wasn't alarmed at first, not until I went out looking for him and came across his gear." He paused a moment. "I guess I shouldn't have waited, but I really hated to call in search-and-rescue until I knew for certain it was necessary. Those fellows are all volunteers. They have to leave their jobs and families."

"Volunteers? You mean it's not the police searching for him?"

"They're involved. But volunteers do most of the legwork. This is a remote area. It takes pilots volunteering to fly people in, Anchorage businesses donating foodstuffs. You have to appreciate how much people have come together on this."

Crysta had heard of search-and-rescue teams, and she admired the volunteers for their dedication. But when it came to Derrick, she wanted the very best trackers looking for him—professionals, if at all possible. Fear knotted her stomach. She yearned to hear Derrick's voice, to hear him laugh, to feel the warmth of his hand on hers.

"Are you saying the search for my brother is being left to amateurs?" Despite her attempt to be calm, Crysta couldn't keep the note of hysteria out of her voice.

When Sam Barrister spoke, his tone was silken and patient. "Search-and-rescue teams are well qualified. In addition to them, Blanchette Construction made arrangements to bring in a Huey helicopter with infrared devices that detect as much as a two-degree variation in temperature. Everything that can be done is being done. Bank on that."

"And has the helicopter detected anything?"

"Not yet, no. But they didn't start making sweeps until yesterday. There's endless territory to cover. All the high-tech equipment in the world can't perform miracles."

The helicopter sounded impressive, but beyond that, Crysta pictured a handful of unqualified men stumbling around in the woods calling Derrick's name. Her throat tightened.

"Do you have a spare cabin I could use?" Derrick was too important to let strangers handle everything. Her mother was right; Crysta should be there. "I'd pay, of course. I'd really like to be nearby, and I know my mom would feel better if a member of our family was up there."

He hesitated a moment. "How's your mom doing? Derrick told me about her heart problems, so I wasn't too happy when I heard the authorities up here had called her. I asked them not to, to try to get in touch with you, but I guess the fellow I talked to went off shift. I tried to get your number through information but couldn't. I figured they might have better luck. First thing I knew, your mom was calling me." He sighed. "I'm sorry about that. I wanted to get word to you so you could be there with her and cushion the blow when she heard the news."

"She's awfully upset, I'm afraid." Crysta fastened her gaze on Derrick's photograph. The concern she heard in Barrister's voice reinforced all the positive things Derrick had told her about him.

"It's an expensive trip, Crysta. I can waive my rates, but that won't help on your airfare or your float-plane flight inland."

His voice was deep and warm, filled with sympathy, yet Crysta detected an underlying tension. Something wasn't clicking here.

"I see."

There was another short silence. "No, I'm afraid you don't. Let's be straight with each other, okay? Your coming up isn't a good idea."

"Why on earth not?"

"What could you actually do to help? This is rugged country. A person who doesn't know his way around could easily become lost. As cruel as this may sound, you'll be more a hindrance than a help. It's pretty primitive up here, and right now every available person is out searching. There's no one to accompany you anywhere."

"I see."

Actually, she didn't see, and she was infuriated with herself for making the same inane response twice. Why was the man trying to discourage her from coming? Crysta knew from Derrick's stories about Sam's lodge that all different types visited there: businessmen, actors, football players, families with children. The main lodge, though rustic, kept food laid out round the clock for any hungry guests who might trail in from the surrounding cabins. That wasn't what one would term *primitive*.

"I knew you'd understand," Barrister replied. "I'll keep you posted, okay? If Derrick's out there, we'll find him—you can count on it."

Bristling, Crysta said, "Derrick is my brother—my twin brother."

"And you love him. But loving him isn't enough in country like this. In fact, it could be a drawback. It's extremely difficult for family members to remain objective. You'll be better off if you stay home. And so will Derrick. Why don't you give me your number. I'll give you a call back tonight to let you know how the search is progressing and if we've found any signs of—"

The phone crackled loudly with static. Crysta pressed the receiver closer to her ear. "Mr. Barrister?"

She listened a moment, then clenched her teeth in frustration. Disconnected. She redialed the number and got a busy signal. Had he hung up on her? His phone might have gone on the blink again, but it seemed like mighty convenient timing.

Dropping the receiver into its cradle, she reviewed her conversation with the lodge owner, becoming more convinced by the moment that there was something he wasn't telling her. She had no idea what that might be, but she was convinced his reluctance to have her up there stemmed from something more than concern over her finances and her safety. What, though? That was the question. Was he hiding something?

Whatever his argument, Crysta knew she had no choice but to fly north. It wasn't just that her mother wanted her to go; Crysta loved her brother far too much to let his fate be decided by a bunch of weekend Rambos. No matter how she tried or how much she wanted to, she couldn't forget her dream.

With grim determination, she flipped the phone book back open. Within five minutes, she had reserved a flight to Anchorage. After that, she called Rosanne, asking her to take over at the shop until she returned, then quickly packed a bag and went to spend the night at her mother's. They both needed a little comforting.

CHAPTER TWO

SAM RAPPED THE phone on the counter, then listened. Nothing. He gave it another rap, then heaved a frustrated sigh. With his luck, Derrick's sister would think he had hung up on her, and if she was anything like her brother, that would be all the impetus she needed to book the first possible flight to Anchorage. He glared at the phone, cursed under his breath and slammed it down. There were days when nothing went right, and this was one of them.

He walked to the window, bracing his shoulder against the frame to stare through the steamed glass at a stand of cottonwoods. He considered sitting down for a moment but quickly discarded the idea. As if he had time to rest.

The lodge's main room, dining and sitting area combined, was filled with the delicious aroma of fried salmon cakes and Jangles's wonderful homemade yeast rolls. His stomach turned. He massaged the muscles in the nape of his neck, tipping his head back to ease the tension. The crackling of the fire usually soothed him, but not today.

What would he do if Crysta Meyers flew up here? Maybe he should have told her about the condition of Derrick's gear. The shredded backpack and scattered contents pointed to a bear attack, except for two minor things: no blood and no body.

That bothered Sam. Derrick was fast on his feet, but not that fast. He couldn't have outrun a grizzly for long, so there should have been at least some blood nearby. Not only that, but bears rarely attacked people in this vicinity unless provoked, and Derrick was too bear-smart to be that stupid. Sam couldn't, in good conscience, intimate to Derrick's relatives that Derrick had been the victim of a bear attack until there was more conclusive proof. Especially not when he had reason to suspect that Derrick had been murdered by men, not animals.

Heaving a sigh, Sam turned from the window and strode toward his office. He had to get started going through those papers in Derrick's briefcase. That alone would be a two-day chore. Maybe he was barking up the wrong tree, but he couldn't rid himself of the feeling there was far more to this than met the eye. If he didn't turn up anything, then a flight to Anchorage was in order.

Meanwhile, Sam could only hope Crysta Meyers took his advice and stayed at home in Los Angeles...where she would be safe.

Alaska from the air.

At any other time, Crysta might have thought this state beautiful, perhaps even mystical, but today her only reaction to it was dread. How could she hope to find Derrick out there? For too long now, the closest thing to a road she had seen was a moose trail. The tundra, dotted with small dark lakes, seemed to stretch into infinity, the snow-draped peaks of Mounts McKinley and Foraker standing sentinel, so immense their tops were wreathed in clouds.

As the tiny plane veered north, she stared down at a tannish-brown glacier river, the Big Susitna, according to her travel pamphlet. Along the river's banks, she saw several uprooted trees, bulldozed by nature when the ice had broken.

"The Yentna River's up ahead," the pilot, Todd Shriver, yelled, trying to make himself heard over the engine noise. "We'll follow her course right in to the lodge."

Crysta craned her neck to see. She had expected something more than spruce, cottonwoods and undergrowth. "Aren't there other lodges out here besides Cottonwood Bend?"

"A few. You have to remember, though, that a real close neighbor in these parts is at least five miles away."

To Crysta, a wilderness area was a well-marked nature trail. Ordinarily, she might have enjoyed visiting a remote lodge. But knowing Sam Barrister wasn't going to be happy to see her made the isolation rather unnerving. To locate her brother, she needed to be here. What if Barrister refused to let her stay?

To take her mind off that unsettling possibility, Crysta tried to concentrate on the landscape. The shaking and shuddering of the Cessna made it impossible. The Cottonwood Bend brochure, which she had picked up at the Lake Hood Airport, had called the float-plane flight up the Yentna a once-in-a-lifetime adventure; it hadn't mentioned that it could well be her last.

She had only herself to blame. Rather than wait until tomorrow, she had bribed Shriver for passage on a supply run this afternoon, not realizing what she was bargaining for. Despite her mother's favorite aphorism, ignorance was not bliss. Her fellow passengers were numerous crates and two fifty-gallon drums of fuel for the lodge's generator. Behind those, she caught a glimpse of a partially open carton bearing an animal skull with macabre black holes where its eyes had once been. She couldn't shake the eerie feeling that it was staring at her. Doubtless Shriver often hauled hunters and their grim trophies to and fro from Anchorage, but she wished she hadn't encountered a victim on her first pontoon-plane flight. She was nervous enough as it was.

Crysta often made buying trips for her dress shop and considered herself a fairly seasoned traveler, but she flew in large jets. Being a passenger on this glorified tin can with no landing wheels was a new experience. The pilot, tall, blond and tanned to a leathery brown, looked as if he should be posing for a macho cigarette advertisement. And he lived up to the image.

In the two hours since meeting her, he had already tried to hit on her, flirting blatantly and inviting her out for a "night on the town." Crysta assumed "town" was Anchorage. No matter. She wasn't here for a fling. Even if she had been, Shriver wasn't her type. She supposed he was likable enough, but when it came to dating, Crysta preferred men of a more serious nature. The handsome bush pilot struck her as the type who probably had a girl in every port-or, in this case, behind every bush.

"Um, excuse me, Mr. Shriver, do you think it's wise to be smoking? The gas fumes are awfully strong back here."

"Not to worry, honey. I haul fuel all the time, and, as you can see, I haven't blown up yet."

Somehow Crysta didn't find that very reassuring. Reaching inside her blouse, she tugged her floral-print thermal undershirt away from her skin, hoping for a whisper of air. As her travel-tips pamphlet had warned, the temperatures here took dramatic swings, and, as advised, she had dressed in layers. Now the chill of the morning was rapidly giving way to steamy afternoon warmth, and she had already discarded her sweater vest and jacket.

The plane shuddered again, making her forget her discomfort. She clutched the edge of her black vinyl seat.

"Won't be much longer now," Shriver called back to her. "You anxious to start catching those big old king salmon?"

"I didn't come to fish. My brother is missing. Derrick Meyers. Maybe you know him?"

He threw her a surprised look. "You're Derrick's sister? You know, I thought you looked familiar. You were twins, weren't you?" A frown pleated his forehead. "Hey, I'm really sorry about Derrick. Enjoyed visiting with him. He knew this country, I'll tell you that. A helluva nice guy. Having him along always spiced up the trip. He was one of my favorite passengers."

"Was?"

"Like I said, he knew his way around out there. He should have been back by now unless he met with an accident or—"

"My brother isn't dead."

In response to that, Shriver shrugged and faced forward again.

Unwilling to let the matter drop, Crysta said, "If he had met with an accident, the searchers would have found his body."

"Not necessarily. You have to remember how many predators are out there."

A wave of revulsion washed over Crysta. She hadn't thought of that. Averting her face, she pretended sudden interest in the Yentna River below. Cottonwoods and an occasional spruce lined its banks. She found herself watching carefully for anything that looked familiar. A lone, wind-twisted spruce in particular. Or a splotch of red flannel.

"Look, ma'am, I didn't mean to upset you. I speak before I think sometimes. I liked Derrick. Why, I've even flown some of the searchers in, free of charge."

Crysta dug her nails into her palms. "I appreciate that. It's just hard, you know?" She studied the back of Shriver's head. "Tell me, have the police considered the possibility of foul play?"

"Foul play?" He nearly twisted his neck off to stare at her. "You serious? Who'd want to hurt Derrick?"

"I'm not certain." Crysta hesitated, then asked, "How well do you know Sam Barrister?"

"Well enough. If you're saying… Well, you can forget that. Sam may be the rough-and-rugged type, but violent? No way."

"How about his guests? Are there many regulars?"

"An easy dozen. Hey, look, if you want to learn more about that, I suggest you question Sam. He knows his guests better than I do. As for foul play, honey, I think you're way off the mark. It's one big happy family out here. You want mystery, go to the city."

Crysta forced herself to leave it at that. Could Shriver be right? Was Derrick dead, his remains devoured by animals? Perhaps that was why Sam Barrister had discouraged her from coming. Had he been trying to spare her? Crysta had been praying for a happy reunion with her brother, clinging to the belief that he would be found alive. Now grisly images flashed through her mind.

Fear made her hands start to shake. She couldn't start

thinking like that. Not about Derrick. He was too much
a part of her. If she lost him… Well, it didn't bear thinking about.

Squeezing her eyes closed, Crysta tried to block out
everything—the gas fumes, the heat, the roar of the engines, the shuddering of the plane. None of that mattered.
Derrick was all that counted—finding him by whatever
means she had, even if it was self-destructive. As well it
might be. Her failed marriage testified to that.

Derrick? She listened to that secret, inner part of herself, praying she would hear something, feel something.
Derrick, answer me. Oh, please, please, answer. There
was nothing. Just a horrible, dead silence.

"Check your safety belt," Shriver called over his shoulder. "We're about to land."

The plane began its descent. Pressing her cheek against
her window, she spotted a bend in the river where a large
log building perched on a rise, surrounded by rustic cabins. The lodge, she guessed. In a clearing nearby, she saw
a group of tents, which she presumed were for the searchers. Miniature people were scurrying about onshore, some
shading their eyes to see the plane, others waving.

The aircraft tipped crazily to one side, then the pontoons touched down. Crysta braced herself for a shuddering deceleration, but the landing felt more like gliding on
glass. In the center of the river, joined to shore by a footbridge, was a small island, where several aluminum boats
were moored. Todd Shriver cut the engines and coasted
the plane toward the strip of land. She felt a jerk when
the pontoons hit bottom.

"Safe and sound," Shriver called as he slid out of his
seat. "When you get out, be careful. Not to say I'd mind

fishing a pretty little gal like you out of the water, but that river's like ice."

A pretty little gal? Crysta nearly groaned. The pilot definitely needed to be metropolitanized. He wouldn't last a day among the women's activists in Los Angeles. Keeping her expression carefully blank, Crysta unfastened her seat belt and scrambled forward to the cabin door. Following Shriver's example, she stepped out onto a pontoon and leaped from there to semidry land. Had Derrick once stood in this very spot?

As she got her balance and turned to look shoreward, a stout man with a shock of grizzled red hair ran up, his arms laden with two large boxes. He didn't spare her a glance as he set the boxes down and struggled to assist Shriver in unloading a heavy barrel.

She scanned the tree-lined riverbanks, glad to finally be here. True, arriving was only a start, but Derrick was out there somewhere. He had to be. And she was determined to find him.

She heard Shriver and the redhead talking, their voices low. She strained to hear what they said, but the brisk breeze snatched their words away. She turned and spotted her luggage, tossed down on the soggy dirt alongside a gas drum and a galvanized tub filled with salmon, bloody water streaming down its sides. Caring less about her expensive suitcases and more about having clean, dry clothes to wear while searching for Derrick, she quickly pulled the suitcases to dry ground.

As Shriver removed the last crate of supplies from the Cessna and set it down by the others, he said, "Well, I wish you luck, hon. Hope you find him, hale and hearty."

As he headed back toward the plane, Crysta called, "Thanks for making room for me."

"No problem."

The redhead stowed his boxes inside the airplane, then turned to look at her. From the curiosity she read in his expression, Crysta guessed that Shriver had told him who she was. His unwavering regard made her uneasy. At a loss, she turned away.

The scenery seemed familiar, very much like the terrain in her dream. People fished the river in boats, but otherwise, there was nothing, just water and dense cottonwoods. Her one link to civilization, the plane, was about to leave.

"Um…Mr. Shriver. Hold up a sec."

The pilot doubled back, blue eyes quizzical. "Problem?"

"No, not exactly. I was, um, just wondering. I may have some business to take care of in Anchorage. If I call you, can you pick me up that same day?"

"Depends."

"On what?"

"We fly VFR out here."

"What's that?"

"Visual Flight Rules. If I can't see, I don't go. Rain storms, low clouds."

"Oh." Anchorage suddenly seemed light-years away. She might want to visit Blanchette Construction's warehouse there if Derrick wasn't found soon. Just to see if the building in any way resembled the one in her dream. "And how often does inclement weather interfere?"

"That depends on Mother Nature. Like most females,

she's pretty unpredictable. For the most part, though, I fly in at least once a day."

"Then I can catch a ride?"

"If there's room, you bet. I never turn down a pretty passenger." He gave her shoulder a consoling pat. "Hey, if there's anything I can do to help—fly you around so you can search from the air—anything, you let me know."

Ignoring the unwanted intimacy, Crysta asked, "How expensive would that be?"

"If it's worked in around my flight schedule, I'll only charge for the fuel."

"I may take you up on it."

"I hope you do."

The wind picked up, dragging wisps of her long hair across her eyes. Through the reddish-brown strands, she studied Todd Shriver's features. In the sunlight, she could see things she hadn't detected inside the plane: a smattering of freckles across his nose, a chin that wasn't quite squared enough to offset the sharp angle of his cheekbones. All in all, though, it was a nice face. A little too cookie-cutter handsome for her tastes, but nice.

Except for his eyes. Maybe it was their ice-blue color, but they seemed expressionless to her. Her aunt claimed the eyes were windows to the soul, and Crysta guessed that might be true in Shriver's case. With his lighthearted outlook on life, she doubted many serious thoughts crossed his mind. The lack thereof showed in his gaze. She thought of Derrick's expressive eyes, which reflected grief as well as joy. Her heart grew heavy at the comparison.

"Again, my thanks, Mr. Shriver, for everything." Her voice sounded a little shaky, but she couldn't help it.

Shriver clasped her shoulder, flashing her a smile. "Thank me when there's something to thank me for, hmm? And forget what I said earlier. Positive thinking can work miracles." Dropping his hand, he swung around and strode toward the plane. "See ya, Riley. Don't clean the river out of fish!"

The redhead chuckled. "It'd take a better man than me. You have a safe flight."

"Always. Hey, buddy, keep an eye on the lady for me, would ya?" Shriver jumped onto the pontoon, his footing sure from long practice. Crysta fastened her gaze on his rubber boots. Military-green with yellow trim. Catching the door frame, Shriver swung one leg through, pausing to add, "If she needs anything, help her put a call through to me, okay?"

Riley nodded. "Sure, I can do that. If I'm here, anyway."

As Shriver disappeared inside the plane, Crysta glanced at Riley's feet. His boots were the same avocado green, trimmed with yellow.

The plane's engines roared to life. Loneliness knifed through Crysta as the Cessna pulled away from the island. Thus far, Shriver was the only person she knew in Alaska. Now that he was gone, she was on her own. Shoving her hands into her jeans pockets, she took a deep breath of astonishingly pure air and headed toward the footbridge. No sense in putting it off. She might as well confront Sam Barrister now.

The footbridge felt unsteady when she stepped onto it, and she found herself wishing for handrails.

"Hey, lady!" Riley yelled as he shouldered a box of supplies. "You forgot your gear."

Crysta had hoped the lodge would have an employee to carry guest luggage ashore. She sighed and started to retrace her steps. As she did, the bridge gave under additional weight.

Glancing over her shoulder, she saw a tall, dark-haired man striding toward her, his every step making the water-soaked structure bounce and sway. Preoccupied though she was with keeping her footing, she noticed three things about him. He was without question one of the biggest men she had ever seen. He was as attractive as he was tall. And he looked angry.

CHAPTER THREE

CRYSTA TURNED TO meet the man head-on. It was a narrow bridge, and the approaching stranger took up most of its width, not with fat but sheer bulk, every centimeter lean muscle. There was an air about him—the loose-jointed way he walked, the set of his broad shoulders, the gleam in his brown eyes—that made him seem at home in the rugged country around him. She sincerely hoped the unlucky person he was so furious with was somewhere behind her.

No such luck. He drew to a stop dead in front of her and said, "Crysta Meyers, no doubt."

"And you must be Sam Barrister."

He squinted against the sun, tiny lines creasing the corners of his eyes, his long lashes casting shadows on his cheeks. The wind lifted his hair, drawing it across his high forehead in unruly black waves.

Crysta shoved her hands deeper into her pockets. For some reason, she had never pictured Sam Barrister as so attractive or virile. A red sweatshirt molded itself to the impressive contours of his chest, its snug fit accentuating his narrow waist and flat belly. Faded denim skimmed the muscular length of his legs. A knife scabbard rode his hip. Like Riley and Shriver, he wore a pair of yellow-trimmed green rubber boots. Obviously her running shoes were inadequate for the terrain, but it couldn't be helped. She hadn't had time to go shopping before leaving home, and galoshes weren't among her usual accessories.

Crysta returned her gaze to his face. The sun touched his unshaven jaw, highlighting a sprinkle of silver whiskers among the black. Late thirties, early forties? She chose to ignore his anger and kept her voice carefully polite. "Is there any more news about my brother? How's the search going?"

"If I could have reached you last night, you would know the answer to that. I wish you had called back. After we were disconnected, I got the phone working again, but with your unlisted number, I couldn't get through to you."

"I stayed at Mom's. She's terribly upset, naturally."

Something flickered in his eyes. Concern? It was gone as quickly as it came. "Maybe you should have stayed there with her." He clipped the words short. "I told you your being here wasn't necessary."

"If it was your brother missing, where would you be?"

She had him there. His gaze shifted, as if he couldn't quite look her in the eye. "As much as I sympathize with your concerns, I don't have space for you." He nodded toward the group of tents. "All the cabins are full."

"If you have a spare sleeping bag, I'll manage. I tried to bring my own, but passengers are limited to two pieces of luggage on the pontoon flights. I had to leave it in a locker at the airport."

Silence hung between them. His gaze met hers again, hard and unyielding. Then he swiped at his cheek with the back of his hand, leaving a smudge of dirt along his jaw.

Crysta shot a glance at the cluster of tents. "I can always sleep under a tree."

His eyes warmed with a weary smile. "With the bears?"

"Bears?" Crysta echoed. She scanned the area again. It hadn't occurred to her that wild creatures might venture this close to the lodge. Still, if the volunteer searchers could sleep outdoors with nothing but canvas to protect them, she could make it through a few nights in the open. "Right now, my main concern is finding Derrick. If a spot under a tree is all you have available, then I'll settle for that."

He seemed amused by her reaction to the idea of bears, but she also detected a flicker of admiration in his expression at her willingness to brave it out. The smile in his eyes finally touched his mouth. "I think I can do a little better than that."

Crysta noticed that the warmth in his expression transformed his features. He was even more attractive when he smiled. "I appreciate your help—and I apologize in advance for any inconvenience I might cause. I didn't realize so many people would be here."

Tipping her head back to study him more closely, Crysta noted once again that he was not what she had expected. Derrick had described Sam, of course, but "big and rugged" didn't do him justice. He was at least six-five, maybe more, with a set of shoulders most of the weight lifters in Los Angeles would kill for. At five-ten, Crysta seldom met a man so tall and with enough breadth to make her feel petite.

His dark gaze searched hers. "I should be the one to apologize—for the surly greeting. I haven't slept more than a couple of hours at a stretch in days. I've been trying to run this place, organize the search parties, make sure the volunteers are fed, keep beds ready and in between all that, I've been trying to search for Derrick myself. I'm afraid it puts a strain on congeniality."

Now that Crysta was looking for them, she could see the faint shadows of exhaustion beneath his eyes.

"A few minutes ago, one of my guests got a fishhook stuck through his finger," he added. "The ordeal of trying to get it out while he threatened me with a lawsuit destroyed what was left of my sense of humor." With a wry twist of his mouth, he admitted, "Not that I had much left to destroy."

A wave of guilt washed over her. Now she could see why Sam Barrister might not have wanted her here. She licked her lips. "I didn't realize so much responsibility for the search had been laid on you."

"It wasn't laid, I took it. Derrick's my best friend."

"I don't suppose an extra pair of hands might be useful? I worked one term during college as a short-order cook, so I might be a help in the kitchen."

"Somehow, I pictured you wanting to accompany the searchers."

"I want to go look for him. I won't deny it. But if I'll be more useful working here to free someone more experienced for the search, you won't hear me arguing. He's my brother. I have to help. Can't you understand that?"

"Of course I can. It's just that the thought of you getting lost out there scares the hell out of me. Derrick's being missing is bad enough." He placed his hands on his hips. "Let's get your luggage. It looks like you're stuck here, at least until tomorrow. We may as well make the best of it."

Crysta took one of the suitcases, and Barrister grabbed the other. He led the way back onto the footbridge. Crysta watched the rhythmic shift of his shoulder blades as she followed him. In all fairness, she really couldn't blame him for resenting her arrival. In the city, she could handle just about anything, but she was definitely out of her element here. He logically expected her to be more trouble than help. Crysta was determined to prove him wrong.

When he reached the end of the bridge, he leaped over a wash of mud to dry ground, then turned to hold out a hand for the suitcase she carried. Since she lacked his length of leg, Crysta didn't demur. Once unburdened, she gauged the distance and jumped.

As she drew abreast of him, he retained both suitcases but made little concession for her shorter stride. Crysta gave him a measuring glance, taking in his chiseled profile and clenched jaw. Deep within, she experienced a purely feminine response to him.

That surprised her. Normally she was attracted to a man more by his personality than by his looks. She laid her reaction off on nerves. Since learning of Derrick's disappearance, she hadn't been herself. Sam Barrister was the epitome of masculine strength; frightened and unsettled as she was, it was natural that she should feel drawn to him.

He headed toward the large log buildings set apart on a knoll. By the time Crysta made it up the incline, she felt as if she had run a footrace. He didn't slow until they reached the lodge entrance and then paused only to push the door wide with his shoulder.

He stepped back to let her enter first, juggling suitcases so she could slip by him. A blast of warmth hit her in the face, and she glanced at the stone hearth where the dying remains of a fire crackled, the feeble flames casting golden shimmers on the knotty-pine paneling. Around the hearth was an arrangement of sturdy wood furniture with orange-and-brown plaid cushions that lent the spacious sitting area a cozy feeling.

Had Derrick lounged there? She pictured him kicked back in a chair, leafing through one of the magazines about Alaska that were fanned across the coffee table. A heavy ache centered in her chest. What if Derrick never visited this lodge again?

At the far end of the room stood several planked tables, one laden with food, another occupied by three men whose low conversation and laughter blended with the crackling of the fire. Judging by the men's clothes, she didn't think they were searchers. Guests, more likely. Crysta scanned the walls, expecting to see hunting trophies. She was both relieved and puzzled not to find any.

"Mr. Barrister, when I asked you earlier how the search was going, you never answered me. Has any progress been made? Have they found any sign of Derrick, any clues as to what happened?"

Sam glanced at the three men in the dining area. "Let's discuss that when we have some privacy," he said in a low voice.

Her reluctant host stepped behind a cluttered check-in counter, then through a doorway. As she followed him, she spied a dog-eared calendar on the wall, a dingy picture of Mount McKinley at its top. Her attention was caught by some sloppy writing in the box for the fifteenth. *Phone due back—have check ready.* She paused. Today was the seventeenth of June. Derrick had called their mother, supposedly from the lodge, last week. How could he have if Sam Barrister's phone had been gone?

More determined than ever to press the man for some answers, Crysta stepped through the doorway into a small, untidy living room with another stone fireplace and more of the same rustic furniture. The back of the sofa was toward her. She spotted two very large white-socked feet propped on the wooden armrest at one end.

"My son," Sam whispered as he set her luggage down in a corner.

Crysta heard a low snore, a sputter and then a surprised grunt. In a husky, sleepy voice, the boy said, "Dad? I thought you were gone."

"Didn't leave yet. There's a guest you should meet, Tip. Derrick's sister, Crysta Meyers."

A dark head shot up over the back of the sofa, and Crysta found herself looking at one of the handsomest boys she had ever seen, a younger version of his father. His pale blue T-shirt struck a sharp contrast to his deep tan and liquid-brown eyes. His sleep-tousled hair and nervous grin only added to his appeal. She guessed him to be about sixteen.

"Hi—hi. I'm p-pleased to m-m-mmeet y-you, Cr-Cr—" He dipped his head and swallowed, his face suddenly aflame. "Cr-Cry-sss—"

Crysta's heart went out to Tip as she watched him struggle to say her name.

Sam laid a hand on the boy's shoulder. "It's all right, son." Throwing Crysta a warning look, Sam added, "Tip gets a little tongue-tied when he first meets strangers."

"Tongue-tied, hmm?" Anxious to put the boy at ease, Crysta moved forward and extended her hand, remembering that Derrick had mentioned Sam's son was handicapped. "Well, we'll be fast friends, then. When I meet new people, I trip over my own feet."

Tip stared at her outstretched fingers. "Y-you d-do?"

"You should have seen me when I tried to be a waitress. I lasted two hours, and all my wages went to clean some poor lady's dress. I dumped a platter of spaghetti down her front."

"Y-you did?" Tip's eyes grew round.

"Yup. And the little meatballs went down inside her— Well, it was really a mess. I got canned before the dinner hour was over."

Tip's eyes grew even rounder. "Canned? Like a salmon?"

Sam's stern visage softened. "No, son. That's another way of saying she lost her job."

Tip finally grew bold enough to grasp Crysta's extended hand, his mouth spreading into a lopsided grin. "W-well, you don't have to w-worry around us. If you t-trip, we'll j-just help you up. R-right, Dad?"

Sam glanced at Crysta. "And you offered to help out in my kitchen? Help like that may put me out of business."

"Just don't serve spaghetti."

She thought she detected a hint of a smile at the corners of his mouth, but he squelched it before she could be certain. Then Tip distracted her by carrying through the handshake with such enthusiasm that he jolted her arm clear to the shoulder.

Before she thought, Crysta said, "Easy." Tip froze. When he tried to draw back his hand, though, she held on. Smiling at him, she modified the pumping action. "There, you see? The same way, just not quite as hard."

Tip glanced at his father as he released her hand. "I forgot. You d-do it soft with ladies."

"That's right." Sam glanced at Crysta. All trace of warmth had left his face.

Crysta squirmed. She certainly hadn't meant to offend. Would it have been better to endure a painful handshake with Tip, and then avoid letting him touch her again?

"I'm sorry, C-Crys— Crys—"

"Just call me Crys. Derrick used to when we were younger, and I kind of miss it."

"Crys." Tip appeared pleased when he had no difficulty with the shortened version. And, unlike his father, he didn't seem upset that she had corrected him about the way he shook hands. "I like n-nicknames. My r-real name's Sam, just like my dad's. Only when people c-called me, he answered, and when they called h-him, I did."

Crysta gave the boy another warm smile. "So you're called Tip?" She pretended to consider the name for a moment, then nodded. "I like it. It suits you, somehow."

Tip nodded. "It's b-because my dad won't let m-me work for f-free. He says I help p-people as good as the m-men he hires, so I sh-should get paid tips like they do. One guest said h-he had to pay me so m-many times, my m-middle name should be Tip."

"And the name stuck," Sam inserted.

"You wanna see my p-p-pictures, Crys?" Tip asked.

Actually, Crysta had a dozen questions for Tip's father: where Derrick had been heading the day he left the lodge, who had known his destination, where his gear had been found, whether any of it was still missing, what area the search was covering right now. She needed to procure a forestry map to help her keep track of the search. She also wanted to do some sleuthing as soon as the opportunity presented itself. But faced with the eagerness in Tip's expression, she held her tongue. Five more minutes would make little difference to Derrick, and she had a feeling they would mean the world to Tip.

"What kind of pictures?"

"Just p-pictures." Tip tugged his drooping socks up

and sprang off the sofa, as lofty as his father when he straightened. "C-ome on. I have them in here."

He hurried to a door across the room and threw it open. Remembering his manners, he stepped back so she could precede him. In his excitement, he wasn't stuttering. "I do them without any help. Huh, Dad?"

"Tip, Crysta may want to freshen up. She's had a long trip, and she's worried about Derrick. Maybe you could show her later when—"

"No, really," Crysta cut in, "I'd like to see them."

When she stepped into the unfurnished bedroom, she felt as if she had entered an art gallery. Every inch of wall from floor to ceiling was taken up with oil paintings, mostly nature scenes but portraits, as well, one of Sam, another of Todd Shriver.

"Oh, Tip." That was all Crysta could say.

"Do you like them?"

"Like them?" Crysta took a step back to absorb the full impact of a lone wolf on a snow-swept knoll. The moonlight, the layered clouds against a slate sky—every last detail was perfect. She could almost hear the animal's forlorn howl. "I'm in awe."

Tip threw a questioning glance at his father. Sam flashed a weary smile. "That's a compliment, son."

"You're very talented, Tip. Have you given any shows yet?"

"Tip paints for pleasure," Sam inserted brusquely.

Crysta cleared her throat. Clearly, any talk of art shows was taboo. "When I can, I'd like to spend some time in here admiring each painting, Tip, and hearing the story behind it. Did you see the wolf in a book, or take a picture of him outside? The detail you've captured is breathtaking."

"Tip paints from memory." Sam's piercing brown eyes met hers. "With one glance, he sees more than most of us do after staring at something for an hour."

Tip rushed to the easel in the center of the room. "Come and see this one."

Crysta stepped around to view the canvas in progress. For an instant, when she spied the cinnamon-colored hair and hazel eyes, she thought it was an unfinished portrait of herself. Derrick. His facial features were still sketchy, not yet brought to life by Tip's brush. As her gaze lowered from Derrick's face to his shoulders, her heart began to slam.

"As you can see, Derrick's been on Tip's mind a lot," Sam said softly.

Crysta licked her lips. "That shirt. When did you see Derrick wearing it, Tip?"

"Wh-when he left that day. R-right before he got lost." Shadows crept into the boy's brown eyes. "I'm s-sorry. I didn't m-mean to make you sad."

For a moment, the room seemed to spin. In the portrait, Derrick was wearing a Western-style, red flannel shirt with pearl snaps, just as he had in her dream.

CHAPTER FOUR

TWENTY MINUTES LATER, Crysta still hadn't completely recovered from the head-on collision between her dream and reality. As she followed Sam Barrister behind the lodge for a tour of the buildings, she scarcely heard what he said. Derrick had been wearing a red shirt the day he disappeared. If that much of what she had dreamed was right, how much of the rest was? She couldn't forget the explosive noise that had ended her dream. Had her brother been shot?

"Are you listening to me?"

Crysta jerked herself back to the present and looked up at Sam's brooding features. "I guess I was woolgathering. What did you say?"

"I was telling you how to go about bathing in the sauna. It's more of a steam bath, actually. Luckily, it's pretty self-explanatory. All the toiletries you'll need are in the anteroom. And, as you can see, the fire is kept stoked most of the time. We all use the same steam room, and, for safety's sake, there's no lock. Turn the sign to read Occupied when you go in so you don't get company. Right around the corner, you'll find the necessary house. Again, there's only one for both sexes, so latch the door."

Still feeling separated from reality, Crysta noted a string of smoke trailing from the sauna building's chimney.

"Seeing that portrait really upset you, didn't it?"

She forced herself to focus, dismayed that he had cued in so easily on her feelings.

"I'm really sorry. Tip means well. He just doesn't think beyond the moment sometimes. You went so white, I thought you might faint."

"Tip's great. And the portrait is going to be wonderful. It was just—" She shifted her gaze, afraid he would see too much, read her too well. "I wasn't prepared, that's all."

He watched her closely. Too closely.

"Crysta..." His facial muscles tightened. "We both know I didn't bring you out here for a tour. Aside from the fact that you've got dozens of questions to ask me and would probably like to talk to the search coordinator, there's something I need to tell you before you hear it from someone else."

He looked so somber that she braced herself.

"It's about the condition of Derrick's gear when I found it. It looked like a—"

"Hey, Mr. Barrister?"

Sam turned at the call, focusing on a weary-looking man in soiled jeans and a safety-orange shirt. As the man strode toward them, Crysta noticed he carried a dark green garbage bag in one hand. Her stomach tightened.

Looking back at her, Sam said, "That's one of the searchers. Hold on a second, okay?"

Crysta nodded and watched Sam walk down the slight slope. The two men met about twenty feet away from her, but it was so peaceful here that she could hear everything they said.

"I wanted to report the news to you first thing. We finally found him—or what little was left of him. Several miles downstream. I'd guess it was at least five miles from where you found his gear. Bear, no doubt about it. Must be a renegade in the area."

The ground seemed to dip beneath Crysta's feet. Sam threw her a concerned look. "Jim, this lady is—"

"Still no body, I'm afraid," Jim rushed on, inclining his head at Crysta to acknowledge her presence. "But we found plenty of bear tracks and blood at the scene. He was either completely ingested or dragged away. We'll probably never know. In the surrounding brush, we found remnants of his shirt. At least we assume it's his." Jim stuck his hand into the garbage bag and pulled out a shredded piece of red flannel. A pearlescent snap shimmered in the sunlight. "The lab will run tests, of course, to check the blood type. I know there isn't much left of it, but could this be part of the red shirt you described?"

A cry tore from Crysta's throat. Sam spun and hurried back to her. "Crysta—"

"They're saying he's dead?" She couldn't drag her eyes from Derrick's shredded shirt. She would have recognized it anywhere. Had a bear's claws ripped it that way? "Derrick's dead?"

Sam gripped her arm, the pressure of his fingers firm enough to support her but strangely gentle. "Jim, this lady is Derrick's sister."

"Oh, hey, I'm sorry. I had no idea."

Crysta fastened pleading eyes on Sam's. "He can't be dead. I'd know it. I'd feel it. Don't you see? He can't be dead."

Sam said nothing, and his silence drove the horrible news home. Crysta threw a bewildered look at the retreating searcher, her thoughts a jumble.

"It can't have been a bear," she whispered. "I would have known. I know I would have."

"Crysta… Let's go up to the lodge, okay? I'll fix you some Irish coffee. Maybe you can lie down and rest."

The silken tone of his voice made Crysta realize how hysterical she must sound. She nodded, numbly following the lead of his hand. The searcher had sounded so positive. Surely they couldn't make a mistake like that. Bear tracks and blood. Maybe her dream had meant nothing, after all.

"They—they could be mistaken, couldn't they?" she asked, looking up at him.

"I—" He broke off and swallowed. "Jim Sales is one of the best trackers in the country. I've never known him to make a mistake. He wouldn't blame it on a bear unless he felt positive."

The walk back to the lodge passed in a blur for Crysta. At some point, Sam put his arm around her, and she dimly realized he was not only steering her but allowing her to lean into him. His strength became her only reality.

One foot in front of the other. She tried not to think. It hurt too much. A bear. Every time the horror of it skirted her mind, she shoved it away. *Not Derrick. Please, God, let it be a mistake.* Sam Barrister's lean strength and the warmth of his body gave Crysta something solid to hang on to. Derrick's friend. She didn't resist when he drew her closer to his side.

She had a vague impression of the lodge as Sam led her through it, of his private quarters, of being lowered to a sofa. She was seeing it all through a layer of cotton. Sam spoke to her, his voice low and gentle. Tip's voice rang out intermittently. Crysta felt separated from them, not registering reality because she couldn't bear it.

Time passed. How much, she didn't know. Her mind began to let the truth seep in, a fact at a time. Derrick was gone. Not just dead, but gone. No body. No funeral so she could say goodbye. Just gone, as though he had never existed. A bear. She couldn't envision the animal—nothing in her imagination was monstrous enough. Then Sam whispered, "I'm sorry," and it became a reality. People didn't say they were sorry in a shaky, rough voice like that unless something unspeakable had happened. "I'm sorry." She tried to focus on his face. His being sorry didn't make it hurt any less. How would she ever tell her mom?

Raised by proud, very private parents, Crysta seldom cried and never in front of people. She had broken her arm once in two places and hadn't shed a tear. At her dad's funeral, she had survived listening to the eulogy dry-eyed and with her head held high. But now her pride eluded her. The tears welled in her eyes, carried up from deep within her on the crest of a ragged moan she could not stifle. If only Sam and Tip would go away so she could be alone.

Instead, Sam tried to take her in his arms. Maybe he had been Derrick's friend, but to her, he was still a virtual stranger. In addition, he was extremely handsome, definitely not the type who could carry off a brotherly embrace. Though she knew Sam meant well, she felt self-conscious instead of comforted, and she pushed against his chest. He backed off instantly.

"I'm sad f-for you." Tip said softly.

Perhaps it was Tip's lack of pretense, that he didn't say he was sorry or pretend to understand how she felt, just a tremulous whisper that cut straight to her heart, but Crysta felt her self-control begin to slip further. Looking at him, at his stricken brown eyes swimming with tears, was a mistake. Her shoulders started to shake. "Oh, Tip. I don't want you to feel sad."

"Why? You're sad."

As if it were the most natural thing in the world, he sat

next to her and drew her into his arms. His embrace was awkward, his hands clumsy as he stroked her hair, but Crysta buried her face in the crook of his shoulder. He was solid and warm, something real to hang on to while the horror of her brother's death sank in. Mauled to death by a bear. Crysta couldn't think of a more awful way to die. The images assaulted her mind, faster and faster, until a scream welled in her throat.

No. She wouldn't do this to herself or Tip. Curling her hands into fists, she forced the pictures away and focused instead on the boy who held her. She breathed in and out, concentrating on the rhythm. Don't think about how Derrick died.

Her tears slowly dwindled, drying to stiff trails on her cheeks. When at last she felt more like herself, she straightened. She gave Tip's hand a gentle squeeze. Words didn't seem enough, somehow.

"B-bears aren't bad," Tip whispered.

Until that moment, Crysta hadn't realized she had spoken her thoughts aloud. A denial sprang to her lips, but she swallowed it back. Tip was right. All bears weren't bad.

"D-Derrick liked the bears. They eat breakfast in our g-garbage heap every day, and he liked to watch them. We gave them all n-names. There's Grumpy and Snaggletooth. And Hog, because he won't share. Derrick'd be sad if you started hating them. He said the bears need f-friends to help protect them. Stupid people shoot them and make rugs out of their f-fur. I found a c-carcass yesterday." His eyes darkened with sadness. "They killed it for its head and f-feet."

Crysta stared at him, not quite registering the words.

"The t-teeth and c-claws can be sold f-for jewelry," Tip elaborated mournfully.

Crysta could barely control a shudder. "I won't start hating the bears, Tip. I promise."

As if he knew the shock had chilled her to the bone, Sam had built a fire, and soon the small living room was cozily warm. Though Crysta knew she should move away from Tip, she couldn't find the will. She had come here fired up with plans to find Derrick. And now there was nothing to find. She remembered how she had tried and failed to sense her brother's presence on the float-plane. Had that been a sign? Despite the fire, a cold numbness seeped into her mind and through her body.

"I'm going to go talk to the searchers," Sam said softly. "I really don't think it's necessary for you to come. You can review the official reports later, when you feel more up to it."

Crysta agreed with a nod. She couldn't handle hearing the gory details of Derrick's death, not yet. She sat straighter and finger-combed her tangled hair. Flashing both of them a quavery smile, she said, "I'm sorry for losing it like that. You scarcely know me. It was just such a shock to hear that—" She broke off, unable to put it into words.

Sam started to speak, but Tip beat him to it. "We're fast f-friends. You s-said so."

Puzzled for a moment, Crysta suddenly realized that to Tip her prediction that they would be fast friends meant they would become friends quickly. It followed that pretense between them was unnecessary. Patting the boy's hand, she said, "I guess we are, aren't we?"

Tip beamed. "I'm glad. You make me feel nice."

The feeling was mutual. Tip was special, and Crysta knew she was richer in some inexplicable way for having met him. Not even her grief over losing Derrick could completely overshadow that.

THREE HOURS LATER, when Sam slipped back into his apartment, he saw Crysta had fallen asleep on the sofa. A blanket was tucked around her—Tip's doing, he guessed. Sam pulled the blackout shades on the windows so the light wouldn't disturb her rest. At this time of year, from midnight until around three in the morning, Cottonwood Bend experienced twilight, but darkness never descended. For someone unaccustomed to it, Alaska's midnight sun could make sleep difficult, and Crysta needed her rest. Tomorrow would be draining.

After drawing the last shade, Sam turned from the window. Shadows now obscured Crysta's features. He studied the outline of her face, a pale oval in the dimness. He felt an inexplicable urge to move closer. Something about her drew him, made him want to hold her, to—Sam cut the thought short, amazed at himself. He scarcely knew the woman. And he certainly was in no position to befriend her, not until this was over.

With only a few words, he could have eased her pain somewhat, but he hadn't. And he wouldn't now. She might insist on staying until he told her everything. It was better that she believe Derrick the victim of a bear attack so she would go home, where she would be out of harm's way.

Despite what the searchers believed, Sam didn't buy the theory that a bear had killed Derrick Meyers. He might have if it had appeared that Derrick had been killed near the site of his initial encounter with the animal. But Derrick's shredded gear had been found five miles from the scene of his death. The way it looked, the bear had taken exception to Derrick's presence in its territory, which wasn't unheard of, had torn up his gear and then chased him for five miles before killing him. No man could out-run a grizzly for five miles.

Sam knew the searchers felt satisfied with the evidence. After all, grizzlies sometimes did strange things. Sleeping campers had been known to disappear, bedding and all, never to be seen again. To the searchers, this was just another bizarre grizzly incident, and they were willing to call it a closed case as soon as the lab reports came back. They had no reason to suspect foul play.

But Sam did.

Straightening his shoulders, he went into the adjoining bedroom to check on Tip. When he was satisfied the boy was sound asleep, he slipped from the apartment and went to his office. From a cupboard along one wall, he withdrew a briefcase. Derrick's papers were inside. With luck, the name of his murderer would be there, as well.

DIZZINESS SWIRLED IN Crysta's head. Light flashed before her eyes, and she felt as if she was falling. Mud. Cold and slick. It was everywhere. All over her arms, globbed on her hands. She was on a slope, an extremely steep slope, and sliding backward. Instinct took over, leaving her no time to wonder how she had gotten there. She looked down and saw white water surging around craggy boulders. If she lost her precarious hold, she'd plunge to her death. She clawed at the slimy earth. Pain. Like the mud, it seemed to surround her. White-hot pain so intense it took her breath away. She longed to rest but didn't dare. Panic filled her. She was slipping.

Crysta dug into the mud with her toes and fingers. She scrambled upward, blocking the agony from her mind. The roar of the water below filled her ears. So cold. So

*tired. She found a foothold and rested a moment, her
lungs convulsing. A shudder racked her. Lifting her head,
she gauged the distance she must scale to reach the top
of the mud slide. It wasn't far, and desperation drove her.
Arm over arm, one toehold at a time.*

*When she reached the top of the slope, Crysta rolled
onto her back to rest. Turning her head, she spied a rickety log cabin nestled among some trees. It's chimney pipe
rose above the roofline, one side badly bent. Smoke. They
were still there. At the thought, her mind spun with questions. They? Fear clenched her guts. She couldn't waste
time wondering who. Run, run, before they find you.*

*She struggled to her knees. Pain exploded in her shoul-
der and chest when she put weight on her left arm. She
glanced down. Blood. Crimson ooze coming from a black
hole over her heart. She gained her feet, still staring at
the wound. The mud seemed to be staunching the blood
flow. She took a step; knifelike pain shot through her right
thigh. She gritted her teeth. There was a lake nearby, a
deserted cabin. She'd be safe there.*

WITH A GASP, Crysta woke. The sofa cushion pressed
against her face, the weave of its fabric warm and slightly
scratchy. Still gripped by terror, she lifted her lashes. A
blur of brown and orange swam before her eyes. She jackknifed to a sitting position and grabbed her right thigh.
Her head reeled. For a moment, she hovered between
nightmare and reality, aware of her surroundings but still
able to see the mud and blood. Frantic, she began brushing at her chest and arms.

"Are y-you okay?"

Tip's voice made her start. She stared at him, her hands

frozen in midmovement. Then she threw wild looks around the room, taking in the plaid upholstery, the fire, her clean clothing and hands. Slowly the last traces of her nightmare disappeared.

"Y-you scr-screamed," Tip whispered. "Y-you said you were b-bleeding. Did you cut yours-s-s-self?"

"No." Crysta swallowed. "No, Tip. I guess I was having a bad dream."

He relaxed his stance. "Oh. I have b-bad ones sometimes. My dad'll let you s-sleep with him if you're still scared."

Heat crept up Crysta's neck. "I'll be fine out here." Her gaze shifted to Sam's closed bedroom door. "Thanks for checking on me, Tip. I'm sorry I woke you."

"I c-can tell you a story for a w-while. My dad's taught me some really good ones."

Never had Crysta known anyone as sweet as Tip. "That's thoughtful of you. Maybe another time? I'm awfully tired. I'll bet you are, too."

"Kind of." He looked reluctant to leave. "Good n-night."

She watched Tip disappear into his bedroom. After his door closed, she rested her elbows on her knees and dropped her head into her hands. What was happening to her? Even now, though she was wide-awake, her right thigh still throbbed, and her shoulder felt stiff. Crazy, so crazy. Or was it?

A sudden flare of hope jerked Crysta's head up. She remembered the explosive noise that had ended her last dream, her certainty that it had come from a gun. The blood. The black hole in her flesh. A bullet wound? She leaped from the sofa, nearly falling before she disentangled herself from the blanket. Pressing her hands to her cheeks, she stared into the dying fire. Was she losing her mind? Or could Derrick still be alive?

CHAPTER FIVE

IF THERE WAS a possibility that Derrick was still alive, Crysta had to do something. Finding her brother was the first priority, but she knew that only a fool would strike off searching for Derrick alone in so vast a wilderness. She needed help—from someone who knew the country. Who better than Sam Barrister, who was, according to Derrick, one of the best guides in Alaska?

When a soft tap on Sam's bedroom door failed to rouse him, Crysta ventured out to the front of the lodge, vaguely aware of a humming sound somewhere outside. A generator? Watery light came through the dining-room windows. Crysta glanced at her watch. Two o'clock. For a moment, she thought she had slept through the night and into the next afternoon. Then she recalled that Alaska didn't have darkness at this time of year, only twilight. The feeling of nighttime in Sam's apartment was due to blackout shades.

A glow of lamplight spilled from a partially open doorway to her left, and through the crack she glimpsed someone moving. She veered toward the door, raising her fist to knock. Then she hesitated. Through the opening, she saw Sam Barrister seated at a large desk, his dark head bent over a pile of papers, his forehead furrowed in a scowl.

Rapping softly on the door, she gave it a push and took in the cozy work area at a glance. A gorgeous painting of an elk hung behind Sam's desk. It was unmistakably

Tip's handiwork. The pine walls shone in the aura cast
by the reading lamp, and the rich aroma of coffee teased
her nostrils. "Mr. Barrister?"

Sam Barrister flinched at the sound of her voice and
jerked up his head, his piercing dark eyes arresting her
as she started to step across the threshold.

"I, um, need to speak to you," Crysta said, feeling suddenly wary. Why was the lodge owner so jumpy? His behavior was completely at odds with the stories Derrick
had told her about him. "Do you have a minute?"

"Sure." With a casualness belied by the tautness of
his mouth, Sam shoved the papers he had been studying into a familiar-looking brown briefcase and snapped
it closed. He lifted it from his desk and stowed it in a
drawer. "Come on in."

He shoved back his chair and stood up, giving the bottom of his red sweatshirt a tug in an attempt to cover his
smudged undershirt. Crysta closed the door behind herself, then immediately wished she hadn't, her hand tightening on the cool knob.

She tensed as Barrister stepped out from behind the
desk. In the small room, he seemed even larger than he
had before, his long, well-muscled legs skimmed with
worn-soft denim, massive shoulders emphasized by the
undersized sweatshirt. He was the only man Crysta had
ever met who made her feel small. Given the circumstances, she could have done without that.

"Coffee?" he offered, voice strained. "Just made fresh."

Crysta's gaze slid to his desk. It was impeccably neat,
the wood surface agleam with wax, which clued her that
Barrister's untidy apartment and unkempt appearance
were probably uncharacteristic of him. She longed to walk
over and open the side drawer to look more closely at the

briefcase he had hidden from view. "Yes, please. Hot coffee sounds wonderful."

He strode to a battered white serving cart near the window where an automatic coffeemaker was giving its final sputter. Crysta noted that the coffee utensils were in tidy order, too, a curious contrast to their unshaven, weary-looking owner.

He took two mugs from a wooden wall rack and sloshed coffee into each. Derrick aside, Crysta was accustomed to men in suits and polished dress shoes, nails manicured, the pads of their hands as soft as hers. Sam Barrister was anything but soft.

"Don't you ever sleep?" she asked.

"Cream? Sugar?" He glanced over his shoulder at her.

"A lump of sugar, thanks."

"In answer to your question, yes, I do sleep. But these last few days, I've been too busy to do it much."

As he spoke, he moved toward her, extending one of the steaming mugs. She crooked a finger through the handle of the cup and murmured still another thank-you, feeling self-conscious and uncertain of what to say next. Gesturing toward a spare chair in front of his desk, he relieved the silence. "Have a seat."

As she lowered herself onto the leather cushion, he perched a hip on the desk, one leg straight to support his weight, the other slightly bent. There was an air of the woodsman about him, even indoors. Crysta decided his dark, rugged looks probably gave most women butterflies.

Not that she herself didn't find him attractive— amazingly so, considering that he had made no effort to look his best. Once again she noted the dark circles of exhaustion under his eyes and the telltale specks of silver peppering his unshaven jaw. His age was stamped in tiny lines upon his countenance, those bracketing his mouth deeper than those at the corners of his eyes, both giving testimony that he had laughed at life and wept over it. She got the impression he didn't realize how handsome he was or else didn't count it important. She liked that in him.

She couldn't help wondering what was so pressing that he had passed up a chance to shower and sleep to come in here and work. She shifted her attention back to the top of his desk and the papers lying on the blotter. The direction of her gaze seemed to make him uneasy.

"What was it you wanted to talk to me about?"

Crysta took a sip of coffee, then lifted her gaze to meet his. "Where are my brother's personal effects?"

"I'm sorry. I thought I told you. They were found along a trail…destroyed by the bear."

"Derrick carried his briefcase when he went hiking?"

One of Sam Barrister's eyelids twitched, but otherwise his expression remained poker straight. "I didn't realize Derrick even carried a briefcase."

"In his line of work, Derrick had contacts to make even during his off-hours. He was worse about carrying his briefcase than most women are about their purses."

Shrugging one shoulder, Barrister frowned. "Maybe Cottonwood Bend was the exception. He did come here to get away from it all, you know. And with mobile phone rates as costly as they are, he seldom contacted people from here. Maybe he left his briefcase behind in the hotel safe at Anchorage."

The skin across Crysta's cheekbones felt as if it were smeared with drying egg white. Tight-lipped, she studied this man whom Derrick had called friend. She felt certain he had just lied to her about Derrick's never bringing his paperwork to the lodge.

"Speaking of your mobile phone, Derrick called my mom from here last week, yet I noticed a note on your calendar that leads me to think your phone was being repaired. How did Derrick place a call from here when there wasn't a phone?"

Sam shot a glance toward the doorway. "Since mine was on the fritz last week, Riley O'Keefe let me borrow his."

"Riley O'Keefe?"

"He's a regular here at the lodge—the stocky redhead you saw on the island when you arrived?"

She recalled the man. "How well does he know my brother?"

"Fairly well. Riley works for Blanchette Construction."

"In what capacity?"

Barrister hesitated. "He's a warehouse supervisor."

"Are there other Blanchette people who come here regularly?"

Barrister searched her gaze, his jaw muscle flickering. "Several. Steve Henderson comes the most—the tall, brown-haired kid? Maybe you didn't notice him. Riley brings him along fairly often, probably to take Steve's mind off things at home."

"He has problems?"

Sam's eyes clouded. "A sick son. Leukemia. He's just a little tyke. It's hard on Steve. I don't think the financial squeeze he's under has helped any."

Acutely aware of the compassion revealed in Sam's eyes, Crysta remembered her original reason for coming here. Surely a man who cared so deeply about another man's sick child could be trusted. Emotion clogging her throat, she blurted, "I don't believe my brother was killed by a bear."

His eyes went deadpan. "What do you think killed him, then?"

Careful, Crysta. "I—I don't think he's dead."

Sam grew unnaturally still, watching her in that unnerving way he had that made her feel he could read far more from her expression than she wished.

"Let me rephrase that," she whispered. "I *know* he isn't dead."

He gave a nervous cough. "How can you possibly know he's not dead?"

Wrapping her fingers around the warm mug, Crysta bent her head, staring at the coarse weave of her denim jeans, fighting back the urge to tell him about her dreams. Her credibility was on the line; she mustn't forget that.

"I just know, that's all. I want to resume the search. It's imperative. We have to find Derrick before it's too late."

There followed another taut silence. Then she heard the click of porcelain on wood. With no warning, he leaned forward and grasped her shoulder, making her start. "Crysta, I know how difficult it must be for you to accept Derrick's death, especially the way he died. It's natural to go through a time of denial, even rage. Is there anything I can do to help you?"

Crysta kept her head bent. The heavy warmth of his hand and the concern she heard in his voice tapped emotions she had been fighting to ignore. Weakness. The need to be consoled. This was the same man who allowed his frightened teenage son to sleep with him, the same man who told bedtime stories to chase away nightmares. Isolated as she was from the rest of the world, Sam was the only person she could turn to. Derrick was out there somewhere. She wanted, needed, to believe in Sam Barrister, to know that he cared. "You can help me find my brother."

The request rested heavily between them. Slowly, Crysta lifted her head.

"What makes you think he's alive, that there's—" He relinquished his grip on her shoulder and shoved strong-looking fingers through his dark hair, avoiding eye contact with her while he uttered the distasteful words that followed. "What makes you think there's anything left of him to find, Crysta? You heard what the searcher said."

When he looked back at her, Crysta's turmoil increased. Sam Barrister seemed like a nice man, and she instinctively liked him. Was she responding to his good looks? To Tip's revelations about him? Or did she feel she knew him better than she actually did because of the many stories Derrick had told her about him? She knew foul play factored into Derrick's disappearance and she should trust no one at this lodge, but she needed help.

"I just know he's alive," she whispered, her voice ragged.

"You just know?"

He seemed to consider that. With the incredulous tone of his question still hanging in the air, Crysta was forced to ask herself how much or how little she could trust her own instincts. Looking at it from Sam's point of view, she had to admit that her convictions sounded absurd. Yet they stemmed from a lifetime of experiences, and she couldn't discount them, not when Derrick's life might hang in the balance. She didn't care if she looked the fool.

He finally broke the silence. "If you have one iota of proof, I'll organize a search. But, please, understand I can't do it without a darned good reason. Those men have jobs to return to in the morning, families to support."

"I'd feel it if he were dead. We're twins. Twins are— more attuned to one another than other siblings."

That was as close as Crysta dared get to the truth about her relationship with Derrick. And it wouldn't be enough. If she read Barrister right, he was a facts-and-figures man, the pragmatic sort who discounted anything he couldn't see, hear or touch.

Feeling defeated but defiant, she set her mug of coffee on Sam's desk and pushed to her feet, feeling very like a disobedient child called onto the carpet. He studied her, his expression unreadable, his jaw set in a stubborn line.

"If you won't help me look for him, then I'll hire a guide."

The corners of his mouth tightened. "The guides up here are booked for months in advance. Finding a reputable one on such short notice would be nigh unto impossible."

Crysta's flare of hope died with his words. She knew by the look in his eyes that he was telling the truth; she'd never be able to find a guide in time to help her brother. She stood there staring at him, her hands knotted into fists. Never had she felt so impotent. "Then I'll look for him myself. You'll at least steer me in the right direction, won't you?"

He raised his hands and shook his head. "No. Another lost person is the last thing I need. We're talking a bear attack, Crysta! Raw power, enough to take your head off with one swipe of a paw. You're not going out there alone. I won't allow it."

Her frustration mounting, Crysta cried, "You won't allow it? Excuse me, but I happen to be over twenty-one. You have no authority over me."

"Oh, yes, I do. This is my lodge. You're here as my guest. You get yourself killed, and I'm liable."

"I'll sign a disclaimer."

"You'll stay within sight of the lodge, that's what you'll do. In court, a disclaimer wouldn't be worth the paper it's written on. I know the dangers out there, you don't. It would be criminal to let you take the risk. Like it or not, I'm responsible for you as long as you're here. And my livelihood depends upon my reputation."

"You let Derrick take off hiking."

"Derrick was an experienced woodsman. You aren't. If I let something happen to you, it'll be a clear-cut case of negligence."

"Please…" she whispered. "It's my brother out there."

Sam met her gaze, his own stony. He had the look of a man who longed to say yes but couldn't. Sensing that he was teetering on the edge, she stood her ground, hoping he'd relent.

When the silent waiting became unbearable, she spun and left the office, trembling with frustration and fear for her brother. She felt utterly helpless, and she hated that. In her everyday world, she prided herself on being a take-control type, someone who could think quickly on her feet.

Once outside the office, she pressed a hand over her eyes, so confused by her conflicting emotions and thoughts that she couldn't make sense of anything. She wanted to trust Sam Barrister, yet common sense told her she shouldn't. Derrick's friend or his enemy, that was the question, and Crysta had no answer.

Her neck stiff with tension, she stared at the closed office door. Had that been Derrick's briefcase on Sam's desk? There was only one way to find out.

SAM STUDIED THE closed office door, his ears tuned for the sound of Crysta Meyers's footsteps so he could determine what direction she took. Outdoors. He heard the front door hinges squeak as she let herself out.

"I'd feel it if he were dead." Sam knew better than to take that statement lightly. Whether or not the Meyers twins were actually able to communicate telepathically wasn't an issue Sam cared to wrestle with at the moment. The important thing was that both twins believed it. Sam knew, through his long association with Derrick, that if Crysta had a feeling about her brother, she'd act on it as if it were fact.

Weary and discouraged, Sam tipped back his head and studied the shiplap planks in the ceiling. Crysta Meyers posed more problems than he had ever anticipated. She could be in danger if she stayed here, and Sam didn't know from what quarter the danger might come, which made it impossible to protect her. Yet how could he convince her to leave?

Being curt and unfriendly hadn't worked, and telling her the truth was out. If he revealed to her that he thought Derrick had been murdered, that he believed Derrick had stumbled across some sort of criminal activity being perpetrated by Blanchette Construction employees, she'd be determined to stay until she brought her brother's killers to justice.

Taking a slow sip of coffee, Sam cast a worried glance toward his desk drawer, wondering if Crysta had recognized Derrick's briefcase. If she had, she'd press the point until he told her the truth. He couldn't let it come to that. He wanted her safely out of here. He owed Derrick that much.

An ache centered itself behind Sam's eyes. He groaned and set aside his coffee mug to knead the back of his neck. Self-recriminations did no good, but Sam couldn't stop himself. If only he had listened more closely to Derrick when his friend had mentioned his suspicions.

I don't want to make any wild speculations at this point or finger innocent people, so I won't elaborate right now, but something fishy is going on up here in Alaska, Sam. I'm not sure what, not yet. But I'll find out, mark my words. When I do, I'll hang the creeps.

Sam, preoccupied with a discrepancy he had found in his books, had been tense the evening Derrick had come to him and had listened with only half an ear. Now the conversation haunted him.

All Sam could do was follow a paper trail in hopes of discovering what had made Derrick suspicious. Some kind of proof, that was what he wanted, something he could present to the authorities. If he approached the law empty-handed, no one would heed anything he said. *"Something fishy."* Sam had to find out what. And he had to find out quickly, before Crysta Meyers started asking the wrong people unsettling questions—people who would do anything to avoid answering.

THERE WAS MORE than one way to skin a cat.

Raised as she had been by an aphorism-prone mother, Crysta had a wealth of adages stored in her memory for every situation she encountered, and she didn't have it in her to give up easily. Going to Sam Barrister had proved a dead end, but that didn't mean she was going to stand back while the search for her brother was terminated. If Sam wouldn't or couldn't help her, she'd go above his head, directly to the search coordinator himself.

Panic nibbled at the edges of Crysta's mind. The clock was continually ticking, the seconds mounting into minutes, the minutes into hours. Time was being wasted, time that could mean the difference between life and death for Derrick.

As she walked down the slope, she scanned the circle of pup tents among the cottonwoods, hoping someone in the search team would be awake. She wasn't disappointed. Outside one tent, a man sat on a stump, a clipboard angled across his knees, one hand clasping a pen, the other holding down the paper he was writing on so the wind coming in off the river wouldn't ruffle it. She approached him slowly, trying to compose herself and rehearse what she was about to say.

"Excuse me, sir? I'm Crysta Meyers, Derrick Meyers's sister. Is the search coordinator up and about anywhere?"

The man paused in his writing and glanced up. Crysta immediately recognized him as Jim, the man who had approached Sam on the slope and broken the bad news. "You're looking at him."

Crysta couldn't believe her good luck. "Could I ask you some questions?"

His gray eyes skimmed her rumpled clothing and softened with sympathy. "I'm real sorry about your brother, ma'am. If answering questions will help you through this, I'll field any you have until our plane picks us up." He indicated a stump next to his own. "Take a load off."

Crysta perched, pressing her hands between her knees. Gazing at the nearby fire, which had burned down to coals, she recalled camping trips she had taken with Derrick, sitting on a stump or rock, her cheeks warmed by the fire, singing along while he strummed his ukulele and made up silly ditties. Pain washed through her, and her sense of loss was so acute, she ached with it. In the recent past she had wished that she could distance herself from Derrick and have a normal life. Now she would give anything to hear his voice whispering inside her head, to feel connected to him again.

"Without a—a body, how can you be positive my brother is dead? Couldn't you continue looking for him for a couple more days?"

Jim shoved his pen behind his ear and gazed off into the cottonwoods. Crysta focused on the grizzled tufts of brown hair that curled down over his upturned shirt collar. He needed a haircut and a shave. She wondered if he missed his family, if he understood her grief. She decided he must. He wouldn't be here, volunteering, if he were an uncaring man.

"It isn't easy to lose someone this way," he said softly. "I know that. But you have to accept it. We found parts of his shirt, shredded and soaked with blood. There were bear tracks and signs of struggle all around the scene."

Straightening her spine, Crysta asked, "Did you search for any evidence of foul play?"

"Foul play?" The look he gave made her feel the question was ridiculous. "No. Why would we look for something when there was no indication we should?"

Because I heard a gunshot. Crysta nibbled her lip. "Did you notice any human footprints?"

"Naturally there were some. Your brother's."

"Any others?"

He was beginning to look irritated. "We didn't make any plaster molds and compare the shoe marks, if that's what you mean. There were signs of a violent struggle, slide marks in the mud, bear tracks, blood, broken branches on the surrounding bushes, dislodged rock and your brother's shredded shirt."

Not to be deterred, Crysta pressed on. "Aren't bear tracks common up here?"

"Of course it's common."

"Were the bear tracks indicative of an attack?"

A flush crept up the man's neck. "Everything was indicative of an attack."

"Were the bear tracks just ordinary tracks? You mentioned slide marks. Were any of those marks made by the attacking bear? Or were they all made by boots?"

The muscles in his face tightened. "Ma'am, it was a clear-cut case of a renegade bear attack. There's no reason, absolutely none, to think otherwise. The authorities are satisfied with our findings. Why can't you be?"

"You found blood, but how do you know it's my brother's?"

"Whose would you guess it to be, the bear's?" He pinioned her with a steady stare, then sighed. "I'm sorry. That was uncalled for. Tests will be run, ma'am. If it isn't your brother's type or if it's animal blood, we'll resume the search."

"By then it will be too late!"

"We'll get preliminary reports back this afternoon."

"And if there's any question that it's his blood, you'll come back and begin another search?"

"It's a promise."

Crysta blinked and glanced away. Out at the island, she saw the redhead, Riley O'Keefe, disembarking from a boat. She wondered if he had been night fishing. Her brother was missing. How could people go on as if nothing had happened? "I don't think my brother's dead. We're twins, and because of that, we're closer than most siblings. I'd know. You understand?"

The search coordinator gave her a pitying look. "It's hard to accept, I know it is."

"No, you don't under—"

Crysta broke off, struggling to stop the violent shaking

that had attacked her limbs. It was such a horrible feeling to pour out her heart to people and not be able to reach them. If only telepathic phenomena didn't make people so wary! But Crysta had learned long ago that she must guard her words. Saying the wrong thing could alienate this man even more than he already was. She felt badly about grilling him, but she had so many questions and so few answers.

"Do you ever get a gut feeling? Deep down, you just know something, and you can't really explain how?"

He continued to study her, clearly at a loss.

Crysta leaned toward him, as though drawing closer would somehow convince him when words alone failed. "I know my brother isn't dead. He's out there somewhere, and every wasted second decreases his chances of survival. Please don't call off the search. Please."

"Ma'am, the evidence is overwhelming. I can't keep these fellows here. Our organization would never sanction more expenditures to cover their wages, not on the strength of a gut feeling. I'm sorry."

"Their wages?"

"Like it or not, it's a consideration."

An image of Derrick's face flashed through Crysta's mind. Her brother, whom she loved so dearly, and he was being written off because of expenses. Heartbreak prodding her, Crysta shot up from the stump and whirled on the coordinator. "So the bottom line is money, is that it? How can you place a price on a man's life? You can't just give up and leave him out there!"

Her voice had risen to a wail. When she realized how she sounded, she swallowed and swiped her sleeve across her mouth, acutely aware that the surrounding tents probably sheltered sleeping searchers who needed and deserved their rest. She gazed upriver, fighting for control, watching Riley O'Keefe bounce along the footbridge toward shore. From the surreptitious glances he shot her direction, she guessed that he had heard her outburst and probably thought she was hysterical. Not that he was far off the mark. Derrick needed her, and her ignorance of the area held her trapped here, unable to make a move on her own.

The sound of a snapping twig made Crysta glance around. A thin, brown-haired man in jeans and a powder-blue sweatshirt strode through the trees. For an instant she wondered if he had been eavesdropping on her conversation with the search coordinator, then discounted the suspicion as ridiculous. She couldn't distrust everyone she saw.

Crysta swallowed again and took a bracing breath, returning her attention to the coordinator. "I—I'm sorry for raising my voice. I should be thanking you for all you've done."

"Don't be sorry, ma'am. As hard as it is for you to believe, I understand how you feel, truly I do. I wish I could continue the search, but I can't. Not without cause. If you'd like, you can call headquarters and see if they'll authorize our staying. Or the police in Anchorage. All I need is a go-ahead."

A sense of futility swept over Crysta. Nothing she could say or do would change things, not even if she blurted out the entire story and gave them a blow-by-blow account of previous instances when she had experienced telepathic communication with her brother. Who would believe her? Except for her parents, Derrick and her aunt Eva, who had ever believed her? Not her ex-husband, certainly, not the family doctor, not her analyst. Why expect more from a bunch of strangers?

"I don't suppose you'd be interested in hiring yourself out as a guide?"

He gave her a regretful smile. "Like everyone else, I have a job I have to get back to. My boss excuses me for official searches, but when those end, he expects me back."

Crysta swallowed. "Could you recommend a guide to me, then?"

"An easy dozen, but none will be available. Their time is usually booked up well in advance, sometimes as much as a year."

"Where exactly did the bear attack occur?" she asked softly, hoping he would be more informative than Sam had been.

His gaze sharpened. "You're not thinking about going out there, are you?"

What did he expect her to do? Nothing? Crysta knew she was a lousy liar, so she chose silence as an answer.

"No way." He jerked his pen from behind his ear, suddenly all business, his body language clearly stating that, as far as he was concerned, their conversation was over. "I'm really sorry about your brother, ma'am. If you have any more questions, you know where I am."

"I have a right to know all the pertinent facts."

"If you wanna get yourself killed, you'll do it without my help."

"You're withholding information from next of kin."

He leveled a stubborn glare at her. Then, eyes revealing nothing, he pointed downstream. "The scene of the attack was thataway."

The sarcasm made Crysta want to shake him. "How far?"

He seemed to consider the question. "Several miles."

"Several meaning three, four, five? How many would you guess?"

"More than two, less than ten. I didn't log the exact location."

"Was it along the river, at the mouth of an inlet, along a slough?"

He frowned, feigning bewilderment. "I think it was along the river, but then again, it could have been a slough. It was definitely along the Yentna somewhere, and it'd be hard to miss if you came across it. We flagged the area."

Blazing with anger and fighting off tears, Crysta turned away before she lost her temper. It certainly wouldn't help Derrick if she alienated everyone who might be able to find him. As she walked up the slope back to the lodge, she weighed her options, trying to decide what she should do next. It didn't look as if she was going to convince anyone else to resume the search for her brother. She needed a map of the area.

Weariness blurred her thoughts, and the maze of disjointed ideas in her head made her wonder if she wasn't losing her ability to be rational. Overwhelming evidence indicated that Derrick was dead, the victim of a bear attack. Was she insane to believe otherwise?

A gust of wind caught Crysta's hair, whipping it across her face. She stared through the reddish-brown strands, wondering if she would ever again see her brother's hair gleaming in sunshine, ever again hear him call her name.

As a greenhorn in rugged country, she would be taking a perilous step if she ventured far from the lodge alone. She must think things through, plan her strategy. If her dreams were accurate, there was a whole lot more than bears out there to worry about. She would need all her wits about her, that was a certainty. Maybe a hot bath would clear her head.

She slipped quietly into Sam's apartment and gathered fresh clothing from her suitcases, then slipped quietly out again, relieved that she hadn't encountered Sam. As she approached the sauna building, the hair on her nape prickled. Hesitating, she glanced uneasily around. When she spied no one, she shrugged off the sensation, blaming it on exhaustion and raw nerves.

Proceeding up the steps to the building, she flipped the sign over to Occupied, as Sam had told her to do, and opened the heavy outer door to the anteroom. After hanging her fresh clothing on the provided hooks, Crysta selected a few chunks of wood from the supply along one wall, then opened the stove door and refueled the fire. Grabbing soap, shampoo and a towel off the stack, she stepped through the interior doorway into the steam room, pulling the massive door closed behind her.

Amazed at how effectively Sam's rustic sauna system worked, Crysta deep-breathed the steam. The structure had soaked up the mist until the foot-thick walls were swollen and airtight. Now she could appreciate Sam's reasons for not putting latches on the doors. The air was so hot and thick that someone less fit could easily stay in here too long and get woozy.

Crysta felt as though a hundred years had rolled away. On one side of the room was a recessed area in the planked floor, bedded with rock that was somehow heated by the wood stove. A huge galvanized tub sat on the rock, the simmering water within sending up a continual mist of steam. Nearby was another tub, filled with cool water. The opposite wall supported handmade steam benches. The slatted floor provided drainage.

She had always imagined coming to the lodge with Derrick, to have him be the one to show her around.

Remembering only sketches of Sam Barrister's instructions, Crysta was on her own in figuring out the bathing procedure. Feeling uneasy because there was no latch on the door to guarantee privacy, Crysta undressed, then sloshed water over the rocks so she could enjoy the calming effects of the steam. She filled the large bucket by the tub of hot water, added cold water to get the temperature right and dumped the contents over herself. Definitely not the Ritz, but she guessed that was the appeal of Cottonwood Bend. People came here to escape the strictures of their citified lives.

After a brisk shampoo and scrubdown, she returned to the anteroom and dressed, forgoing makeup and giving her hair only a few cursory swipes with a brush.

En route back to the lodge, Crysta spotted a flash of red down by the river. Riley O'Keefe. Remembering that Sam had said the Irishman worked for Blanchette, Crysta decided to talk to him, just to see if she might glean some new information. Stowing her damp clothing by the lodge entrance, she struck off toward the river, shivering as a cool breeze whipped up off the water to cut through her denim shirt and jeans. For the first time since coming to Alaska, she wished she had on her thermal undershirt.

Riley O'Keefe, who had been cleaning fish, smiled when she approached. Scooping a wad of chewing tobacco from inside his cheek, he shook his hand clean and spat. "Sorry to be caught with a chaw, but I wasn't expectin' company this time of morning. Nice to know I'm not the only night owl up and around."

Appalled that anyone would stick a fish-bloodied finger in his mouth, Crysta hid a shudder and said, "It doesn't seem like night to me." She shot a glance at the sky. "It's kind of like twilight, isn't it?"

"Yeah, but this time of year, it's the only nighttime you'll get. Makes for a great growing season, but newcomers often have trouble sleeping. It'll catch up with you, though, and when it does, you'll crash and sleep like the dead."

The dead. Everything reminded her of Derrick and her race against time. Crysta raked her fingers through her wet hair, forcing herself to smile. "I understand you know my brother."

"I knew him."

Crysta flinched at his use of the past tense. "You work for Blanchette, Sam tells me."

"That's right." Opening a Coleman cooler that sat beside him, Riley fished out a dripping can of beer. "Want one? Might help you sleep, and I've got plenty more where this came from. I'm heading into Anchorage later. Shriver's making the loop today, so I can put in a few hours at work, pick up another rack of beer, then pull a U-turn and do more fishing. The life of Riley." He chuckled at his joke, then arched an eyebrow. "Wet your whistle with me?"

Crysta couldn't help wondering how Riley O'Keefe could afford frequent trips to the lodge and all the beer he wanted to drink on a warehouse supervisor's wages. Maybe she was in the wrong line of work. "I'm not much of a beer drinker unless the weather's extremely hot. Thanks for offering."

He pulled the can tab. Tipping back his head, he guzzled, his larynx bobbing. For a moment, she thought he meant to drain the can. Giving a satisfied burp and an apologetic smile, he wiped his chin with his shirt sleeve.

"I guess you're the type who comes prepared," Crysta said lightly.

"How's that?"

"Well, you have a stock of brew." She inclined her head at the cooler. "And I understand you travel with your phone. You lent it to Sam last week, didn't you?"

"The mobile phone?" He nodded. "Yeah, I brought mine up. His was gone for repairs. In a remote place like this, a phone is a must. Never know when an emergency might come up."

Crysta's throat tightened as she glanced downstream. "Yes, my brother's disappearance proves that."

Riley finished off his beer, tossed the can into a sack beside him and promptly reached into the cooler for another. Nearby, Crysta saw a pile of discarded beer cans in the brush, and she was surprised that Riley's hadn't joined them. His regard for the environment made her reverse her first unfavourable impression of him. Just because a man had poor chewing-tobacco habits didn't mean he wasn't a nice person.

"I'm real sorry about Derrick, by the way. Started to tell you so when you landed, but I wasn't sure what to say."

The sympathy in his expression made a lump rise in Crysta's throat, and her eyes started to burn. To maintain control over her emotions, she gazed at the beer cans in the nearby brush. Alaska wouldn't remain beautiful and untouched very long if people threw litter all over the place. She wondered why Sam didn't lay some ground rules for his guests. Perhaps he had, and some simply chose to ignore them.

"I guess there isn't much anyone can say," Crysta finally replied, dragging her gaze back to Riley. After a moment, she asked, "You wouldn't happen to know exactly where my brother's clothing was found, would you?"

O'Keefe gave her a knowing look. "Why don't you ask the search coordinator?"

"I did, but he was rather vague."

His voice gentle with concern, he asked, "You aren't thinking about going down there, are you?"

"I might. That's my decision."

"True. Unfortunately, I don't know the exact location. Just that it was downriver somewhere."

Frustration seethed within Crysta, warming her skin. She had a hunch O'Keefe knew more than he was telling. "If you do know, I'd appreciate your telling me. I realize the risks."

He gave her a pleading look. "Don't put me on the spot. It's not my business, you know? I'm just a guest here. If I get on Sam's bad side, my weekend retreat is shot all to hell, and I like coming here."

Crysta could see pressing him for more information would be fruitless. She understood everyone's concern and appreciated their reasons for trying to protect her, but it was frustrating, nonetheless. She decided to explore another subject. "I gather you come here a lot?"

"Every chance I get."

"Must be nice. Most people can't afford the rates or the airfare in."

"All the pilots give me a break on my airfare, and Sam gives me a discount."

"It still must be expensive. Especially if you bring your friend often. What's his name?"

"Steve Henderson. He's not the only guy from work I bring, but I do bring him the most. It's all what your priorities are, I guess. Me, I'm single, don't have kids. I figure I may as well enjoy myself. And if a few weekends away help Steve to cope, it seems little enough for me to do, paying his way up. Nice kid, Steve. Closest thing to a son I'll ever have."

"It's good of you to care. Nowadays, too many people don't." Crysta focused on O'Keefe's wristwatch, wondering if it was a genuine Rolex or an inexpensive lookalike. "I gather you and Sam must know each other well."

He nodded. "Sam's good people."

"You like him, then?"

"Everybody likes Sam."

"I know my brother did."

Riley O'Keefe took another swallow of beer, sighing with satisfaction as he drew the can from his mouth. "Yeah, they got along real well. Most of the time, anyway."

Crysta's skin prickled. "Most of the time?"

O'Keefe shrugged. "Nobody gets along a hundred percent."

"I wasn't aware they ever disagreed."

"Wasn't any big deal."

Crysta took a moment to phrase her next question, not wishing to sound too eager. "When were they on the outs?"

He squinted and leaned over to retie the laces on his boot. Another green boot with a band of yellow at the top. "Derrick had been coming up a lot lately, more than usual. You know how it goes. Too much of a good thing. Don't misunderstand—they were good friends. Hell, Sam's been half out of his mind since Derrick came up missing. They just didn't see eye to eye sometimes, that's all."

That was news to Crysta. "I guess we all feel cross at

times." She caught the inside of her cheek between her teeth, worrying the soft flesh, her gaze fixed on O'Keefe's ruddy face. "They weren't quarreling last week, were they? Right before Derrick disappeared?"

He glanced up, his eyes sharpening. "What if they were?"

Crysta shoved her hands into the pockets of her jeans. "Just curious. That could account for Sam's re-action to Derrick's disappearance. He might feel a lit-tle guilty, which always makes losing someone hurt all the more."

He seemed to relax. "It was no big deal. Something silly, I think. Sam was a little hot when Derrick left, but he would have been over it by the time your brother got back."

"So you haven't any idea what they were upset about?"

"Even if I did, it wouldn't be my business to repeat it."

She gave a shrug, feigning an unconcern she was far from feeling, questions burning within her. Press-ing O'Keefe for answers right now might be unwise. He could relate her curiosity to Sam, forewarning the lodge owner that she knew he had quarreled with Der-rick. Crysta preferred to spring that knowledge on Sam when he didn't know it was coming and when it might be to her advantage.

She studied the trees, filled with resentment toward Sam, pretending she had run out of things to say. "Well, I guess I should at least try to sleep. It was nice talking to you, Mr. O'Keefe."

"Same here. And, once again, I'm really sorry about your brother. He was a favorite around here, a real nature enthusiast and a helluva nice man to work under. I'll miss him, in more ways than one."

Crysta bit back a rebuttal. Derrick wasn't dead. She just knew he wasn't. Not yet.

CHAPTER SIX

A DELICIOUS SMELL wafted to Crysta as she approached the lodge. Curious about who would be up cooking at this hour, she followed her nose, circling the building until she came upon a plump Indian woman busily placing trays of salmon on racks in a makeshift smokehouse. Though Crysta had little interest in salmon-smoking techniques, she was keenly interested in learning all she could about Derrick's last visit here. If this woman worked at the lodge, she might have answers to some of Crysta's questions.

"Hello," Crysta called softly.

Stooped over a burdensome tray, the woman turned slightly at the waist and fixed her black eyes on Crysta, her square face expressionless. Making no attempt to be friendly, she grunted and returned her attention to her work. She was bedecked in jewelry, her arms striped with colorful bangles, her neck with gaudy strands of beads and ivory pendants, her earlobes weighted with dangling ovals of scrimshaw. Even her black braid was interwoven with handmade jewelry.

"I'm Derrick Meyers's sister."

"I know who you are," the woman replied, her voice toneless.

"You have me at a disadvantage."

The woman ignored that.

"If you know who I am, then you must know my brother."

She graced Crysta with another glance. "I knew him."

Crysta's heart caught, and she glanced uneasily at the ground, struck speechless by the woman's ill-concealed animosity. What reason could the Indian cook have for disliking her?

"He would not want you here."

The words were spoken so softly that Crysta almost thought she had imagined them. She looked up, confused and shaken. "Why do you say that?"

"Because it is true. The Tlingit Indians speak only truth. You walk in the shadow of the great black bird, Crysta Meyers. Death is your companion. Go home. Back to the living. There is nothing for you here but sorrow—great sorrow."

So she was a Tlingit. Crysta knew very little about the Alaskan tribes, but it seemed to her she had once read that the Tlingit hailed from the southeast section of the state. If so, this woman was a long way from where most of her people lived. "Wh—what do you mean?"

"What I said. Go home." The woman returned her black gaze to the salmon racks. "Go now, before it is too late."

With that, she closed the smokehouse door and walked toward the lodge, an emptied tray swinging in one hand, her colorful gathered skirt swirling around her plump calves, her braid bouncing along her spine. Crysta longed to pursue her and demand that she elaborate.

She longed to but didn't. The people at Cottonwood Bend were not what they seemed. Sam Barrister had quarreled with her brother right before he disappeared. Now this Indian woman spouted veiled threats. Crysta had a bad feeling, a very bad feeling.

She circled the lodge and retrieved her bundle of clothing. As she drew up at the front entrance, Sam Barrister was coming through the doorway. He was looking back over his shoulder and speaking to someone, so he didn't see her. Though Crysta tried, she couldn't sidestep him quickly enough to avoid a collision. Stunned, teeth snapping together on impact, she dropped her clothes, staggered and would have fallen if not for Sam's quick reaction.

Seizing her shoulders, he righted her. "Are you okay? I should have been watching where I was going."

"I—" Crysta closed her eyes, then opened them, still disoriented. "I'm fine, just a little rattled."

Focusing on the lodge owner's dark face, Crysta could have sworn his concern was genuine. His grip on her shoulders tightened, hinting at the leashed strength in his hands. She looked past his arm into the dimly lit lodge. "It seems to be my day for unsettling encounters. I just had a skirmish with a Tlingit."

"A Tlingit?" One of his eyebrows shot up. "Jangles?"

"Is that her name? She was so busy trying to scare me, she didn't introduce herself."

Sam's mouth quirked. Releasing her, he bent to pick up her clothes. "Don't mind Jangles. Her heart's in the right place. She's just a little abrupt at times."

He called that abrupt? "She threatened me."

"Jangles?" He looked amused by the thought. "That doesn't sound like her. Threatened how?"

"She told me to go home, back to the living, before it was too late. Something about walking in shadows."

Sam pressed the bundle of clothing into her arms, his

expression turning wry. There was something different about him, but she couldn't pinpoint what. She only knew he was even more attractive than she had first thought, which was unsettling, and she missed the comforting warmth of his hands on her shoulders, which was doubly so.

"Probably her superstitious nature coming out," he offered. "Some of the natives are frightened by death or any dealings with it. Maybe she's afraid because you've come here searching for Derrick."

"Are Tlingits particularly superstitious?"

"Most Indian cultures are rife with superstitions."

Crysta had to admire the neat way he had avoided giving her a direct answer. Somehow, she felt sure Sam knew as much about Tlingits as he did about Alaska. She wondered if he would be equally evasive when she cornered him about his quarrel with Derrick.

Shoving the door open wider, he stepped aside to allow her through. "You're sure you're okay?"

Crysta's mind raced, trying to sort the questions she wanted to ask him. All she could manage was a weak "I'm fine."

Since she couldn't just leave him standing in such an awkward position, bracing the door open, she ducked under his arm, amazed, even in her agitation, that he was so tall. So large a man would have no difficulty overpowering someone Derrick's size. It was an unsettling thought, but one she couldn't banish once it slipped into her mind.

Sam inclined his head, then continued on through the doorway before Crysta could voice any of the questions she had hoped to ask him. When the door swung closed behind him, she stood staring at the wood. Only then did she realize what was different about Sam Barrister. He had showered, changed clothes and shaved. The brown plaid shirt he wore was far more flattering than the grungy sweatshirt he'd sported earlier.

After stowing her soiled clothing in Sam's apartment, Crysta returned to the front of the lodge. On the check-in counter, she spied a rack of maps, some of them the forestry type that plotted the surrounding wilderness. Helping herself to one, she sat at one of the long dining tables, smoothing the large map open on the planks. Within seconds she was absorbed in the spidery network of lines, trying to decipher the small print and pinpoint where along the river Derrick might have been when she had dreamed of men chasing him.

"I DON'T BELIEVE Derrick is dead. I know he isn't." The words ate at Sam. After sharing a few pleasantries with Riley O'Keefe, Sam stared downstream, his thoughts fragmented. What if Crysta was right and Derrick was out there someplace, alive and in need of help, while he wasted precious time going through a briefcase for clues?

In his mind, Sam relived every detail of his initial search for Derrick, which had culminated with his finding Derrick's shredded backpack and scattered camping gear. Had he overlooked something, some telltale clue?

Torn, Sam cast a furtive glance at the lodge, then sauntered toward the trees. One thing was for sure, he didn't want Crysta to realize he'd given credence to anything she said. If she found a single chink in his armor, she'd work at it until he confessed everything. And then she'd be in on this until the bloody end.

The word *bloody* stuck in Sam's thought grooves like a scratchy needle on a phonograph record. He circled the lodge, then struck off through the trees, hoping the indirect route would prevent anyone from noticing his departure. It was quite a trek to the spot where Derrick's gear had been found, a good twelve miles, but Sam knew he could pace it off, do a more thorough search of the area and return before anyone became unduly alarmed by his absence. Sometimes, though not often, his long legs were an asset.

A MOVEMENT CAUGHT Crysta's attention, and she glanced up from the map. Through the window, she saw Sam Barrister skulking through the cottonwoods and casting furtive looks over his shoulder, as though he didn't want to be seen. With the mystery of her brother's disappearance foremost in her thoughts, Crysta deduced that the lodge owner's secretive excursion involved Derrick. She didn't take time to think beyond that.

Shooting up from the bench, she raced outside, determined to follow Barrister without his knowing it. She could only hope Riley O'Keefe, who still sat on the riverbank, had drunk so many beers that he wouldn't notice her as she slunk around the sauna and darted into the woods.

Before long Crysta was cursing Sam Barrister for his lengthy stride. Not an easy man to tail. She was forced into a trot half the time, just to keep him in sight. Along the riverbank, the brush was thick and tall. While it provided her with necessary cover, it presented a problem when it came to following someone.

Sam disappeared from view. Crysta strained to catch a glimpse of him through the tangled undergrowth, then increased her pace, cringing at the noise she was making.

At a run, it wasn't easy to be quiet, and she had no ready explanation if he should turn around and discover her.

Three miles later, Crysta's side ached from exertion. She stopped a moment to catch her breath, scarcely able to believe Barrister or any other man could cover ground so quickly at a walk. Peering through the trees, she once again tried to spot his brown plaid shirt. He was nowhere in sight. Momentary panic set in. Not only did she hate to lose him, but she wasn't too thrilled about being out here alone.

A crackling noise made Crysta whirl to look behind her. Footsteps? Frustrated by the low rushing sound of the river, she strained to hear, eyes scanning the woods for movement, heart racing, her senses bombarded by unfamiliar smells and sights. Poised for flight, she felt the muscles in her legs quiver. Suddenly, all the conversations of that morning came back to taunt her. What if everyone else was right, and she was wrong? What if her brother was indeed dead?

One word bounced off the walls of her mind. *Bears*. Still, if there was anything as big as a grizzly out there, surely she would see it. Or hear it. A renegade bear wasn't likely to be furtive before it launched an attack. A picture of Derrick's shredded shirt flashed in her head, and her stomach lurched. She listened a few more seconds, flinching when leaves, caught by the wind, rustled overhead. Nothing. Whatever she had heard, it was gone now. She hoped.

A more cautious person probably wouldn't be out here. It was a fault of hers, acting before she weighed the consequences. She drew little comfort from her proximity to the river, by which she could retrace her footsteps. After all, bears ate fish, didn't they?

Bears or no, Crysta knew she was out of her element and should follow the river back to the lodge. But she didn't want to. What she wanted was to dog Barrister's heels and see where he was going. Was she going to let thoughts of a four-legged man-eater scare her off?

Determined, she slogged through a narrow slough, wetting her jeans to the knee. Common sense told her that since Barrister had followed the river this far, he wasn't likely to alter his course. If she discovered that he had, she could turn back.

She ran across a stretch of marshy grass and back into the brush, darting right and left through the maze of dappled cottonwood trunks and undergrowth. Straining for a glimpse of the lodge owner up ahead, Crysta was taken totally off guard when a dark shape hurtled out at her from the thick brush.

A bear? Fright flashed through her, but there was no time to react. One instant she was on her feet, and the next she felt as if a brick wall had mowed her down. She spied a blur of brown plaid. Then coarse wool grazed her cheek. Sam Barrister. When she tried to move, she found herself vised in a tangle of muscular arms and legs. The instinctive scream that had welled in her chest came out as a grunt when he rolled, flattening her body with his, slamming her face into the dirt.

It quickly occurred to Crysta that Sam Barrister must think he had tackled a man. She was proved correct an instant later when he clamped a palm over her breast and froze. The contact made Crysta's nerves leap.

"Son of a— What in the—?" He jerked his hand away. "Don't you know better than to sneak up on someone like that? It's a good way to get yourself hurt."

With her face buried in dirt and moldy leaves, Crysta

couldn't have replied if she wanted to. It was all she could do to gather her wits and regain her shattered composure. Her skin still tingled from the touch of his hand, and the unwelcome, purely feminine reaction at such an inopportune moment made her unreasonably angry, with him and herself.

Twisting her face to one side, she spat out dirt and other things she didn't want to identify. Then she ran her tongue over her throbbing front teeth, none too sure they were all intact.

He muttered something that sounded suspiciously like a curse, then rolled, came up on one knee and extracted his arm from around her. "I could hear you but couldn't see you. If I'd known it was you, I—" He let out a ragged sigh. "I'm sorry. I just reacted."

Crysta pushed up on her elbows, shoulder throbbing, scraped cheek afire. He reached to help her, seeming uncertain where to touch. By the flush rising up his muscular neck, she guessed that he was as unsettled as she by the physical awareness that had flared between them.

"I'm really sorry. I didn't mean to— Is anything broken?"

"I'm fine." Squelching her anger, which she knew was due more to embarrassment than outrage, Crysta gave her sleeve a tug and brushed debris from her hair, taking advantage of the brief silence to mend her shattered dignity. Testing her shoulder, she said, "You pack quite a wallop."

"It never occurred to me it might be you, and with everything that's been going on, I decided to act first and ask questions later."

Crysta focused on only part of what he said. As she flicked the leaves and dirt off her favorite denim shirt, she countered, "Exactly what *has* been going on?"

━ The flush on his neck deepened. He flexed his shoulders, bracing one arm on his upraised knee. The breeze ruffled his dark hair across his forehead, and Crysta had a sudden urge to smooth it with her fingertips. She stifled the wayward impulse, determined to ignore the attraction she felt to him. For some reason beyond her comprehension, she was drawn to this man in a way that defied all her attempts to squelch it.

Frustration mounting, Crysta fired another shot. "You've been keeping things from me. I know you have."

His eyes met hers, teeming with indefinable emotion, but he said nothing.

"You quarreled with Derrick right before he left. Do you deny that?"

"No."

"What did you argue about?"

His jaw tensed. "That isn't any of your concern."

His response so infuriated Crysta that she shot to her feet. How could she allow herself to be attracted to this man? He clearly wasn't being up front with her, and his reasons for that remained to be seen. She could only assume the worst.

"Not my concern? My brother is missing! Anything involving him is my concern! Don't play games with me, Mr. Barrister. I don't appreciate it."

"Sam."

"I hardly think we should be on a first-name basis. I want answers."

"I'm your brother's best friend, have been for nearly ten years. Doesn't that count for something? How can you possibly think I had anything to do with what happened to him?"

"If that bothers you, then level with me!"

For a moment, Crysta thought he might do just that. The shutters lifted from his dark eyes, and she saw pain reflected there. In that instant, she would have sworn he loved her brother, possibly as much as she did. With Derrick's life at stake, though, she couldn't afford to go on intuition. She also wasn't sure, judging from the tangle of her emotions when she was near this man, that she could trust her instincts.

"How about your leveling with me?" he retorted. "What makes you so sure Derrick's alive? Why did you come to Alaska when I asked you not to? Why are you acting as though some*one* hurt your brother when you've been told repeatedly that he was the victim of a bear attack? And why on earth did you follow me out here?"

Crysta clenched her teeth to keep from answering those questions. A part of her wanted to tell him everything. She also reasoned that she was out here alone with him. With his size as an advantage, he needn't engage in a war of words for long. On the other hand, he had to realize that two disappearances in less than a week were bound to raise eyebrows.

Reassured by that thought, she said, "If you're so certain my brother was killed by a crazed bear, Mr. Barrister, then why aren't you carrying a gun?"

She could see the question caught him unprepared. Her determination bolstered, she rapped out another question. "Where were you going?"

"For a walk."

Crysta knew that no one would take such precautions to avoid being seen simply to go for a walk. She braced her hands on her hips. "I know whatever it was you intended to do somehow involved my brother, and I want to know what it was."

He gave her a look far too innocent to be genuine. "You must read too many mysteries. I came for a walk, that's all."

"I *never* read mysteries." Two could play this game. Crysta shrugged. "I saw you coming out here and decided to join you. Nothing mysterious about that, either, is there?"

His expression registered *touché* as clearly as if he had spoken. Pushing to his feet, he regarded her steadily. Then, with a half grin, he reached to pluck a leaf out of her hair, his hand lingering longer than was necessary, his thumb grazing her temple. "You not only *look* like Derrick, you act like him."

Crysta had the uncomfortable feeling that he was trying to distract her, and she was loath to admit that the tactic might work. The notion and all it implied frightened her in some indefinable way she didn't have the energy to deal with right now. "Why do I get the feeling that isn't a compliment?"

His grin broadened. "Possibly because you know Derrick as well as I do. When they came up with the word *bullheaded,* it was with him in mind."

Drawing on the store of maxims her mother used so frequently, Crysta quipped, "Birds of a feather flock together. According to Derrick, you two were very close." She paused, gauging the seconds so her next words would catch him off guard. "Is that why you quarreled, because Derrick's bullheaded?"

His face tightened. "Like I said, that's not your concern."

"If my inferences bother you, why keep secrets? Your having a quarrel with Derrick looks bad. Even you have to admit that. If it was over nothing important, why hide it?"

He arched an eyebrow. "Excuse me, but do I in any way resemble a bear, Crysta? A quarrel wouldn't look bad if you would take things at face value."

"Face value isn't good enough, not when my brother's life rides on it. I want answers, and I'm not getting them, not from you or anyone else. You've no right to keep secrets from me."

His eyes gave her no quarter. "And you've no right to accuse me of things without proof."

"But I do have every right to see where my brother's gear was found, where this *alleged* bear attack occurred. Yet you refuse to tell me where either of those places is. And you've seen to it that no one else will tell me, either. I resent being treated as if I were a child."

"A child? This is Alaska, not the Los Angeles zoo. A renegade grizzly could spot you in his territory from a mile away and go into attack mode. Grizzlies don't cotton to interlopers at the best of times. Hikers learn to respect their habits and go out of their way to accommodate them. But a crazed bear? We're talking totally unpredictable."

"Then why don't you escort me downriver? I'd be safe with you, and I could satisfy my curiosity."

"You *wouldn't* be safe with me, that's just it. Do you see a large red *S* emblazoned on my shirt?" The sound of a snapping twig caught his attention. He glanced over his shoulder, looking uneasy. Crysta wondered if his behavior was a ploy calculated to frighten her. She scanned the woods behind him. When he looked back at her, she met his gaze. "I couldn't protect myself from a grizzly, let alone you," he finished.

"Come on, Sam. Derrick's told me what an expert guide you are. You're as at home out here as in your living room. You don't let grizzlies or any other bears stop you from hiking."

"Under ordinary circumstances, no. It's safe enough, if you know what you're doing. But these aren't ordinary circumstances, and that's no ordinary bear out there. And, contrary to what you seem to think, I'm a very ordinary guy. Besides, I told you flat out before you came that I didn't have time to escort you downriver."

"Yet you have time for a walk?" Shaking with anger, she gestured upstream toward the lodge. "Shall we head back? Or do you want to *stroll* a little farther?"

Sam bit back a frustrated groan. She had pluck, he'd give her that. But there was such a thing as being too fearless for one's own good. If he was correct and Derrick had fallen victim to foul play, the last thing Sam needed was a daring and stubborn sleuthing partner. He wanted Crysta on the first flight out, safely away from here before she followed the wrong man into the woods or pressed the wrong person for answers. So much for re-examining the spot where he had found Derrick's gear.

"We may as well head back," he growled.

She glanced around. "How much farther is it?"

So exhausted that he was operating on automatic pilot, Sam said, "It's about—" and then caught himself. She had almost nailed him. "You don't give up, do you?"

"Would you?"

Her hazel eyes lifted, filled with such pain and fear that Sam yearned to comfort her. The answer to her question was no, if it was his brother missing, he would never give up, but he couldn't admit that. Nor could he acknowledge, even to himself, that her expression tugged at his heart.

Over the last ten years Sam had formed a vague picture of Crysta from Derrick's stories about her, but even so, she'd been little more than a name to him. Now the reality of her was hitting him like a well-placed blow to his solar plexus. She was a living, breathing, feeling person, grappling with grief and terror. And he was helpless to do anything about it. The fact that she appealed to him more than any other woman ever had made the situation he found himself in even more difficult.

ONCE BACK AT THE LODGE, Sam dropped Crysta off at the door and went down to the river, presumably to oversee his paying guests but in actuality to think and wait for a more opportune moment to sneak away. Until he was certain Crysta wouldn't follow him, he didn't dare go downstream again.

A feeling of helplessness dogged Sam everywhere he went. Derrick. He couldn't get his friend off his mind. *"Something fishy."* What had Derrick meant by that? And whom had he suspected? Sam was totally in the dark. Surely Derrick had come across an illegal activity of some kind within his company. But what? *"Something fishy up here in Alaska,"* he had said. *"I'll hang the creeps."* Derrick had suspected something serious, definitely. Something so serious that the perpetrators had killed him to protect their anonymity.

Or had they? *"I don't believe my brother is dead. I know he isn't."* Sam sat on the riverbank, arms braced on his knees, shoulders slumped with weariness. There was only one consolation in all of this. If Derrick was indeed alive, he was an expert woodsman and could survive in the Alaska interior for quite some time. Unless, of course, he was badly hurt. In that case, he probably wouldn't have lasted this long.

MORE DETERMINED NOW than ever to search for her brother on her own, Crysta returned to her map the moment she got back to the lodge. She was deeply engrossed when Tip's voice snagged her attention. She glanced up to spy him walking across the dining hall, hair rumpled from sleep, his cheek lined from where it had pressed against his pillow.

"H-hi, Crys. Wh-what are you d-doing?"

His shy smile made it impossible for Crysta to say she was busy. She patted the table across from her. "I'm looking this map over. Have a seat."

"Am I b-bugging you?"

Crysta forced a smile. "Certainly not. Whoever said such a thing to you?"

"Lots of people." He swung a jeans-clad leg over the opposite bench and sat astraddle the wood, one elbow propped on the table's edge. "I don't bug my dad, but he loves me."

Crysta was pleased to note that the boy's stuttering had stopped, a sign that her warm welcome had put him at ease.

"Well, I *like* you. Does that count?"

His cheek dimpled as he smiled, giving Crysta an idea of what Sam might look like if his expression wasn't so stern all the time. Cocking his head, Tip regarded the map. Jabbing a finger at a spot upriver from their location at the lodge, he said, "I walk to that place a lot."

"Do you?"

It occurred to Crysta that Tip might know the area well enough to give her some direction. But before she could pursue that train of thought, he jerked her offtrack.

"D-do you really think my p-pictures are good enough to sell?"

The return of his stammer told Crysta just how important to him her reply was. Recalling Sam's disapproval of this subject, she hesitated, but she couldn't bring herself to lie. "I not only think they would sell, but for premium prices. I believe you could become famous if you showed your work."

Beaming with pleasure, Tip shot up off the bench. "I'm going to go paint."

Crysta gazed after him, momentarily distracted from her worries about her brother. Tip clearly wanted to display his paintings, yet Sam wouldn't allow it. Crysta couldn't imagine why. Surely Sam could see that his son wanted and needed to excel in something, that he yearned to be accepted by others as an equal. It was cruel to keep him secluded here, exposed only to the guests. In addition, many people who patronized an establishment seemed to feel it acceptable to snipe at those who worked there. As a designer and dress-shop owner, Crysta had been on the receiving end of such behavior. Someone like Tip couldn't understand that the jabs made at him weren't personal.

With a weary sigh, Crysta eyed a nearby window. As much as she might like to champion Tip and to make Sam understand his son's needs, she didn't have time right now to play family counselor. Pushing to her feet, she sidled over to the glass and peered out at the river to see if Sam had tried sneaking off again. Sunlight glanced under the eaves, making her squint. It should be dark outside at this predawn hour, yet it wasn't. Was Derrick out there somewhere, gazing at that same river? Hurt, possibly, and growing weaker? The thought made Crysta ache, and the need to be doing something hit her with such force that she stiffened.

She saw Sam Barrister in one of the boats out on the

river, helping a guest wield a large fishing net. As she watched him work, it occurred to her that as long as he was thus occupied, she had a perfect opportunity to snoop.

A tingle crept up the nape of her neck as she turned from the window to contemplate the closed office door. Was it locked? Her heart picked up speed. Invading some-one else's privacy wasn't something she felt comfortable doing, and yet, how could she not? She wouldn't rest until she examined the familiar-looking sienna briefcase she had seen on Sam's desk. Was it Derrick's, as she sus-pected, or a look-alike?

The few feet to the office seemed like a mile as she moved across the rustic planked floor. Checking over her shoulder, Crysta made sure no one was watching before she tried the doorknob. It turned easily. Afraid of being discovered, she pushed quickly into the room and eased the door closed behind her, leaning her back against the wood. Her heartbeat resounded in her ears while she stood there, half expecting someone to burst in after her.

To her dismay, she felt no lock button when she glided her fingers over the cool surface of the doorknob. Some-one might walk in and catch her there. She sped to the desk. The more quickly she checked the briefcase and got out of there, the better. A good plan, except for one thing: she felt like a common thief. When she reached to open the drawer, her hand hovered over the handle, fin-gers trembling.

Her love for Derrick strengthened her resolve. This was no time to be a faintheart. Taking a deep breath, she jerked the drawer open. Disappointment coursed through her when all she saw was a thick, leather-bound book, the same shade of brown as Derrick's briefcase. Was this what she had seen on Sam's desk?

No, she distinctly recalled Sam shoving papers back into a folder, closing the briefcase and pressing the latches. She had been tired, yes, but not so exhausted that she had started imagining things.

Was this a plant, then? Had Sam hoped she would come here, see the brown book and believe her eyes had tricked her? The thought unsettled her. If such was the case, she was dealing with a very crafty fellow. Removing the book from the drawer, Crysta flipped it open.

The heavy pages parted about a third of the way through. Crysta stared at a lock of dark hair affixed to the paper with clear tape. To the right of the hair was a notation, written in bold, masculine longhand, *Eighteen months*. On another page was a tiny tooth, stained a peculiar lavender shade, with the footnote, *Tip's first tooth, lost at six years when learning to blow bubbles with grape bubble gum.*

Feeling an irresistible need to learn all she could about Sam Barrister, Crysta leafed through several more pages. Snapshots of Tip. Crayoned artwork done by a child's clumsy hand. An arrowhead. Dried flowers. All annotated in that manly script. Crysta's mouth inched into a reluctant smile. A scrapbook, filled with a father's treasured memories.

She could almost see Tip, as a much younger child, eyes bright with excitement, scurrying into the lodge with surprises for his dad. It said a great deal on Sam's behalf that he had not only saved everything but had so painstakingly recorded the memories. One of Tip's crayon drawings depicted a stick-figure man holding a child on his lap, a storybook opened on his knee. Knowing Tip's penchant for detail, Crysta guessed Sam must have read to his son frequently. Was a man without feeling capable of loving so deeply? Crysta didn't think so.

Shoving the scrapbook back into the drawer, she checked all the other desk compartments, then went to the cupboards along one wall. Door after door revealed nothing but lodge-related paperwork—daily sheets, receipts and past years' tax documents. Dust burned in her nostrils as she shifted stack after stack of papers.

Then Crysta opened a middle cupboard. The edge of a brown briefcase peeked out at her from beneath a pile of yellowed folders. She recognized the case by the deep, Z-shaped gouge at one corner, put there by Saksi, her mother's Pekingese, during one of his puppyhood teething frenzies. Derrick had teased Ellen for weeks about the damage.

With quivering hands, Crysta pulled the case off the shelf, all sense of guilt vanishing. Sam Barrister had lied to her. Not only had he lied, but he had tried to throw her off by planting a sentimental scrapbook in the drawer where he had known she would look first.

Was he a loving father, as he clearly hoped she would believe, or a killer?

Shaken by the implications of her discovery, Crysta carried the briefcase to Sam's desk, emboldened by her sense of outrage. Now if Sam caught her in here, he would have as much explaining to do as she did. As she popped open the brass latches and lifted the lid of her brother's briefcase, another thought ricocheted through her mind. Sam wouldn't have hidden this unless there was something inside he didn't want her to see. But what?

Crysta spent the better part of a half hour trying to find an answer to that question. The documents in Derrick's file folders were simple and unmysterious, records of Blanchette business transactions, inspections sheets, purchase orders, job assignments, return credits, jotted notes. Nothing Sam Barrister should have been afraid for her to see.

So why had he hidden the briefcase? Maybe there had been something in one of the folders, something incriminating, and before Sam could remove it, she had burst unexpectedly into his office. Put on the spot, he had been forced to say he hadn't seen the briefcase, and once he had lied, he had no alternative but to keep the case hidden, even after the incriminating evidence had been removed.

The slamming of a door outside the office brought Crysta's head up. Heavy footsteps crossed the dining hall. Heart pounding, she closed the briefcase and returned it to the cupboard where Sam had hidden it, expecting him to walk in on her at any moment. All her bravado evaporated. If Sam was involved in her brother's disappearance—and it certainly looked as if he might be—it wasn't likely that raised eyebrows would stop him from getting rid of her if he thought she was on to him.

When the footsteps faded away, she felt limp with relief.

Since she hadn't been discovered, Crysta saw little point in abandoning stealth now. The less Sam knew of her activities, the more chance she would have to watch him. She crept to the door, tensing at the smallest noise. After a final glance at the room to be certain she hadn't left anything out of place, she slipped out of the office and wandered over to the sitting area, pretending interest in one of the magazines.

Her skin prickled. The picture on the front cover of the magazine was of a beheaded walrus. Crysta had never seen anything so gory. An inset in the upper righthand corner of the cover showed a lonely stretch of Alaska beach littered with similarly mutilated corpses. The headline read: Walrus Killings Continue. Repulsed, she let the magazine drop from her fingers back onto the table.

Had anyone seen her sneak from Sam's office? She didn't want to appear suspicious by glancing over her shoulder, so she brazened it out, half expecting a heavy hand to clamp over her shoulder.

When no one confronted her, Crysta allowed herself to relax a little. Then it occurred to her that Sam might wonder what she'd been up to during his absence. After their run-in downriver, he'd never believe she'd been lounging around reading, no matter how convincing her act.

She should look busy, but doing what? The clatter of pans from the kitchen reminded her that she had promised to help out in any way she could. There was nothing like killing two birds with one stone, and she had a feeling that Jangles, the cook, would be a font of information, if only she could be persuaded to talk.

Striding toward the rear of the lodge, Crysta pushed open the swinging door to the huge, antiquated kitchen. Jangles spared her only a glance before returning her attention to the batter she was stirring inside a gigantic metal mixing bowl.

"I was hoping you might let me help," Crysta offered in her friendliest voice. "I promised Sam I'd carry my own weight while I was here. Could you use a hand? I understand you've been overworked since the searchers arrived."

"I've survived worse," the Tlingit woman replied. "And I only have one more meal to get through before they all fly out."

"Still, the work load has been heavier than usual, and

you must be running behind. Maybe I can help you catch up. I'm pretty good in a kitchen." In actuality, Crysta's forte was designing fashions for the problem figure, not preparing the calories that created it. Playing it safe, just in case she might be asked to cook something unfamiliar, Crysta added, "I can fetch and carry, wash dishes, scrub floors. Just name it."

Jangles's dark eyes gleamed with unspoken challenge. "You can clean those fish behind you."

Heart sinking, Crysta rolled up her sleeves and approached the double utility basins along one wall. One tub was chock-full of salmon, all of them staring at her with round little eyes that made her skin crawl. The fish she had encountered up to now had already been beheaded, cleaned and arranged attractively on beds of ice at the neighborhood market.

"I thought the guys cleaned their own fish down at the river," she ventured weakly.

"Some do, others don't. My pay is the same no matter what the work, so I do not complain."

Planting her hands on her hips, Crysta stared into the tub and wondered how one went about cleaning a salmon. It wasn't something the average Los Angeles woman learned. Behind her, Jangles bustled about the kitchen, opening oven doors and banging pans. Ellen Meyers's voice piped into Crysta's mind. *"Use that head of yours for something besides a hat rack, Crysta."* Cleaning a fish couldn't be that difficult. Nauseating, perhaps, but not difficult.

Picking up the knife that rested on the edge of the sink, Crysta advanced on a dead fish, her gorge rising as she began the nasty task. If it hadn't been for her brother's plight, she might have begged off. But getting on Jangles's good side was crucial.

One fish later, Crysta was mentally calculating ways Derrick could make this up to her. Dinner at Navaho's, one of the glitziest restaurants in her neighborhood, would be nice. By the time she finished the second fish, she was thinking more along the lines of a Caribbean cruise, all expenses paid. It was a cheering thought, imagining Derrick, alive and well, trying to make good to her on a debt. And he would definitely owe her when this was over.

"When you get finished, it would be nice if there was some meat left to eat," Jangles said matter-of-factly.

The sound of the other woman's voice so close to her elbow made Crysta jump. She turned and raised an eyebrow. "Can you give me some pointers?"

Jangles's mouth quirked, but she didn't smile. Taking the knife from Crysta's hand, she picked up another fish and, with a few deft strokes of the blade, gutted and scaled it. "It is simple," she said as she tossed the cleaned salmon into the other sink. "When you finish, rinse them all, and then we will fillet them and cut up the steaks."

Crysta eyed the next fish, none too eager to resume her chore, but determined. She read Jangles as being a woman who had little use for wimps. Not that Crysta did, either. It was just that in her environment, it wasn't considered wimpy to do one's fishing over a meat counter.

A soft knock at the outside door brought Crysta's head up. It would be just her luck that the caller was a guest bringing more fish. Sighing, she returned to her task. Jangles threw a wary glance over her shoulder as she went to answer the knock. Then, the instant she cracked the door, the Indian woman stiffened.

"What is it?" she asked in a sharp voice. "I told you not to come here."

A masculine voice replied in a language Crysta couldn't understand. Jangles abandoned her use of English and responded in kind. Then, after throwing a worried look at Crysta, she opened the door wide enough to slip outside.

Crysta rose on her toes and angled her body across the utility sink, trying to see out the window. She glimpsed Jangles and a stoutly built Indian man hurrying away from the lodge. Before Crysta could get a clear look at the man's face, the two entered the trees. There, beyond earshot, they stopped. It looked to Crysta as though they were arguing. Heatedly. Jangles kept casting glances over her shoulder, as if she feared she might be seen.

Perplexed, Crysta rinsed her hands and turned to regard the various pots Jangles had left unattended on the stove. She turned down the flame under a huge skillet of frying potatoes, then gave them a cursory stir with the oversize spatula. What could the man have said that was so important that Jangles had dropped everything to talk to him?

Crysta wandered back to the sink and looked out the window to see Jangles scurrying back to the lodge. When the Tlingit woman reentered the kitchen, she looked breathless and agitated. Crysta busied herself cleaning another fish.

"I turned down the flame under the potatoes."

"Ah. Thank you."

Crysta hoped Jangles might explain who the man was, but she didn't. "A friend of yours?"

The Indian woman threw Crysta a stony look and didn't answer. Crysta wondered if perhaps the man was

Jangles's lover. Maybe Sam had rules against his employees socializing during the work week, and the woman feared that Crysta would tell on her. It was difficult to imagine the plump little Indian woman caught up in a torrid affair, but what other explanation was there? If the man had come to the lodge for a legitimate reason, Jangles wouldn't have reacted the way she had.

Crysta grabbed another salmon and went to work on it, trying not to think about the cold, scaly skin against her palm. In between fish, she threw longing glances out the window at the dense cottonwoods, wishing she had the know-how to strike off on her own to search for her brother. If only Derrick had become lost in intercity Los Angeles, where she maneuvered like a pro, then she wouldn't be wasting precious time, elbow-deep in raw salmon.

It was little comfort knowing that she had come in here not to waste time but to pry information from Jangles. Though Crysta made several attempts at conversation, the Indian woman remained distant. When the fish were all cleaned, Crysta stood beside the Tlingit at a large work center in the middle of the room, watching to see how she filleted the pink meat. When Crysta felt she had the technique down pat, she began filleting herself.

After several minutes had passed with no conversation, Crysta could bear the silence no longer. "Have I done something to make you dislike me?"

Jangles continued slicing salmon steaks without pause. "I like you fine. I think you should leave, that is all. Derrick would want you to."

Crysta considered her next words carefully. "Why do you feel I should leave, that my brother wouldn't want me here?"

Jangles at last stopped working to pin Crysta with her black gaze. "Because you are in danger here."

"Other people are here. Are you telling them to leave?"

"They are different," the woman rasped. "You are walking in shadows, courting death."

"That's nonsense."

"Is it? I speak seldom. My silence makes many forget that I have ears. Leave, Crysta Meyers, before it is too late. You cannot help your brother now."

"What have you heard?" Crysta pressed. "Oh, please, Jangles, tell me. My brother isn't dead. I know he isn't. I need your help."

"And I am giving it. *Leave.*"

"You believe someone harmed my brother, don't you? You don't think it was a bear that got him. Have you told anyone? Mr. Barrister, the search coordinator, anyone? You must, Jangles, you *must.* They're abandoning the search for him. He could be alive out there!"

"I know nothing," the woman said. "Bits and pieces that make no sense. There is nothing I can do, nothing you can do. You take great risks staying here, asking questions and following Sam. Desperate people can be dangerous. Leave before it is too late."

Desperate people? "Convince me." Crysta met the woman's gaze. "Stop talking about birds and shadows. Tell me something concrete."

Jangles averted her face. No matter how Crysta tried to prompt her, she refused to say anything more. They finished filleting the salmon in taut silence, Crysta so frustrated she wanted to cry. Jangles's vague references to having overheard something suspicious was the closest thing to a clue Crysta had unearthed. How could she give up and leave the kitchen when she knew Jangles had information that might save her brother's life?

CHAPTER SEVEN

IN THE END, Crysta felt she had no choice but to stay to help Jangles prepare breakfast. *"Desperate people can be dangerous."* The woman's words replayed ceaselessly in Crysta's mind. She tried not to reveal her disappointment when the Tlingit woman refused to say any more about Derrick's disappearance.

When the meal was cooked, Crysta remained true to her word about making herself useful and busied herself carrying food to the dining room, arms aching from the heavily laden serving trays as she maneuvered her way through the doorway and down the aisles between tables. Hotcakes, salmon and beef steaks, cottage fries, eggs, toast, biscuits, sweet rolls. Cholesterol heaven. She couldn't believe the variety or the amounts of food Jangles had provided.

Guests and soon-to-be-departing searchers trailed in to eat as the items were placed in the warming pans along one wall and on the tables. Crysta tried not to get angry about the aborted search for her brother. Her mother having often reminded her that one could attract more flies with honey than vinegar, Crysta forced herself to smile at each man who offered her his condolences.

The rich food smells made her feel a little nauseated, probably a result of not having eaten in so long. Now that she came to think of it, she couldn't recall her last meal.

When she had finished helping Jangles, Crysta filled herself a plate and sat at an unoccupied table, determined to eat at least a few bites. As she chewed a piece of steak, she felt someone staring at her. Glancing up, she met the gaze of a lanky, brown-haired man with worried blue eyes. She recognized him as the same young man she had seen in the woods earlier when she was conversing with the search coordinator.

The intent, anxious way he watched Crysta unnerved her. The meat in her mouth turned to sawdust. With an effort, she managed to swallow. Averting her gaze, she studied the remaining food on her plate, her determination to eat vanishing.

"You have to get something under your belt," a deep voice chided her. "You can't run on willpower and caffeine for long. Trust me, I know."

The sound of Sam's voice made Crysta leap. As he sat down across from her with his plate piled high, she prayed he wouldn't read the guilt on her face. Had he gone to his office yet? Would anything out of place clue him to her visit there? "It's hard to eat when I feel I should be doing something." She met his gaze. "Time is slipping by, and so far, I've accomplished nothing."

"You've only been here—" He glanced at his watch. "It's only been about twelve hours, tops."

"It seems like days." One table down, a fisherman hooted with laughter. Distracted by the sounds of merriment, Crysta glanced in that direction, then back at Sam. "It's my brother out there. I keep telling you that, but it doesn't seem to sink in."

After a lengthy pause, he replied, "Oh, it sank in, believe me. It's just that there's nothing you can do. I tried to tell you that over the phone before you wasted airfare coming here."

Visions of Derrick swept through Crysta's mind, and she felt angry tears welling in her eyes. "I disagree. I think there's plenty I can do, and I intend to."

Crysta knew that was an overstatement. She had failed to convince Jim Sales to continue the official search. There were no guides available. At the moment, her only option seemed to be searching for Derrick on her own. She knew that doing so would be dangerous and that only a fool would try it. She was no fool. But she was desperate. Desperate enough to risk her life if she had to.

"Why don't you start by trusting me?"

Trust him? If Crysta hadn't been so upset, she might have hooted with laughter herself. She had to hand it to him; the husky concern in his voice sounded so real, he deserved an Oscar. She wished he truly did care. Never had she needed a friend more.

The scalding tears in her eyes spilled over onto her cheeks. She made an angry swipe at them, outraged with herself for losing control again in front of him. He wasn't what he seemed. The proof of that lay hidden in a cupboard in his office. For an instant, she considered telling him that Jangles might know something, just to see his reaction, but caution ruled that out. She mustn't betray Jangles to anyone—least of all to him.

"You expect me to trust you?" she countered. "Why won't you trust *me?* You could start by answering my questions. No one here will so much as point me in the right direction so I can look for Derrick."

The dark depths of his eyes eddied, the swirl of emotion revealed there too fleeting to identify. His jaw tightened. "I don't think you're equipped to look for him on your own. Do you?"

Crysta knew she wasn't, but she couldn't bring herself to admit it to him. It struck her as ironic that a brief pontoon flight had plucked her out of a world in which she felt capable of handling almost anything and had deposited her in a place so foreign to her that she was rendered all but helpless.

"You're very frightened for your brother," Sam went on in a soothing, reasonable tone. "Fright can lead anyone to make unwise decisions."

"If so, then the consequences of those decisions would be my own fault."

"And mine for allowing you to make them. You're in unfamiliar country and under a great deal of stress. You're also exhausted. You can't be thinking clearly right now."

"Do you always take responsibility for other adults?"

The corner of his mouth lifted in a halfhearted smile. "Only when the circumstances dictate. Besides, you're not just anyone—you're my best friend's sister."

"Yes, and your best friend is lost out there, possibly dying. How will you live with it if you don't do something to save him?"

He studied her for a long moment. "Don't judge me on appearances, Crysta. Derrick trusted me. Why won't you?"

"Because you—" Crysta bit back the words. She had nearly mentioned the briefcase. An ache of exhaustion spread across her shoulders.

He sighed and shoved his plate to one side. "Crysta, why don't you fly back to Anchorage with the volunteers? Why torture yourself like this? Let me handle the search for Derrick."

"What search?" she cried, a little more loudly than she intended. The dining room went suddenly quiet, but she was beyond caring who might hear her. "Show me one person who's been out there looking for him today!"

"What if I were to promise I'd go on looking? Would you consider leaving then?"

Once again thinking of the briefcase, Crysta could scarcely credit how worried about her he looked. His duplicity made her long to reach across the table and slap him. A dozen accusations crawled up her throat. She voiced none of them. "If you're going to search for Derrick, there's not a single good reason I can't accompany you."

"No, there are more like a dozen—the first, a killer bear. I'll have my hands full just keeping my own hide safe."

Passing a hand over her eyes, Crysta glanced down the table. The man with the worried blue eyes was still staring at her. "Who *is* that man? He keeps staring at me."

Sam followed her gaze. "Steve Henderson. He's probably not staring so much as spacing out. He's the fellow with the sick son."

Crysta's heart caught. No wonder there was such a worried expression in his eyes. She felt a sense of kinship with him.

"I'm surprised he's not at home, spending every spare moment with his son," she whispered.

"He says the doctor advises that family members continue with their regular activities. If not, the kid will sense how desperately ill he is and may not respond as well to treatment. He doesn't enjoy himself here, as you can see. Half the time, he just sits, gazing at nothing. When I try to imagine how he must feel…" The muscles in Sam's face tightened. "Sometimes I feel guilty because I'm so glad it isn't Tip."

Crysta curled her hands around her coffee mug, wishing she could do something to help Steve Henderson, knowing she couldn't. Just as no one seemed able to help her. "Is there any hope?"

"Maybe a bone-marrow transplant. They're waiting for a match, and then he'll be flown down to Seattle for the procedure. If they can afford the initial fees, that is."

"Won't it be horribly expensive?"

"More than a hoister driver like Steve can afford. His insurance had a ceiling amount per illness, and that's been exhausted. From what Riley O'Keefe tells me, Steve's in debt already." Sam poked at a clump of scrambled eggs with his fork, looking none too hungry. "We took a collection last month for a television and VCR for Scotty's bedroom, so he can watch movies when he's too ill to leave his bed. But that's only a scratch on the surface. He wants a Nintendo. He wants to visit Disneyland. They'd like to buy him some tutoring videos so he won't fall behind in school. The costs are endless."

Pictures of Steve Henderson and his wife hovering at their dying child's bedside filled Crysta's mind. The pain they must feel. A knot lodged in her throat. She didn't even know Steve Henderson and his little boy, Scotty. It was insane to feel so perilously close to weeping.

"Crysta..." Sam's voice trailed off, and he reached to grasp her wrist, his fingers curling around her flesh like heated bands of steel. "You're exhausted. Why don't you lie down for a while. My bed has fresh linen on it. If I get a chance to rest, I can bunk in Tip's room."

Gazing at his handsome face, Crysta decided he was the epitome of the romantic hero: tall, dark, powerfully built, and irresistibly attractive—the proverbial bridge over troubled water, the sort a woman could fancy herself leaning on. But what lurked beneath the facade Sam Barrister presented to the world? Was he as mysterious on the inside as he was on the outside? It occurred to her that if she accepted his offer, she might be using the bed of her brother's murderer. The thought made her skin crawl.

"I couldn't take time for sleep." Crysta blinked and straightened. "After I help Jangles clean up, I want to study one of those forestry maps again."

"Why? So you can go out and get lost? Do you think Derrick would want that?"

Crysta wanted to say that Derrick had called to her, pleading for help, but that wasn't within Sam's scope of reality. Her dreams were her curse, never to be shared with anyone, unless she wanted her sanity questioned. "I'm going out to look for him. I don't suppose you have any spare pairs of rubber boots?"

He gestured toward a wall cupboard with his chin. "They're mostly men's sizes. I don't know if any of them will fit you."

Crysta made a mental note to check the boots later. "Before I go, I need to study the area, so I have my bearings." She turned her mug within the circle of her palms, forcing Sam to release his grip on her wrist. Recalling her last dream and the ramshackle structure she had seen in it, Crysta licked her lips and let her gaze trail past Sam's shoulder. "Are there any cabins downstream from here?"

"No. Why?" His voice sharpened, compelling her to look at him.

"In case I need shelter," she lied. "There must be a cabin out there someplace."

"Abandoned cabins pepper the interior, but there are

none nearby along the river. At least if there is, I haven't come across it. We aren't exactly in a metropolis out here." He raised one dark eyebrow. Clean-shaven, his strong jaw line complemented his striking features even more than before, perfectly offsetting his prominent nose and angular bone structure.

There was something about Sam Barrister, possibly the sheer size of him, that undermined her usual self-assurance. Under other circumstances, she would have deferred to his judgment. He knew this country; everything about him testified to that. It would be foolish to disregard his warnings. Yet she had no choice.

"Is there anything I can say to dissuade you?" he asked softly.

Instead of answering his question, she replied, "I'll take every precaution."

"If you lose your bearings, can you read a compass?"

"I'm not expert at it, but it can't be that hard. Besides, there's always the sun to guide me."

He laid his fork down on the edge of his plate. "You're forgetting we don't get the same sunrises and sunsets here that you're accustomed to seeing."

"I'll figure it out."

"You'll get lost, that's what you'll do."

"That's my risk to take."

"And my livelihood you're gambling with."

"I said I would sign a disclaimer."

He leaned forward, his eyes glittering. "I'll have it engraved on your headstone, shall I? Do me one favor. At least get some rest before you go out there. Otherwise, you'll collapse five miles from the lodge."

With that as a parting shot, he left the table, looking far angrier than Crysta felt he had any right to be. What did he care if she got herself killed? She didn't buy that his primary concern was his reputation. It was a free country; he couldn't be held responsible for every ding-a-ling city slicker who ignored his advice and insisted on taking risks.

It wasn't until after he was gone that Crysta realized he hadn't touched his meal. She eyed her own with mounting distaste. Only her realization that she needed nourishment prompted her to once again pick up her fork.

AFTER CRYSTA HELPED Jangles clean up the kitchen, she checked the boot cupboard to see if any of the spare rubber boots came close to her size. All were far too wide and would rub blisters. Disappointed, she abandoned the closet and followed her earlier plan of action, retrieving the map she had been studying from its rack on the check-in stand. Spreading it open on the table, she traced a finger along the spidery network of lines, trying to make sense of them. When she noticed the mileage scale in the bottom right corner, her heart sank. An inch represented fifty miles? Crysta sat back, taking in the map with renewed dread. She hadn't realized until now just how large an area she was trying to familiarize herself with.

Panic fluttered in her stomach. Sam was right; she had no business attempting a search on her own. She hadn't the vaguest idea how to find her way around out there. To her, one tree looked exactly like another.

A picture of a wind-twisted spruce flashed in Crysta's mind, rekindling her determination. The tree of her dream had been growing along the bank of a waterway. She need only find it to know she was hunting for Derrick in the right area. The problem was that there were probably numerous rivers in this region, not to mention hundreds if not thousands of small sloughs. Which waterway had Derrick been following?

So weary that she ached, Crysta slumped over the map, staring blindly. As she contemplated the enormity of the task she was undertaking, a frisson of fright coursed through her. She'd be risking her life out there, and if she got lost, as Sam predicted, her death might not be swift. Regardless, she had to search for her brother. If she didn't, she'd spend the remainder of her life hating herself.

Black spots danced before Crysta's eyes. With a defeated sigh, she passed a hand over her forehead. Sam was right on another count: she had to grab a little sleep. If she didn't, she'd be dead on her feet before she had walked a mile. Her sleeve cuff brushed against her nose, and the strong smell of salmon hit her. Grimacing, Crysta drew back and glared at the stained denim. She needed another bath, thanks to Jangles's tub of fish.

Wrinkling her nose, Crysta pushed to her feet and refolded the map, tucking it under her arm. There wasn't time for another bath, not until she found her brother. After a couple of hours' sleep, absolutely no more than that, she had a search to begin. God willing, it would lead her to Derrick.

SAM BARRISTER'S BEDROOM was a reflection of the man himself, the colors earthy and quiet. Remembering her ex-husband's penchant for chrome and glass, Crysta decided she much preferred Sam's plain and simple approach. This was a place where one could stretch out and not worry about leaving fingerprints.

His furniture was large and sturdy, the finish, like its owner, handsomely weathered and marred. The rumpled quilt on his bed, a wedding-ring pattern, was hand-stitched yet somehow masculine, the clean cases on his king-size pillows as crisp and white as Alaskan snow. The leather boots sitting neatly by the bedstead were stained mud-brown. Above the headboard hung a painting of the northern lights captured so beautifully in oils that Crysta stood mesmerized for a moment. Was it any wonder Sam loved Alaska?

Crysta pictured him living a hundred years ago, a big, rugged man carving out an existence in the wilderness, his gaze always fixed on the horizon. Perhaps that was why he lived in Alaska, where the wave of civilization had not yet struck.

She picked up the book on his nightstand. Scanning the title and blurb, she ascertained that it was about wolves and the human threat to their survival, the sort of material she might have found in Derrick's library. Clearly, Sam and her brother had a great deal in common.

Everything led back to Derrick.

Sighing, Crysta returned the book to its resting place, feeling lost and frightened. She knew why. There were no whispers inside her head. Was Derrick still alive? If so, why the ominous silence? Maybe he was deep in a dreamless sleep. Or unconscious. Please, God, let him be alive.

As she turned from the bed, Crysta realized this was the perfect opportunity to search Sam's room. Not that he would have offered to let her sleep here if he had hidden anything from Derrick's briefcase in the drawers. Still...

Methodically and thoroughly, she searched everywhere, even going so far as to run her arm under the mattress. She found nothing. Heavy of heart, she drew the blackout shade, plunging the room into darkness. *Hold on, Derrick. I'm coming. I won't let you down.* As she peeled off her clothes, Crysta thought of Sam in this room, tugging his shirt off over his head, sitting on the bed to doff his boots. The picture made her feel self-conscious, as if he were here with her, watching. The masculine scent in the room, his scent, added to that illusion, a pleasant blend of flannel and denim, fresh air and aftershave, laced with faint traces of musk. Cool air washed over her skin, making her shiver.

She hoped Sam remembered offering her the use of his room and didn't barge in on her. Drawing on her flannel nightgown, she wriggled her toes against the braided rug and stretched her aching arms. A wind-up clock on the headboard drew her attention, its loud ticking reminding her of just how quickly each second passed. Time had become her enemy. And Derrick's. With numb fingers, she set the alarm so she wouldn't oversleep.

Flipping back the corner of the quilt, Crysta slid into bed, pleased to feel that the crisp linen was stretched tight. From the rumpled condition of the quilt, she had half expected wrinkled sheets, one of her pet peeves. Punching the pillow, she arranged it just so under her head and angled a forearm across her forehead, so exhausted that she felt wired. Determined, she closed her eyes.

The sickening stench of dead fish crawled up her nostrils. Crysta frowned and drew her forearm away from her face, wondering how the smell could possibly still be clinging to her. She had washed her hands and wrists thoroughly, and now her soiled shirt lay in a heap by her suitcase.

Rolling onto her side, Crysta drew up her knees, snuggling her cheek against the pillow, bent on ignoring the odor. She had more important things to worry about than personal hygiene. Warmth stole over her, and her muscles slowly relaxed. The hypnotic ticking of the clock began to soothe her. She closed her eyes, twisting her hips slightly so one leg was angled forward.

Something cold pressed against her knee—something cold and wet. Crysta stopped breathing and lay motionless, her skin prickling. There was something in the bed. For an instant, the years rolled away and she felt like a child again, afraid of the dark and tormented by Derrick's stories of bloody hands reaching under the covers to grab her.

It took all Crysta's strength of will to extend her hand toward the wet lump. Her fingertips encountered something cold and slightly rough. She slithered away, pushing up on her elbow. Throwing back the quilt, she stared through the shadowy gloom at a long, dark shape against the white backdrop of sheet. What on earth?

Reaching behind her, Crysta grasped the shade and gave it a jerk, sending it into a rattling ascent on its roller. Sunlight spilled into the room.

"Oh, my God!"

Crysta sprang from the bed, eyes agape, frantically rubbing her hand clean on her nightgown. A huge king salmon lay in the center of the mattress, its gill gaffed with a wicked-looking hook, its guts spilling forth from the jagged rip in its underbelly. Crysta glanced down to see that her gown was smeared with gore. She recoiled a step, stomach heaving.

"Oh, my God…"

SAM'S OFFICE DOOR flew open with such force that the doorknob cracked against the wall. He glanced up, amazed to see Crysta standing in the doorway, a white bundle clutched in her arms, her slender, jeans-clad legs spread wide as if she were trying to keep her balance on rocky seas, her auburn hair in a glorious tangle around her fury-whitened face, her hazel eyes afire. For a moment, he was so taken aback that he forgot he had Derrick's briefcase out on his desk, in plain view.

"I want to talk to you, Mr. Barrister!"

It was more a hiss than a request. And then she advanced on him like a general coming to do battle. There was no time to gather Derrick's papers. Sam snatched the briefcase off his desk and shoved it into a drawer, uncertain what had set her off but hoping, all the same, that she was so mad she hadn't noticed her brother's briefcase.

As insurance, Sam decided diversionary tactics were called for and opted for counterattack. "Good, I've been wanting to talk to you, too. Now's as good a time as any. I was speaking to Tip a little while ago. You've been filling his head with nonsense about his paintings making a big splash in the art world." Sam shuffled papers, trying to hide those belonging to Derrick beneath some of his own. Then he shoved back in his chair, striving to look irritated rather than unsettled. "I want nothing more said to him on the subject. Is that clear?"

Crysta swept around his desk. Anger became her, heightening her color, adding a sparkle to her already beautiful eyes. With a cry of indignation, she tossed the white bundle at him, keeping one of her fists knotted in the linen. The sheet unrolled, and something heavy plopped into Sam's lap. When he saw what it was, he nearly shot from his chair. As accustomed as he was to salmon, he'd never had one dumped in his lap, gaff, guts and all.

"What in the hell?"

"I took you up on your offer to use your bed. Somehow, I found the other occupant offensive, to say the least!"

Sam looked up to find a slender finger wagging before his nose. No one could ever say Crysta Meyers was easily intimidated. She leaned toward him, and Sam had no doubt she was angry enough to punch him if he chose to stand up.

"Your son and his wasted talent is your business. I won't say another word about his paintings. By the same token—" her finger drew closer "—my brother is *my* business, and your sick little prank won't change that."

"This was in my bed?" Sam inched his head back as her finger advanced . "Crysta, I didn't—"

"Get this straight, Mr. Barrister, once and for all. I'm not leaving here until my brother is found. It'll take more than bears and fish guts to scare me off. Is *that* clear?"

It was crystal clear. Sam hadn't been confronted like this in years, not by a man, let alone a woman he towered over. "I didn't put this in the bed, Crysta. How could you think—"

She grabbed a fistful of the papers on his desk and waved them before his face. "How could I think you'd do something so despicable? What are these, Mr. Barrister? Papers from my brother's briefcase, which, according to you, didn't exist! I was in here earlier and found them myself. I've listened to enough of your lies!"

Sam stared at the papers crumpled in her fingers. The game was up. Like it or not, he had to tell her everything. Her presence was making someone uncomfortable. The fish in her bed was proof of that. If he didn't level with her, she might blunder her way right into a deathtrap. "Please don't rumple those," he said quietly. "They may prove helpful in discovering what happened to Derrick."

"Really?" She slapped the documents down. "You mean to admit, at long last, that a bear didn't make him his main course for dinner? Congratulations, Sam! The truth for once. Please, don't stop while you're on a roll."

"We need to talk. But not here." Gingerly, Sam lifted the stinking salmon from his thighs and rewrapped it in the sheet. "Let's go to my apartment where we won't run the risk of being overheard."

Dumping the linen-wrapped fish into the waste basket, he glanced up just in time to see the wary expression that crossed her face. Now that her anger was flagging, she was clearly having second thoughts about coming here. For all she knew, he might be planning to get her off alone so he could shut her up—permanently.

That thought strengthened Sam's resolve to tell her everything. Crysta wasn't the sort to avoid confrontations. She was more the type to say what was on her mind, the devil take tomorrow. It was a quality Sam admired and tried to cultivate in himself. But if Crysta confronted the wrong person, her straightforwardness might land her in a situation she couldn't get out of.

She retreated a step when he met her gaze, looking none too thrilled at the prospect of accompanying him to a more private setting. He didn't suppose he blamed her for not trusting him. He was doing an awfully quick about-face and, from her viewpoint, without any reason.

"Crysta, the dining room is within yelling distance of my living quarters."

She took another step back, giving her head a toss to get the hair out of her eyes. "If I was able to yell."

Sam stood. Though she was tall for a woman, Crysta's head barely cleared his shoulder. And after their tussle in the woods, both of them knew he had the advantage physically. Sam decided to challenge her pride. "Running scared, Crysta? Maybe you're not as much like Derrick as I thought."

Her chin shot up, and her eyes flared. "Lead the way."

Sam did, painfully aware that she wasn't about to turn her back on him.

A LOG SHIFTED in the grate, sending up a spray of sparks. Crysta, who had settled herself onto the sofa and was waiting for Sam to speak, stared at the fireplace, hands clasped in her lap, spine rigid, trying, unsuccessfully, to appear relaxed. Sam sat in the recliner, arms braced on his knees, shoulders forward, feet planted wide, looking ready to jump up at any second. After their wrestling match in the woods that morning, she had no delusions. Sam was big, strong and fast. If he should leap at her, she didn't stand a chance of escaping him.

"I don't know where to start," he said.

The sudden sound of his voice in the brittle silence made Crysta jerk. He cast her a knowing glance.

"Why not start with the quarrel between you and Derrick?"

His mouth tightened. "That's peripheral to the entire situation."

"So you say."

His eyes narrowed. "If you must know, it was about Tip. Like you, your brother has an irritating habit of interfering, and I told him so. We had words. End of subject."

"Not the end of your friendship?"

"Our friendship was as strong as ever. It wasn't the first time we've gotten into it over Tip, and pray God it won't be the last. Friends can agree to disagree, Crysta."

Crysta took a moment to digest this new tidbit of information. "Am I right in assuming that the argument was over Tip's artistic talent? It's the only thing I've come anywhere close to interfering in."

"With a bang," he amplified, shooting her another look, this one bordering on a glare. "You have Tip all but ready to pack his bags and head for the big city."

"He asked me a question. I told him the truth. Should I have lied?"

"The truth as *you* see it. He's my son. I know better than anyone else what he's been through, and I know what's waiting for him out there. I've seen how people—" He broke off, his mouth twisting with disgust. Raking a hand through his hair, he sighed. "Like I said, my argument with your brother has nothing to do with Derrick or what happened to him, so let's drop it."

Crysta inclined her head, acquiescing. He was telling the truth about the quarrel. The fire in his eyes told her that. But if he was innocent, why had he hidden Derrick's briefcase? Why had he tried to sneak off downstream?

"I see your point," she said softly. "The argument about Tip was none of my business, and I can see why you felt it unnecessary to tell me about it. I'm sorry I kept pressing you."

He ran his fingertips along his jaw, making a faint rasping sound on the growth of beard that had cropped up since his last shave. "Yeah, well…I should have just told you what it was all about. I'm sorry I didn't, but the truth is, it isn't easy even to think about it. We, um…" He turned to stare out the window, his voice going suddenly husky. "I let him leave without telling him goodbye. I was ticked, he was ticked. If he is dead, it was a hell of a way to end a ten-year friendship."

Crysta returned her gaze to the fire, resisting the urge to comfort him. His pain was evident in his voice, but was it real? From the corner of her eye, she studied him, alert to his every move.

"Why did you lie about having Derrick's briefcase? Why did you try to discourage me from coming here?" Crysta fixed him with a relentless gaze. "Why did you try to slip away from me? I want to trust you, Sam, but you haven't given me a single reason to."

He smiled slightly. "No, I haven't, have I? Can we take that one question at a time, beginning with the second one? I didn't want you coming here because I was afraid it might be dangerous."

"Dangerous? As in bears?"

His eyes met hers. "I was more worried about two-legged killers, Crysta." Briefly, he told her about the night Derrick had visited the office. "He had come across something at Blanchette that looked *fishy*—his word, not mine."

"Something fishy." Intent, Crysta scooted forward to the edge of the cushion. "Did he say what? And how do you know it was something at Blanchette and not somewhere else?"

"He wouldn't elaborate. You know Derrick and his ethics. Until he had some solid evidence, he didn't want to make any accusations. As for it being in Blanchette, that's an assumption on my part. *'Something fishy going on up here in Alaska'* was what he said. I took that to mean it was something he'd run across that wasn't occurring at the construction sites in the lower forty-eight. That's why I'm going through his briefcase, looking for clues. So far, I've found nothing."

The nape of Crysta's neck prickled. She couldn't help recalling her dream, the report of a gun echoing in her ears. "So you think Derrick came across something illegal within Blanchette and that the perpetrators tried to silence him?"

"Exactly."

"And earlier, when you sneaked off downstream. Why didn't you want me to know?"

"I didn't want you involved." He pinched the bridge of his nose between thumb and forefinger, sighing. "When you seemed so certain that Derrick wasn't dead, I got to wondering if maybe the searchers had missed something. I figured you'd never leave if you knew what I suspected, so I kept up the pretense about the bear."

"Is my knowing such a bad thing?"

"It will be if you start pressing the wrong people for answers. You could end up a bear statistic, like your brother."

"That goes for you, as well. I'm a big girl, Sam."

"And Derrick's sister. I wanted to put you on the first flight out, safely away from here. He would expect that of me."

Some of the tension eased out of Crysta's shoulders. She wasn't entirely convinced he was telling her the truth, but at least this story made a lot more sense than the bear-attack theory.

"Flying me out to safety isn't in the cards, I'm afraid. Until Derrick's found, I'm here to stay."

His mouth twisted in a smile. "Well, if you're bent on staying, Derrick would want me to keep an eye on you."

Crysta rolled her eyes. "Let me set you straight, Sam. Derrick is the twin who usually needs caretaking."

"Humor me."

Pushing up from the sofa, she walked to the fire, hugging herself and rubbing her arms. "I want to be involved in everything. I won't be set on a shelf. If that's your idea of looking after me, it won't work."

"I was planning to go downstream while you were asleep."

"Then I'm going with you."

"It's a long walk. And you're already tired. You might slow me down. I don't think—"

"I'm not that tired," she insisted, though she was.

He stared past her at the fire for a moment. "All right. At least if you're with me, I'll know you're safe and not following me or searching on your own."

Crysta had expected more of an argument. She hesitated, studying him. If he was deceiving her, it would be much easier for him to harm her once they left the lodge.

CHAPTER EIGHT

As a precaution, Crysta made it a point to let Jangles, Riley O'Keefe and two other guests know that she was leaving the lodge to go for a walk with Sam. As they struck off along the river, Sam flashed her a knowing grin.

"Are you sure you wouldn't like to invite someone else to come along?" he asked. "There's safety in numbers."

Crysta felt heat rising up her neck, from embarrassment or anger, she couldn't be sure. On the one hand, if Sam was on the level, it was inexcusable to let him know she didn't trust him. Just the same, she preferred to play it safe, and if that offended him, there was very little she could do about it.

Her second trip downriver seemed far less strenuous than her first, due, she was sure, to the slower pace Sam set. The fact that he altered his stride to match hers was reassuring. Surely it wasn't second nature to a killer to be so considerate.

When they reached the slough, he searched for the narrowest place, leaped across, then turned to give her a hand. The distance she had to jump was intimidating. Even as tall as she was, she couldn't compete with a man of Sam's stature. She hesitated to take his hand, reluctant to give the impression she needed coddling. She had waded through the slough only hours ago, though, and knew how chilly the water was. It would be foolish to risk getting soaked again.

"Coming?" he asked.

The trace of impatience in his tone prompted her to take his hand. His warm grip was disconcertingly strong. She was in big trouble if he had brought her out here to get rid of her.

Gauging the distance, Crysta tightened her fingers around his and leaped. When she landed, right foot first, her running shoe slipped in the mud. Sam braced himself to catch her. When he did, he lost his footing, as well. Crysta thought they were both in for a mud bath, but at the last second Sam scrambled and found purchase on the slick bank, catching her around the waist with a steely arm.

Crysta's breath caught. With her back arched, her thighs were pressed intimately against his, and her breasts were flattened against the broad ladder of his rib cage. They both froze.

Sam's dark eyes fixed on hers. Unbidden, a frisson of electricity shot through her. Until this instant, she had been so suspicious of Sam and so worried about her brother that she had fought her attraction to him. Now all her reasons for doing so seemed to have disappeared. As Sam bent his dark head toward hers, Crysta remained perfectly still, wanting his kiss in a way she couldn't fully comprehend. For a fleeting moment, just as his warm, silken lips touched hers, she wondered what it was about him that so disarmed her. Then sheer sensation wiped rational thought from her mind.

His kiss began in the predictable way, a hesitant exploration, but in less than a heartbeat the shyness vanished, replaced by a raw, primal hunger that Crysta sensed in him and felt within herself. Forgetting all else, she let the strong circle of his arms pull her closer and allowed her body to mold itself against him.

As suddenly as it had begun, the kiss ended. With a dazed and unmistakably incredulous expression in his dark eyes, Sam gently set her away from him and proceeded along the riverbank as though nothing had happened. But Crysta sensed his discomfiture in the long strides he was suddenly taking. She guessed that he had been taken as off guard as she.

At any other time, the situation might have been amusing, given the fact that for years Derrick had tried fruitlessly to get Crysta and Sam together. This wasn't another time, though, and Crysta had far too much on her mind to deal with overactive hormones, hers or Sam's. Clearly, Sam felt the same.

She lengthened her stride to catch up. Within minutes she was panting with exertion, the sounds issuing from her throat short and shallow. Sam cast her a surprised glance and slowed his pace.

Relieved to have the tension between them eased, Crysta fell in beside him again. But her nerve endings were sensitized now to his nearness, and her gaze kept shifting sideways to rest on the coarse blue denim stretched tight over the corded muscle of his legs.

She had no business thinking of Sam as anything but a means to her end, which was finding Derrick. What was wrong with her? She couldn't be certain Sam was even trustworthy. She sneaked a look at his profile. Sunlight glinted in his hair where it fell in tousled waves across his forehead.

Crysta laid her feelings off on the desperateness of her situation. Though she might manage to search for Derrick on her own, the odds of her success were slim. Sam Barrister's assistance was her only hope. Her emotions were a powder keg, and he was merely the spark to set them off.

The seconds became measured by the steady thud of their feet on the earth, her sneakers tapping out a soft counterpoint to the heavy impact of Sam's boots. Crysta became lost in the rhythm, her thoughts focused on Derrick as her legs churned to keep up with the man beside her.

They had to cross two more sloughs, each wider than the last, which gave Crysta her first glimpses of the tranquil marshlands and meadows that lay beyond the camouflage of trees along the river. She had no idea how much time passed. A great deal, judging by the ache in her thighs. She began to get the disconcerting feeling that she and Sam were the first people ever to have come here. On occasion, though, she spotted footprints that dispelled that notion, probably left there by the men who had searched for Derrick.

How far had she and Sam walked? Five or six miles? The only sounds that drifted to her ears were those of the water, the rustling leaves, the wind. She could see why her brother loved it here.

"So what do you think?"

She glanced up. "About what?"

"About that fish in the bed. Who do you think put it there?"

Wondering why it had taken him miles of walking to address that issue, she replied, "My first inclination was to blame you."

He snorted. "Put a stinking fish in my own bed? Besides, give me credit for *some* brains. It would take more than a few fish guts to send a woman like you running."

It was an offhand compliment, but a compliment just the same. She didn't know why it mattered to her what he thought, but, strangely enough, it did. "Who do you think did it?"

"The dining room was full of people. Any number could have heard me offer you the use of my room. My question is, was it someone's sick idea of a joke, simply because you're an attractive single woman here alone, or was it an attempt to frighten you into leaving?"

"I lean toward the latter. When I thought you'd done it, my first assumption was that you were trying to scare me off. Let's face it, fish guts aren't very funny."

Sam stepped around a bush. "I agree. Now that that's settled, the question is who?"

"I haven't been here long enough to make enemies. Jangles, possibly. I don't think she cares for me."

Sam shook his head. "Jangles likes you fine. She's just bent on getting you out of harm's way."

Crysta tensed, then plunged ahead, praying she wasn't subjecting Jangles to danger. "She knows something. She won't say what, but she doesn't believe Derrick was eaten by a bear any more than I do."

"I sensed that, too."

"And you haven't questioned her?"

"I tried." He shot her a troubled frown. "Jangles is one of the last of a dying breed, clinging, in many ways, to the old customs, fiercely proud of her Tlingit heritage, even though she's the only one in this immediate area. She loves Alaska, its natives and its wildlife, with a passion. And she prizes the strength often found in silence. If she takes it into her head not to talk, for whatever reason, she won't. Trying to force her is—" He lifted one shoulder in a shrug. "One thing I know—she'd never put a gaffed fish in your bed. Sneaking around behind a person's back isn't her way."

Crysta remembered the animosity that had gleamed in the woman's dark eyes. "I realize she's a friend of yours, but—"

"That's not the only reason I'm so convinced it wasn't her. Don't forget, whatever else Jangles may be, she's Indian. Heritage is extremely important to her. Even today, many Tlingit homes feature lineage crests."

"Lineage crests?"

"Totem poles," he explained, a smile touching his mouth.

Crysta found herself recalling the touch of those firm, silken lips on hers, how mesmerizing they had seemed.

"Courage and honesty are very much a part of that heritage," he continued. "I'm not saying she's above doing something mean, but if she does, she'll do it right to your face. To sneak would be cowardly."

He seemed so convinced that Crysta decided to concede the point. "Do you realize she has a gentleman caller? A Tlingit?"

Sam gave her a sharp look. "A caller?"

"A boyfriend, I assume. He came to the kitchen door this morning. She seemed upset and told him he wasn't supposed to come to the lodge. Then she went out into the woods and appeared to be arguing with him."

Sam's forehead creased in a thoughtful frown. "You're sure he was Tlingit? Not to say there couldn't be others in the vicinity, but if there are, I've never met them."

"He spoke in another language, and Jangles replied in kind. If they weren't talking in Tlingit, then what?"

As if he was considering that, Sam gazed ahead of them for a moment. "It's possible she knows more than one of the native languages. Or maybe the guy *was* Tlin-git."

"Have you any idea why she would want to keep his visit secret from you?"

"No." He turned worried eyes on her. "She knows her friends would be more than welcome at the lodge."

A tingle crept up Crysta's spine. She had gotten the impression that Jangles hadn't wanted anyone to see the man. If Sam had laid down no rules restricting employees from having callers at the lodge while they were on his time, why had she hustled the man off into the trees?

"Is it possible she's up to something she doesn't want you to know about?"

"If she is, I'm sure it's nothing for me to worry about. The bottom line is, I trust her. Completely."

Crysta could see from Sam's firm expression that pursuing the Jangles angle would be fruitless. She wasn't quite so trusting, however. She made a mental note to keep an eye on the Tlingit woman.

"So, if not Jangles, then who?"

"Someone staying at the lodge—that much is a given. If I'm right that Derrick was referring to Blanchette when he talked about finding something fishy, then we have to assume the culprit is someone who works for the company."

"Any suspicions?"

Sam hesitated. "I don't like accusing people without proof."

"Let's forget the innocent-until-proven-guilty thing and toss ideas around. We aren't going to do irreparable damage to anyone's reputation if it's just between you and me. That was Derrick's mistake, remember? If he had pointed the finger at someone, we'd have an idea now of who to go after. As it is, we're shooting in the dark."

Sam gave a fleeting smile. "We? You sound as if you might be starting to trust me."

She jumped over a marshy spot, then dragged the soles of her shoes clean on the grass. With more certainty than she felt, she said, "You think I'd be out here with you if I had any doubts?"

"Unfortunately for my peace of mind, yes. You take too many risks, Crysta, without weighing the consequences. Like following me today. Then searching my office. And then confronting me about the fish. Did you even once stop to think what might happen if I caught you or turned on you?"

"I considered it."

"Did you? Somehow I doubt it. Understand something, okay? This isn't Los Angeles. The cops can't drive up to your door within five minutes of your call. You're a female, and you're alone. The modern woman's mind-set could get you into big trouble up here."

"I've taken self-defense training. I can handle myself."

He braked to a sudden stop, squinting against the sun at her. The impact of his gaze brought her to a halt. Looking up at him, she found her training in self-defense small comfort.

"We're about seven miles from the lodge," he reminded her. "I outweigh you by at least a hundred pounds. You don't have a weapon of any kind as an equalizer. You can't outrun me. I'd say that could spell trouble—in capital letters. What's your solution? A karate chop to my neck? What if I brought you here to shut you up? Have you thought of that?"

Crysta had indeed thought of that. "I told several people I was taking a walk with you. It'd cast you in a pretty bad light if something happened to me out here," she retorted. "As for my self-defense training, my instructor taught me to aim much lower than the neck."

Her pulse leaped at the grim twist of Sam's mouth, but before she could react, he struck off walking again.

"And what if I did away with you and made it look like an accident? Don't trust anyone—that's all I'm asking. Not *anyone,* is that clear? You're right—we are shooting in the dark. My first instinct is to suspect Riley O'Keefe, but since I'm not positive Derrick was referring to something fishy at Blanchette, I can't act on that. Besides, Riley flew back into Anchorage with Shriver shortly after breakfast, so it isn't likely he would have had time to sneak something into my bedroom."

He heaved a weary sigh and ran his hand over his hair. "I suppose Derrick could have come upon something here at Cottonwood Bend," he went on. "It's a possibility we can't ignore, anyway. There are two other lodges within five miles. Planes galore fly in round the clock. People and cargo of every conceivable kind come and go."

Crysta scrambled after him. When he entered a line of trees and stopped to wait for her, she slowed her pace. He settled a thoughtful gaze on her, his lips softening.

"I didn't mean to sound condescending a minute ago. It's just that—" He grasped her arm to help her over a fallen cottonwood. "You weren't sure of me when you agreed to come out here. You can't deny that. It was foolish to take such a chance. It scares the hell out of me to think you might do it again, next time with the wrong person."

Crysta opened her mouth to retort, but before she spoke, she remembered how vulnerable he had made her

feel a minute ago. As much as it rankled, he had a point.
It was lucky for her that he hadn't brought her out here
to kill her. Against an ordinary mugger, her self-defense
training and the element of surprise might stand her in
good stead, but the odds were considerably poorer here,
with no one to intervene if she cried for help.

"I realize Derrick's your only concern right now," he
added patiently, "but as much as you hate to think it, he
may be dead. If he is, sacrificing yourself won't help him."

"I'll do whatever I have to."

He tightened his hand on her arm. "Crysta, if he's alive,
he can survive out here for an indefinite period of time."

"Not if he's hurt!"

"A small cut on the head can bleed a great deal. The
blood the searchers found isn't necessarily an indication
that Derrick was badly wounded. He's bear-smart. If an
enraged grizzly was on his heels, he might have taken
off his shirt and tossed it down as a distraction. Sometimes an animal will go after anything with its prey's
scent on it. That could explain the shirt's being shredded
by a bear's claws."

A picture from her second dream flashed in her
mind—of the puncture wound over Derrick's heart.
"You don't believe that. You don't even believe a bear
was involved. You think it was a man." She gestured at
his empty hands. "If you thought for one minute a killer
bear was out here, you'd be carrying a gun."

He pinched the bridge of his nose and heaved a weary
sigh. After a long moment, he dropped his hand. "I can't
make sense of any of it," he said in a husky voice. "There's
only one thing I'm certain of at this point. I don't want
something to happen to you."

The sincerity in his expression made Crysta forget

whatever it was she had intended to say. For an instant she experienced an almost overpowering need to feel his arms around her again, to pour out her frustrations and fears, to believe he could somehow make everything all right.

She knew it was a childish wish. But, like Sam, she was so weary of trying to make sense of it all that she could scarcely think straight. A respected tracker was convinced Derrick had been slain by a bear. Yet Derrick had said things that gave Sam reason to believe her brother had been the victim of foul play. Who was right? Had the men who harmed Derrick staged a bear attack to throw the searchers off track? Crysta didn't know. And if all that wasn't enough, she had her dreams to consider. Were they telepathic visions, sent to her by Derrick? Or was she losing her mind?

At the moment, Crysta was none too sure of her sanity. Nothing seemed clear to her except that she felt inexplicably drawn to Sam Barrister. Yet common sense warned her that she still couldn't be entirely certain she should trust him.

As if he sensed how close she was to tears, he took her arm and drew her into a walk beside him. They emerged from the dappled shade into bright sunlight. Crysta blinked, momentarily blinded. When her vision cleared, her footsteps dragged to a stop.

"What's wrong?" Sam whispered.

Crysta stared ahead. "This is the place where it happened."

Sam glanced around them. "It's a little farther, I think. I found Derrick's destroyed gear farther ahead."

"No," she said with certainty, her attention fixed on a wind-twisted spruce on the riverbank several feet ahead of them. "No, Sam, this is the place."

Sam began scanning the ground, his expression dubious. Crysta stood frozen, her head swimming with images. This was the spot along the river that she had dreamed of, where the three men had caught up to her.

"You're right," Sam said softly, pointing at something to her left.

Feeling strangely numb, Crysta turned to follow his gaze. A flutter of orange caught her eye. She focused. Someone had driven a flagged stake into the ground to mark the spot. Sam moved cautiously forward, head bent to search the area.

"This is it. That's amazing—that you knew, I mean."

Still with that same feeling of separateness engulfing her, Crysta followed him, her gaze fixed on the ground. The toe of her running shoe touched a black splotch. She stopped to study it, then recognized it as dried blood. Derrick's blood, according to the search coordinator. Her knees went weak.

"It's just like Jim said, plenty of bear track, lots of blood." Sam touched the broken branch of a bush, his expression grim. "God, they're right. I've been off all along. It *was* a bear attack."

His voice, thick and husky with emotion, raked down Crysta's spine like chalk skidding over blackboard. Nausea rolled up her throat. Closing her eyes for an instant, she whispered, "No," the sound almost inaudible.

Sam glanced up. "What do you mean, no?" He pointed at the many bear tracks. "The proof's staring us in the face."

Crysta's feeling of unreality wouldn't dissipate. She turned to stare at the twisted spruce. There couldn't be another tree exactly like it. Derrick had been here. Men had been chasing him. She wasn't losing her mind. She didn't care what evidence there was to the contrary. The bear attack had been faked; she knew it as surely as she did her own name.

"It wasn't a bear that got him," Crysta amplified.

Like a sleepwalker, she strode toward the water, envisioning herself lying there, dazed from a blow to the head. In her dream, she had been trying to reach safety someplace up ahead and the twisted spruce had been to her right. Crysta turned, putting the tree to her right, and found herself looking back the way she and Sam had just come. Derrick had been trying to reach Cottonwood Bend…and his friend, Sam Barrister.

More images from her dream assailed her as she drew closer to the water. A flash of silver arcing over her shoulder to plop into the water. Derrick's buckle. She had bent to pick it up and had put it in her left breast pocket.

Sudden excitement shot through Crysta, making her forget, momentarily, that there were some things best left unsaid. She bent at the waist to scan the earth. "Was Derrick's silver-dollar belt buckle found in the pocket of his red flannel shirt?"

"The shirt he was wearing when—?" Sam broke off. "No, I don't think so. Jim would have mentioned it."

"Then it must be here somewhere. When they picked him up after shooting him, it must have fallen from his pocket." Crysta waded into the water, peering through the murky ripples. "Help me, Sam. It's here, it has to be."

"What are you talking about? What buckle? And what shooting? You aren't making sense."

"I'm making perfect sense. Help me look. In my dream, I put the buckle in my pocket. Then someone hit me. I fell, stunned. When I turned over, they were talking about getting rid of him. Not *her,* Sam, *him!* I heard a gunshot right before the dream ended and—" she pressed a hand over her heart, lifting her face to stare at him "—I woke up with a terrible pain in my chest. Don't you see?" She waded from the water onto shore, not caring that her feet were soaked. "I knew this place because I had seen it before, in my dream! It wasn't me I was dreaming about, but Derrick! They shot him. And then they tried to make it look as if a bear got him."

In a rush, she went on to describe the dream in more detail. So intent was she on recounting everything exactly the way she had seen it that she scarcely noticed the wariness crossing Sam's face, growing more pronounced by the moment.

"And all you saw of the men were their legs and boots?" He arched an eyebrow and glanced at his feet. "Green boots with yellow bands at the tops? Crysta, everyone up here wears them. I'm sorry, but that's not particularly conclusive."

"You have to believe me, Sam. Derrick's life depends on it." Her breath caught, and she swallowed. "Derrick and I, we aren't like other brothers and sisters. Though we're not identical twins, somehow there's a special link between us."

"A link?" He avoided meeting her gaze.

"We—" She caught her lip between her teeth and paused, feeling as if she were about to leap off a cliff. Sam was going to think she was crazy, she just knew it. "Our minds are linked, telepathically linked."

"Interesting theory."

"It isn't a theory, dammit!"

Her curse brought his gaze careening back to her. After studying her a moment, he said, "You're serious."

"Of course I am. Do you think I'd joke at a time like

this? Derrick can send me thought messages, kind of like…" she made a futile motion with her hands. "Sort of like radio waves. Only sometimes I get pictures, too. In turn, I can contact him." Crysta knew how insane she sounded, but she couldn't stop herself. Sam had to be convinced. "It's happened. I swear it."

In a rush, she told him about several instances from childhood when Derrick had been ill or hurt and she had been simultaneously stricken. "I was miles away from him, Sam. Every single time. There was no way I could have known."

"So why are we out here searching and playing guessing games?" A challenging glint crept into his eyes. "Why don't you just *call* him and find out where he is?"

The sarcasm in his voice was veiled, but there. Crysta swallowed down anger. And pain. "I can't. He isn't answering me. But he called to me for help, Sam. Forty-eight hours before the police contacted my mother. That's how I recognized this place. I'd seen it before! In my dream."

He cast a dubious glance around.

Crysta moved toward him. "I didn't tell you before because I was afraid you'd think I was crazy. But more importantly, I was afraid to let on how much I knew! If you were involved, Sam, my link to Derrick would be dangerous to you."

"So why are you telling me now?"

"Because now I know you had nothing to do with it." She gestured toward the spruce. "In the dream, I was running, trying to reach safety up ahead. That tree was on my right. I was running toward Cottonwood Bend, Sam! Don't you see? I wasn't dreaming about myself, but about Derrick. You were the safety he was running toward! His friend. He knew you'd help him."

In her desperation, she grabbed Sam's shirt. As quickly as she could, she recounted her second dream, in detail.

"You have to believe me! He isn't dead. It wasn't a bear."

Sam grasped her shoulders. The frantic appeal in her eyes caught at his heart. Derrick had told Sam about the "link" between him and his sister, but until now, Sam hadn't truly understood how deeply they both believed in it. Or how much it might mean to Crysta that he believe in it, as well. By nature, Sam was a doubting Thomas. He found it extremely difficult to believe in anything he couldn't see or touch or feel. But, for Crysta's sake, he was willing to try.

Giving her a slight shake, he said, "Crysta, I believe you. Just calm down. I believe you."

It was the first time in Crysta's life anyone had said that—other than family, of course, who had seen the proof—and she was momentarily taken aback.

"You believe me?" Her amazement came through in her voice. "Does this mean you'll bring the searchers back?"

Sam tightened his grip on her shoulders. "I think you dreamed the dreams, exactly as you described them, and that you believe with all your heart that they were messages from Derrick."

Her heart sank. "You believe I'm telling the truth, as I see it, in other words."

"I'm *trying,* Crysta. You can't blame me for having reservations."

Frustration welled within her. She jerked away and turned her back on him to stare blindly at the water. People had been skeptical all her life. Just once, why couldn't someone believe her? "I should have known not to say anything. You'd think, after all these years, that I'd learn. But, oh, no, I never do."

"Crysta…"

She waved a hand. "No, no! It's all right. I'm used to it. At least I should be." She gave a bitter laugh. "Have you any idea how many friends I've lost over this? I can even list my marriage as a casualty. You get a thick hide after a while."

"If only you had some proof," he said quietly. "There's a great deal at stake here."

She whirled around. "Like your reputation? Your credibility? Other than that, what have you got to lose?"

"Not me so much. I have to think of the searchers. I can't keep them from their jobs without some tangible proof to go on."

"I *can* prove it!" she cried. "The buckle, Sam! If it wasn't in his shirt, it has to be here someplace."

She began another frantic search. For several seconds Sam stood back, looking nonplussed, but then he began helping her comb the area. Ten minutes later, Crysta admitted defeat.

"Well it isn't here." She lifted her hands and shrugged. It was all she could do not to cry. Derrick had counted on her to come through for him, and she was failing, miserably. "I guess as far as tangible proof goes, we're back to square one and the bear theory."

Sam, who stood a few feet away, clamped a hand around the base of his neck, tilting his head back, clearly exhausted.

"In my second dream, I saw a wound over Derrick's heart." A cool breeze came in off the river, funneling around them. She wrapped her arms around herself, shivering. "In the first dream, he picked up the buckle and slipped it into his left breast pocket. What if the bullet went through the buckle, Sam? It may have been damaged. If those men found it, they wouldn't have dared leave it. It would have been evidence of foul play."

"You're grasping at straws, aren't you?"

"Maybe, but right now, I'll grasp at anything!"

"Crysta…" Sam walked slowly toward her. Taking her by the shoulders again, he said, "Honey, I know how upset you are and that the dreams seemed real to you. But isn't it possible that they were products of wishful thinking? That you love Derrick too much to accept the unthinkable—that he's dead and you'll never see him again? There's no sign here of two-legged attackers. Other than the more recent footprints of the searchers, there's nothing to indicate Derrick encountered anything other than a bear. I looked, believe me."

"Two things," she said, placing a hand on his chest to keep a distance between them. "One being that I had the first dream forty-eight hours before I was notified of Derrick's disappearance, which rules out wishful thinking. The second is, don't call me honey. It's condescending and infuriating. You wouldn't consider using an endearment like that if you were having this conversation with a man, would you?"

"I suppose not." His eyes filled with irritation when she pulled away from him. Folding his arms across his chest, he fell into step beside her as she headed back upstream. "Where are you going?"

"Back to the lodge. We've seen what we came to see. I'm going to study the map to familiarize myself with this area while I have Jangles pack me some food. Then I'm coming back here."

"To do what?"

"To look for my brother."

"Where?"

"Everywhere. I'll comb every inch of the area."

Sam sighed.

Crysta rounded on him. "Look, I understand that you don't believe me. That's your choice, and I really can't blame you. That doesn't mean I'm giving up." She struck off walking again. "I know what I know. I can't prove it, but there it is. I'm coming back, and nobody, including you, is going to stop me."

"Even though you just saw the evidence of a bear attack with your own eyes?" he countered.

Crysta raised her chin. "Evidence can be faked."

"It might be a little difficult to get the bear to cooperate," he came back.

A sudden thought hit her. "Not if it was dead." Her gaze flew to his. "The bear carcass, Sam—the one Tip said he found, minus its head and paws. What if Derrick's attackers used the teeth and claws to tear up his clothing? Bear track is common everywhere, right? They wouldn't have had to fake that. If they were extremely careful about the other evidence they left, not even a forensics lab could tell by examining the clothing. Naturally, the searchers would be fooled."

His eyes narrowed in thought. "It's possible, I suppose. It'd be a mighty clever trick, using a dead bear, but if it was done right, even an expert might be misled by the hair and saliva traces left on the clothing."

"So you admit it's possible."

"Possible, yes."

"But unlikely," she added hollowly. With a little shrug, she accepted that and picked up her pace. "For me, a possibility is enough."

"What if I was to say I'm willing to go on your instincts?"

The question made her falter. "What do you mean?"

"That I'll forgo proof and logic, just this once. I can't have the searchers resume their hunt, but that doesn't mean I can't continue the search."

"I'm not one to look a gift horse in the mouth, but why?"

"Let's just say, for now, that I concede there may be such a thing as mental telepathy and that it might manifest itself between twins. There *was* a bear carcass found, a fresh kill, at just the right time. I care a lot about Derrick, and as long as there's a possibility he's alive, I'd be a fool to ignore what you're telling me."

"Oh, Sam, I could kiss you!"

"Kiss a man who calls you demeaning names like honey?"

She ignored the dig. "So you'll come back here with me?"

"I didn't say that."

"Sam, in my dream, Derrick was badly wounded! We have to make finding him our first priority!"

He shook his head. "If the wound was that serious, time has already run out. If not, then Derrick will manage to hang on until we reach him. A frenzied search isn't the answer. We have nothing to base it on." He held up a staying hand. "I know you saw a cabin in your dream. That's great, but it doesn't help. There are a lot of abandoned cabins in the interior. We might waste days searching and not find it."

"It's a sure bet we won't find it in Derrick's briefcase."

"We may get a lead there. You dreamed about a warehouse. If your dreams are messages from Derrick, that's proof my suspicions about Blanchette are accurate. If we can find out what Derrick found, we may be able to identify his attackers."

"Marvelous. Without Derrick to testify, we'd have culprits, but no evidence against them. What good would that do?"

"The 'culprits' can tell us where Derrick is, or at least point us in the right direction."

"Why would they be so accommodating? They'd be incriminating themselves."

"If we find them, Crysta, I think I can persuade them to cooperate," he replied in a silken voice.

She glanced down to see that his hands were knotted into fists. As frightening as it was to envision Sam losing his temper and using those fists on someone, it was also strangely reassuring. For the first time since coming to Alaska, she felt as if she had a friend in all this, someone who would stand by her and help her find her brother.

As they walked along, she noticed that Sam paused frequently, as if to listen, and scanned the surrounding area.

"What are you looking for?" she whispered.

His mouth settled in a grim line. "Grizzly sign. Territorial markings. Like it or not, we can't disregard what we saw back there. Where there's smoke, there's usually fire, and I'm not willing to risk our lives gambling that all that bear sign was planted."

The hair on Crysta's neck prickled. "If there *is* a renegade bear out here, what'll we do? You haven't got a gun."

"More fool I. I should have known Jim wouldn't have been so convinced of a bear attack without plenty of reason."

"Can grizzlies climb trees?"

He grimaced. "They usually just knock them down."

He settled somber dark eyes on hers. "If we run across a bear, drop to the ground, pull yourself into the fetal position, tuck your head under your arms and play dead. If it mauls you, try not to move or cry out. If you're lucky, after a while, it'll grow bored and leave you alone."

"And if I'm not lucky?"

Sam's response to that was to scan the woods again. The worried look on his face was answer enough for Crysta.

CHAPTER NINE

DURING THE RETURN trip to the lodge, Crysta's legs grew quivery with exhaustion. The slightest projection in her path caught the toe of her sneaker, making her stumble.

With no warning, Sam touched her elbow and nodded toward a grassy sweep of high ground. "I need to take five."

He sat down and she stumbled after him, drooping to the ground like an overcooked strand of spaghetti. Despite the breeze coming off the water, her face felt hot, her forehead filmed with sweat. Sam stretched out on his back, head on his folded arms. With far less grace, she flopped over on her stomach.

She knew he had stopped not for himself, but for her. His legs were accustomed to long treks; hers were not. She drew a shaky breath, running her parched tongue over dry lips, longing for a drink. The river water looked too muddy for consumption.

As if he had read her mind, Sam removed a small flask from his belt and offered it to her. "Care to wet your whistle?"

Crysta uncapped the canteen and took a drink. After wiping the mouth of the container, she handed it back to him and watched as he took a long swallow and sighed with satisfaction.

"You okay?" he asked as he clipped the canteen back

onto his belt. "This is quite a trek for someone not used to it."

After she had tried so hard to keep up with him, the husky concern in his voice pricked her pride. "I'm fine. How about you?"

The comeback was ridiculous. He would have to be blind not to see how trembly her muscles were. However, just because her body had given out on her didn't mean she should lose her sense of humor. "If you don't think you can make it the rest of the way, I'll let you lean on me," she offered.

She heard a choked laugh. "I appreciate that."

Abandoning pretense, she rolled onto her side and tipped her head back to study his profile. Against the backdrop of thick grass and swaying cottonwood, he struck a contrast to the wildness, yet seemed strangely a part of it. "Are we walking uphill?" she asked.

"The incline is pretty slight."

"Tell my legs that."

His firm lips inched into a wry grin. "I'm sorry. I should have stopped sooner. I had my mind on other things."

Crysta wished her own thoughts could transcend the physical. The last mile or so, even her obsessive musings about Derrick had dimmed, edged out by muscle fatigue and the struggle to keep walking. "What other things?"

"Derrick's papers. I've gone through at least half of them, possibly more. My instincts tell me there's something there, something I'm missing." He closed his eyes. "There *has* to be something. It's our only chance."

Crysta made a fist in the grass, giving the tender shoots a twist. The bittersweet smell drifted to her nostrils, making her think of the times in high school when she had tussled with Derrick on their front lawn while he practiced his wrestling moves. The memories brought a lump to her throat. She needed to share the pain and seek reassurance.

Since their talk at the site of the alleged bear attack, Crysta felt more at ease with Sam. She had revealed a side of herself she seldom shared with anyone, and he hadn't mocked her.

"Sam, tell me honestly, do you think Derrick's dead?"

He turned his head to look at her. "I did. Now that you've told me about your dreams, I'm not so sure." As if he sensed how desperately she needed a friend's assurances just now, his eyes softened, delving deeply into hers. "If he's contacting you, he can't be dead, can he?"

"That's just it. Since I had that dream last night, he hasn't." A shiver coursed through her, cold as death. "There's just silence now—an awful silence. For as long as I can remember, I've always *felt* him. I can't explain. I suppose you think I'm insane. It's part of me I don't often share. People—even those I thought were good friends— tend to shun me if I talk about it." Her mouth trembled as she tried to form the next words. "I can't feel anything, Sam. It's as if Derrick's gone."

"I don't think you're insane." His voice turned gravelly, but it soothed her in some indefinable way. "And even if I did, what difference would it make? Those people you thought were friends? You're you, Crysta. Your feelings, your relationship with Derrick, the telepathy thing—that's all uniquely you. Anyone who shuns you for being yourself isn't worth your time."

"I'm frightened," she whispered.

"I know you are."

Such a simple answer, yet somehow, it was exactly what she had needed him to say. No judgments, no analytical preaching, no cruel gibes. She hadn't expected him to understand, and perhaps he didn't. Maybe no one could. But that wasn't important. What counted was that Sam accepted her as she was.

She had been longing for a friend. Now she realized she had one. Tears sprang to her eyes. "Thank you for that."

It might have been a silly thing to say, given his response, but he seemed to understand. He shifted onto his side and placed a hand on her cheek, his fingertips feathering lightly over her ear and the tendrils of hair at her temple. As recently as this morning, Crysta probably would have pulled away. But now the familiarity seemed right. She supposed circumstances might be fostering emotions between them that they might not feel at another time—Derrick's best friend and his sister, drawn together by fear and grief—but it didn't seem like that.

His hand was large, warm, heavy. Even though she knew he only meant to comfort her, his touch made her skin tingle. She let her eyelashes drift closed, absorbing the solidness of him. He said nothing. When she thought about that, she realized there was very little else he could say. His touch was enough. It helped to know that he cared, even though he couldn't comprehend.

"Maybe he's unconscious," she whispered raggedly.

"Maybe," he agreed. "Or too exhausted to communicate. You're weary, too. That has to have some bearing."

She was glad for his seeming acceptance, but she still had to face the reality that the channel of communication between her and Derrick had gone dead. She might need to assimilate, deal with and accept what that might mean.

"I love him more than a sister usually loves a brother. I guess it's not true of all twins, but with us, there's a closeness, a sense of oneness." She opened her eyes. "Even when we fought, as brothers and sisters always will, the bond was there between us."

"I know. Derrick and I go back a long way. I could tell you two had something special, just by the way he spoke of you."

"I need to call my mother, update her. I'm not sure what I should say." Her throat closed around the words, making them sound tinny. "If he's dead, how will I—"

Sam moved his arm slightly, his thumb grazing her lips to silence her. "Crysta, if he *is* dead, your mom will deal with it. You'll both survive and go on living, just like everyone else who's lost someone dear. Until you know for sure, though, you have to concentrate on finding him. Not on what people might think. Not on what you should tell your mom."

She took a deep, steadying breath. "You're right. I know you are. I'm sorry."

"Don't be." He withdrew his hand from her cheek and sat up, looping his arms around his knees. The wind ruffled his dark hair. "You're handling this better than most people would. If the roles were reversed, Derrick would be over the edge."

Crysta pushed to a sitting position, keeping an arm braced behind her. "Yes, Derrick was—" She broke off, shattered that she was referring to her brother in the past tense. "He *isn't* so strong sometimes. Especially not since his breakup with Eileen. Emotionally, he's been walking a tightrope, and sometimes he—he loses his footing." Brushing hair from her eyes, she stared hard at the river, still fighting tears. "He changed after she left. Then there was the car wreck.... Without Eileen, the only comfort he seemed able to find was at the bottom of a bottle." She glanced sideways at Sam. "You knew him then, didn't you?"

"Yes. I visited him at the hospital, in fact. Drinking and driving. I couldn't believe it when I found out."

"I'm surprised we didn't run into each other. I practically lived outside the intensive-care unit."

"If I remember correctly, you had gone to pick up your husband at the airport that afternoon. We probably just missed each other. I didn't get to visit Derrick for long. I was lucky even to get in, not being a relative, but they made an exception because I'd come so far."

Unpleasant memories assailed Crysta. Now that Sam mentioned it, she recalled that afternoon vividly—the grudging trip she'd made to the airport to pick up Dick, their ensuing argument over Derrick, Dick's ultimatum. She had been forced to make a choice that afternoon, a choice no woman should ever have to make.

The memories still hurt, not because of any undying love for Dick—bitterness had killed that long ago—but because a marriage that should have been strong had crumbled. Crysta knew Dick had tried his best, and so had she. The problem was that no marriage could survive the intrusion of a third party, and Derrick had intruded constantly.

Facing those memories now was too much for Crysta. She shoved unsteadily to her feet. "I'm rested enough to go on."

Sam rose beside her, his eyes hooded. Crysta wondered if he already knew why her marriage to Dick had failed. Had Derrick told him? Unsettled by the thought, she struck off walking.

Sam fell in beside her, setting his stride to match hers. The silence between them, at first uncomfortable, slowly mellowed. Then, without warning, Sam grabbed her hand fiercely. Crysta spun to a stop to find Sam looking over his shoulder. Tension radiated from him. His gaze, alert and suspicious, scanned the woods. Then, so slowly the movement was almost imperceptible, he stepped between her and the brush.

"Wha—what is it?" she whispered. Envisioning a hungry grizzly, she clutched the back of his shirt and instinctively moved closer to him. "Did you hear something?"

He motioned for her to be quiet. Crysta stared into the trees, afraid on the one hand, yet not nearly as frightened as she might have been had he not been there. After a moment, he relaxed and resumed walking, keeping his hold on her hand.

"My imagination, I guess. I thought I heard something."

Crysta had heard nothing. "A small animal, do you think?"

He smiled. "Probably. I've gone so long without sleep, I must be getting wired. Jumping at shadows."

His hand, callused and warm, tightened around hers. Crysta fell into step with him, acutely aware that the pace he had set was a comfortable one for her.

Touched by his regard, she returned the pressure of his grip. He glanced up from his study of the ground ahead of them, his dark eyes molten and probing. The impact made her miss a step. He hauled back on her hand to keep her from stumbling, which brought her hip into contact with his thigh. Awareness once again crackled between them. She knew he felt it by the sudden tightening around his mouth. This time, though, he didn't increase his pace to put distance between them, and he didn't pretend nothing had happened.

Her heart picked up speed. This was crazy. And to say it was bad timing was an understatement. Sam Barrister wasn't her type, and she wasn't his. An Alaskan lodge owner and a fashion consultant? Ludicrous. So why was she feeling such a strong pull toward him?

Crysta had no answer and no energy to explore her emotions to find one. Derrick was all that mattered. She couldn't lose sight of that.

TODD SHRIVER'S CESSNA was floating up to the island when Sam and Crysta rounded the last bend in the river before reaching the lodge.

"Looks like Shriver brought Riley back with him. I swear, Riley could keep every pilot in the area going with all the flights he makes."

Crysta cupped her hand over her eyes, trying to spot the redheaded warehouse supervisor. "This morning he said he had to go on a beer run."

"He does that frequently."

"Does he have a drinking problem?"

"I'm not sure *drinking* is the word. *Guzzling* might better describe what ails him. At any rate, the luggage restrictions on the pontoon planes make it impossible for him to bring in more than one case of beer per trip, so he quite often runs low and flies back to town for more."

"How can he afford the airfare?"

"His father died recently. I understand he inherited a substantial amount of money."

Crysta wrinkled her nose. "It won't last long."

"Nope, but that's not my business. I give him discounts because he stays here so much and brings so many friends. Maybe Shriver and the other pilots give him special deals, too."

The sound of voices drifted on the air to them. Crysta veered toward the lodge, envisioning a tall glass of water and a thick sandwich. She tried not to think about her upcoming telephone conversation with her mother; some things were better left until you had to face them. No use borrowing trouble, as Ellen would say.

"Hey, Barrister!" a masculine voice called.

Crysta drew up beside Sam, watching as Todd Shriver came toward them, long legs scissoring along the muddy bank. Upon reaching them, the pilot passed an arm over his forehead, laughing and out of breath. "Guess I'm not as young as I used to be."

Looking at him, Crysta tried to catalog his features to decide what it was about him that bothered her. He had an infectious smile, and he was quite friendly. For want of a better explanation, she decided it was not so much his looks, which were above average, but the fact that his face had no character lines. Lines upon the face were like words upon a page; they made a statement. Her tastes ran to men who were a bit older, she decided, with features that bore the marks of their emotions. Laughter, tears. A man or woman had no real depth until they had experienced the heights of happiness and the depths of despair. Evidently Todd still had all of that ahead of him.

"Are any of us as young as we used to be?" Sam flexed his shoulders, making no attempt to hide his own exhaustion. "We've been on a long walk, Todd. Right now, we'd kill for a glass of water. Can it wait until later?"

Todd's grin faded, and he turned his ice-blue gaze on Crysta. "Sure, no problem. Fact is, I'm staying over to do some fishing, so I'll be around longer than usual. Before we took off downriver in the boat, I wanted to offer my condolences to you, Ms. Meyers. I heard about what the searchers found." He shook his head. "A bear—can you believe it? And to Derrick, of all people."

"It can happen to the best," Sam countered, his gaze intent on Shriver's youthful face. "Not often in these parts, though."

"Which makes it all the more a shame. Why here? Why him? I'm really sorry." Todd inclined his head toward Crysta. "You can't know how much."

Crysta noticed that the pilot kept glancing toward the river, as if he was worried that he might miss his fishing expedition. She wanted to accept his condolences graciously, but part of her couldn't. Like Steve Henderson, she found it difficult to accept that other people went on enjoying life when her own was being torn apart. She supposed it was self-centered of her. To Todd Shriver, Derrick had been an acquaintance, nothing more.

"I appreciate your concern," she said. "But let's not forget that his body hasn't been found. I still have hope."

"I don't blame you there. Never give up hope." Shriver flashed a slow smile, calculated, she was sure, to make her pulse escalate. "And like I said before, if you need me to fly you around, it'll only cost you for the fuel." Glancing toward the river, he retreated a step. "Better go before all the boats leave without me."

As Shriver walked off, Crysta gazed after him. More to herself than to Sam, she whispered, "Was I ever that carefree? Right now, the most important thing on his agenda is catching the biggest fish. There's a little-boy quality about him, isn't there?"

"Shriver?" Sam threw her a disbelieving look. "Most of my female guests go cow-eyed when he comes on to them like that."

She shrugged. "Fish, women. To fellows like him, both are candidates for the trophy rack."

Sam laughed, a little uneasily, she thought. "And what a way to go?"

Crysta angled a grin at him. "Looks only run skin-deep. He's a little too young for my taste. Life's still nothing but a big game to him."

Sam's answering grin warmed his dark eyes. Placing a hand on her shoulder, he pressed her into a walk. "He's not a bad fellow. It's nice to know, though, that not all women fall for a pretty face. There's hope for guys like me, after all."

Crysta threw him a sharp glance. Surely a man as handsome as Sam couldn't truly believe himself to be homely. "Do you?" she countered. "Fall for a pretty face, I mean."

He studied her. "Only if it belongs to an especially nice lady."

The response, coupled with the intensity in his eyes, brought a rush of heat to Crysta's cheeks, and she quickly glanced at the ground to hide her discomfiture.

WHILE SAM STOPPED by the kitchen and asked Jangles to bring them a plate of sandwiches, Crysta put in a call to her mother, dreading the moment when she would have to admit that she still had no idea where Derrick was. When her aunt Eva answered and explained that Ellen was asleep, Crysta sagged with relief. Being careful not to mention either of her dreams about Derrick, Crysta updated Eva on the situation.

"I wouldn't mention the bear theory to Mom," Crysta warned. "I'm convinced Derrick's still alive, and hearing that would only upset her. Just tell her I've arrived, and that I'm—" Crysta broke off. "Tell her I'm doing everything possible to find him."

"You worry too much about your mother's health. Sometimes I think she uses that heart condition of hers to manipulate you. One minute she's having an angina attack, and the next she's eating bonbons. I'm four years her senior, you know, and I have a heart condition, too. You don't see me clutching my chest every time things don't go my way."

Crysta stared at the calendar picture of Mount McKinley. Perhaps her mother's heart condition had become a sort of leverage she used to manipulate her children, but Crysta loved her mother too much to take that chance.

A brief silence hummed over the line. Then Eva said, "Crysta, this catastrophe with Derrick isn't your fault, you know. Your voice sounds so strained that I'm beginning to feel more worried about you than I am about him."

"I'm fine, Aunt Eva."

"Are you?"

Crysta shoved her hair from her eyes, acutely aware of the loving censure in the other woman's voice and the static on the phone line. "I'm positive. Listen, Aunt Eva, the rates on this telephone are astronomical. I really should get off. Will you tell Mom I love her?"

"I'll tell her—as if she could fail to know." Eva sighed. "Don't be too hard on yourself. Do I have your promise on that?"

Crysta smiled in spite of herself. "I'll do my best."

Just as Crysta hung up the phone, Sam and Jangles emerged from the kitchen. Jangles stared at Crysta and said, "Sandwiches are on the way."

"Great. I'm famished," Crysta called to the Indian woman as she and Sam entered his office.

She took a seat by his desk, watching while Sam poured a pot of water into the automatic coffeemaker. Then, he grasped the waist of his shirt and tugged the tails free of his jeans, unfastening the snaps as he strode toward her. "Hope you don't mind, but I've got to shed a layer."

"It is warm in here." Averting her gaze from the ripple of chest muscle revealed by his snug T-shirt, she leaned around to open the right drawer of his desk, pulling Derrick's briefcase out. Glancing down at the wastebasket, she frowned. "The salmon is gone."

"Jangles must have dumped it."

"Efficient lady, Jangles."

"Do I detect some animosity?"

"Did you notice that look she gave me a second ago? She's against my being here, and I can't understand why."

"Like I said, it could be superstitious nonsense. Don't read too much into it."

"She didn't even mention the fish. That seems suspicious to me."

Sam smiled. "Crysta, the only place at this lodge where a salmon is out of the ordinary is in my bed. Why would she mention something so commonplace?"

Crysta realized he was right and sighed. "I guess maybe I'm looking for things because she isn't very friendly."

Sam nodded, bracing an arm on the desk to lean over her while she began leafing through the papers in Derrick's briefcase. Crysta had seen most of the documents that afternoon when she had come in here snooping, and hopelessness filled her. "Have you any idea what we're supposed to be looking for, Sam?"

He sighed and eased around her to claim the captain's

chair behind the desk. Shuffling through the papers on his blotter, he located the stack of records he had been studying earlier when Crysta had burst in so unexpectedly, brandishing the salmon. "I wish I did. Something out of the ordinary."

She scanned an invoice. An idea struck her. "What if they're buying inferior material? There's big money in that."

"Skimming from the budget, you mean?" Sam shook his head. "I thought of that and called a contractor friend of mine in Anchorage. I gave him a quick rundown on the purchase orders. He said it sounded as if the company was ordering from reputable firms, up to code and getting more than enough stuff. When skimming occurs, a contractor generally buys from a disreputable outfit, using lower-grade materials or less than is required by law."

Crysta groaned and tossed down the invoice. "Then what *are* we looking for, Sam? This isn't a solution, it's a time waster. Wouldn't it be more expedient to return downriver and search the area around the attack site for signs of Derrick?"

"Do you think the searchers haven't done that?"

Crysta knew they must have. "But he can't have gotten far. Not if he was wounded."

Sam's expression grew grim. "If your dream is an accurate account, his attackers must have removed him from the area."

"You're a good tracker, aren't you?"

"Jim, the search coordinator, is a far better tracker than I. If there was a trail out there to follow, he would have spotted it. There is no sign, none at all, that anything but a bear was in the vicinity."

Suddenly it occurred to Crysta just how much faith in

her Sam was exercising by even *trying* to believe in her story. "There has to be something we can do besides this."

He glanced up from the documents he was scanning. "Maybe, but the briefcase is the most obvious place to start."

Crysta longed to contradict him, but, remembering the map she had studied, she didn't.

Within ten minutes, the coffee had finished perking and Jangles had delivered a plate of delicious steak sandwiches. After Crysta ate, she began to feel drowsy. Determined to keep working, she poured them each a second mug of coffee and sat back down to study more papers.

She could see what Sam meant about the quantity of merchandise being ordered by Blanchette. She was no expert, but it seemed to her that the construction company bought plenty of everything, especially conduit. And all from reputable firms.

Exhaustion blurred her vision. She blinked and sat up straighter. Seconds later, she shifted in her seat and stretched, the battle to stay awake growing more difficult.

Glancing up from his desk, Sam studied Crysta a moment, biting back a smile. Her head was nodding, and her grip on the sheaf of papers in her lap was growing lax. He returned his gaze to the paper work, wishing she'd go lie down but knowing she'd resist if he suggested it. Because of the long hours of daylight in Alaska during the summer months, Sam was used to operating on little if any sleep. Crysta wasn't, especially not after the strenuous walk she'd just been on.

Moments later, a soft snore interrupted Sam's concentration. He looked up to see that Crysta had slumped sideways in her chair. Her head lolled on her shoulder. Sam watched her for a moment, smiling each time he heard the purring noise that feathered past her lips. Not exactly a rafter shaker, but definitely a snore. He decided he liked the sound.

The clock on the wall ticked rhythmically. Every once in a while, the coffeemaker sputtered. Soothed by those sounds and Crysta's soft snore, Sam settled in to work.

SWEAT STREAMED DOWN Crysta's sides to the waistband of her jeans. Her chest felt as if a red-hot coal was buried in it. With a groan, she struggled to open her eyes, wondering why the soft leather cushion of her chair felt so hard and uneven.

She stared into thick gloom. She was no longer in Sam's office but sitting on a fireplace hearth, feeble flames flickering in the grate to one side of her. The room around her was dark with shadows and smelled of smoke, dampness and dust. At one end was a broken window, the remaining glass filmed with grime and draped with cobwebs. Struggling to breathe, she leaned her head back against the rock face of the fireplace and stared at the layers of smoke hovering like cumulus clouds below the exposed rafters of the ceiling.

Sick, so sick. Her body felt afire. She looked down and saw that she held a knife in her hand. Her arm shook as she directed the blade toward the small black hole in her chest. The bullet. If it didn't come out, she'd die of infection.

Pain lashed Crysta as she pressed the tip of the knife into her flesh. Swirls of red blinded her. It took all her courage to sink the knife deeper, and then she had to call upon sheer desperation to probe for the lead. Her body began to shake more violently. Sweat streamed down her face.

Please, God.

The knife tip grated against something metallic, and the pain, already excruciating, amplified, flashing across her left breast. The room began to swirl, slowly at first, then faster. Blackness encroached on her vision until she was seeing the wound in her chest through a tiny peephole that was narrowing at an alarming speed. The lead at last popped free and bounced away across the floor, bloody-black and misshapen.

So weak. The knife slipped from her hand and clattered onto the stone hearth. She knew she mustn't lose consciousness, not yet. Through the tiny sphere of her narrowed vision, Crysta stared at the blood spurting down her belly, keeping time with her heartbeat. The bleeding was good; it would clean the wound. She groped for the knife, found it. Summoning all her remaining strength, she extended her arm, holding the blade over the flames until the steel turned a muted red.

Tightening her grip on the knife handle and clenching her teeth, she withdrew the blade from the heat and slapped the red-hot metal over her wound. Body rigid, she hissed, quivering as the stench of searing flesh turned her stomach.

"CRYSTA! CRYSTA, HONEY, wake up."

Crysta swam up toward the light and Sam's voice, frantic for air, for a release from the pain. His face burst through the swirls of blackness, muscles taut with concern, his eyes frightened. She swallowed down another wave of nausea.

"It hurts! It hurts, Sam."

"What, where?"

"My chest—my chest."

Sam's arm encircled her shoulders. Crysta leaned against him, not caring when she felt his other hand tearing at the top buttons of her shirt. Cool air wafted across her collarbone. Warm, callused fingers pressed against the side of her throat. She realized he was checking her pulse.

In one smooth motion, Sam lifted her out of the chair and laid her on the floor. "Be still, honey. Just be still and trust me, okay? I'm trained in first aid. You'll be fine."

Frantic to somehow rid herself of the pain, Crysta clutched at her chest. He clasped her wrists, forcing her arms to her sides. Another wave of nausea washed over her, and she tried to sit up, gagging.

Sam cradled Crysta's shoulders, forcing her to lie back against his arm. Fishing his handkerchief from his back pocket, he wiped her pale face, frightened for her yet uncertain precisely what was wrong.

"It's all right, Crysta. Relax, relax."

She pressed a shaking hand over her left breast. Sam stared at her colorless skin, at the taut pull of her facial muscles, and listened with half an ear to her babbling description of what could only have been a dream. A bullet? A knife? Derrick, wounded and alone, in a ramshackle cabin? Sam could tell by looking at Crysta, by the way she quivered, that the dream she was recounting had been no ordinary nightmare.

With an inexplicable feeling of dread, he drew her hand from her chest and stared at the angry red welt rising on her ivory skin, beginning above the cup of her white bra and angling downward under the lacy cloth. Goose bumps rose on the nape of his neck.

Slowly, she began to quieten. Sam held her, stroking her hair, whispering to her. Her breathing evened out. A quick glance told him that the red imprint on her skin was fading. Questions crowded into his mind. Had she caused the red mark herself, clutching at her chest? Could he have done it while opening her shirt?

"He's alive, Sam. He's alive!" She arched her neck to look up at him. "We have to find him. Soon!"

Sam swallowed, uncertain what to say to her. "Calm down, Crysta. It was just a bad dream, a bad dream."

"No." She shook her head, struggling to escape him. "Not a dream. You have to believe that."

During his military training years ago, Sam had watched films on torture techniques. He knew how powerful the mind was. There were documented cases in which blindfolded prisoners, expecting to be touched with hot steel, had actually developed burns when touched with harmless, frosted metal. Was it possible that the mark on Crysta's chest had been put there by her absolute belief that Derrick had placed a hot knife against his chest? Or was it true that Crysta and Derrick, so genetically similar, shared some strange and incomprehensible mental link that enabled one to feel what the other suffered?

"Please, Sam, listen to me. We're wasting precious time! Maybe if we went to the police we could convince them to do something."

"With what as proof?" he asked gently. "Your dreams, Crysta? Jim Sales is one of the best trackers around. He says Derrick was attacked by a bear, and even I have to admit the evidence points to that. What chance have we of convincing the police otherwise?"

"What if we did an aerial search? We might spot the cabin he's in."

As patiently as he could, Sam once again explained to her that the interior was dotted with abandoned cabins. As versatile as Todd's float-plane was, it couldn't land unless the conditions were ideal. Even if they narrowed their scope and chose only a few cabins to investigate by foot, it would take days, possibly even weeks, to reach them all.

"But what about the helicopter you told me about?" she cried. "A helicopter can land almost anywhere."

"The Huey? Crysta, that was a military chopper, brought in especially for the search." Sam studied her pinched face, wishing that he could make her comprehend how vast Alaska was. "Have you ever seen a map of Alaska superimposed over a map of the lower forty-eight? It's mind-boggling how large it is."

"We could rent another helicopter. Surely some pilot would take us up!"

"That'd cost a fortune. We're not talking a few hours, but possibly days. I have some money in savings, but not nearly enough." Sam sighed, his thoughts straying to Tip and the exorbitant costs for his special schooling during the winter months. "I'm sorry, Crysta. I just don't have the resources for something that expensive."

"I don't, either," she admitted in a quavery voice. "But, Sam, we can't just poke around in a briefcase!"

Sam helped her to sit erect. He could see she was becoming frantic and that she wouldn't be satisfied with spending any more time going through Derrick's papers. Her pallor alarmed him. It was fast becoming a toss-up what concerned him most, trying to find out what had happened to Derrick or playing along with Crysta to make this as painless as possible for her. This couldn't be an easy time for her, and with every passing hour Sam's hopes of finding Derrick, alive or dead, diminished.

Smoothing her hair, he said, "Okay, I'll admit that the briefcase may be a dead end. The next place to look is in Anchorage." His gaze locked on hers. "You say you dreamed of walking through a warehouse, right? I think we should fly to town with Todd Shriver and get permission to tour the Blanchette warehouses. Maybe we'll find the building you dreamed of."

"And possibly find a lead?"

She looked so grateful to him that Sam felt a twinge of guilt. He *wanted* to believe in her dreams, but his pragmatic side balked. "Possibly," he offered noncommittally. "Before we leave, though, both of us have to get some rest."

"Rest?"

Sam feathered his thumb across her cheek. Dark shadows formed crescents beneath her eyes, all the more noticeable now because she was so pale. "I'm running on sheer willpower."

"But Derrick— We can't take time to sleep, Sam! Time is running out. Derrick needs me. Don't you understand?"

"We have to get some sleep. I've been operating on short naps for five days. I'm beat. My mind is fuzzy. We'll both be better equipped to find and help Derrick if we're refreshed."

With obvious reluctance, she acquiesced with a nod, her eyes haunted. Sam pushed to his feet and offered her a hand up. When she stood, he gazed down at her for a long moment, fighting off an almost irresistible urge to draw her into his arms.

"Why don't you go down to the sauna and freshen up?" he suggested. "It'll relax you and help you sleep. I promise to set the alarm so we don't sleep long."

Too weary and disheartened to argue, Crysta turned to leave, reasoning that the sooner she got some sleep, the sooner she and Sam could fly into Anchorage. At the door, she stopped and looked back over her shoulder. "You'll tell Todd not to leave without us?"

"I'll have Tip go down and give him the message."

EN ROUTE TO THE SAUNA, Crysta noticed Steve Henderson sitting under a cottonwood, back braced against the trunk, one knee bent to support his arm. He looked so desolate that she veered toward him, uncertain what she could say to comfort him but driven to try. It couldn't be easy watching your little boy slip away, especially when all it might take to save him was a donor match. She could only imagine the frustration he must be feeling, his impotent rage at fate.

About ten feet from him, she called out a hello.

He jumped as if she had stung him. His blue gaze rose to her face. She immediately noted how thin he was, almost wasted, as if he were the one stricken with a grave illness.

"I'm Crysta Meyers, Derrick's sister." Suddenly feeling foolish, Crysta let her gaze trail off into the trees. "I, um, heard about your little boy, Scotty. I just wanted you to know I'll be praying that they line him up with a donor soon."

When he said nothing, Crysta returned her gaze to his ravaged features. He was staring through her, past her, as if he found eye contact with her disconcerting. Crysta realized her arrival was probably an unwelcome intrusion on his solitude, that he had come here to grieve and didn't appreciate her company.

"Why would you care about my son?" he asked in a shaky voice. "Who's he to you?"

The wind whipped her shirt tightly around her torso. She dragged her hair away from her eyes, wishing she hadn't come. Maybe he saw her as a morbid curiosity seeker; he clearly resented her condolences. "I'm sorry, Mr. Henderson. I walked up on impulse. I, um, just wanted to—" She shrugged. "You've heard about my brother. Sometimes I feel as if no one cares but me. I know it must be a thousand times worse for you."

His eyes cleared and seemed to focus on her. "That's life, isn't it? No one else really cares. Your world falls apart, but all around you there's laughter."

"Yes." Crysta swallowed, her throat suddenly dry and burning. "That's life. It's not true of everyone, though. Some people *do* care. I just wanted you to know that."

He averted his face and let out a ragged sigh. She noticed that he was clenching and unclenching his fist. She had intended to comfort him, not make matters worse.

"Well…" She gestured at the bundle of clothes she carried under one arm. "I was on my way to the sauna. Better get on down there before someone else beats me to it."

With that, Crysta spun and walked off. She could feel Henderson's eyes boring into her back. His hostility unnerved her, yet she couldn't condemn him for it. *"Your world falls apart, but all around you there's laughter."* She knew how the sounds of gaiety hurt when someone you loved might be dying.

It took an effort to put the uncomfortable meeting with Henderson into perspective. She had offered to commiserate with him; he had rejected her. No big deal. She had problems enough of her own. Trudging up onto the sauna steps, she flipped over the sign, then let herself in the door. Sam was right, a good steam bath was what she needed—a nice long one so she could forget her most recent dream and relax enough to once again fall asleep.

STEAM ROSE AROUND Crysta in a thick cloud. She tipped her head back and poured water from the bucket over herself, rinsing off the soap. The heat soothed her aching body. She grabbed her towel off the hook and wrapped it around herself, tucking a corner between her breasts. Giving in to exhaustion, she sank to the steam bench and braced her back against the wall.

A muffled thump came from the anteroom. She cocked her head, peering through the swirling steam. Before coming in, she hadn't looked at the sign to see what side was up. Had the previous sauna occupant forgotten to turn the sign back over when he left? If so, she might have put the Occupied side toward the building, unintentionally inviting company.

"Is someone there?" she called.

No one answered, but Crysta sensed a presence. Why would someone ignore her?

Before she could think of an answer to that unsettling question, a rumble vibrated through the planked flooring. Startled by a noise, Crysta shot up from the bench. It sounded as though the woodpile in the anteroom had collapsed.

Unable to see clearly through the steam, she moved carefully in the general direction of the door. She heard the echo of booted feet crossing the floor in the other room, then a creak of metal as the stove door opened. More thunks, which sounded like lengths of wood being shoved into the fire, brought a relieved smile to her mouth. Someone must be replenishing the wood supply. She remembered seeing Tip carrying wood in here earlier.

"Tip, is that you?" Uncertain exactly where the door was, Crysta stepped closer to the wall, groping with flattened palms. "It's me, Crysta. I forgot to check the sign before I turned it over. I don't mind that you brought in wood, but could you come back in a few minutes to stack it? I'll hurry and get dressed."

No answer. She thought she heard the stove door clank shut. Were the walls of the sauna so thick and airtight that she couldn't be heard? Possibly the ducts from the stove piped sound into the sauna, but not vice versa.

She didn't consider herself overly modest, but she drew the line at communal baths. At any moment, an unsuspecting fisherman might stroll in. She found the door and pressed her palm against it, intending to shove it open a crack and peek out.

It wouldn't budge. For an instant, Crysta thought perhaps the door opened inward, but when she ran her palm along its edge, squinting to see, she couldn't find a pull handle. Her heartbeat accelerated slightly.

"Yoo-hoo? It's me, Crysta Meyers. What happened? Did the woodpile fall?" She pushed harder on the door. It still wouldn't move. Giving a little laugh, she leaned closer. "I think the door is blocked."

No answer. Crysta shoved on the door again, putting all her weight against it this time.

"Hello! Is anyone out there?"

A panicked scream worked its way up her throat. She swallowed it down, moving back a step and lunging forward, hitting the door with her shoulder.

"Tip! Somebody! Answer me!"

The sound of her own voice, muted by the steam, bounced back at her off the moisture-soaked walls. She turned to peer through the roiling mist. Was it her imagination, or was the temperature within the sauna rising? Remembering the sound of wood being shoved into the stove, she turned back to the door, horror washing over her. Had someone deliberately blocked her only exit and built up the fire?

"Oh, my God..."

Crysta clutched her throat. There was no point in letting her imagination run away with her. It was probably a simple case of someone coming in with a load of wood, accidentally knocking over the woodpile and not being able to hear her yelling.

She knew from her occasional visits to the health club in Los Angeles that a healthy person could safely remain in an extremely hot steam bath for at least twenty minutes, and she had only been in here about fifteen. If the wood had toppled, which she felt certain it had, then the person she had heard in the other room had probably gone to get help to restack it.

The thing to do was remain calm and— The thought fragmented. And do what? her mind mocked. Slowly parboil? What if the person who had knocked over the wood didn't realize she was in here and took his time coming back? She could suffocate.

Crysta stumbled along the wall, fanning her foot across the floor and patting the shelves with her palm. Surely there was something in here that she could use for leverage on the door. A crowbar would be nice, though she didn't imagine Sam would leave anything metal in here to rust.

Crysta circled until her knees connected sharply with the end of the steam bench. So much for finding a tool of some kind. Pausing a moment to listen, she forced herself to breathe evenly. The last thing she should do was overreact and exert herself.

Sweat streamed down her body. The air tasted hot and thick as it rolled across her tongue. Too thick to breathe.

Had the mysterious wood bearer opened the damper on the stove? *Stay calm.* She couldn't hear any voices filtering in from outside. If she screamed, would anyone outside be able to hear her?

Crysta moved toward the door. Her knees felt strangely weak and shaky. The extreme heat was already sapping her strength. This couldn't be happening. Someone would come. When she didn't return to the lodge, Sam would surely come down to check on her.

Feeling somewhat reassured, Crysta walked face-first into the door and staggered backward, cupping her hand over her nose. *Stay calm.* Sam would come. As nightmarish as this was, she would laugh about it later. Hot air rises. If worse came to worse, she could lie on the floor. Her head already felt light, her body leaden. How much longer did she have before she succumbed to the heat?

"Help! Someone, help me! I'm in the sauna!"

Crysta screamed again and again. She lost track of what she said or how many times she called out. She leaned against the door, trying to work her fingers into the cracks. If she could find purchase for a grip, perhaps she could open it against its hinges. Her fingernails tore. Her hands began to throb.

She had no idea how much time passed. She only knew that her thoughts were growing disjointed and that every breath she drew seemed to go about halfway down her throat and stop there. She sank to her knees, giving way to panic, clawing frantically at the wood. She had to get out of here. Frightened now, really frightened, she began to pound futilely with her fists, screaming until her throat felt raw. No one responded. In the back of her mind, she realized her voice was growing weak.

She sank onto her side, pressing her face to the seam

of the threshold, praying that cool air might be seeping in. "Sam! Sam!" A sob caught in her chest. Dizziness rolled over her.

CHAPTER TEN

"Where's Crys?"

At the question, Sam glanced up from his desk, focusing on Tip, who had just wandered into the office. A smear of paint angled across the boy's cheek, and his hair looked as if he had stuck his head in the blender.

"She's taking a nap."

Tip looked perplexed. "Uh-uh. I just knocked on the bedroom door, and she didn't answer. I, um, wanted to show her my painting of Derrick."

Sam dragged his attention from the paperwork again, fighting down irritation. He'd been neglecting Tip for days. Who could blame the boy for wanting some attention? "She's probably sound asleep, Tip. She's really tired."

A flush crept up Tip's neck. "She isn't in bed. I peeked."

"You what?"

"I knocked first."

"Tip, you know you shouldn't open a lady's bedroom door. She might have been asleep and out from under the covers. Some people don't wear pajamas. I've explained that to you."

"She wasn't in there." Tip turned a deeper red. "I wouldn't look if she was undressed, Dad."

Sam grinned in spite of himself. "Tip, it's a little hard

not to look if a naked lady pops up in front of you. Rules are rules. Don't intrude on Crysta's privacy again. She's probably down at the sauna. When she comes back, I want your promise that you won't open her door again, unless she invites you in."

Tip sighed and rolled his eyes. "I promise." He gave an exaggerated shrug. "I don't see the big deal. I see you, and you see me."

"That's different."

"How come?"

Sam leaned back in his chair, studying his son. He sincerely hoped this wasn't a sign that it was time for a serious discussion about sex. As much as he hoped Tip might one day have a normal life and possibly even marry, Sam was too exhausted today to tackle such a weighty subject. "Ladies are different." Sam made a vague gesture at his body.

Curiosity gleamed in Tip's eyes. "I know *that,* Dad."

Sam sighed. "Anyway, they're extremely…" He paused, searching for a word Tip would understand. "*Bashful.* Like you are when you show your paintings? They don't like it when fellas barge in uninvited and see them without clothes."

"How come they have their pictures taken naked, then?"

Sam stiffened. "Pardon?"

"You know, like in those magazines."

"What magazines?"

Tip blushed, shrugging. "Just magazines some of the guests bring. You know the kind."

"You never mentioned that some of our guests had pictures of naked ladies, Tip."

"There were only a couple, and I figured you knew."

Sam cleared his throat, fighting down a surge of irritation toward the unnamed men who had shown so little discretion in exposing a young innocent boy to graphic sexual photos. He didn't want Tip's attitudes toward women molded by such trash. "I'd really rather you didn't look at that kind of picture again, Tip."

"Is it bad to look?"

"No, not *bad* exactly. But those types of magazines exploit women, and I disapprove." Sam could see that was over Tip's head. With a sigh, he braced his elbows on the desk and smiled. "I think we need to talk. This afternoon I'm very busy, and I'm worried about Derrick. But by next week, things should calm down. We'll take a lunch up Antler Slough. How's that sound?"

"Fun." Tip scratched his cheek, frowning when he felt the paint. Wiping his fingers on his shirt, he added, "I won't look at any naked lady pictures again."

"Good." Sam started to scold about the paint smear but decided Jangles would probably scold enough for both of them when she found the shirt in the laundry. Heaving another sigh, Sam waved his hand. "Get out of here, you rapscallion. We'll talk later, okay?"

After the door closed, Sam gave a weary chuckle and cupped his hand over his eyes. Did the complications of parenthood never cease?

FIVE MINUTES LATER, the door to Sam's office crashed open again. Tip stood in the doorway, his face washed of color, his mouth working. Sam could see something was wrong. The last time Tip had made an entrance like this, an extremely hefty guest had fallen out of a boat, and the three men on board couldn't haul her back in.

"Calm down, Tip. Take a deep breath."

Tip gasped for air, his eyes bulging. "Crys—Crys—wood—the door. I—I tried to m-move it, but I was t-taking too long. You g-gotta c-ome. Qu—quick!"

Sam leaped up from his chair. "Crysta? Where is she?"

Tip fought to speak, waving wildly behind him. "The s-sau-sauna."

"Oh, Lord!"

Sam raced from the lodge, Tip riding his heels. It seemed as if it took forever to reach the sauna. Sam lunged up the steps and threw the door wide. The sight that greeted him made his blood run cold. The pile of firewood had toppled, blocking the interior door. Crysta's clothes hung on the wall hook.

She was inside.

Sam began tossing wood out of his path. Tip dived in to help. The fire in the stove was roaring, throwing off so much heat that Sam could scarcely breathe. Due to the amount of wood in his way, it took at least two minutes to clear a swath, every second of which resounded inside Sam's head like the ticking of a time bomb. *Hurry, hurry.* He kicked aside the last piece of wood, grabbed the door and threw it wide. A wall of steam spilled over him. He stumbled forward, fear clawing at his guts.

"Crysta!" His boot bumped into something soft. Sam dropped to his knees, groping, afraid of what he might find. His hands connected with feverish flesh. "Crysta!"

Lifting her limp body into his arms, Sam stood and shouldered his way past Tip to get outdoors. Tip came running out behind him, holding Crysta's towel. Sam wasn't sure covering her was a good idea. He laid her gently on the ground and pressed his fingertips to her throat, feeling for a pulse. At first he detected nothing. Then he felt a weak flutter.

"Tip, run and soak that towel in the cool water tub. Wet down several and bring them back here. Hurry, son!"

Uncertain if Crysta was breathing, Sam quickly shifted her to a position that would give him access for resuscitation. Relief filled him when he felt her chest rise and fall on its own beneath his hands. Tip returned with the towels. Sam wrung them out over Crysta's body. Steve Henderson came running up.

"Is she—alive?"

"Yes, thank God." Sam scooped Crysta into his arms, grabbing a towel from Tip to cover her. "Steve, go tell Jangles. Hurry. She'll know what to do."

CRYSTA SURFACED TO consciousness slowly, aware of the light touch of a man's hand on her hair and the ceaseless timbre of a deep voice. Slitting her eyelids, she peered upward. Sam Barrister's dark face came into focus. Behind him, she saw Tip, worrying his pale bottom lip between his teeth.

Then she remembered.

"Sam!" she cried in a hoarse voice, trying to sit up. Her body felt strangely heavy.

"Whoa…" He caught her shoulders, pressing her back down. "It's over now. You're safe in bed."

"The door—it wouldn't open!" Crysta swallowed, wincing at the fiery rawness of her throat. "I screamed and screamed."

"Tip found you." He cupped his hand over her cheek. "You're one lucky lady. A few more minutes and it would've—" He trailed his thumb along her cheekbone. "Want some water? The doctor says we have to pump fluids down you."

"Doctor?"

"We called the hospital in Anchorage. Luckily, Jangles is a fair nurse. A little unorthodox, but she gets the job done." Sliding an arm under her shoulders, Sam helped her sit partway up and held a glass of cool water to her lips. "Not too fast."

Crysta gulped greedily, sucking air when he withdrew the tumbler. It took all her concentration to lift her arm and swipe the sleeve of the lightweight cotton shirt she wore across her mouth. Judging by the shirt's large proportions, she guessed it to be her host's. Exhausted from the supreme effort it had taken to move, she managed a weak smile. "I feel like I've been run over by a train."

He eased her back onto the pillows. "I can't believe it happened. The wood has been stacked along that wall for years, and it's never fallen like that before."

Crysta closed her eyes for a moment. If she lived to be a hundred, she'd never forget how frightened she had been. She tried to reposition her hips, then abandoned the idea. Her muscles felt as if they were made of cold rubber. She shivered and made a feeble tug at the crisp bed sheet, wondering who had changed the linen. "I'm freezing, Sam. May I have a blanket?"

"Not for a while. The reason you're so cold is that we've been rubbing you down with water, trying to lower your body temperature. If I pile blankets on you, it'll defeat our purpose."

A fleeting image of Sam running wet cloths over her naked body hit Crysta, but for the moment she was far too exhausted to expend energy worrying about it. She shivered again, hugging the sheet closer with arms that felt strangely disconnected from her body. "I'm freezing."

"Your temperature is probably still a little high, and

your skin is chilled from the ice water. It's like getting chills with a fever. It'll pass."

"My head hurts. Can you draw the blind?"

He quickly accommodated her, then sat back down on the bed.

Crysta licked her lips, longing for more water but too weak to reach for it. She thought of asking Sam for some, but since she'd just had him draw the blind, she hesitated.

"Someone came in there—with wood, I think," she whispered. "Then the woodpile toppled. I called out, but I guess my voice didn't carry to the anteroom. Whoever it was stoked the fire and left without answering. When I tried to open the door, it was blocked."

Sam took one of her hands in his, examining her torn nails. Glancing over his shoulder at Tip, he said, "Didn't you do your chores this morning, son?"

Tip's eyes widened. "I d-did them."

"Did you forget to restock the sauna's wood supply?"

"N-no. I took two loads in. And I stacked it real nice, j-just like you sh-showed me."

Crysta angled an arm across her forehead, squinting through the gloom at Tip. He looked worried about being blamed for her mishap. The throbbing ache in her temples grew worse. "I saw Tip carrying wood in that direction earlier today. There was plenty when I went in, and the pile was neat as a pin."

Sam's gaze rested solemnly on hers. "There's something you're not saying."

Tension knotted Crysta's stomach. "It's so silly that I hate to bring it up."

"Humor me."

"Well…" She drew her arm down from her forehead. "I sort of panicked, I guess, and while I was trying to get out, the thought occurred to me that someone might have—" She broke off and toyed with the sheet.

Sam glanced over his shoulder at Tip. "Son, go and ask Jangles if she'd mind making Crysta a cup of tea. It might take her chills away."

Tip's brown eyes sharpened. He gave Crysta a curious study. Sam reached out and gave the boy a playful punch on the arm. "Go on, Tip. *Now*."

After Tip left, Crysta waited for Sam to speak. He raked his fingers through his hair, heaving a tired sigh. "You think someone did it on purpose, don't you?"

"The thought crossed my mind." Crysta pushed up on her elbow to take another drink of water. Wooziness hit her. She blinked, trying to bring the spinning room into focus. With a trembling hand, she reached toward the nightstand. "It was probably silly, but one tends to think all kinds of weird things when something like that happens."

Sam helped her steady the glass and press it to her lips. "I'm not so sure it was silly. While Jangles was sponging you off to get your temperature down, I went to the sauna. The damper on the stove was wide-open, and the firebox was completely filled with wood. We never put that much in there."

Crysta's scalp prickled. "You aren't saying—" She let him take the glass. Sinking back against the pillows, she stared at him. "But, Sam, I could have died in there."

"You very nearly did."

Crysta closed her eyes. "It's crazy. Who would want me dead?"

"Maybe no one. It could have been an accident. It's possible your voice didn't carry to the anteroom, just as you said. And given the near-disastrous outcome, I really can't blame someone for not coming forward and admitting he toppled the wood. Maybe I'm jumping at shadows again."

He turned to gaze at the shade-covered window, then, at the sound of footsteps outside, he leaped up and jerked aside the blind.

"Sam, what is it?"

He stepped close to the wall, peering sideways through the glass. "It was Jangles," he said in a thoughtful voice. "She's going down toward the river, toward the trees. There's a man with her."

"The Indian?" Crysta asked hoarsely.

Sam nodded, a frown pleating his forehead. "If a friend of hers is coming to visit, I wonder why she doesn't just ask him in."

Crysta had no answer to that unless Jangles wanted to keep the man's visits to herself. "A boyfriend, do you think?"

Sam watched them for a moment. Then a halfhearted smile touched his mouth. "I guess. He just hugged her goodbye."

That revelation eased Crysta's mind somewhat. "Maybe she's afraid you'd disapprove."

He sighed and rubbed his forehead. "I'd worry, more than likely. If she gets married and I lose her, I don't know what we'll do without her. It's not easy to find help who's willing to live this far from Anchorage for half the year." Returning to sit beside her, he waved the subject of Jangles aside and said, "Back to more immediate concerns. I want you to be more careful from here on in. Try to stay around people—me, Tip, Jangles. I'd rather be safe than sorry."

"I just went to take a steam bath," she reminded him.

"Next time, I'll go down with you."

Remembering the thick steam, she suppressed a shudder. "It'll be a while before I go back."

"It's going to be a while before you do much of anything. The doctor says you have to rest for twenty-four hours. He wants us to pour at least four gallons of fluid into you."

"Twenty-four hours!" Despite her weakness, Crysta could scarcely bear the thought of being confined to bed that long. "Sam, no! We have to go to Anchorage."

"You're dehydrated."

"So? I'll drink water on the way!" She tried to sit up again and immediately felt dizzy. Sam caught her shoulder to steady her. "I'm not staying in bed an entire day!"

She threw her legs over the edge of the bed and pushed to her feet. A wave of dizziness washed over her, and Sam had to catch her from falling.

"There, you see?" he said. "You're ill, Crysta, and you're going to follow doctor's orders and stay in bed if I have to sit on you." He helped her to lie back down. "Feel fortunate I didn't have you flown in to the Anchorage hospital. If Jangles hadn't assured me she knew how to take care of you, that's what I would have done. Getting trapped in a steam room and losing consciousness is no laughing matter."

Crysta could see by the grim set of his mouth that he wouldn't waver, no matter how she argued. "Then why don't you go?" she cried in a voice thick with frustration. "I can describe the building. Maybe you could find it."

"There are several warehouses, and I'm sure they'd all look pretty much the same to me. Besides, I'm not leaving you." He shot a nervous glance at the window. "Not after finding that stove stoked full and the damper wide-open. Prepare yourself for a day of constant company."

"I'll go crazy lying here."

"We'll go through Derrick's papers some more."

"A lot of good that will do Derrick!"

Thoughts of her brother were Crysta's undoing. The tears in her eyes spilled over onto her cheeks, prompting her to avert her face and rub blindly at them with the sleeve of Sam's shirt. She knew Sam was right; she was too weak to go anywhere. Feeling so helpless infuriated her.

"If we run out of papers to go through, I'm a great hand at chess," he offered in a gentle voice.

She groaned.

"Rummy?"

No longer caring if he saw her tears, Crysta turned to look at him. "Bring on the briefcase."

IN ADDITION TO GIVING Sam and Crysta further opportunity to study Derrick's papers, the day's delay, though frustrating, afforded Sam, Crysta and Tip a getting-acquainted time, during which they began to forge strong bonds of friendship. Crysta, with some tactful questioning during one of Tip's absences, discovered that Tip's mother, an ambitious interior decorator who couldn't cope with the hardships of raising a learning-impaired child, had walked out before the boy's second birthday. As much as that knowledge made Crysta's heart ache for Tip, she felt even sorrier for Sam. The pain and disillusionment his wife had caused him still lurked in his eyes when he spoke of her.

When Tip left the bedroom again to make some popcorn, Crysta lay back against the pillows and absently shuffled the deck of cards. "I guess we all have our heart-breaks," she said softly. "It makes you wonder if love is all it's cracked up to be."

"Janet didn't know how to love," Sam replied matter-of-factly. "Doesn't say much for my preferences in women, does it?"

"Maybe the fault lay in her, Sam. You can't beat up on yourself for making one bad call."

"It wasn't just a bad call, not with a child involved." His jaw tensed. "Janet lacked the nurturing qualities you need to be a parent. Somehow, I failed to see that, and my son paid the price. Tip was like a toy to her. She loved to play with him when the mood struck, but her energies were mainly directed toward her career, and when it became apparent that Tip would demand far more time than she could comfortably give him, she walked out."

Crysta couldn't think of anything to say, so she said nothing.

"When I look back on it, I don't know how I could have thought I loved her." He made a feeble gesture and shrugged. "I was young—too young, I guess. She was pretty and vivacious and lighthearted. I didn't see the self-ish side of her until she settled into marriage and stopped putting her best foot forward." He looked up, straight into Crysta's eyes. "For Tip's sake, I tried to make the mar-riage work, and even that turned out to be a mistake. She stayed just long enough for Tip to love her and then dis-appeared from his life." His eyes grew distant and shad-owed. "I never could understand how she could abandon Tip. Me, yes, but not him."

Crysta had no answers. In the short time she had known Tip, she had already lost a piece of her heart to him.

"Those first few weeks after she left, I wanted to go

after her and throttle her," Sam admitted raggedly. "Hearing my son cry for her, knowing she was probably out on the town with a bunch of yuppies, not even thinking of him...it made me crazy. Sometimes I'd lie awake imagining how satisfying it would be to strangle her."

After an extremely long silence, Crysta touched his hand. "We all get a little crazy sometimes. If you ever meet Dick, ask him about the condition of the bed sheets I gave him when he moved out."

Some of the seriousness eased from Sam's eyes. "There's a story in there somewhere."

Crysta smothered a smile. To this day, the memory gave her a feeling of satisfaction. "He did say that he wanted to *split* the sheets. Far be it from me not to accommodate him."

Sam shouted with laughter. Crysta grinned.

"The moral is that we all get a little radical if someone pushes the right buttons. For you, it was seeing your son suffer. For me, it was taking a backseat to silk sheets. The fact that he already had a girlfriend had absolutely *nothing* to do with it." She slanted a smile at him. "Well, maybe a little."

He was still smiling, though sadly. "You still loved him?"

"Truthfully?" It was Crysta's turn to shrug. "Yes. The divorce was his decision, not mine, though I didn't fight it. He took exception to the fact that my brother intruded into our lives so much."

She took a deep breath and let it out slowly. "Anyway, live and learn. In this day and age, marriage isn't the be-all and end-all of a woman's existence. My life is full now. My shop is thriving. I have lots of friends. And, living alone as I do, it doesn't matter if I wake up from a dream in the middle of the night, convinced my brother needs me."

Sam studied her thoughtfully. "Is it so bad to be needed?"

The skin across her cheekbones felt tight as she forced a smile. "Only if there's a husband around to come unglued. To Derrick and me, that kind of thing seems normal. Not that it *is*." She swallowed. "My analyst believes our mother brainwashed us, and that because Derrick and I are so convinced our dreams are based in fact, we manipulate events to make them come true."

"And do you believe that?"

"I've tried."

His eyes darkened. "Your analyst's theory sounds like hogwash to me. What's *normal* anyway? I have a problem with that word."

"Be that as it may, I've spent three years and thousands of dollars on counseling since the divorce, trying for that enviable state." She bent the cards backward and let them rain onto her lap. "What you said about being uniquely me hit home. We can't change what we are, no matter how we might try."

"The right man will come along."

She shook her head. "No man would put up with the intrusions in my life, not Dick or anyone. I was the one who couldn't fit into the mold."

"Crysta, the *right* man would understand about Derrick. Don't sell marriage down the river just because you tried it once and failed."

"You're a fine one to talk. You're not ready to risk getting burned again. I can see it in your eyes."

He gathered the cards from her lap and gave them an expert shuffle, tapping them into line on his bent knee. "I met another woman. About five years ago." He flashed a humorless smile. "That time, I thought I was going into it with my eyes open, choosing a woman who was the opposite from Janet—a homebody, not particularly attractive, more serious in nature." His mouth twisted. "I didn't love her. At that point, I was still convinced my child needed a mother. I liked her, and after the experience with Janet, that seemed more important to me than romance."

"What happened?"

He cut the cards, turning up a three, which seemed to amuse him. "With my usual unerring accuracy, I'd chosen badly. If you want lessons on how to strike out every time you go to bat, just give me a call and I'll give you pointers."

"I've done fine with no help," she inserted with a laugh.

"A few days after I gave her the ring, I saw some notes by her telephone. I asked her what they were about. She hedged and then finally admitted she was checking on boarding schools for Tip. End of relationship."

"There are lots of women who would treasure a son like Tip."

"There are special problems raising a handicapped child. A lifetime of them. It's a rare woman who would take them on when the child wasn't hers. These last few years, I've come to realize Tip is doing fine just as things are. I'm content to remain single."

"Content or merely resigned? Tip's handicap isn't that debilitating. The right woman will love him, Sam."

"Will she? You've no idea how often he's been hurt by people. Here, in this setting, he's shielded. The real world is cruel, and kids like Tip get kicked in the teeth. I can't subject him to another rejection."

"Is that why you get so upset about the idea of him showing his paintings?"

His face tightened. "Is it so wrong for Tip to take joy from his art as a hobby? If I let him enter an art show and some critic lacerates him, he'll never again recapture the magic he feels for painting. Painting is Tip's *life.*"

"Living life to its fullest means being shot down sometimes. You're holding Tip back, in the one arena where he can excel. Maybe he will get lacerated by art critics. Most big talents usually are. But then again, maybe he'll set the world on fire. Have you considered that?"

"You sound just like Derrick."

She arched an eyebrow. "My brother and I tend to think alike." Growing quiet, she studied his dark face, remembering his scrapbook of Tip's childhood and her initial feeling that Sam was an exceptional father. "I know you love Tip. More importantly, Tip knows. Let him take his knocks, Sam, and be there for him when he needs support. That's what parents are for."

"You're forgetting that Tip is handicapped."

"So was Beethoven."

A soft knock cut their conversation short. Sam got up to answer the door. Todd Shriver stood framed in the doorway.

"I invited myself in," he explained. "I knocked on the front door, but you didn't hear me. Didn't want to be too loud for fear Ms. Meyers might be asleep." Flashing a grin at Crysta, he added, "I heard about your mishap. Now I see I was worrying over nothing. You look fit as a fiddle."

Crysta raised a delicate eyebrow. "I wish you could convince Sam of that."

"Wise fellow, Sam. After what you've been through, a day's rest is probably a good idea."

"Except that I have far more important things to be doing."

Shriver smiled. "Careful. You don't want to earn yourself the reputation of being a difficult patient."

"Impossible is more like it." Sam settled laughing brown eyes on Crysta. She was relieved to see that he didn't seem angry with her for speaking so candidly about his son. "I'll be glad when we're on our way to Anchorage tomorrow so she'll stop needling me."

"Tip mentioned that you two wanted to fly back with me. Going to have her checked over by a doctor?"

Sam shook his head. "No, actually, we have some other business there. Although, her seeing a doctor isn't a bad idea."

"Bite your tongue, Mr. Shriver. Now see what you've done?" Crysta rolled her eyes. "I'm perfectly fine, I tell you."

Returning to sit on the bed, Sam braced an arm behind him, his side pressing warmly against the sheet that covered Crysta's legs. To the pilot, he said, "It's not a problem, your staying overnight, is it? If so, we could probably hop a flight with someone else."

Todd rested his shoulder against the door frame. "I wouldn't hear of it. Tomorrow evening the lodge upriver from here is due for a delivery of gasoline. After I get the plane loaded, I have a bunch of errands I can attend to. Taking you out and bringing you back will work out fine for me."

"Good," Sam said.

Shriver's gaze slid to Crysta. "Planning to pick up Derrick's personal effects?"

"Um, yes, I suppose I might do that while I'm there."

"Well, I'm glad to get a chance to help out."

Sam rose from the bed and moved casually toward the door, effecting Shriver's dismissal without having to suggest it. "We'll see you first thing in the morning, then."

THE WINDUP CLOCK struck midnight, its steady ticking a comfort to Crysta. Sam had lain with his head on this pillow. Being in his room, warmed by his quilt, she felt far more secure than she probably should have.

She lay staring at the twilight beyond the bedroom window, her thoughts on Derrick. As horrible as her last dream had been, she no longer had the frightening sensation that Derrick was dead. The intermittent communication from him proved he wasn't. Her earlier suspicion that the silence inside her might be due to Derrick's being unconscious now had merit. It was a slender thread of hope, but at least it was hope.

The creaking of the door brought Crysta's gaze around. Sam poked his head into the room, then, upon seeing her awake, stepped inside. In one hand, he held some papers. "How's the head?"

"Much better."

He glanced toward the jug of water on the nightstand. "Looks like you've got the third gallon almost whipped."

"Almost."

Crysta checked the buttons on the shirt she wore, feeling suddenly self-conscious. During the endless hours of enforced bed rest, she had been afforded plenty of time to contemplate her state of undress when Sam had rescued her from the sauna.

"You feel up to talking?" he asked.

"Sure." Crysta pushed herself up against the pillows, pulling the sheet high. The mattress sank under Sam's weight as he sat beside her. She noted that his eyes seemed shadowed.

"Jim called a while ago."

Crysta stared at him, knowing what he was going to say. "The blood was Derrick's, wasn't it?"

"Preliminary tests show it's the same type."

She took a deep breath. "It's no more than I expected."

He held the papers aloft. "I think maybe I've found something."

Her heart leaped. "What?"

"Now, don't get your hopes up. It could be nothing."

"*What,* Sam? The suspense is killing me."

He spread the papers out, some on his lap, some on hers. "Invoices for conduit, all marked returned. Some have question marks and notes in the margins in Derrick's handwriting."

"So?"

Sam glanced up. "Crysta, don't return shipment documents for each order strike you as odd?"

"Not particularly. If you order way too much of something, you return it. Why keep your capital tied up in stock?"

He held up a staying hand. "You're thinking small-business practices. Think West Coast corporation a minute. Blanchette has a lot of building sites in Alaska, and several warehouses, so storage space isn't a concern. If you'll need conduit at another site within a few months, does it make good sense to return your surplus? When you reorder, you have more shipment costs. Prices might go up. Double whammy, and not cost-effective. You're the retailer. Am I off base in my reasoning?"

Crysta's mind clicked into gear. She sat more erect. "All right, I see your angle. It *doesn't* make sense to rack up extra shipping costs to return something you'll have to reorder soon thereafter." She quickly scanned the papers Sam had spread across her lap. "But what's the point, Sam? It may be odd, but why would someone do it?"

"I'm not sure. I only know it struck me as odd when I noticed it, and—" he tapped Derrick's initials on one of the invoices "—I think Derrick may have picked up on it, too. It isn't much to go on, but at least it's something."

Crysta slowly nodded, excitement building within her. Glancing at the clock, she said, "I can hardly wait to leave for Anchorage. Maybe we'll find that warehouse I dreamed of, Sam. Maybe we'll find out what it was Derrick went there about."

"Maybe. At least it's a lead. Which is more than we had."

Gathering up the documents, Sam avoided her gaze, still uncomfortable when she alluded to her dreams. Earlier today, he had, on two occasions, encouraged Crysta to be true to herself. He had insisted that those people who were incapable of accepting her as she was weren't worthy to be her friends, that the *right* man would understand her relationship with Derrick. Now Sam found himself in the unenviable position of wanting to be Crysta's friend—possibly even more—but at the same time, doubting her.

To believe or not to believe, that was the question.

CHAPTER ELEVEN

THE FOLLOWING DAY was overcast. After another harrowing flight in Todd Shriver's Cessna, Crysta was eager to leave the Lake Hood Airport in the cab Sam commandeered. She settled back in the seat beside him, fighting down a rush of anxiety as the cab wound its way through the city's streets toward the outskirts of town, where Blanchette's Anchorage offices were located.

Sam seemed as nervous as she, shifting position and glancing through the rear window. When they had nearly reached their destination, she noted his odd behavior and followed his gaze.

"Is something wrong?"

Sam looked a little sheepish. "I thought there was another cab following us. Shadows again. I think it turned off about three blocks back."

Memories of being trapped in the sauna washed over Crysta. She turned forward again and folded her arms, shivering. The smell of new vinyl inside the cab made her feel slightly nauseated. Sam could lay his paranoia off on jumping at shadows all he liked, but that didn't alter the fact that someone might have tried to kill her.

"Cold?"

The weather was oppressive enough without her dragging Sam's spirits down with hers. Hesitant to admit she had shivered with foreboding, she opted to tell a small white lie. "A little chilly."

Sam immediately slipped an arm around her shoulders and drew her against his side. Still feeling a bit self-conscious about his seeing her unclad the previous day, Crysta stiffened at the unexpected familiarity and glanced up. The dark depths of his eyes heated, catching glints of light, warming her.

"Don't," he whispered.

"Don't what?"

He tightened his arm around her and settled himself more comfortably against the door. "You know perfectly well what. The entire incident is a blur to me, and that's the truth."

Crysta, who should have been an old hand at having her thoughts read, felt her cheeks flush. Sam wasn't Derrick, and his perceptiveness made her feel vulnerable. She started to avert her face, but Sam caught her chin so she couldn't.

"I mean it. You're feeling embarrassed over nothing."

Crysta nibbled at her bottom lip, fastening her gaze on his chin, which was far more comfortable than making eye contact with him. "It's silly for me to be embarrassed, at any rate."

"You wouldn't be normal if you weren't," he whispered. "And as I recall, being *normal* is of great importance to you."

His teasing tone sliced through the charged atmosphere, relieving her tension, which, if she was honest, wasn't totally due to embarrassment. There was Derrick's plight, the attempt on her life, the days of ceaseless worry, all of which had her nerves worn raw. His invitation to banter offered her an escape from the serious, no matter how brief, and lured her irresistibly. She slid her gaze to his and flashed a dubious smile.

"You honestly don't remember anything? I'm not at all sure *you're* normal, if that's the case."

It was his turn to grin. "I didn't go stone blind, exactly. I just—" He broke off and chuckled. "Crysta, there's looking at someone, and then there's *looking.* Let's just say that if you stood in a lineup of a dozen women, I couldn't pick you out. Is that any comfort?"

"On the one hand, yes. On the other, though, I'm not sure it's very flattering."

He barked with laughter. The cab pulled up in front of the Blanchette offices just then, and he released her to fish in his jeans pocket for cab fare. Crysta beat him to the draw by pulling some ready cash from the side pocket of her purse.

"Lunch is on me," he grumbled as they exited the cab.

The sky hung low above them, a depressing, heavy gray. Crysta took a deep breath of the salty air. "We're trying to find my brother. I should pay the expenses."

"Correction, we're trying to find my friend. Therefore, I should pay the expenses. Besides, he did get lost while staying at my lodge." Crysta had already come to realize how proud Sam was, but she also knew he didn't have much cash in reserve, and she hated for this trip to become an expense he could ill afford. "Look, you've waived all my lodging costs, so how about if we go halves from now on?"

"Fair enough."

They fell into step with each other, breaking apart to circle a wash of mud. Crysta inclined her head toward the office. "Since I'm Derrick's sister, I'll handle this, okay?"

"Fine by me."

The closer they came to the office, the more tense Crysta felt. What if she couldn't finagle her way into the warehouse? Sam took the steps two at a time, reaching the door to sweep it open for her. Once again in a teasing tone, he said, "I suppose you're the type who insists on paying your share when a man takes you out."

Crysta, grateful for his attempt to keep her spirits rallying, rose to the challenge with what she hoped was an impish grin. "Is that an invitation?"

Sam followed her inside. "I'm old-fashioned when it comes to that. If we go out, I insist on paying."

"How quaint." She aimed her footsteps toward the visitors' information desk, then glanced back over her shoulder. "When?"

"When what?"

"When are we going?"

His eyes lit up with laughter. "When I *ask* you."

"You *are* old-fashioned. I was thinking about asking you."

"I accept."

He slowed his pace, drawing up behind her as she approached the blonde at the desk. Crysta introduced herself. After listening patiently to the receptionist stress how sorry she was to hear about Derrick, Crysta homed in on her purpose for being there.

"I was wondering if my friend, Mr. Barrister, and I could take a tour of the warehouses. I, um…" Crysta didn't find it hard to look as if she might burst into tears. "I'd like very much to see where my brother worked. I always planned to come, you see. He wanted me to. And now…"

"I understand," the pretty blonde inserted in a kindly voice. "And it's no problem at all. In fact, we issue visitor passes all the time. But, Miss Meyers, Derrick didn't have an office. He traveled from site to site, you see, and carried his paperwork with him. I'm afraid that—"

"No, no, I came in hopes of visiting the warehouses."

"Well, that's no problem at all. Let me make you up a list of addresses. We have maps of each complex, too."

Within moments, Crysta had two visitor passes in her possession, and Sam, exiting the office beside her, was studying the list of warehouses.

"The main warehouse is right here in this complex," he told her as they stepped out onto the porch.

A gust of wind hit Crysta, so strong she nearly lost her footing. Sweeping her hair from her eyes, she leaned into the current and went down the steps. "Point me in the right direction."

"You don't recognize anything?"

Crysta shot him a knowing glance. "I didn't dream about the outside of the warehouse, Sam. The dream started inside, walking down the aisle. If you're going to test me, at least be fair."

"I'm not trying to test you."

"Yes, you are."

"Okay, I am. You've no idea how relieved I'd be to see some tangible proof that there's something to those dreams of yours."

Crysta wondered if that was true. As they rounded the office building and struck off toward the aluminum-sided warehouse, she found herself hoping she could provide Sam with that proof. For some reason that she wasn't quite willing to analyze, it had become extremely important to her that he believe, truly believe, in her dreams.

BLUE-WHITE LIGHT BATHED the interior of the building, coming from fluorescent tubes suspended in rows from the lofty rafters. The musty-sweet smell of lumber and the heavy fumes of engine exhaust tainted the sea air that breezed in through the massive bay door. Crysta stopped just inside, scarcely noticing the bright yellow hoister that bucked past them.

"This is it," she whispered.

"You're sure? One warehouse looks like another."

"I'm sure." Crysta moved forward, her skin chilled, her legs oddly numb. "I can't explain, but I know this is it."

Looking into Crysta's eyes, Sam had the uneasy feeling that she was no longer really with him. She struck off walking, not watching where she put her feet, her gaze distant. He hurried to catch up and grasped her arm. A forklift nearby grated its gears and lifted a bundle of shingle siding. Another hoister bounced across the loading zone. Neither driver seemed aware that two visitors had entered the area. Tiers of building supplies peppered the broad expanse of concrete floor.

"Crysta?" Her arm felt brittle under his fingers. His gaze shifted to a crane, which suspended an ominous-looking load of three-foot culvert above their heads. In a place like this, an oblivious person could all too easily become a grease spot on the concrete. "Don't get spacey on me."

She kept walking as if he hadn't spoken. Sam tightened his hold on her, attempting to guide her footsteps. At first she seemed to wander, then he felt her pick up the pace. She was heading toward a center aisle. As they stepped into it, Sam had the sensation that he had entered a narrow hallway, except, of course, that the walls were rows of packing boxes.

When the end of the aisle came into view, Crysta slowed her steps. "The crates and boxes I saw are gone."

Sam followed her gaze to some empty pallets. Crysta

started forward again, scanning the concrete floor. When they came upon a splotch of green paint, her slender body stiffened. He increased the pressure of his grip on her arm, frightened without knowing why, possibly because of the expression on her pale face.

"The paint, Sam! It's here, just as I dreamed it was."

To Sam's discomfiture, Crysta jerked free from his grasp and dropped to her knees by an empty pallet. Lying forward over her thighs, she shoved her arm under the framework. He glanced uneasily behind them. If someone happened along and saw her, Sam had no idea how he would explain her odd behavior.

"It's here, I know it is!"

"Crysta, get up from there. What are you doing?"

Ignoring him, she fanned her arm under the slats of wood. "I have to find it. It'll be proof, don't you see? *Proof,* Sam!"

"Proof of what? What are you looking for?"

"It fell from his buckle! Right here, Sam! By the paint!"

"Crysta, warehouses always have paint spills on the floor."

She gave a cry of triumph and pulled her arm from under the pallet. Scrambling to her feet, she turned to face him, clutching something in her hand. Her eyes bright with unshed tears, she extended her arm toward him and unfurled her fingers. Upon her palm rested a silver dollar. An amateur numismatist, Sam knew by the muted sheen of the coin's finish that it was not only pure silver but also extremely old.

He stepped forward, his pulse accelerating. The 1906 dollar that Derrick had had fashioned into a belt buckle had been a gift from Sam. Finding a silver dollar under a warehouse pallet might be odd yet still explainable, but if that dollar in her hand was a 1906, even Sam would have to admit it was too much to be coincidence. With tense fingers, he lifted the coin from her palm to read the date.

Shifting his gaze from the coin to Crysta's face, Sam saw that her mouth was quivering. "I'm *not* crazy. This is proof, Sam."

Curling his fingers around the coin, Sam stepped toward her, realizing, suddenly, how terribly important finding this coin had been to her. It went beyond providing proof for his benefit; it was proof for herself, a vindication after years of self-doubt. Forgetting about onlookers, not really caring at this point who might see, Sam caught her around the shoulders and hauled her against his chest to give her a comforting hug.

"Of course you're not crazy. I never thought you were."

"You didn't believe me, not completely."

"I had my reservations, but I didn't think, even for an instant, that you were crazy, Crysta."

"Do you believe me now?"

Drawing his arm from around her, Sam opened his hand and stared at the coin once more. "Yes, Crysta, I believe you. No doubts, no reservations."

The tension went out of her, and she leaned against him, pressing her face against his shoulder. "You'll never know how much it means to me to hear you say that."

"I only wish I'd said it earlier," he replied huskily.

She gave a wet little laugh and drew away, tilting her face up to meet his gaze, her own still bright with tears. "You were willing to stand by me, to be my friend, even with the doubts. That's what counts, Sam, more than you'll ever know."

Sam's throat tightened. Her friend? He didn't know when it had happened or why, but his intentions had subtly altered. Friendship with Crysta, as enjoyable as that might be, was no longer all he had in mind. That admission rocked him, and he wasn't yet ready to ask himself just what, exactly, he did have in mind.

Moving away from her, he said, "Well, we hit a dead end in one way." He nodded at the pallet. "No crates, no boxes. That adds up to no leads. Now what?"

Wiping at her cheeks with the sleeve of her jacket, she sniffed and glanced around them. "We check the other warehouses. Maybe the crates and boxes I dreamed about have been moved."

"And if the other warehouses turn up nothing?"

"Then we regroup and try to decide what to do next." A glint of determination crept into her hazel eyes. "From here on in, *defeat* isn't in my vocabulary. We aren't giving up."

"No." Sam flipped the coin into the air, palmed it and slipped it into his pocket. "Let's go call a cab and hit the next warehouse."

NOTHING.

The word resounded in Crysta's head as she and Sam left the last warehouse. In the center of her chest, an ache began to spread, radiating down into her belly and up into her throat. Three warehouses, and they had found absolutely nothing. Images of Derrick, digging a bullet from his chest, swam in her mind. Her brother was dying out there while she toured warehouses in Anchorage. Never had she felt so frustrated...or so horribly guilty. This was her fault, all of it.

"Crysta?"

Sam's voice tugged her back from the nightmares to reality, which wasn't much better. Even the weather, misty and drab, seemed to spell doom. A car sped past, sending up a spray of water from the gutter. The way her luck was running, Crysta was surprised she hadn't been drenched to the skin.

"If you're going to ask me what we ought to do next, I don't know," she said in a shaky voice. "I'm fresh out of ideas."

He placed a warm, heavy hand on her shoulder. "Look, just because we've struck out so far doesn't mean we should give up. We're on to something here. We have to be."

Crysta glanced up and met his gaze. For several seconds they simply stood there, visually communicating what neither could verbalize. Something indefinable was happening between them, and Crysta sensed they would never totally forget or manage to sever the bonds they were forming today.

But what were those bonds? Friendship? That tag seemed pitifully inadequate. It was more of a melding. Sam had stood by her, following through on only the strength of her dreams, with no proof to motivate him. Because of that, she felt closer to him in some ways than she ever had to anyone, even Derrick.

"No, we can't give up." She took a deep breath and exhaled slowly, shoving her hands deep into her jacket pockets. "Not until there's no hope left. And as long as I'm getting periodic flashes of Derrick, there *is* hope."

For the first time since she had found the silver dollar, it struck Sam what all this meant. Her dreams were a reality. Derrick was still alive. There was a chance that he and Derrick would see one another again. If that happened, Sam vowed that he'd never again part company with his friend when either of them was angry. One couldn't count on tomorrow.

"Let's walk," he suggested. "I think better on the move."

Crysta fell into step beside him, staring down at their feet. Today, Sam had doffed the green rubber boots he usually wore in favor of the high-top leather ones she had seen sitting beside his bed. Jeans, boots, a flannel shirt. Not exactly sophisticated garb, but on Sam, it looked wonderful and right.

As they left the fenced enclosure, a Blanchette truck edged up to an open gate, braked, then spun out in the gravel and merged with the traffic. Crysta watched it travel down the street.

"Probably going to pick up a load at the docks," Sam said.

Crysta gnawed her lip. The truck was now a tiny orange blur, nearly lost to sight. "Sam, that's it!"

He scowled after the truck. "What's it? You've lost me."

"What if those boxes in my dream held something illegal? There were no others in any of the warehouses like them! What if they weren't supposed to be there?"

Clearly perplexed, Sam seemed to consider that angle. "Can you back up and run through that one more time? I'm not following."

Excitement soared within Crysta. "Think, Sam. Someone has been ordering too much conduit and sending the surplus back to Seattle. We've already concluded that doesn't make sense. Derrick agreed, or he wouldn't have made all those notes in the margins of the invoices!"

He nodded. "I follow that much."

"Last night, we couldn't figure out *why* someone would

over-order and then return the surplus. We only knew it was odd. Think smuggling, Sam! An illegal commodity. How could you get something illegal out of Alaska and down to Seattle, where it could be marketed in the lower forty-eight?"

His gaze sharpened on hers, and his lips pursed to emit a low whistle. "Inside the conduit crates?"

"Exactly! Order too much, hide the commodity inside the crates of surplus, and return them! If you had someone waiting at the other end in Seattle who could remove the commodity from the crates before it was discovered, you'd have a perfect setup."

"Crysta, you're incredible!" He threw another glance down the street. "How did you get all that by seeing a truck?"

"Because of what you said! Picking up a load at the docks! It could go just the other way, returning stuff to the docks."

He nodded. "Of course. Brilliant of me to bring it up, wasn't it?"

She laughed softly and rolled her eyes. "So now, Mr. Brilliant, put on your thinking cap. What could have been in those smaller boxes that I dreamed of?"

"Something illegal?"

"Sam, this is serious."

"I'm being serious. Something illegal. The problem is, I don't have an inkling what. I'll leave it to you. You're the one on a roll."

Crysta pressed her back against the tall chain-link fence. "I haven't an inkling, either." She stared at a crack in the concrete. "So let's play what if."

He took a spot beside her, his arm pressing against her shoulder. "What if?"

"Yeah, what if. It goes like this. What if Derrick noticed the surplus of conduit, discovered it was being returned and came up with the same idea that I did, that someone was using the returned crates to transport an illegal commodity?"

"Then he'd try to figure out what the commodity was."

"How?"

"I imagine he'd come to the warehouse and open the crates that were about to be returned."

"And what if, when he came, he saw some smaller boxes, stacked near the crates, that didn't belong in the warehouse?"

Sam nodded. "If it were me, I'd open one."

"And when you were about to, what if the culprits came?"

Sam, clearly warming to the game, glanced down at her. "I don't know about you, but I'd run like a scalded dog."

"And what if, while you were running, your silver-dollar buckle came loose from your belt? You couldn't risk going back for it."

"I'd pray the culprits didn't find it, because if they did, they'd recognize it and realize I might be on to them."

"And if they did find it?"

"They'd be edgy." Sam met her gaze, his mouth tightening. "Depending on the size of their operation and the money they stood to lose, not to mention the prison sentence they might face, they'd weigh their options. If the costs would be steep on all counts, they'd get rid of me so I couldn't squeal."

"And what if, after they got rid of you, your sister flew to Alaska, asking questions and not accepting that you were dead?"

Sam's eyes took on a shimmer of anger. "They might try to scare her off with a gaffed salmon in her bed. If that failed, they might try to kill her, making it look like an accident."

"More than that, they'd probably decide to bring their operation to a halt for a while. Wouldn't you? Think of it, Sam. You're missing. Your sister is stirring up suspicion. They wouldn't dare continue as usual."

He threw a quick glance over his shoulder at the warehouse. "They'd stop the smuggling operation until things cooled off and hide the evidence someplace."

"And the *last* place they'd hide it would be in one of the company warehouses!"

Sam frowned again and stroked his chin. "It wouldn't be easy to hide a lot of boxes. You couldn't very well bring them home—neighbors and guests might notice. You'd have to find someplace where storing a bunch of stuff wouldn't raise suspicion."

"Someplace dry, probably, and locked up, so no one could stumble across the evidence."

Sam nodded. After a long moment, he snapped his fingers and pushed away from the fence. "Come on! We've got some phone calls to make."

"To whom?"

"Public storage!"

Crysta caught his arm, pulling him to a stop. "Sam, we can't just start calling public-storage places. What will we do, ask if anyone's unloaded a lot of boxes in one of their units recently?"

"Not just anyone, Riley O'Keefe."

"Riley? What makes you suspect Riley?"

"Number one, I don't like him. Number two, he's spending money like it's water. Number three, he's a warehouse supervisor. He could be responsible for placing orders or be in cahoots with someone in purchasing. Add that up, and you've got a logical place to start."

CHAPTER TWELVE

FROM A NEARBY public phone booth, Sam called several public-storage companies, impersonating Riley O'Keefe. With an adroitness Crysta couldn't help but admire, he told each clerk that he had lost the keys to his storage unit and, unable to get inside, was wondering if he couldn't beg an extra set. The first phone calls ended with the clerks trying to find his file and informing him that he must have mistakenly called the wrong place of business.

Just when Crysta was beginning to fear his plan would turn up nothing, Sam connected with a man who recognized O'Keefe's name. From what Crysta could glean from the conversation at her end, spare keys were, as a safeguard for customers, unavailable. If Sam's were lost, he would have to call a locksmith.

With a low laugh, Sam said, "You know, now that I think of it, I tossed out my copy of the rental agreement, since the number of my unit was on the key. I'll need it if I'm going to bring out a locksmith. Could you look it up for me?"

After a short wait, Sam thanked the clerk and hung up the phone. Turning in the restrictive confines of the phone booth, he graced her with a discouraged smile. "Well, I found O'Keefe's storage company, but it doesn't look like an easy entry into his unit is in the cards. A locksmith would demand identification to be sure he wasn't accessing someone else's unit."

Mind racing, Crysta stared at the phone book dangling from its chain. "Is *easy* a key word in that prognosis? Or are we at a dead end?"

Sam, clearly agitated, smoothed his windblown black hair with his palm, his brows drawn together in a thoughtful scowl. "We're so close. We can't let one little hurdle stop us."

Crysta's lips felt like rubber. "Sam, the only way into that storage unit is breaking and entering. That's illegal. We could get into serious trouble if we were caught, as in *jail*."

His gaze slid to hers. A long silence fell over them. Then, with a challenging grin, he said, "Maybe we can be roomies. Are you game?"

Crysta stared up at him, not quite able to believe that this man, so practical and analytical up to now, was suddenly willing to throw caution to the wind. "What about Tip?"

"We're not talking a life sentence here, Crysta. Jangles would take care of Tip. Right now, Derrick's life is hanging by a thread. I have to think of him."

Her throat felt suddenly tight. "Tip needs you, Sam. I don't want you doing something you may regret later."

His eyes darkened with emotion. "I can't let the possibility of a stint in jail stop me. Derrick might die. It won't be easy on Tip if I have to be away from him, but he'll survive it. The way I see it, I don't have a choice."

Crysta remembered all the times she had suspected Sam of being involved in Derrick's disappearance. She wished she could go back and undo that, but she couldn't.

"Well, in that case, I can't think of anyone I'd rather have as a cell mate."

"Do you realize what all this means? Your what-if-game led us right to Riley. We're inches away from finding out what's going on. Once we do, we'll know who's involved and be able to question them. That means we could be inches away from finding Derrick."

Crysta couldn't contain a soft cry of joy. "Oh, Sam, how will I ever thank you?"

"For what?"

"For coming here with me, even though I had no proof to substantiate my dreams."

Sam gave a low laugh and, catching her totally unprepared, encircled her waist with one arm, hauling her against him. "The important thing is, we came! We're almost home free, Crysta!"

He ran his hand up the curve of her back. A shock zigzagged through her. Sam's grin faded, cuing her that what he had intended to be a quick, innocently affectionate hug had suddenly turned dangerous. She could feel his heart picking up speed.

Dropping her head back, she stared up at him with surprise on the one hand and a feeling of inevitability on the other. Since their forced embrace yesterday after nearly falling into the slough, both of them had been becoming increasingly attuned to the other. This was a natural, spontaneous culmination of that phenomenon.

"This is crazy," he whispered in a gravelly voice.

Before Crysta could agree, he lowered his head and touched his lips to hers in a shy, tentative caress. Then his arm tightened, pulling her more snugly against the hard contours of his body, destroying all illusion of separateness. The pressure of his arm forced her breath from her lungs, and, by necessity, her lips parted to release it, affording him a taste of her mouth and her a taste of his.

Crysta had been kissed many times and had long since come to the conclusion that kisses were, by their very nature, pretty much the same. Years before, she had abandoned any hope of breathless surrender and starbursts. A nice fantasy, but such things didn't happen in real life. Not to her.

Being so convinced of that, it was with considerable alarm that she realized she couldn't feel her sneakers touching the ground. For a moment she wondered if Sam, being so lofty, had plucked her off her feet. Then she realized that, though her eyes were open, she was losing her grasp on her sense of place. The phone booth began to swirl around her. The world had diminished to encompass only one thing: Sam Barrister. His mouth, deliciously sweet and hungry. His arms, like velvet chains. His body, hard and demanding, making hers throb with longing in every deep, dark, secret place she had.

Coming up for air, Sam skidded his lips across her cheek, tasting her skin, his breath hot and quick. "I can't believe this," he rasped.

Crysta blinked, becoming aware of her surroundings by degrees. More than a little dazed, she pressed her cheek against his chest, listening to the wild beat of his heart as she looked through the glass wall of the booth—directly into the bemused face of an elderly man who stood outside, patiently waiting to place a call.

"Sam?"

"Don't say it. I'm sorry. I don't know what came over me. You must think—"

"Sam, there's a man staring at us." Crysta tried to disentangle herself from his arms.

Sam finally registered what she said and dropped his arms from around her, reaching for the booth door to effect their escape. The man outside winked at her and grinned.

"Sorry," Sam called.

"No problem. Most entertaining wait I've had in a long time." The old man tapped his cane merrily as he walked into the phone booth.

After putting several feet between themselves and their inadvertent voyeur, both Crysta and Sam blushed. Sam turned up the collar of his shirt and lengthened his stride. Crysta hurried to keep up, glad that the wind was tossing her hair around, hiding her face.

"Do you realize that I'm going to be forty-two years old next month? *Forty-two!*" Sam raked his fingers through his hair, looking so agitated that Crysta had to smile. "I can't *believe* I did that."

She shrugged, pretending an unconcern she was far from feeling. "We've both been in a pressure cooker for days. You let the lid off, that's all."

He slid questioning eyes to hers. "*Is* that all?"

The directness of his gaze made her cheeks grow warmer. "For now, it has to be. Until Derrick's found, Sam, I don't have the emotional energy for anything more."

He returned his attention to the sidewalk, his jaw muscle working. "I'm sorry I stepped over the line like that."

"No harm done."

The words echoed in Crysta's mind as they proceeded down the street. Though she would never admit it, she wasn't entirely sure she had emerged from the embrace unscathed. Sam Barrister could prove dangerous to the safe, comfortable world she had created for herself since her divorce.

AFTER THROWING HIS jacket over the barbed wire above them to protect them from injury, Sam made a stirrup out of his interlocked fingers and braced a shoulder against the six-foot chain-link fence that encircled the public storage yard. Grabbing the fencing, Crysta placed her foot in the cradle of his hands and pushed up, her heart skipping when Sam shoved her skyward so she could throw her other leg over the slanted guard of barbed wire at the top. Crysta felt so conspicuous that she cringed.

"You aren't supposed to do things like this until it's dark."

"We can't wait for darkness, Crysta. This is Alaska, remember? Waiting until after hours was the best I could manage."

In an attempt to dispel her nervousness, Crysta said, "I almost wish Todd Shriver had botched this idea by saying he couldn't wait for us. I've just discovered I have vertigo."

"Just fall in the right direction and land on your feet."

"That's helpful of you. You'd sing a different tune if it was your fanny planted up here."

She thought she heard him laugh and was pleased that he wasn't the type of person who clung to relentless grimness in sticky situations. Over the years, Crysta had found that a well-timed joke could make unpleasant circumstances a little easier to handle.

"Did Derrick ever mention to you that he wanted you and I to get together?" Sam called softly up to her.

Precariously straddling the wire fence, Crysta registered the question with puzzlement. "How on earth is that significant right now?"

"I was just thinking that he was right—we make a great team," he called back in a teasing tone.

At the moment, teamwork was the furthest thing from

Crysta's mind. A sharp steel prong was biting through his jacket into her bottom. She gazed at the ground, which seemed a lot farther down on her side than it had on Sam's. To divert herself from the very real possibility that she might twist an ankle while jumping, she opted to focus on something unlikely. "What if they have Dobermans guarding the yard?"

"You read too many mysteries. Just jump."

"I do not." Crysta swallowed. Heights had always bothered her.

"If there are dogs, I'll hop over and play Tarzan. *Jump,* Crysta. If I try to come over while you're hanging up there, that barbed wire will cut you to pieces."

"It already is."

As carefully as she could, Crysta swung her other leg over and pushed off, suddenly airborne. An instant later, her flight came to an abrupt end when she hit the ground.

"I said to land on your *feet!* Are you all right?"

Crysta scrambled up, brushing dirt off her jeans. "So far. Hurry, would you?" She glanced over her shoulder, lowering her voice. "Someone's going to see us."

He chuckled. "You just don't want to be supper for a pack of Dobermans without me."

With amazing agility for so large a man, Sam scaled the fence. Never touching his torso to the barbed wire, he braced hand and foot on the top string and vaulted, landing beside her with far more grace than she had displayed. He tugged his jacket down from the top of the fence and pulled it on.

He flashed her a grin. "Jealous?"

"Since fence-climbing isn't on my list of necessary accomplishments, no. I only resent the fact that you didn't become a human pincushion up there." She fell into step beside him, rubbing the back of her leg. "That stuff is wicked."

His expression turned serious. "Are you okay?"

Crysta threw a worried glance at the fence. "I was until I looked up and saw that barbed wire from this side. How will we ever get out over that guard?"

"I'll find something for us to stand on."

As they rounded the corner of a storage building, they were confronted by a bounding, snarling Rottweiler, fangs gleaming. The dog, which at a quick guess weighed at least a hundred and fifty pounds, spotted them and came to a fast halt, swinging his massive head and snapping the air. Crysta's legs turned to water.

"Get behind me. Move slowly," Sam commanded in a smooth, silky voice.

Crysta was too frightened to move. Sam settled the matter by stepping forward and sideways, putting himself between her and the dog. Then, to Crysta's absolute horror, her protector sank to his knees, commanding her to do likewise. If she was going to be eaten alive, she wanted to die running.

"I said get down," Sam whispered. "Put your palms on your knees. It's a nonthreatening position."

Shaking, Crysta dropped as if someone had dealt a blow to the backs of her legs. The Rottweiler tipped his head and threw one ear forward, clearly perplexed. After studying them a moment, he licked a string of foamy slobber from his chops and sat down, whining in bewilderment.

"Good dog," Sam praised him gently. Very slowly, he lifted his arm, hand dangling at the wrist. "Come here, boy. Let's get to know each other, hmm? Come on."

The Rottweiler snarled. Crysta's skin prickled. What

if there was more than one dog? She longed to look behind them but was too scared.

"Speak to him," Sam ordered.

Crysta's throat closed off. Working her mouth, all she
could manage was a squeaky "Hello, doggie."

The Rottweiler barked, a deep, soul-shaking bark that
made Crysta jerk. Then, as if he had looked them over to
his satisfaction and judged them to be trustworthy, the dog
stood and slowly approached, twisting his hindquarters
about in what Crysta presumed was an attempt to wag
his bobbed tail. Upon reaching Sam, the animal lowered
his head and whined, bringing his nose up under Sam's
palm. Sam visibly relaxed and smiled, accommodating
the dog by scratching him behind his floppy ears.

"Some watchdog you are," he said with a laugh.

"Some Tarzan you are," Crysta inserted. "Down on
your knees."

She placed a shaky hand on the Rottweiler's squared
head, smiling in spite of herself. "Aren't you a nice doggie."

The creature responded by bathing her face with
kisses. Crysta reared back, trying to protect her mouth.
The dog butted her, and she nearly toppled. Sam grinned
and rose to his feet.

"It seems to be your day to be attacked by overzealous males," he observed drily. Grabbing the dog by the
collar, he offered Crysta a hand up. "Come on, we've got
a storage building to break into."

The Rottweiler accompanied them through the rows
of buildings as if it were his role to play guide. Crysta,
giddy with relief, had to laugh at how friendly he was.
"You can tell he's used to having people come in here
during the day."

Sam threw the dog a measuring glance. "His looks are enough to scare most people off. It really isn't necessary for him to be vicious."

When they reached Riley O'Keefe's storage building, they found themselves faced with a new problem. Studying the door, Sam said, "We need a crowbar to bust the lock."

With that, he left Crysta to wait by the building with the dog. Several minutes later, he returned with a crowbar.

"Talk about luck. Where did you find it?"

Sam quirked an eyebrow. "Would you believe it was lying on the office porch?" He inserted the tip of the crowbar under the edge of the garage-style door. "Remind me never to store my stuff here." Sam heaved downward, and on his third try, something inside the door gave a loud pop. An instant later, he shoved the portal up on its runners.

Giving the crowbar a toss, he flashed her a grin. "How's *that* for Tarzan?"

"You're getting there." Crysta stepped into the enclosure, squinting to see. Boxes, several rows deep, lined all three walls. Each container was about two feet long and over a foot wide. Recalling boxes exactly like these in her first dream, Crysta related that information to Sam and grinned with delight. "Pay dirt."

Wasting no time, Sam stepped around her and seized the taped lid of a box, ripping it open. Rising on tiptoe, Crysta peered inside. Small round tins gleamed up at her in the dim light. "What is it?"

Sam swore under his breath. "Canned salmon!"

With the explanation, he unended the box, dumping cans and cardboard dividers on the concrete floor. Using the toe of his boot to scatter them even more, he swore again.

"Nothing! Can you believe it? Nothing but canned salmon."

Crysta dropped to one knee, seizing a can. "Let me have your knife. Let's open a few and check what's inside."

Sam pulled his knife from its scabbard and took the can. Jabbing the lid with the blade tip, he cut around the rim in a rocking motion. Peeling back the lid, he said in a dry voice, "Surprise, surprise—salmon."

Unwilling to give up so easily, Crysta busied herself opening more boxes while Sam checked the contents of several other cans. In the end, their findings were the same. The boxes in Riley's storage building held nothing but canned salmon, which was not, by any stretch of the imagination, an illegal commodity.

When it became apparent that their visit to the public storage unit had proven a dead end, Sam glanced at his watch. "Shriver's expecting us back at the airport in forty minutes. We'd better close down and get out of here."

Working in tandem, they returned the tins of salmon to the boxes, discarding the few they had opened in a garbage can outside. When the evidence of their visit had been erased, they left the storage area, and Sam drew the door closed.

"With any luck, they won't know the lock's been broken until Riley makes another visit," Crysta said.

To her relief, Sam found an empty oil drum outside one of the buildings so they could stand on it and climb back over the fence. Once they had gained the other side, Crysta poked her fingers through the chain-link to bid the friendly Rottweiler goodbye.

DURING THE ROUGH FLIGHT back to Cottonwood Bend, Crysta's spirits plummeted and gave way to a numbing sense of defeat. Time was running out for Derrick. All her and Sam's efforts had gotten them nowhere. She had to think of something, fast, or her brother was going to die.

Shriver seemed intent on guiding the small aircraft through pockets of turbulence, a result of the inclement weather. Stomach knotted with anxiety, she softly quizzed Sam about small cabins near the lodge where her brother might have gone to hide.

With a preoccupied expression on his dark face, Sam turned to look at her. "There were several, like I told you, most of them miles from the river near small lakes."

"Could we check some of them out?"

Sam's expression altered to one of exasperation. "I suppose we could ride double on the all terrain four-wheeler and go to one tomorrow. We'd have to go partway on foot, so it would probably involve an overnight stay. We'd be wasting two days, which we can ill afford to lose."

"In other words, no."

His eyes held hers with unwavering intensity. "Crysta, it's your brother. I won't say no. But understand that if we pick out a cabin and go there, it's a crapshoot. Do you want to take a gamble, knowing how precious time is?"

"Well, it's better than doing nothing. I'm out of ideas. Aren't you?"

"For the moment. That doesn't mean I'm not thinking about it, or that something won't come to me. Let me regroup."

Crysta leaned away from him to gaze forlornly out the window. The endless sweeps of landscape she saw only served to depress her. Sam was right, and she knew it. They couldn't help Derrick by wandering aimlessly around out there.

Crysta's silence afforded Sam a chance to think. Pressing his knees against the seat in front of him, he leaned back, closed his eyes and carefully reviewed their day. Up until he had opened that box of canned salmon in the public storage unit, he had been certain Riley O'Keefe was their man. Now he was no longer so sure. Canned salmon? The amounts Riley had stockpiled boggled Sam's mind, but, like it or not, canned salmon was in no way suspicious. Maybe Riley was selling the damned stuff, making spending money on the side.

Had Sam aimed his suspicions at the wrong man? It was a possibility he couldn't ignore. Which would mean that he and Crysta had wasted an entire day. Maybe picking out one cabin at a time and investigating it wasn't so impractical an idea.

WHEN THE PLANE pulled up to the island, Crysta followed Sam out onto the wing, silently accepting his hand as she made the jump to dry land. Turning to Shriver, she expressed her thanks to him for allowing them to ride free of charge. Then she struck off along the footbridge. When she reached shore, she veered toward the trees.

Halfway there, Sam caught up with her. "Can we talk a sec?"

The last thing Crysta needed was company. At the moment, what she really needed was privacy. "What about?"

He drew up beside her. "I want to apologize. If you want to check out a cabin or two, let's do it."

Perilously close to tears, Crysta wandered off a few feet toward the trees. Over her shoulder she said, "No, Sam. You're right. It'd be a crapshoot, at best. I'm sorry that I keep circling back to that idea, but when I run out of things to do, I start to feel frantic, you know?"

"I know."

She glanced over her shoulder at him, wishing he hadn't followed her. There were times when something hurt so badly, one's only alternative was to weep; this was one of those times for her.

"I, um, think I'll take a little walk."

"I'd really rather you didn't," he said in a gentle voice. "After what happened yesterday in the sauna, I'm not sure it's safe."

The gentle whispering of the cottonwood leaves beckoned to her. She wanted to weave her way through the shadows and lose herself. "But, Sam, right now I need to be alone."

He stepped around so he could see her face. "Are you so upset you can't even talk about it?"

Trying to keep her features carefully blank, she ignored his question. "I'll stay within shouting distance of the lodge."

"Crysta, come here." As he spoke, he clasped her arm and pulled her toward him. "This is no time for you to be alone."

"Yes, it is. Please go, Sam."

He drew her against him, looping an arm around her shoulders and cupping a hand to the side of her face.

"Don't," she whispered. "I don't want company right now."

"I know." Pressing her face against his chest, he hunched his shoulders around her. "There's a problem with that, though. I can't walk off and leave you."

"I'm going to cry," she squeaked, "and when I cry, it's not a pretty sight. I never have figured out how some women manage it without turning red and getting all puffy."

He ran his fingers into her hair and rested his cheek atop her head. "Do you always try to joke when you're upset or frightened?"

"The alternative is worse."

"I'll risk it."

"I don't want you to see me like this."

"I'll wring out my shirt afterward and never tell a soul."

A sob caught in Crysta's throat. Leaning against him, she lost her battle to control her tears. They rushed from her eyes, streaming down her cheeks in hot rivers. "Oh, God, Sam, I'm afraid for him. Time is running out. I can feel it."

"We'll find him. If he's lasted this long, Crysta, he can hang on another day or two."

"What about infection? Or blood loss? Not to mention food and water. No one can hang on forever."

"We'll find him."

"Maybe not in time, though." A tremor shook her. "I need to call my mother, but what can I say to her? He's alive, Mom, but I can't find him? Prepare yourself for the worst?"

Sam's guts wrenched at the pain he heard in her voice. Closing his eyes, he tightened his hold on her. Her hair, thick and vibrant, slid over the back of his wrist like warm silk.

"Have you ever wished you could just run away from who you are?" she asked in a tremulous voice. "My mom will never understand my not being able to find him. Never. She'll think I haven't tried, that I'm blocking him out!"

"Why in heaven would she think that? You love Derrick. Anyone can see that."

"Because..." Going tense, she made fists in his shirt and pressed closer to him. "Oh, Sam, because I've tried to do just that. God forgive me, I've tried to do just that."

Suddenly, it was brought home to Sam just how difficult Crysta's life had been. A telepathic link. To an onlooker, it sounded almost fun, being able to communicate with someone without words, receiving messages long distance, seeing images. But it hadn't been fun for her. Nor for Derrick. And now, the telepathic link between them had turned Derrick's disappearance, which would have been horrible for anyone, into a nightmare. Crysta felt responsible for finding her brother in a way other people couldn't comprehend. If he died out there, it was possible she might never recover from it.

"I guess we all wish we could be someone else sometimes," he whispered raggedly. "But in the end, we're stuck with being ourselves. All you can do is your best, Crysta. No one can expect more than that from you—not your mother, not Derrick and not you. Don't set yourself up for a big fall in this."

"I should be able to *find* him. Can't you understand that? I should be able to see where he is, and I can't."

Sam grasped her shoulders and set her a step away from him so he could look into her eyes. He wondered if he was plunging in way over his head, but the pain in her expression made him take the leap, anyway. "Can you tap into Derrick's thoughts at will?"

"No, but—"

"You listen to me, okay? You're asking things of yourself that other people wouldn't even consider—all because you have a gift? You can only see snatches, not the entire picture. It's unreasonable to blame yourself."

She gazed up at him with injured, tear-bright eyes, her pale face streaked with wetness. Sam winced when he realized how stern he sounded. She needed a good listener, not a lecture.

"Come on, let's go sit down for a while."

Taking her by the hand, he led her to a nearby stand of cottonwood. Picking a grassy spot, he sat down, bracing his back against a silvered trunk, pulling her down beside him. She withdrew her hand from his, looping her arms around her knees. The anguish in her face made him long to wrap his arms around her.

"Talk to me, Crysta," he said softly. "You know what I'm hearing in your voice? Guilt. Layer upon layer of guilt. Why? There's more to this than your not being able to find Derrick, isn't there? Something you're not saying."

She took a moment to answer. When she did, she turned haunted eyes on him. "You're Derrick's friend. You'll never forgive me if I tell you."

"Try me."

With a soft moan, she dropped her head onto her knees. "All right, you want to hear the real truth, Sam? As much as I love my brother, there's a part of me that—"

She began to shake. Sam saw her throat go taut, but the words she was trying to say wouldn't come.

"You hate him just a little, don't you?" he asked her.

She swallowed and lifted her head. "I don't *hate* Derrick. But there's a part of me that resents what he's done to my life." She swiped at her cheek with her sleeve and sniffed. "For a while there I really believed I had escaped him. I was beginning to buy into the analyst's theory— that it was all nonsense that our mother had drilled into our heads. That all I had to do was ignore the dreams, and they would go away."

"Was that what you wanted, for it to be nonsense?"

She fastened bewildered eyes on him. "Yes. Do you remember what I said to you, about marriage not being the be-all and end-all of my existence? It was a lie, Sam. I wanted children, a family. For as long as I can remember, that was what I wanted more than anything. Derrick stole that chance from me."

"Did he, Crysta? Or was it simply that you fell in love with the wrong man?" Before she could protest, he held up a hand. "Oh, I know, it isn't easy to admit. Loving the wrong person hurts like hell, and it isn't easy to face. I think I know that better than almost anyone. But it happens."

"You don't understand. It wasn't Dick's fault."

"Make me understand, then. From what I've been hearing, the guy sounds like a selfish jerk."

"He wasn't, though. No one would put up with what he did. My getting constant flashes of Derrick? You've no idea…."

"Tell me."

"Sometimes, the flashes come at difficult moments." She pushed her hair from her eyes, then plucked a piece of grass. "It wasn't so bad the first couple of years of our marriage. I'd get flashes of Derrick, sometimes, but I never saw anything alarming. Then he broke up with Eileen." She paused and licked her lips. "Derrick went off the deep end for a while. He started drinking. He had terrible mood swings. And my emotional balance went on the roller-coaster ride with him. Once, Dick and I had just gone to bed, and right—" her face went crimson "—in the middle of everything, I got a flash of Derrick breaking a whiskey bottle against the sink. He put the jagged edge to his wrist. I jumped up and left Dick with his face planted in the pillow. At that time, Derrick only lived a few blocks away, and I felt I had to go to him. Dick was furious."

"Furious?" A surge of anger shot through Sam. "Surely he could understand that you had to get up. What were you supposed to do, let Derrick slash his wrists?"

"You have to remember that Dick didn't believe in my gleanings. He thought the entire thing was baloney. He wanted me to put Derrick out of my mind, out of my life."

"And when you couldn't?"

Another flush crept up her neck. "He accused us of—" She broke off and averted her gaze. "He started feeling jealous. To him our relationship went beyond the acceptable, and he began to suspect that perhaps there was something unhealthy going on."

"Something incestuous, you mean?"

"Yes."

"And how does that relate to your feeling that your mother will hold you to blame for all this?"

"Dick insisted that I choose between him and Derrick, never understanding that I *had* no choice." Fresh tears filled her eyes. "I loved Dick, so I tried. I stopped seeing Derrick. I even stopped seeing my mom. But the dreams still came, the flashes still came, and Dick just kept getting more and more paranoid. Then Derrick had the car wreck. I woke up in the middle of the night and started packing. Thirty minutes later, I was on my way out the door to the airport. That was it as far as Dick was concerned. Soon after, he walked out on me."

Sam tipped his head back, staring at the canopy of leaves that shimmered above them. "Taking his exit when you needed him the most."

"What man wouldn't have? That's why I continued the counseling. I realized I would never be able to lead a normal life unless I somehow grew separate from Derrick." She closed her eyes, worrying her bottom lip between her teeth. "I wanted to be free of him. And now I am."

The pictures came clear for Sam. "And your mother knows you wanted to be free."

"Yes. But worse than that, *I* know it."

"Crysta." Sam finally gave in to his urge and wrapped his arms around her. "Honey, you can't wish someone gone. Besides, what you were really wishing for wasn't Derrick's disappearance, just a chance to have what other people have—love and kids and a normal home life. It's not wrong to want those things."

"It's my fault I can't connect with him!" she cried. "Can you understand that? I tried and tried for so long not to feel anything from him, and now, when his life depends on it, I can't! Don't you see? My mother will never forgive me, and I don't blame her."

Sam did see, with a clarity that cut clear through him. He also saw that there were no words that could possibly soothe her. Barring Derrick's rescue, Sam wasn't sure anything ever could. If Derrick returned, he and Crysta needed to talk this out and toss away the emotional garbage both of them were lugging around. But what if Derrick didn't return?

The sound of a snapping twig caught Sam's attention, and he glanced over his shoulder to see Todd Shriver approaching through the trees.

"She okay?" the pilot called. "Not an easy trip for her, huh?"

"She'll be fine," Sam replied. "Right now, she just needs to be alone."

Shriver nodded in understanding and immediately re-traced his footsteps. Sam sighed and tucked in his chin to study the top of Crysta's bent head. He had no easy answers for her. He only knew that he had come to care about this woman he held in his arms, that he shared in her pain. Suddenly, he had a double stake riding on his finding Derrick alive: his own peace of mind, and Crysta's.

CHAPTER THIRTEEN

FIRELIGHT DANCED UPON the knotty-pine walls of Sam's living room, bright and cheerful, in direct contrast to Crysta's somber mood. The blackout shades were drawn, casting the room into shadow, giving her a much-needed feeling of privacy. Sam had thoughtfully left her here alone for a while, taking Tip with him, so she could regain her equilibrium before she called her mother.

She wandered listlessly, stopping to gaze at framed snapshots of Tip and Sam, sometimes managing a smile because the camera had caught them clowning. Tip was a very lucky boy, she decided, to have a father like Sam. Very lucky, indeed. In every photo, Sam's unconditional love for his son shone through in his expression.

Setting her jaw, Crysta left the apartment to use the mobile phone, almost wishing that the thing wouldn't be working properly so she could put off this necessary chore. No such luck. The call went through without a hitch.

"Have you got news?" Ellen cried.

Crysta glanced up at the sound of a bell jingling and saw Steve Henderson coming through the front door of the lodge. He veered to the right to take a seat at one of the dining tables. As always, he looked sad and troubled.

"No, Mom. Not much news, at any rate. Derrick is

alive, though. I'm certain of that much. You mustn't worry."

"He's contacted you again, then?"

Crysta's throat tightened. "Yes…a couple of times."

"Oh, Crysta, darling, you can't know how glad I am to hear you say that. These last few years, I didn't know what had gotten into you. All that nonsense about distancing yourself from your brother and living your own life." She gave a relieved laugh. "Where *is* he? I've been worried sick."

Crysta leaned against the counter and tightened her grip on the phone. "I haven't figured out exactly where he is, not yet."

"What do you mean, not yet?"

"He's all right, Mom. And I'll find him. Alaska covers a lot of territory. These things take time."

"But you said he contacted you."

"He did. But the pictures aren't—" Crysta closed her eyes. "I'm just getting blips. Not enough to pinpoint his location."

"Have you *tried?*"

"Of course I've tried. How can you ask that?" Crysta pushed away from the counter, struggling for calm. She mustn't lose her temper with her mother. "I'll find him, Mom, I promise."

"Oh, darling, I know you will. Just knowing he's alive is a great relief." Ellen grew quiet for a moment. "I've been so worried—about Derrick *and* about you."

"Me? I'm fine, Mom, really."

The rest of the conversation passed in a blur for Crysta, the only reality the fact that she had promised her mother something she might not be able to deliver. *"I'll find him, Mom, I promise.*" The same old trap was closing in around her.

After hanging up, Crysta returned to the apartment. With the promise still ringing in her ears, she sat on the sofa and stared sightlessly into the fire, trying to clear her mind.

Derrick? Can you hear me? Silence bounced back at her. She pressed a trembling hand over her eyes, remembering all the times she had gotten flashes of Derrick. Now, when his life depended on her, she saw nothing, heard nothing.

What had she done? Dear God, what had she done?

Less than an hour ago, Crysta had come to the conclusion that some things hurt so badly, tears were the only solution. Now she realized that some pain ran too deep for tears.

She lurched up from the sofa, heading for Tip's gallery. When she opened the door, the sharp, heavy smell of oil paints wafted to her. Stepping into the room, she closed the door and moved slowly toward the easel.

Tip was doing an incredible job of bringing Derrick to life on canvas. Looking into her brother's face, Crysta momentarily lost her sense of identity. He looked so real, Crysta could almost hear him laughing, feel the wind whipping his curly, cinnamon-colored hair. She looked into his eyes. The sensation was very like looking into a mirror. How was it possible to love someone so dearly, yet feel chained to him?

Her gaze trailed to the background of the portrait, taking in the detail Tip had so painstakingly recorded. Incredible. Todd's Cessna was pulled up to the island. The cottonwood trees were blowing in the wind. Near Derrick's feet lay a string of gigantic king salmon.

Sighing, Crysta moved about the room, admiring Tip's work, glad for a distraction from her thoughts. A canvasback duck. A caribou. A wolf. A winding slough surrounded by a sweep of marshy grassland. Crysta had never seen such lifelike paintings.

She paused before a portrait of Todd Shriver, smiling to herself when she noted that Tip had captured to perfection the weakness of the pilot's chin and the inexpressiveness of his eyes. Todd stood on the river island, the Cessna behind him. Tip had recorded every detail, right down to the lace hooks on Todd's boots.

With an odd sensation that she was missing something important, Crysta shifted her attention to the luggage and cargo Tip had painted on the ground near Todd. Her gaze was riveted. Boxes of canned salmon. With building urgency, Crysta shuffled through the other paintings that leaned against the wall, searching for more portraits. She finally found one of Riley O'Keefe, also standing on the island. Once again, Tip had painted boxes of canned salmon sitting near the airplane.

Crysta raced through the apartment and out the lodge door. She spotted Sam down by the footbridge, talking with Gary Nelsen, one of the men from Blanchette who frequently flew in to fish here with O'Keefe.

Trotting down the slope, Crysta called, "Sam! Can I talk to you for a moment?"

"Sure." Bidding Nelsen goodbye, Sam strode up the bank, his dark eyes searching her face. "Is something wrong?"

Crysta could scarcely contain her excitement. "No. In fact, something might finally be going right. Can you come up to the lodge with me? I want to show you something."

SAM STOOD BACK from the painting of O'Keefe, his gaze resting on the boxes of canned salmon, his forehead pleated in a frown. Then he looked at all the other paintings Crysta had dragged out.

"I can't believe I never noticed how much canned salmon came and went around here," Sam murmured.

"Kind of fishy, isn't it?"

Sam's gaze flew to hers. "You think Derrick intended that comment as a double entendre?"

"I'm certain of it." Crysta raised an eyebrow. "He has a twisted sense of humor sometimes. I'm convinced something more than fish is being hauled around in those boxes, though."

"I think you're right. It's the perfect cover. Boxes of canned salmon are as common up here as noses on faces. No one would ever question why you had them or what was in them."

"Look at this picture." Crysta hauled a painting over in front of him. "It's of Jangles, but look at the background, Sam. Todd Shriver's climbing down from the Cessna. From the looks of it, he's just brought in a load of supplies."

"He could be getting ready to leave with a load."

"No. Look at the water behind the plane, Sam." Crysta touched a fingertip to the V-shaped wake that foamed behind the Cessna's tail. "He had just landed."

"You're right," Sam whispered. "You've got quite an eye for detail, lady."

Crysta laughed. "Me? Tip's the one with the eye for detail. His paintings are like photographs. That happens with the handicapped sometimes, you know. It's as if God compensates for their shortcomings in other areas by giving them some special talent. With Tip, it's a photographic memory and the ability to reproduce it." She trailed her finger to the cargo door of the Cessna. "Look inside, Sam."

Sam leaned forward. "Canned salmon."

"Exactly."

Sam straightened and scratched his temple, looking perplexed. "Salmon comes in, then it goes out. I think I must be slow on the uptake, here. It doesn't make sense to me. First we suspected that an illegal commodity was being transported inside the conduit crates. Now we're guessing that they're using these boxes of fish up at this end to smuggle something out? Are you saying—" His voice broke off. "That something illegal is slipping right past me?"

She flashed an excited smile. "Sam, think about it! You just admitted that you never noticed how much canned salmon came and went. The reason you never noticed is because everyone who visits Alaska is hauling it around! It's the perfect cover, absolutely perfect. Riley brings a few boxes to Cottonwood Bend, puts whatever it is he's smuggling inside the boxes, and then flies them back out again to Anchorage to the warehouse. After business hours, he moves the illegal commodity from the canned salmon boxes into the crates of conduit, which are about to be returned to Seattle!"

Sam whistled, his eyes taking on a glint. "No pilot would pay any attention to canned salmon. He'd haul the stuff around, no questions asked."

"Exactly!"

Sam took another long look at each painting. "Okay, I can buy it. I think you're on to something, Crysta, I really do. Now all we have to do is figure out what in hell he's smuggling. I can't very well call in the cops without evidence."

Crysta threw up her hands. "I'm drawing a blank on that. I've tried and tried to think what, but I can't imagine. Why can't we just waylay Riley before he takes off on the plane next time and open the boxes?"

"He's not planning to leave again until tomorrow. Time, right now, is something we're running short on." A distant expression crept into his eyes. "That night when Derrick came into my office, he was really upset. 'I'll hang the creeps'—that's what he said. Whatever it is that's being taken out of here, it's something he felt so passionately about that he risked his own neck. Secondly, if Riley's smuggling it in those boxes, it has to be relatively small."

"Drugs, maybe? Derrick would be livid about that."

Sam shook his head. "Look at it from a practical angle. It's too remote here for drug running. That usually occurs along the Coast, near a big city for ease of distribution, or along the Mexican border. And, if you're thinking of a lab, the chemicals needed would be far too bulky to be hidden among cans of fish."

"Then what?"

"I'm thinking maybe it could be animal hides. Derrick can really get angry about poaching, especially up here. The thought that the wildlife might be depleted infuriated him."

"Do hides bring that much money?"

Sam sighed. "I suppose you could turn a tidy profit, but not nearly enough to make it cost-effective when it would take so many trips to transport them. Not only that, but a sizable animal hide probably wouldn't fit in a box that size, not if you left in any cans as camouflage."

"What, then?"

Sam looped an arm around her shoulders. "Let's have a cup of coffee. I'm drawing a blank. Sometimes if I just let a problem rest, the answer will come to me out of the blue."

While Sam went for the coffee, Crysta tossed another log onto the fire. When he returned, they sat together on the sofa, shoulders inches apart, taking reflective sips from their steaming mugs as they gazed into the flames.

"I can't think what they could be smuggling that would bring enough money to bother with," Sam muttered.

Crysta leaned forward to set her mug on the coffee table. "There has to be something. We're just overlooking it." She turned toward him. "Oh, Sam, we're not going to find him in time, are we? After all we've done, we're still going to fail."

Looking into her eyes, Sam could see how frantic she felt. After placing his mug beside hers on the table, he ran his hand under her hair and curled his fingers around the nape of her neck. Her skin there felt as soft as down. Drawing her toward him, he leaned back against the cushions, pulling her head to his shoulder. "I don't know, Crysta. I just don't know."

Pressing his cheek against her silken hair, he gazed into the fire, his heart twisting because he couldn't ease the pain in hers. Closing his eyes, Sam moved his arm down to encircle her back, slipping his hand between her arm and her side. Beneath his fingertips, he could feel the fragile ladder of her ribs. Whoa, this was not the time to let physical desire cloud his thinking. Above all else, Sam was a practical man. But, practical or not, dammit, he wanted her.

The realization struck him like a blow. Worse, wanting wasn't even sufficient to describe the emotions roiling within him. He wanted her, yes, but in a way he had never wanted any other woman. So much that he trembled. So much that he felt frightened. There was a rightness between them, a magical sweetness. Holding her like this filled the emptiness within him, made him feel complete in a way he had never experienced. So perfect... yet so impossible.

Sam came as a package deal, saddled with a troublesome man-child who would never mature to adulthood. Loving Tip as he did, he harbored no resentment and didn't feel in the least put upon that Tip needed so much attention. But he couldn't expect a woman who was not Tip's natural mother to be so charitable. Especially not Crysta, who had her own life in Los Angeles, a busy, fast-paced life that precluded mothering a handicapped boy.

Sam's first duty lay with his son. He couldn't allow himself to forget that, even for an instant. And yet he had needs, needs he had ignored for far too long. Was it so wrong to steal a magic moment with this very special woman?

He shifted his hand so the pads of his knuckles grazed the soft swell of Crysta's breast. An ache rose up his throat. Making love to her right now would be insanity. One taste, and he might never be able to get enough.

To his surprise, she turned in the circle of his arm and tipped her head back, her eyelashes casting shadows over her cheeks, her lips parted. "Sam?"

Sam responded to the question in her voice by lowering his head. Crazy, so crazy. But he couldn't stop himself. Just one sweet kiss. Surely God would grant him that much—one kiss to be remembered during the long, cold, empty winter nights to come. One kiss to last him a lifetime. His lips touched hers, so lightly, so gently, but the electricity was there again just the same. Two-twenty, with no ground, and he knew he was a goner.

She tasted like toffee, her mouth warm and sugary from the coffee, her lips moist. Sweet, so incredibly, wonderfully, impossibly sweet. Sam, usually so responsible, forgot everything—that the door wasn't locked, that Tip might walk in. His mind went blank, automatic pilot kicked in, and before he knew it, he had pulled her down beside him on the sofa.

At five foot ten, Crysta fit his body the way a woman should. He wasn't even aware that the sofa wasn't long enough. If Sam had feet, he couldn't feel them. She moaned and let her head fall back over his arm. Sam accepted the invitation and feathered his mouth along the graceful slope of her neck to her collarbone. And then lower.

The top buttons on her shirt opened as if he had magic in his fingertips. His heart slamming, he peeled the cloth back and trailed kisses down her chest to the shimmering mounds of her breasts, breasts that seemed to beg for his lips to explore them above the lacy edge of her bra. Her skin was as flawless and as creamy-white as ivory, silken, warm, vibrant.

Sam stiffened, his hand frozen on her breast, his mind stunned. *Ivory!*

Crysta heard Sam curse, and her eyes flew open. He was suspended above her, his body rigid, his eyes filled with what could only be described as disbelief.

"Sam?"

He shot up from the sofa and smoothed his hair, staring down at her. "Ivory, Crysta." He barked with incredulous laughter. "Your skin is as flawless as *ivory.*"

It wasn't a very original line, and Sam's delivery needed work, but Crysta accepted the compliment with as much grace as she could muster. Quickly buttoning her shirt, she said, "Thank you…I think."

"*Ivory,* Crysta! That's it, don't you see? That's what they're smuggling! I can't believe I was so dense! It's been making all the headlines recently. Walrus tusks. There have been several killing fields discovered, some on the islands, several up north!"

"Ivory?" Crysta sat up, trying to gather her shattered composure. Then what Sam was saying began to register, and excitement coursed through her. "Ivory! Of course! They could make a mint on that!"

"A mint? A head mount brings over a thousand dollars! One head mount, Crysta. Have you any idea how many they may have smuggled out of here? And that's only for starters. Scrimshaw would bring astronomical amounts. Have you any idea how much one small piece costs? Once they had the ivory in the States, they could commission someone to work it into scrimshaw, then launder it some- how onto the open market."

"Wh-what's a head mount?"

"The front portion of the walrus's skull, with the tusks still attached."

Crysta recalled the magazine cover she had seen with its gory pictures of the beheaded walrus corpses litter- ing a lonely beach. A feeling of revulsion swept over her. And something elusive tugged at her memory.

"That *bastard!* He's slaughtering walrus! No wonder Derrick was so upset!"

Crysta pressed her fingers to her temples, her senses still reeling. She swallowed and closed her eyes. "Wait,

Sam. We're not near the coastline. There are no walrus around here."

"Of course not! He's flying them in. It's perfect, Crysta. He hits a beach, slaughters the animals, hacks off the heads and transports them here to be cleaned. He'd have to clean them before taking them to the warehouse in Anchorage. If he didn't, the smell coming from those conduit crates would bowl a person over. And what better place to do it than someplace near Cottonwood Bend? Daily flights out, lodging, isolation!"

"So he cleans them somewhere around here, hides them in the canned salmon boxes, then brings them to the lodge to be flown out to Anchorage? But, Sam, a walrus head with tusks wouldn't fit in a box two feet long."

"It would if you removed the tusks. You can dismantle a head mount, then put it back together."

"And if the mounts were concealed inside the canned salmon boxes, the pilots hauling the ivory would never even realize what they were hauling!" Crysta pushed up from the sofa. "Sam, you're a genius! It fits perfectly! Derrick must have discovered what Riley was doing!"

"And probably followed him."

She held up a hand. "Wait, we're forgetting something. In my dream, I saw three men. He must have helpers."

"That goes without saying. No one could do something on this scale without help. There's probably more than just three men involved. We've already deduced that there must be a contact in Seattle. Then there would have to be at least two or three guys working at the killing fields." Sam's excited grin faded. "Crysta, from here on in, this can only get more and more dangerous. Until Riley's caught redhanded with some boxes that contain ivory, we don't have enough evidence to go to the police. I'm not so sure I want you involved."

"Oh, no, you don't! Questioning Riley is my only hope of ever finding out where Derrick may be. I want to be damned sure the man's caught. I'm in on this to the end, Sam."

His eyes darkened. "I don't want you getting hurt."

"And I don't want you hurt, either. We've done well so far as a team. Let's not rock the boat."

"We have, haven't we?" he whispered, his expression far more eloquent than the words he spoke. After a long, emotion-packed moment, his mouth quirked in a sad smile. "I'm sorry about—" His gaze shot to the sofa. "Not very chivalrous of me, popping up that way."

Crysta laughed softly. "No, it wasn't. But given the reason, I'll reserve judgment until next time."

Would there be a next time? Sam wanted that more than he could admit, but part of him knew that both of them would be better off if the occasion never again rose. Crysta had her own set of problems; she didn't need to take on his.

"Well." Sam wandered over to the fire, not quite able to look her in the eye. "All that's left is for us to unearth the ivory. If we can find the cleaning location, there should be enough evidence there for us to go to the police. Then we can have the searchers brought back in."

Crysta could scarcely contain her excitement. "If we need them. If I see anything familiar at the cleaning location—something I've seen in my dreams—I might be able to find Derrick myself."

Sam glanced up, a grin touching his mouth. Despite the fact that time was running out for him and Crysta, this was a major triumph; a moment for joy. He would share in that with her and worry about tomorrow later.

"The quickest way to find a possible cleaning location would be from the air. It's probably convenient to the river, for ease of transport by pontoon plane."

"Todd's still here. Do you think he'd take us up?"

"I'm sure he would." Sam strode across the room to her and clamped a hand on her shoulder. Guiding her toward the door, he grabbed her windbreaker off the chair and handed it to her. "Let's go commandeer ourselves an airplane, shall we?"

Just as Sam reached for the doorknob, Tip burst in. "Where are you going, Dad? It's almost bedtime."

"Crysta and I have some things we have to do," Sam replied gently.

Tip looked crestfallen. "I thought maybe we could read to each other for a while. I bet Crysta likes to read."

"As a matter of fact, I do."

Guilt stabbed Sam. He had been ignoring Tip for days, and it bothered him to be leaving the boy alone again. Tip often had nightmares and sought Sam out for reassurance. "I'm sorry, son. Maybe we can read before bedtime tomorrow night."

Tip's gaze slid to Crysta. "Will you r-read with us? The book we're d-doing now is really good. It's about buried treasure."

Crysta took Tip's hand and gave it a warm squeeze. "You know, Tip, if we find Derrick, he might be ill or hurt. If he is, he'll have to be taken to a hospital. Since I'm his sister, I'll want to go with him. I may not be here tomorrow night."

Tip's face fell. "You won't come back, will you?"

Crysta hesitated, but only for an instant. "And never

see you again? Not on your life, kiddo. We're fast friends, remember?"

Tip's mouth arched in a reluctant grin. "For real?"

"Of course, for real. For always, Tip. I'll come back. Maybe with Derrick. Wouldn't that be fun? We could make popcorn, and all of us could read together."

"I'd like that. W-would you like that, Dad?"

Sam couldn't say how much. "Hey, Tip, how about if I ask Jangles to stay with you tonight? I bet she'd enjoy some company."

"Okay." Tip brightened visibly. "Maybe we can make popcorn."

After leaving the apartment, Sam glanced at Crysta. "I have to talk with Jangles. Mind waiting a few minutes?"

As anxious as Crysta was for them to be on their way, she knew Sam had other obligations, as well. "Not at all. We'll both feel better if we know Tip's all right."

The sincerity Sam saw reflected in Crysta's gaze made his stomach tighten. Was it remotely possible that maybe, just maybe, he'd finally found a woman who wouldn't resent Tip? As he hurried through the lodge to find Jangles, Sam cautioned himself against reading too much into Crysta's behavior. She might sing a different tune entirely when faced with a lifetime of making allowances for Tip.

Bitter memories washed over Sam. He couldn't let Tip be hurt again. Setting himself up for a big fall was one thing, but putting Tip through another rejection would be criminal.

CHAPTER FOURTEEN

THE CESSNA CIRCLED, rattling and shaking as it lost altitude. Crysta pressed her face against the window, scanning the landscape below. The sunken roof of a cabin came into view. She groped behind her for Sam's hand and gave it a squeeze.

"I don't think that's it," he whispered so Shriver wouldn't overhear. "There's no trail leading from the river, no sign of traffic."

From up front Todd said, "What is it you two are looking for? I'm pretty familiar with the area. Maybe I can help."

Before boarding the plane, Sam and Crysta had decided the less said to anyone about their suspicions, the better. Sam followed through on that feeling now by ignoring Shriver's question. He leaned forward. "Bank to the left, Todd. The place we're looking for should be fairly close to the lodge."

Todd did as instructed. Watching the man's skilled maneuvering of the plane, Sam considered the repercussions Todd or any other pilot might suffer if he were caught smuggling ivory. It would be insane to take that risk. Undoubtedly the pilots involved were blissfully unaware of their illegal cargo. Anger welled within Sam. People who slaughtered walrus obviously didn't have much in the way of conscience. They didn't care who they took down with them.

That thought led Sam back to the most troubling question of all. Who were the culprits? Their uncertainty had been the main reason he and Crysta had decided to reveal as little as possible about their reasons for this air search.

Focusing along the wing, Crysta spotted another cabin. She reached back to jab Sam's shoulder.

"That could be our baby," Sam said softly. "There's a path winding up from the river." In a louder voice, he said, "Circle around, Todd, and swing in low."

Crysta's pulse accelerated. As the plane swooped toward the earth and she got a good frontal view of the cabin, a feeling of déjà vu washed over her.

"Sam!" she whispered, her tone urgent.

He turned to look at her, lifting an eyebrow. "You say yes?"

She gave an emphatic nod.

"Hey, Todd, can you land along this stretch of river?"

Todd took a pass, giving the waterway a thorough study. "It looks good from here. Wanna try her?"

"Yeah, set us down."

AFTER LANDING THE PLANE, Todd insisted on accompanying Sam and Crysta to the cabin even though Sam assured him that they were, at this point along the river, within walking distance of the lodge.

"Hey!" Shriver said, lifting his hands. "Why go off and leave you to walk? I've got nothing better to do."

Even though he preferred that the pilot not come along, Sam could think of no good way to discourage him. Besides, if his and Crysta's suspicions proved correct, Shriver was probably one of the pilots who had been hoodwinked into hauling the illegal cargo. And in that case, it seemed only fair that he be along when Sam and Crysta gathered enough evidence to present to the police.

As the two men struck off walking, Crysta fell in behind them. For some reason she felt uneasy. Was Derrick trying to reach her, perhaps? She tried to clear her mind, but her excitement over finding this cabin made serenity impossible.

About a half mile from the river, Sam stopped and scanned the ground. He looked up and pointed to a thicket of brush. Through the network of green leaves, Crysta spotted something gleaming in the sunlight.

"Four-wheelers!" Sam cried. He and Todd waded into the brush.

"Can you believe it?" Todd pulled back branches to reveal one of the bikelike rough-terrain vehicles. "Who'd leave these here?"

Sam met Crysta's gaze, his own questioning. Since Crysta could think of no way they could conceivably continue this foray without leveling with Shriver, she gave Sam a reluctant nod. Without giving names, Sam explained to the pilot their reason for coming here. He finished by saying, "If we're correct, I'd guess that the smugglers use these all-terrain vehicles to carry the ivory from the river inland."

Shriver gave a low whistle. "Talk about a smooth operation. A plane brings in a load from the killing fields and puts down here on the river. They haul the ivory to this point, load it onto the bikes, and take it to be cleaned. After that, they hide it in boxes of canned salmon, and back onto the bikes it goes! Then from this point they drag it to the lodge, hang around until a pilot is making a flight out and load it up. I can't believe all of us pilots were so dense!"

"You can't blame yourself," Sam replied. "Canned salmon doesn't exactly wave a red flag."

"I suppose not." Todd shook his head, giving the four-wheeler's rear tire an angry kick. "What d'ya say we use these bikes ourselves?"

"No," Sam replied. "There could be someone at the cabin. The noise of the bikes would warn them we're coming."

"That's true." Shriver flashed Crysta a smile. "Looks like we'll have to hoof it."

Once again Crysta fell in behind the men. The trail veered to the right across a meadow and came to a shallow slough. Both Todd and Sam wore the green waterproof boots, but Crysta was in sneakers. Without so much as a word, Sam swept her into his arms to carry her across.

Looking back at Shriver over Sam's shoulder, Crysta watched the pilot step off into the shallow water. Sunlight struck his boots, glistening on the green rubber. A chill of recognition crawled up her spine. Her first dream crystallized in her head. The green rubber boots. Not conclusive, Sam had said. And he was absolutely right. The boots were commonplace up here. But the strange way Todd Shriver tied his laces was not.

Todd didn't lace his boots in a crisscross, like most people, but in a ladder-rung fashion. Tip's painting. While looking at it, Crysta had sensed she was almost, but not quite, grasping something she had overlooked, and she'd begun examining the background. If only she had kept her focus on Todd's boots!

The boots in her dream came flooding back to her. She distinctly remembered now that one pair had been laced horizontally from hook to hook, straight across like ladder rungs. Crysta stiffened.

"What is it? Am I hurting you?" Sam asked, tipping his head back to look at her face. "Crysta, what is it?"

Todd glanced up and halted in the middle of the slough. His gaze met Crysta's. For the first time, Crysta saw expression in those icy orbs. Hostility. She tried to speak, couldn't. Shriver reached into his pocket.

"Sam," Crysta croaked, but she was too late. Shriver withdrew a deadly looking revolver from his pocket and aimed it squarely at Sam's broad back, a target he couldn't possibly miss at this close range. Sam stepped up onto the bank, still oblivious. "Sam? Oh, God, Sam, Shriver's—"

With a quick pull of his thumb, Shriver clicked the gun off safety. The metallic sound stopped Sam cold.

"Go ahead and finish, Ms. Meyers. 'Shriver's in on it'—isn't that what you meant to say?"

The pilot smiled a nasty smile, all attempt at subterfuge abandoned. Looking at him now, Crysta realized what it was about him that had always nagged at her. It wasn't that his face was boyish and a little too perfect. It was the lack of compassion to be read there.

"I had hoped to avoid this until we reached the cabin," Shriver told them. "It would have been so much more tidy that way." He shrugged. "Oh, well, it just brought things to a head sooner than planned. We'll just keep walking, hmm?"

Sam set Crysta on her feet and turned to regard Shriver with glittering eyes. "You weren't an innocent party, after all."

"You're extremely slow at figuring that out. We've been walking on eggshells for two days now, convinced you were only inches away from realizing. Especially after I followed your cab and saw you touring the ware-houses. Riley about came unglued when I told him." He shrugged. "Of course, he's been worried from the start, ever since he followed you into the woods that first day—you remember, Sam, when Ms. Meyers tailed you? The time you tackled her. Riley overheard you arguing and started predicting trouble even then."

"So there *was* something behind me!" Crysta cried. "I thought so, but when I stopped and listened, I couldn't hear or see anything."

"It's not hard to hide in this country," Shriver pointed out. Gesturing with the gun, he added, "Let's start walk-ing. When you guys came and asked me to bring you out here, I got word to Riley before we left. We knew it was the beginning of the end, at that point. From the air, we knew you'd see the trail leading to the cleaning location, then get suspicious and want to see it. My partners struck off in this direction as soon as the Cessna lifted off. It's a ways to walk, but as you've already determined, they're used to it. We're all supposed to meet at the cabin to solve the problem you two present. Riley, as always, has some very inventive solutions."

"Partners?" Sam repeated. "Who else is involved?"

Crysta had a sinking feeling that she knew the answer to that question. A picture of Jangles conferring in the woods with a strange man flashed through her mind. In retrospect, Crysta couldn't believe she hadn't connected the Tlingit to the walrus slayings the moment Sam men-tioned them. It all fit together now. Jangles, a native of Alaska, was the perfect person to help out up here in a poaching and smuggling operation.

Shriver's mouth twisted at Sam's question. "Who else is none of your business. But you'll know soon enough."

"Why you?" Crysta asked. "For the money?"

"Things like this have a way of getting out of hand, you know? Nice guys, trying to make a little extra cash on the side, and, *kaboom,* the first thing you know, Derrick gets suspicious, Riley gets trigger-happy and you're in so deep you can't get out. Do you think I ever intended to kill someone? Once Riley pulled that trigger, it was too late to bail out."

Sam tried to reason with the man. "For God's sake, Shriver, you're not in too deep yet. But if Riley shot Derrick, do you think he'll hesitate to kill us? For your part in that, they'll put you in prison and throw away the key."

"I think one count of murder and ivory smuggling is sufficient to do that." Shriver shook his head. "Not this fella. I'm not doing time. The only reason I got into this in the first place was for a little excitement and some extra cash to impress my ex-girlfriend. She dumped me for a guy with more pocket change. I don't think a prison uniform would turn her on, do you? Besides, why should I rot in a cell? It's not my fault that Riley has a quick trigger finger and no conscience."

"If you go through with this, you're crazy!" Crysta cried.

"It's your fault, you stupid broad!" Shriver waded toward them, keeping the gun trained on Crysta. "One move, Barrister, and she's dead, so don't decide to play hero."

Sam stepped back, keeping his hands in plain sight.

"Why is it my fault?" Crysta demanded. If she could keep Shriver talking, maybe she could distract him long enough for Sam to make a move. It always worked in mystery novels, and as far as Crysta could see, stalling was the only chance they had. "I'm a victim in this."

"An extremely nosy victim." He jabbed her in the hip with the gun. "Turn around, both of you, and keep your hands above your heads. Now, start walking! That's good."

Crysta heard a splash as Shriver exited the slough behind them, the squeak of his rubber boots on the grass. Her back tingled. What if he decided to shoot them now?

"I just came here to find my brother," she said shakily.

"Yeah, yeah. Wasn't the salmon we stuck in your bed warning enough? That should have been your cue to get the hell out while the getting was good, but you stuck around."

"I suppose you'll tell me next that it was you who trapped me in the sauna?"

"No, I don't have the stomach for that kind of thing. That was Riley's special touch."

"But how?" Crysta asked. "You and Riley were both out on boats fishing."

"Correction. You thought we were. We landed downriver and walked back upstream."

"You stood by while he trapped a helpless woman inside a sauna and built up the fire?" Sam asked.

"Hey! He wanted to go in first and have a little send-off party—give her something to go out smiling about. At least I drew the line at that. Don't be offended, Ms. Meyers. That isn't to say I wasn't tempted. You've got the nicest set of—"

Sam stopped and turned. "Shriver, say one more word, and, gun or no gun, I'm gonna make you eat those pearly whites."

Shriver kept the gun aimed at Crysta. "I don't think so, since she'd go first. Besides, I was paying her a compliment."

"She can do without that kind of compliment."

"Fine. Just keep walking."

Clenching his teeth, Sam did as he was told. Crysta fell in beside him, so frightened she felt sick, and not just for herself.

"Shriver, please," Crysta pleaded. "Stop this, now, before Riley gets here. Sam has a son to take care of. What will Tip do without his father? *Think* about what you're doing, the lives it will ruin!"

"It's out of my hands. Riley calls the shots. Just keep walking."

It was the longest journey of Crysta's life. At the edge of the meadow, they entered a line of trees, which bordered another clearing. About a hundred yards away, Crysta spotted the cabin. Following the rutted four-wheeler path through the tall grass, she absorbed her surroundings.

Sam glanced down at her, his expression grim. "This is outside the official search area," he told her softly. "That explains why the pilot in the Huey didn't report it. Using the spot where I found Derrick's shredded gear as a center point, the volunteers searched in a radius they could conceivably cover on foot in a day's time. When they widened the circle, they found the faked bear attack site and ended the search."

"Clever, weren't we?" Shriver boasted. "We made damned sure they'd find evidence of the attack before the search area expanded to encompass our cleaning location. We ran a risk, of course. If the pilot in the Huey had taken note of the trail to the cabin and sent anyone to check it out, we'd have been had. Fortunately for us, he was relying mainly on the infrared device in hopes of finding Derrick by detecting a fluctuation in tempera-

CATHERINE ANDERSON   569

ture. If he flew over the cabin, there was nothing inside to alert him that it wasn't just another abandoned shack like dozens of others in the region."

About fifty yards from the cabin, they came upon an embankment that plunged sharply to a rushing creek. Crysta missed a step, staring down at the jagged boulders jutting up from the water. She remembered them from her second dream. This was the embankment she had been trying to scale. Sweat broke out on her face. She turned slightly to gaze in the direction that she had fled after climbing up the incline. Derrick was out there somewhere, in a dank cabin by a small lake.

"This is where you threw my brother's body, isn't it?"

Crysta turned on Shriver just in time to see his face register his surprise. "How'd you know that?"

"Just a guess," Crysta replied icily. "Why here, Todd?"

"It was far enough away from where we staged the bear attack that the searchers wouldn't find it. With the trees and boulders, his body wouldn't be visible from the air. As you can see, his remains didn't last long enough to be a concern. That's one nice thing about Mother Nature—she cleans up after you rather quickly. Animals—" He broke off. "Well, you get the picture."

Hatred filled Crysta. Shriver deserved a prison sentence. A long one.

"Is that where we'll end up?" Sam asked. "Food for scavenging animals, Shriver?"

"Actually, no. Two more disappearances would arouse suspicion. We can't let nature take its course a second time and risk the authorities finding you. Riley is talking about flying you out over the mud flats outside Anchorage. The beauty of it is, if I fly in low, we can shove you out while you're alive and unharmed. When they find your bodies, it'll look as if you went to show Ms. Meyers the sights and walked out too far." Todd clucked his tongue. "In case you aren't familiar with the mud flats, Ms. Meyers, they can be like quicksand. Not too long back, a man and his wife went out there and got into a bog. A rescue 'copter went in to pull them out. The man didn't make it in one piece. Ripped him clean in half when they tried to lift him."

"I'm a *guide,*" Sam reminded him. "Who'll believe I was that stupid?"

"You're in love. Everyone at the lodge has seen the two of you together. Men can make stupid mistakes when they're trying to impress their ladies, right? Of course, we'll be sure that's the story that gets started, just to cinch it."

Acutely conscious of Sam beside her, Crysta walked the rest of the way to the cabin. She was instructed to enter first, so the pilot could keep close watch on Sam. The stench of rancid blubber and rotting fish hit her the moment she stepped inside. She remembered the odor from her first dream, and nausea rolled up her throat. Along one wall, a pile of ghoulish skulls were stacked, five and six deep. And suddenly she remembered what had eluded her earlier—her glimpse of an animal skull in Shriver's Cessna. A quick count revealed at least fifty head mounts here. The collection was worth at least fifty thousand dollars.

Her gaze shifted to a worktable on her right. A glint of silver caught her attention. Derrick's buckle. At one edge of the ornate scrollwork was a jagged hole. As she had suspected, the bullet fired at Derrick had gone through the buckle in his shirt pocket, leaving telltale evidence of foul play, which was why his attackers hadn't left it to be found in the mangled garment.

Shriver grabbed some rope from beneath the table and tossed it at Sam. "Tie her up," he hissed. "And no funny stuff. I want it tight. Mess with me, and I'll kill her."

"And have a bullet wound in her head to make the police suspicious when they haul us out of the mud flats?"

"We can always think of something else," Shriver retorted. "I do have an airplane."

As instructed, Sam bound Crysta's wrists behind her, then tied her feet. As he finished tightening the last knot, Shriver walked up behind him and brought his gun down on Sam's head, evidently deciding the danger he represented outweighed the risk of any suspicious autopsy findings. Sam crashed to the floor, his shoulder hitting Crysta's leg. Unable to keep her balance, Crysta fell backward, crying out Sam's name.

Stowing his gun in his jacket pocket, Shriver made fast work of tying up Sam. When he finished, he straightened and met Crysta's gaze, his own curiously expressionless, as it had always been.

"If it's any comfort at all, I won't let Riley—well, you know. I do draw the line someplace."

Praying that Shriver wouldn't decide to check the ropes on her wrists, Crysta snapped, "How noble of you."

He shrugged and turned toward the door. "I'll be outside keeping watch for my partners. You wait here, hmm?"

CRYSTA LIFTED SAM'S head in her arms, sending up a silent prayer that he wasn't badly injured. Placing a hand alongside his face, she fought back tears. Seeing him like this brought home to her how deeply she had come to care for him these last few days. Very gently, she ran her fingers over the angry red bump rising on his temple. She was no expert, but it didn't look like a serious injury. He would probably be all right.

It was up to her to somehow keep him that way.

"Sam? Sam, darling… Oh, please, Sam, wake up and look at me."

His eyelashes fluttered open. His dark eyes wandered as he tried to focus on her. "Crysta? We're untied. How did you—"

"It was a trick I learned from a mystery novel. I held the heels of my hands together, with my wrists twisted. It gives you some slack when you straighten your arms."

He licked his lips. "Mystery novels. I *knew* it. You lied to me."

A joyful laugh bubbled up her throat, and tears trailed down her cheeks. "Can you sit up?"

He tried and failed. Crysta tried to help him, but he weighed so much, she couldn't budge him. "Sam, you *have* to get your wits about you."

He fastened bleary eyes on her. "Did you call me darling?"

"Sam!" Crysta caught him by the chin. "Shriver's out there with a gun. Riley will be here anytime. Snap out of it."

He passed a hand over his forehead, wincing when he grazed the bruise on his temple. "What in hell did he hit me with?"

"His gun." Time was running out. Crysta knew if she didn't do something, fast, she and Sam were going to die. She pulled her arm from beneath him and pushed to her feet. Glancing around, she spied a pile of stove wood. "You just lie there, okay? Keep your hands behind you like you're still tied up."

He blinked again, trying to focus on her. "What are you going to do?"

"I'm going to get us out of here." She picked up a hunk of wood, glancing out the murky window as she hefted it in her hands. Twilight had fallen, which meant a great deal of time had passed. Enough time for Riley to have nearly reached them. She glanced back at Sam. "You concentrate on coming around."

He tried to shove up on one elbow. "Crysta, don't be crazy. You're no match for Shriver. He has a gun."

She held up the wood. "This will do if I take him by surprise."

Stepping behind the door, Crysta pressed her back to the wall. Glancing at Sam, she took a deep breath and let out a bloodcurdling scream. He jumped. She screamed again. An instant later, they heard footsteps thumping up the porch. The door crashed open.

Crysta lifted the wood. Shriver stepped into view. With all her might, she brought the wood down on his head with a resounding thud. Shriver staggered, fell against the wall, gave his head a shake and focused on her. Crysta stared at him in horrified disbelief.

"You little—"

Whatever it was he meant to say was cut short. Sam came up off the floor, swinging his massive fist in a wide arc that caught the unprepared pilot squarely on the chin. Head hitting the wall with a loud crack, Shriver rolled his eyes and began a slow descent toward the floor, surprise crossing his face as his legs folded beneath him.

Sam, bracing a shoulder on the wall beside the unconscious pilot, sank to the floor with him. "If we get out of this alive, I'm enrolling you in another self-defense class. You should have hit him above the ear, not dead on."

"How was I to know he has a head like brick? Besides, I only wanted to knock him out, not kill him!"

"Charitable of you," he grunted. "Tie him up. Fast. If he comes around, he won't be half as nice as you, believe me."

Crysta leaped into action. The moment she had Shriver bound, she turned her attention to Sam. "Can you stand up?"

Bracing an arm against the wall, Sam rose to his knees and gave his head a shake. From the way his eyes looked, Crysta knew he was in no condition to walk. Raising his face, he tried to focus on her, his full lips a frightening gray.

"Go without me," he rasped.

"What?"

"You heard me. It's your only chance, Crysta."

She ran to peer out the window. "I'm not leaving you!"

He licked his lips and managed to plant one boot on the floor in front of him. Propping an arm on his knee, he said, "Just this once, would you listen to me? I'll slow you down. They'll catch us, and if they do, we're both dead. Now go!"

"No!"

A little bit of his color returned. He tipped his head back and riveted her with an irritated gaze, his eyes bleary. "Somehow, I *knew* you'd say that. Until I met you, I never realized how boring other women were."

It hit Crysta then, with the impact of a battering ram, that the blow to Sam's head had literally knocked the sense out of him. She ran across the room and grabbed his arm. "Sam, for heaven's sake, this is no time for—"

"Professions of love?" With her help, he gained his feet, staggering sideways, which carried her with him. "What better time? I might not get a chance later."

Crysta took two steps toward the door, hauling Sam with her. His boot caught on Shriver's bound legs. She stumbled, caught her balance and lurched forward again. "Sam, you have to concentrate. Are you listening to me?"

"I'm not deaf, honey, just dizzy."

She gritted her teeth, holding him up with one arm while she threw the door wide with her other. Feeling his solid body stumbling against hers made her heart twist with fear for him. At least she could run. "Our lives are at stake here!" she grunted, steering him out onto the porch.

"Exactly." He tripped down the steps. "Which is why—" He pulled to a stop and leaned forward, planting his hands on his knees while he hauled in a gigantic draft of fresh air. "There are some things you don't leave for later when you aren't sure there'll *be* a later. You're one hell of a lady, Crysta Meyers. I just want you to know that."

"So now I know." She caught his arm again, scanning the line of nearby trees, heart in throat. Riley might appear at any moment. "Now, let's apply ourselves to making sure we *have* a later, Sam. Can you do that?"

He straightened, looking a little better now that he had some clean air in his lungs. Blinking, he pulled his arm from her grasp to drape it over her shoulders and leaned heavily against her. "I definitely want a later, believe me. If I let Riley kill me, I'll never get to investigate that cute little birthmark on your—"

Crysta gasped. "You said you didn't look!"

"I lied, too."

EN ROUTE BACK to the river, Sam had to lean heavily on Crysta to make it. As they crossed the meadow, Crysta felt like a tortoise carrying a load of cement while engaged in a footrace with a hare. Hopelessness filled her.

Fastening her gaze on the line of trees ahead of them, she did the only thing she could think to do: she prayed.

Just as they reached the edge of the tree line, Crysta spotted a flash of movement from the corner of her eye. Red hair, a plaid shirt, blue jeans. She turned her head, fear chilling the sweat on her face. Riley O'Keefe. A tall, slender figure emerged behind him. Steve Henderson? She'd no sooner registered that than a shot rang out and dirt geysered right in front of her feet.

"Sam!"

In response to her cry, Sam shoved her forward, the force of his thrust sending her into a face-first sprawl in the grass. An instant later, his body slammed into the ground beside her. The swampy earth soaked her shirt and jeans. Crysta needed no prodding. When Sam scrambled forward on his belly toward the trees, she was right beside him.

Once under cover, Sam rose to his knees, swayed to get his balance and peered out over the blades of tall grass. His eyes still had a slightly unfocused look, and he was quite pale.

"They're coming this way at a dead run." He jerked his head around, grabbed her roughly by the arm and sprang unsteadily to his feet. Before Crysta realized what he meant to do, he pulled her to a clump of brush and shoved her into the foliage. "You stay put. I mean it, Crysta. Don't so much as breathe, do you understand me? Count to two hundred, then run for the river. They won't be able to track you if you wade in the stream."

With that, he reeled away and took off through the trees. Regaining her wits, Crysta sprang after him. Though still unsteady on his feet, he had already covered a distance of ten yards. Crysta knew desperation was driving him. She broke into a run to catch up.

"Sam! Come back here!"

As if her voice lent him speed, he scissored his long legs to increase the distance between them. Crysta nearly called his name again, but the sound of other booted feet thrumming on the damp earth stifled her. She dived for cover in some nearby brush, eyes riveted to the clearing. An instant later, Riley and Henderson burst into view. They scarcely paused. A crashing sound made them whirl and run in the direction Sam had gone.

Sam was leading them away from her.

Crysta balled her hands into fists, breathing in shallow little gasps. Sam was in no condition to play hero, not after taking that blow to his head. He wouldn't be able to go far. Riley and Henderson would catch him. And when they did, they would kill him.

With a sob, Crysta shoved her way out of the concealing brush. As she gained her feet, fear swamped her. For an instant she stood rooted. Sam was giving her the chance to survive this. If she revealed herself, Riley surely had a bullet in that gun with her name on it. Was she out of her mind?

Like a reel of film being played out in fast motion, Crysta saw herself as she had been before coming here to Alaska. How empty her life had been. Until meeting Sam and Tip, she had fooled herself into believing that she could be happy as a successful fashion designer. Now she realized how pitifully lonely she had been, and how pitifully lonely she would always be if things continued status quo. Sam thought his gift to her was a chance for survival, but she wanted more from him than that; she wanted another chance to live, really live. If that wasn't in the cards, then what did she have to lose? Far less than Sam did.

Crysta sprang forward into a run. She wouldn't let him die because of her. It had been her persistence that had pushed Riley into this in the first place. Her fault, only hers. Bursting from the cottonwoods into the meadow, Crysta focused on the three figures running along the edge of the trees. Sam was keeping himself in plain sight. She could tell by his flagging pace that the blow he had received was taking its toll.

Once again, Crysta felt as if she were watching a film, this one spun out in slow motion. Riley, skidding to a stop and throwing up his arm to sight his gun on Sam. Steve Henderson braking to a halt behind Riley and shouting something. And Sam— Pain twisted inside Crysta's chest when she saw him stop running and look back over his shoulder in her direction. He was making a target of himself! So she could flee.

Crysta screamed. The sound ripped through the twilight. Riley spun around. She waved her arms so he could see her. "Run, Sam! Run! Don't do it! Please, don't do it!"

A shot rang out. The dirt beside Crysta exploded upward, a tiny clod hitting her thigh. She flinched, and a horrible paralysis gripped her legs. Then she heard Sam roar with anger.

"Go back!" Crysta staggered forward, her eyes riveted on Sam as he charged toward Riley. "Sam, go back!" she sobbed, breaking into a run herself.

From that moment, everything happened in a swirling haze of unreality. Riley turned and leveled his gun at Sam. Steve Henderson roared "No!" and threw himself on Riley's back. The two smugglers crashed to the ground in a roll, both fighting for control of the gun. As Crysta reached them, Sam was coming up on their other side.

"I won't let you kill them!" Steve cried. "Enough is enough, O'Keefe! It's over!"

O'Keefe rolled to the top and brought his left fist crashing down into Henderson's face. "Over? One more haul, you stupid bastard, and we'll be *rich*. I'm not letting you screw it up!"

Sam skirted the struggling men and snagged Crysta's hand, dragging her into a run. Behind them, Crysta heard another sickening thud of a fist against flesh, then a roar of rage rent the air. She hauled back on Sam's hand. "We can't leave Steve, Sam! We can't!"

Pale-faced, Sam pulled her into a run, using the advantage of his greater weight. His palm felt sweaty around her hand, and his fingers didn't grip with their usual strength. Crysta would have known he was perilously close to collapse even if he hadn't been staggering.

"He's on his own!" he cried shakily. "I'm getting you out of here!"

Just as Sam and Crysta reached the trees, a shot rang out, the echo strangely muffled. From the look on Sam's face as he braked and wheeled to look back, Crysta knew the bullet had found a target. She saw Riley O'Keefe staggering to his feet, brandishing the gun over Steve, who writhed on the ground, holding his stomach.

"Oh, God!" she moaned.

Reeling like a drunk, Sam passed a shirt sleeve across his eyes, dragged in a bracing breath, then began running again, hauling her along behind him. "It's them or us, Crysta! Run, sweetheart. Run like you've never run in your life!"

The trees seemed to whiz past Crysta. She tried to

focus on the ground, on Sam's churning legs, but everything seemed blurred. Her lungs began to ache. A stitch
knifed into her side. Though his pace began to slow a
bit, Sam still kept running. Across the second meadow,
through the slough, back into the trees.

Sam drew to a stop where the all-terrain vehicles were
hidden in the brush. Like a wild man, he descended on
one of the red four-wheelers, throwing off the camouflage of branches. Crysta hurried to help, terrified by
Sam's waxen pallor and the sheen of sweat on his face.
She knew he was going on sheer willpower now, and that
he couldn't remain on his feet much longer.

"Dammit!" he cried. "They took the key. I'll have to
hotwire it."

"There isn't time. Riley's coming!"

Sam swore again and grabbed her hand. As they broke
into another run, Crysta could see patches of the muddy
river and the Cessna through the trees. She threw a wild
glance over her shoulder, acutely aware that Riley might
appear at any second. They should be going in another
direction. He would guess that they'd head toward the
all-terrain vehicles or the river.

Suddenly Sam's grip on her hand lessened, and he
staggered. Throwing out an arm, he looped it around a
tree, nearly falling. Giving his head a shake, he tried to
use the tree trunk to right himself. "Crysta…" He labored
for air. "I'm finished."

Throwing a fearful glance behind them, Crysta
grabbed his arm. "Lean on me."

"No!" He lifted his head, trying to focus on her. "Go
to the airplane. You saw Todd at the controls."

"I can't *fly* it!" she cried, her voice shrill.

"You can taxi it!" he snarled. "Go, dammit! I hear him coming!"

Crysta heard the footsteps, too. Fright lent her strength. Vising an arm around Sam's waist, she pulled him away from the tree. "I'm not leaving you."

He fell in beside her, the toes of his rubber boots dragging the ground with his every step, his weight pulling her into a crazy zigzag as she tried to head for the airplane.

The Cessna loomed before her. From behind her, she heard the report of Riley's gun. She sobbed and hurled herself into the water, carrying Sam along with her momentum. He fell forward onto the airplane's pontoon, throwing up a leg for purchase so he could climb inside. Crysta jerked open the cabin door and shoved him from behind. "Hurry, Sam, hurry!"

Half dragging himself, half falling forward because she was shoving him so hard, Sam rolled into the cabin. Crysta scrambled in behind him, closed the door and launched herself over him into the cockpit. As she gained the pilot's seat, a bullet popped through the cabin door and hit the windshield.

Crysta's brain kicked into automatic, her hands reacting. She felt Sam's elbow bump her thigh. Just as the engine roared to life, he said, "That's my Crysta. I knew you could do it."

As if on cue, another bullet tore through the cabin door and into the pilot's seat, inches from Crysta's shoulder, barely clearing the top of Sam's head. He bit off a curse. Crysta leaned forward to look out the destroyed door window. Riley was charging toward the plane, trying to aim along the bobbing barrel of his gun.

She threw a terrified look at the controls, at the throttle. What next? She couldn't remember!

"Go!" Sam gasped. "Go for it!"

And Crysta did. She wasn't sure what she touched or what she shoved, but some of it must have been right because the plane lurched forward. The next instant, her feeling of relief was eclipsed by horror. The plane tried to lift off. She screamed. The aircraft banked sharply to the left, the wing diving into the water. Sam fell against her.

"Back off the throttle," he cried in a hoarse voice. "Hold it level. Smooth as melted butter. That's it, honey."

He made it sound as if she were cruising along a six-lane highway in a Porsche. But ahead of them, the river took a sharp twist to the right, and she had no idea how to steer the plane.

"Rudder right!" Sam bellowed. "Rudder right!"

"Rudder what?" she screeched.

Sam groped with one arm, the plane veered and they were executing the turn. Crysta felt as if she might vomit. The river twisted before them, sure death at the speed they were going. But if she stopped, Riley would be following along the bank, ready to empty his gun into their skulls.

"We're not going to make it, Sam! We're not going to make it!"

"Oh, yes, we are." He grasped her knee and dropped his head into the crook of his arm. "We're a great team, you and I. A great team."

Teamwork got them safely down the river, though Crysta wasn't exactly sure how, given the fact that her partner seemed to be only half aware. But somehow, every time she was ready to throw her arms up to shield her face, Sam was there to take over.

After what seemed a lifetime, they rounded the last

bend in the river, and there was the lodge. Crysta aimed for the island.

"Slow down!" Sam barked.

His warning came too late. The Cessna hit the shallows going far too fast and did a belly-skid up onto land, coming to such a jarring stop that both she and Sam were thrown forward against the control panel. The propeller blades thunked into the dirt. The small plane bucked and shuddered. Then, with a cough, the engine died, and an eerie silence blanketed everything.

Crysta, all her muscles watery with fright, oozed downward from the control panel and fell backward. Her landing was softer than it might have been; Sam's chest cushioned the impact.

Dazed, she rolled off him, to be wedged tightly between his body and the seat. He dropped a limp arm around her waist, pressed his forehead to hers and whispered, "Did I tell you you're one hell of a lady?"

Crysta blinked and focused on his dark face, still trying to digest the fact that she had actually maneuvered an airplane along a winding river, that she and Sam, against all odds, were still alive. Though he had come through for her on several occasions, she had, for the most part, guided the plane by herself. "I am, aren't I?" she whispered incredulously.

With a weak laugh, he tipped his head back and closed his eyes, swallowing hard. "We have to get to the lodge. Riley might come, and we have to be ready, just in case. It'll take the cops at least an hour to reach us after we get a call through to them."

Crysta doubted that Riley would approach the lodge. He would realize that they'd be ready for him, and cowards like Riley didn't like bad odds. He would probably try to evade the police in the interior. But with no mode of air transportation out, it would be only a matter of hours before he was caught. She managed to extricate herself from between Sam and the seat.

"Can you make it, or should I holler for help?"

He flashed her a tremulous smile. "I think that, together, we can make it through almost anything. Don't you?"

The question seemed loaded with meaning. Throwing open the door, Crysta glanced out at the lodge, and suddenly, what had seemed so simple back in the meadow took on terrifying proportions. Sam was offering her a whole new world, *his* world. There could be no compromises. This was Sam and Tip's home; they belonged here. The question was, did she?

In a shaky voice, she murmured, "Derrick's still out there, Sam. Right now, I can't get beyond that."

He took her hand and struggled to his feet, crouched so his head cleared the cabin ceiling. His eyes met hers. "The moment the cops have hauled Riley and his friends in, it'll be safe for the searchers to go back out."

"I don't need searchers," she replied with a little more strength. "I know now where Derrick is. There's a small lake a few miles north of the cleaning location. There's a cabin there."

Sam gave a slow nod. "I know the place. The lake's not large enough for a plane to go in for a landing, and the terrain is too swampy to go in on four-wheelers. We'll have to walk."

"If Derrick's survived this long," Crysta said softly, "he'll hold out until we can reach him."

Sam's eyes darkened. "By the time the cops have come

in and cleaned up, I should be recovered enough to go with you."

As Crysta bore the brunt of his weight to help him from the plane, she had reason to doubt that.

CHAPTER FIFTEEN

FIVE HOURS LATER, Crysta stood on the riverbank below the lodge, her ears buzzing from the sounds of airplane engines as they revved to life. Sunlight warmed her face, a direct contrast to the chill coursing up her spine as she watched the police haul Riley O'Keefe past her toward the footbridge. It would be the last time the redhead walked over to the island and boarded a float-plane.

Riley fixed his fiery blue eyes on her and tried to stop walking. The officer holding the cuff chain between his wrists jerked upward, wrenching the smuggler's arms behind his back.

"Keep walking, friend."

Riley spat in Crysta's direction. "If it weren't for you, I'd be vacationing in the Bahamas next week."

Crysta smiled. "But, Riley, it's hot down there this time of year. You might break a sweat."

"You think I don't know what sweat is?" He ran a hostile gaze the length of her. "It was because I was tired of sweating that I did this! It was my turn at the good life, for once!"

Sensing Sam behind her, Crysta pulled her gaze from the departing smuggler and turned. Her heart caught at the seriousness in Sam's eyes. Though he seemed steady on his feet now, his color still hadn't returned completely to normal. "I've gotten four men to volunteer to go with us to the lake. Jangles has packed them food, I borrowed a stretcher, and we're ready to go."

"Sam, it really isn't necessary for you to go."

"You'll have to hog-tie me to keep me from it," was his response.

Crysta pressed her lips together. She knew that Sam was risking a great deal of humiliation should her hunch about Derrick's location prove incorrect. At long last, she had found a man who not only accepted her link with Derrick, but also believed in her dreams.

Sam's gaze shifted to the river island. "Do we have time to go over and see Steve for a minute before they fly him out?"

Wordlessly, Crysta nodded and fell into a walk beside him. A few minutes more would make little difference to the outcome for Derrick. After all, they owed Steve Henderson for their lives.

When they gained the island, Sam hailed the police officers who were preparing to board one of the pontoon planes. After a brief exchange, Sam led her around the plane's wing and into knee-deep water, so they could speak to Steve Henderson where he lay on a stretcher in the already crowded cabin.

"Steve?" Sam said softly.

The thin young man opened his eyes, focused on Sam and Crysta, then managed a weak grin. "So you made it. I'm—" His face contorted, and he clenched his teeth. "I'm sorry, Barrister." He grimaced again. "Never m-meant for anyone to be hurt. Know it was wrong, real wrong, but it seemed a fair enough trade for some money…for Scotty's expenses, not for me."

"The moment I realized you were involved, Steve, I knew why," Sam said softly.

Steve's eyes filled with tears. "They found a marrow match. The wife called last night. He's got a chance, Sam. Shame his old man won't be around to play ball with him again." Closing his eyes, Henderson swallowed. "Stupidest thing I ever did, going after those walrus. First thing I ever poached."

"Jangles told me about the donor match. I'm glad, Steve, really glad." Sam sighed. "I spoke to the police. They know you stopped O'Keefe from killing us. That'll go well for you in court. I also called my lawyer to see if he'd take your case. He's already arranging for bail. All that's left is for you to get that lead out of your gut and regain your strength enough for a flight to Seattle. The lawyer's applying for a waiver, so you can be with Scotty."

"I don't deserve your help, Sam."

"Maybe not, but Scotty does. Besides, the way I see it, your biggest crime was making some bad decisions, and things got out of hand. A judge will agree with me, I think. Scotty has a second chance. I'm going to be there in court to testify—so maybe his father'll get one, too."

Crysta started to say something herself, but before she could, a police officer climbed onto the airplane's wing. "Sorry, folks, but this fella's got to be taken to the hospital."

Sam nodded and drew Crysta away from the wing. Wading through the water and up onto land, Crysta sensed the tension in him. Glancing up, she saw moisture glistening in his eyes. He caught her staring at him and blinked.

"He's a good guy. What was he supposed to do? Let Scotty do without? If it had been me, I'd have gone slaughtering walrus, too, and I detest poachers!"

Crysta couldn't imagine why Sam should be angry with her. At a loss, she lowered her gaze.

"Look, I *know* he was there when Derrick was shot. And I don't blame you if you're ticked at me for going to bat for him."

"I'm not ticked, Sam, not at all. I'm glad."

Sam stopped walking, one foot poised on the bridge. "You are?"

Crysta met his gaze. "Of course. Derrick would be, too. There's no need to defend yourself because you pulled strings to help him. It's obvious he only got involved because of his son and that he later came to regret it. He took a bullet trying to stop Riley from hurting anyone else. That's evidence enough for me."

"Why didn't I do more to help him?"

"You raised all the money you could. That's more than most people do."

"It's a crying shame, that's what it is, and the whole deal makes me feel sick."

Crysta stepped up onto the bridge and slipped an arm around his waist. "Point taken. As soon as we find Derrick, let's get off our duffs and do something about it."

His hip bumped against her as they walked along the bouncing bridge toward shore. "Like what?"

The frustration in his voice made her want to hug him. "I don't know, but we'll think of something. People care, Sam. They'll donate. Scotty Henderson's medical costs will be paid, and he'll get to visit Disneyland."

As they stepped off the bridge, Crysta glanced up to see Jangles and Tip standing onshore, waiting for them. The Indian woman was wringing her skirt with one hand and holding a blue hiking pack with the other, her worried eyes fastened on Crysta.

"I have packed you food," she said softly. "Some special cakes the others don't have. And some very strong coffee, for I know you are tired."

Crysta nodded. "Thank you, Jangles. I appreciate that."

The Tlingit caught her bottom lip between her teeth. After a moment, she whispered, "I have been very bad to you, I think."

Crysta tightened her arm around Sam's waist, recalling all the times she had thought the worst of Jangles. The score seemed pretty even. "Let's put it behind us, Jangles."

"No, you do not understand." She lifted sorrowful eyes to Sam. "Some of my family live up north, near the killing fields where Riley's been slaughtering walrus. Three years ago, some poachers were caught and then set free after serving short sentences. We could not let that happen again."

Sam stiffened. "You knew about the ivory smuggling?"

"I—" Jangles broke off. She slowly nodded. "I watch and listen, like a shadow. Sometimes people forget me, and they whisper their secrets."

Sam made an irritated sound under his breath. Jangles threw a frightened look at Tip. The boy nudged her arm. "Tell him, Jangles. When he g-gets mad, he yells, but then he st-stops."

"You knew about this, Tip?" Sam demanded.

"Not until j-just now. Jangles was c-crying. I asked what was wrong, and sh-she told me."

"There is more," Jangles inserted in a strangled voice. "I knew Derrick had been following Riley downriver."

"I see." Sam's voice rang with bridled fury. Turning the full blast of his gaze on Jangles, he said, "Derrick was my friend. He may be dead. You might have prevented that."

"I was very wrong," Jangles cried. "But I did not think

they would hurt him! Until he came up missing, I thought he was in on it. By the time I realized he wasn't, it was too late! That is why I tried to make Crysta leave—before the same happened to her. She was asking questions. I saw her follow you the first day." She made a feeble gesture with her hand. "She wouldn't accept that Derrick was dead, and I knew she'd come to harm if she stayed here and made the poachers nervous."

She moistened her lips and shook her head. "I know I should have told you. But at the time—" She broke off and lifted an imploring gaze. "Try to see as we see, Sam. The whites come here and kill our wildlife. And they go unpunished! We *must* fight back! When I guessed what was going on, I called my brothers. This time, we decided to follow the old law and punish the poachers ourselves."

"Your brothers? I saw you talking to a man in the woods. That was one of them?"

Jangles nodded. "I was afraid you'd grow suspicious if you knew they had come."

"Jangles, the old ways don't work now. It's sheer folly to take the law into your own hands! And I especially resent your doing it here! I asked you, point-blank, if you knew anything, and you refused to answer me!"

"I am fired, I guess," Jangles said shakily. "It is what I deserve."

Sam rolled his eyes. "Jangles, you're a member of our family. You don't *fire* family. You just—" He sighed and glanced at Tip. "You just yell a little and get over being angry." He reached to take the pack from her hand. "This isn't finished. I have to go find Derrick right now, but when all this calms down, you and I are due for a serious talk."

"Yes," Jangles agreed solemnly.

Tip visibly brightened. "You see?" he said, nudging Jangles's arm. "He's already done yelling."

"Tip," Sam said in a warning voice.

As anxious as she was to be gone, Crysta couldn't smother a grin. Sam glanced down at her, his face lined with weariness. In a low voice, he said, "Let's go before I end up strangling them both."

Signaling to the other men, Sam struck off downstream.

"Can I come, Dad?"

"No, Tip, not this time."

"But I could help!" Tip protested.

Sam paused to look over his shoulder at his son. As much as he wanted to say yes, he knew Tip's jabbering would probably drive Crysta half mad by the time they reached their destination. She had enough to contend with right now. "Son, I—"

"Sam?" Crysta touched his arm. She waited for the other four men to walk past them and get out of earshot. "It's safe enough for him to go along, isn't it? Derrick might be—" She broke off and seemed to search for words. "I'd like having my friends with me, just in case. Tip and I, we're kind of—" She shrugged. "If you don't mind, I'd really like him to be there."

A breeze caught Crysta's hair, draping it across her face. Sam stared down at her, searching her veiled eyes.

"Are you sure?" he whispered. "He'll talk your hind leg off."

"And bug me, you mean?" She leaned closer. "Sam, understand something. I like your son. We're *friends*."

Sam slid his gaze to Tip. "Go get your jacket. You'll have to catch up with us. Can you do that?"

Tip was already racing for the lodge, long legs flying.

Sam watched him a moment, then looked at Crysta. There was a wealth of emotion in his eyes.

Smiling, Crysta turned to look downstream. Her spirits immediately plummeted. It seemed an eternity ago that she had come here to Alaska to find Derrick. Now, the last leg of her search was about to begin. What lay ahead of her? She broke into a walk, her shoulders stiff with tension. Since her dream of Derrick digging the bullet from his chest, she hadn't dreamed of him again or felt anything. It was possible the silence meant her brother was dead.

She curled her hands into fists. She had once yearned to be free of Derrick. If that thoughtless wish came true, how would she ever manage to live with it?

SEVERAL HOURS LATER, the search party crested a knoll. Below them, the cabin sat on a windswept plane of grassland, stark against the horizon, with a smattering of stunted trees on a slope behind it. Though Crysta had seen similar terrain from the air, it looked vastly different from ground level. *Alaska.* She had the eerie sensation that she and her companions were tiny specks in this vast land, so inconsequential that the wind might, at any moment, sweep them away. She had never seen grass so vibrant a green, rolling forever before her. Ribbons of water cut through the marshes, spilling into countless tiny ponds and lakes.

She focused on the small lake before them. Sam had been right. It wasn't a large enough body of water to land a seaplane on.

"Is this it?" Sam asked, taking her arm.

Crysta nodded. She had seen this place in her last dream, and she knew Derrick had to be here. Suddenly, she was terrified. She wanted to race down the incline, but her feet were anchored to the grass. Tip and the other four men hung back, as if they knew she needed to face this moment alone. "I'm frightened, Sam."

"You know, no matter what we find down there, none of this is your fault." When she started to interrupt, he rushed on. "I've been doing a lot of thinking about what you told me the other night. It isn't wrong to want your own life, Crysta. You have to put this thing with Derrick into its proper perspective."

"You make it sound so simple, but it isn't."

"I know Derrick loved you. Alive or dead, he'd want you to feel at peace with yourself. Don't go down there with a load of responsibility on your shoulders that isn't and never should have been yours. You've lived your entire life feeling as if it was somehow your responsibility to not only *know* when Derrick was in trouble, but to somehow *save* him. That's crazy. It was wrong of your mother to encourage that kind of thinking."

"Put like that, it even sounds crazy to me." She straightened her shoulders. "On the other hand, though, my mother has been right, too, Sam. During my marriage and after it crumbled, I tried to be someone I wasn't. This experience has taught me that I can't deny what's between Derrick and me, and I can't shove myself into a mold to please other people—I have to build a life that fits around me. Does that make any sense?"

"Perfect sense," he said huskily. "Just don't forget that there may be a man who'd be willing to help you build that life."

She squeezed her eyes closed. "Will you go down with me?"

"Try to lose me."

Crysta struck off down the slope, her hand enveloped in Sam's, their clenched fingers pulsating everywhere their flesh touched. She couldn't breathe. Her legs felt numb.

"If he's dead, I'll never forgive myself," she whispered raggedly. "Crazy or not, it's how I feel."

She wished she could think of the words to make him understand. Then he gave her hand a squeeze, and she knew, without his saying so, that he did understand. She turned to look up at him.

"Crysta?"

The whisper inside her head made Crysta freeze. With a surge of wild hope, she whirled toward the cabin. "Derrick?" Breaking into a run, Crysta tore down the decline, Sam at her side.

"Derrick!" She hit the rickety, sagging porch in a leap, grappling frantically at the door, which hung awry from its rotted hinges. "Derrick! Oh, Derrick!"

Bursting inside, Crysta hesitated, blinded by the sudden dimness. She heard movement to her left, and a voice rasped, "It sure took you long enough to get here."

Crysta flung herself across the room. Peering through the gloom, she saw her brother lying on a grimy old mattress. He was thin. His eyes were glazed with fever. But he was alive. Sweeping aside an array of empty cans on the floor, she sank to her knees. With a trembling hand, she reached to touch the blood-soaked bandage around his chest.

"Oh, Derrick, what did he *do* to you?"

With a clammy hand, Derrick grasped her tremulous fingers. "He shot me—as if you don't already know." Heavier footsteps behind Crysta caught Derrick's attention. He grinned and closed his eyes, clearly exhausted from talking. "Hey, buddy."

Sam stepped closer, coming to a stop behind Crysta. Leaning forward, he pressed a palm to Derrick's glistening forehead.

"The fever's broken," Derrick rasped, lifting his lashes. "That's why I'm sweatin' like a plow mule. You're too late to play nursemaid, unless you can find something to brace my leg. Broken, I think, in a couple of places." He licked his lips. "You got any fresh water? I made it down to the lake a couple of times. Don't know if it was the rusty can or the water, but it tasted like—" He broke off and smiled. "The food left here wasn't much better. If I never see another Vienna sausage or corn kernel, it'll be too soon. What's the matter? You guys can't talk, or what?"

Glancing down at the empty cans, it struck Crysta as hysterically funny that Derrick was actually *complaining* about his accommodations when she and Sam had been worrying that he might starve. She started to laugh, and she couldn't stop. And then she found herself wrapped in her brother's arms, and her laughter turned to tears.

Aware of his wound, she cried, "Derrick, I'll hurt you!"

"Never. Nothing ever felt so good."

A sob tore up Crysta's throat. Then another. "Oh, Derrick, you'll never know how I felt, not being able to find you."

"I was out of it most of the time. A high fever. Unconscious. I guess that's why you couldn't pick up on me. Crysta, don't do this to yourself. Please."

"But I couldn't *feel* you. I couldn't reach you. All I could think was that it'd be my fault if you died."

"*Your* fault? It was *my* fault, Crysta, not yours." Placing his hand on her hair, he tucked in his chin to look down at her. "Why would you blame yourself for something totally out of your control? How can you possibly take responsibility?"

"I couldn't find you." She sniffed and let out a rush of breath. "For so long, I tried to put a wall between us! And then, when you needed me most, I discovered I had succeeded! Mom tried to warn me I'd regret what I was doing, but I was too selfish to listen. Oh, Derrick, I thought I had lost you."

"Selfish?" Derrick pressed his lips against her hair. "Crysta…" He sighed and hooked a finger under her chin to tip her face back. After studying her for a long moment, he said, "Don't you think it's about time we stopped listening to Mom? If she had her way, we'd be wearing co-ordinating outfits when we were ninety."

Crysta closed her eyes, smiling at the image that conjured. Pulling from his arms, she wiped her cheeks with the sleeve of her jacket. "Look at me, bawling all over you, and you hurt." She reached to touch the stubble on his chin. "Oh, Derrick, I love you. Do you realize how much?"

"Enough to get me some water?"

"I think I can manage that."

Over the next hour, while Derrick got some much-needed first aid, he told everyone what had happened. Much of it Sam and Crysta already knew, but Tip sat spellbound on the floor by the newly built fire, arms looped around his knees.

"One thing bothers me," Crysta inserted. "The staged bear attack wasn't anywhere near the cleaning location. It was at least five miles closer to the lodge."

"I was tailing them. They must have realized, so they led me several miles downstream, then lost me. I stopped to eat. They crept up on me. I ran back toward Cottonwood Bend, leaving my pack and everything behind."

"I found the place were you stopped to eat," Sam inserted. "There was bear track. The pack was torn apart. The obvious conclusion to draw was that you'd been attacked."

"There's bear track *everywhere* here," Derrick put in.

Sam smiled. "I couldn't believe you had been dumb enough to mess with a grizzly. In my experience, you always head in the other direction if you spot territorial markings."

"Oh, I was dumb. Just wasn't a grizzly I was messing with." Derrick sighed. "I wanted so badly to catch them, find out where they were stashing the ivory. Without proof, I knew they'd get off. Pretty cagey of them, making it look like a bear attacked me."

Sam pieced together the rest of what had happened. "When they shot you, they must have thought you were dead. They hauled you away, somehow covering their tracks, and threw you down an embankment."

"Not immediately. First, they threw me into one of their stinking cleaning sheds. I guess they hadn't figured out what to do with my body. I'm not sure how long I was in there. Several hours, because I regained consciousness when they came in to get me. I tried to play dead, but at that point, of course, they realized I wasn't, because rigor mortis wasn't setting in. Lucky for me, Riley didn't have his gun on him, so they settled for throwing me down onto the rocks, which should have finished me, but, by some miracle, didn't." Derrick gestured at his splint. "That's how I got my leg busted."

Crysta remembered the falling sensation she had experienced in her office at the dress shop, the terrible pain in her chest. "And then you lost consciousness again?"

"Yeah, thank goodness. The pain was—pretty bad. When I came around, I was lying wedged between the rocks. The mud had stopped my wound from bleeding, which was probably all that had saved me from bleeding to death or attracting scavengers. By then, I had lost all track of time. I managed to crawl up the bank. I found a tree limb to use as a crutch and came here." Derrick's eyes drifted closed. "I knew you and Sam would come, Sis. Only a matter of time."

"It's a miracle you're here to tell us about it."

"Not a miracle. The belt buckle you had had made for me impeded the bullet and kept the wound from being fatal. By the way, Sis, did you know it was Sam who had given me the silver dollar we used in the buckle?"

Sam touched her shoulder. "We'd better let Derrick rest for a while. It's going to be rough on him making the trip back."

Crysta rose, pulling the blankets they had brought high on her brother's shoulders. Tenderness welled within her.

She and Sam walked outside and dropped wearily onto the porch step, their gazes fastened on the small lake. Acutely aware of Sam beside her, Crysta registered the scenery and realized how soon she would be leaving it all behind. Her time with Sam had been rife with tension and heartache, but now, perversely, she wished it wouldn't end. They had a few hours left, but it wasn't enough.

"Oh, Sam, it's so beautiful here. Now that I know Derrick's all right, I can really appreciate it."

He didn't look at her. "I guess you'll be going back to Anchorage tonight, and heading to Los Angeles from there. I—wish you could stay. It may be pretty here, but it gets mighty lonely sometimes."

She could scarcely speak around the lump in her throat. "I guess it can get lonely anywhere, even in a crowded place like Los Angeles."

He turned to look at her. "I got the impression you kept pretty busy with your business and friends."

She licked her lips. "Yeah...busy."

Her eyes clung to his. Suddenly, she knew what she wanted, more than anything.

He dragged his gaze from hers. "You knew what I was asking there in the plane, right after we beached it. I saw the doubt in your eyes when you looked at the lodge. I guess maybe I was rushing you. I'm sorry." He cleared his throat. "I, um, I was thinking, maybe Tip could show his paintings in Los Angeles. We could visit you while we're there."

She studied his profile. He had listened to her, and he planned to take her advice to heart. He was at last prepared to let Tip take risks.

Footsteps thumped on the porch behind them. "But, Dad, I don't want to see Crysta just on visits!"

Tip's voice made Crysta leap. Sam, more conditioned to the boy's inappropriate timing, turned his head more slowly. Tip planted himself on the step on the other side of Crysta, leaning forward, elbows on his knees, to look at his father.

"That'd be dumb. None of us'd be lonely if we stayed together."

A smile tugged at Crysta's mouth. She turned to look at Sam and found his eyes aching with unvoiced messages. *I love you. Will you stay with us?* With a bit of a shock, she realized that Derrick wasn't the only one with whom she could communicate without words.

Sam's gaze flicked to his son, rested there a moment, then returned to her. "Tip, I think Crysta and I need to take a walk."

"That sounds fun. Can I come?"

Crysta laughed softly and rose from the steps. "Tip, I think you'd better stay here. Your father and I have some talking to do."

Sam jumped off the steps, capturing her shoulders within the circle of his arm. "And don't follow us. If I see even a glimpse of you, I'll snatch you baldheaded."

As they neared the lake, Crysta tipped her head back against Sam's arm and closed her eyes. "The answer is yes."

"I haven't *asked* you yet. I realize you're a woman of the nineties, but can we do this the traditional way?"

She smiled. "All right, but if we're going for traditional, I want you on your knees."

He spun her around and up against his chest, his arm tightening at her waist. "Not *that* traditional. They can see us from the cabin."

She arched an eyebrow at him. "Are you going to ask or not?"

"It won't be easy. Tip demands a great deal of my time. He intrudes at the worst possible moments—*always*. And he may never grow up. Do you understand what I'm saying? It's a lot of responsibility you'll be assuming."

She touched a fingertip to his lips. "Sam, listen to yourself. You sound like a recording of me when I was telling you why Dick left me. When something is right between two people, the external difficulties can be worked out. You have Tip in your life, I have Derrick in mine. I think that makes us a perfect pair."

His mouth curved in a smile, and he nibbled at her fingertip. "You know, six months out of the year, the snow gets so deep up here that we close the lodge and live in Anchorage."

"You do?"

His eyes searched hers. "It wouldn't be inconceivable for us to have two businesses—yours and mine. I've been planning to get my pilot's license. With a double income, we could probably afford a small plane. Our travel costs back and forth during the summer would be minimal. I've never turned my hand to designing clothes, but I'd make a great bookkeeper."

"That's a thought. My partner can handle the shop in Los Angeles, and I could probably use my share of the proceeds to open another shop up here."

"Could you be happy with leaving someone else in charge six months out of the year while we travel back and forth between the lodge and the dress shop?"

"Blissfully. In fact, I may hire a manager full-time and simply oversee things."

"But you'll be giving up so much…"

She placed her hand over his mouth and slowly shook her head. "You're forgetting something. I told you, my lifelong dream was to have a family. The business, my life in Los Angeles, was filler. I'd like to stay in the fashion industry, but that isn't the most important thing to me. I'll want plenty of free time to devote to being a mom. I have a feeling that two businesses, Tip and a couple of sets of twins will keep both of us busy. We'll be glad we have a manager for the dress shop."

"A couple of—" His eyes widened. "Twins run in your family?"

"Obviously."

His mouth curved into a grin. *"Twins?"*

"Would that be a problem?"

"A problem." He looked a little dazed. "No, not at all. I *love* kids! I just never considered having more than one at a time. Fortunately, I'm quite a hand at changing diapers."

"Well, then…"

His face drew closer to hers. "Derrick will be over the moon when we tell him."

Crysta had a feeling Derrick had already tuned in on the news. "You think so?"

His lips brushed hers. "Positive."

A little breathless, she whispered, "You still haven't asked me."

His mouth claimed hers. Crysta melted against him, closing her eyes. Against the blackness of her eyelids, she saw bright little starbursts. Her heart began to slam. With a moan, she gave herself up to the kiss, her senses reeling. The ground disappeared, and there was only Sam.

Some things could be said without words. Sam asked, and Crysta said yes.

* * * * *

Catherine Anderson

77800 SWEET DREAMS   ___ $7.99 U.S. ___ $9.99 CAN.

(limited quantities available)

TOTAL AMOUNT	$ _____
POSTAGE & HANDLING	$ _____
($1.00 FOR 1 BOOK, 50¢ for each additional)	
APPLICABLE TAXES*	$ _____
TOTAL PAYABLE	$ _____

(check or money order—please do not send cash)

To order, complete this form and send it, along with a check or money order for the total above, payable to Harlequin HQN, to: **In the U.S.:** 3010 Walden Avenue, P.O. Box 9077, Buffalo, NY 14269-9077; **In Canada:** P.O. Box 636, Fort Erie, Ontario, L2A 5X3.

Name: _____

Address: _____ City: _____

State/Prov.: _____ Zip/Postal Code: _____

Account Number (if applicable): _____

075 CSAS

*New York residents remit applicable sales taxes.
*Canadian residents remit applicable GST and provincial taxes.

HARLEQUIN® HQN™
www.Harlequin.com

REQUEST YOUR FREE BOOKS!

2 FREE NOVELS FROM THE PARANORMAL ROMANCE COLLECTION PLUS 2 FREE GIFTS!

Join *New York Times* bestselling authors

FERN MICHAELS

and Jill Marie Landis, with Dorsey Kelley
and Chelley Kitzmiller,
for four timeless love stories set on one
very special California ranch.

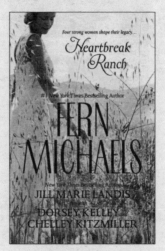

*Heartbreak
Ranch*

Available now!